Charlie's Place

Mick Rennison

Copyright © 2020 by Mick Rennison

All rights reserved. No part of this publication may be reproduced, stored in any form of retrieval system or transmitted in any form or by any means without prior permission in writing from the publishers except for the use of brief quotations in a book review.

ABOUT THE AUTHOR

Since the mid 1970's Mick has made his living as a truck driver, travelling all over Europe and Scandinavia. A globe-trotter and a wanderer, he spent time in his teens as a merchant seaman and in his spare time has driven 5000 miles across the USA and 3000 miles across Canada. He has also toured England on his narrow boat on which he has lived for the past 13 years.

He began his writing career contributing to truck magazines in the late 1980's.

Mick's autobiography, 'Keep on Trucking. 40 years on the Road' was published by Old Pond Publishers in 2016.

Monday

"One two! One two! Good evening ladies, gentlemen, beggars, thieves and truck drivers! Welcome to Charlie's Place! The best truckstop in the whole of the UK! It's Monday night, boys, and we all know what that means!"

Charlie Wheeler, resplendent in his white three-piece suit, paused over the microphone as the assembled truck drivers, in the smoke-filled bar, roared out their approval.

"Yes, it's stripper night!" Stepping back from the whistling mic, Charlie adjusted his bow-tie and waited for the howls of delight to fade. The place was packed out, standing room only.

"And tonight, for your pleasure only, she used to be part of a double act, but sadly the dog died."

"Get on with it!" yelled a voice from the back. They were impatient, they'd waited long enough.

"Ladies and gentlemen, please give a big clap, 'cos if you don't, she'll give it to you, the one... The only... Miss Kitty Le Sadé!"

The cheering truckers drowned out the opening bars of Madonna's 'Like a Virgin' as a leather clad Kitty strode out onto the stage, cracking a bull whip.

"Get 'em off!" they shouted. "Off! Off! Off!"

Stepping down from the stage, Charlie forced his way through the crowd back to the bar. Debbie had his pint waiting, and as he supped, he watched Kitty working up her audience. Another busy night, the lorry park was overflowing, he should have been a very happy man. But nothing could be further from the truth. He had problems, big problems.

This year he would be celebrating his fiftieth birthday, but there was very little to celebrate. True, business was good, the chunky gold bracelet on his wrist and the silver Mercedes parked out back, testified to that. But he'd been doing a lot of thinking lately, as people tend to do when they approached their half-century.

Charlie had got to where he was today with a lifetime of criminality, scams and dodgy deals. Buying and selling, wheeling and dealing, anything you wanted, Charlie was the man to see.

When he was a kid, nicking sweets from the local shop and selling them on to his class mates, he was going to be a millionaire by the time he was twenty. Then at thirty, it was going to be by the time he was forty. But now, at fifty, he had this gut feeling it was never going to happen at all. Not that he was poor by any means, it was all tied up, that's all.

Charlie's Place first took off in the early seventies, and he'd spent the next twenty years building it up to what it was today, here in the nineties, one of the best truckstops in the country. He'd won awards and accolades galore.

But now it amounted to nothing. Sweet FA. The end loomed. This morning, another letter from the Inland Revenue. This time it was serious, they were onto him. For years now the place had been making a loss, on paper. Now they wanted to know where all the money had gone. And where it had all come from in the first place. No longer could he ignore their requests for information, information he couldn't possibly give them. They had him by the balls and they knew it.

He'd given serious consideration to doing a runner. Raise some cash and make a dash. Run for the sun. But he felt he'd left it too late for that. And it would take an awful lot of money to keep Charlie Wheeler in the manner to which he had become accustomed. He was going to get time, no doubt about it. Four years at least, maybe more, depending on how much they found out.

And he'd come out to nothing. Between them, his family and the tax man would clean him out. They'd be fighting over the scraps before the cell door slammed shut.

His wife and kids loathed him; God knows why. He'd struggled all his life to bring them up. Fed them, clothed them, even employed them. But did they appreciate it? Did they hell!

One of his biggest regrets was getting married in the first place. Carol was just a bit of fun; it was never meant to be serious. A bit of a laugh really. Another virgin deflowered, and all behind Tommy's back. Then she got bloody pregnant! His other girlfriends were really pissed off. And so was he! In them days you had to do the right thing and get married. But he felt he'd been trapped. He often wondered how life would have been without a wife and two whining kids on his back.

Carol was five years and at least a generation younger than him. She ran the kitchen. Her constant nagging drove him insane. Just lately, she'd been behaving very strangely. On her evenings off she was down at the local church hall doing good deeds, and Sunday mornings, she'd take herself off to church. Charlie thought it was a bit late in life to start getting into all that Jesus crap, but at least it kept her off his back.

His two kids despised him. Debbie, his twenty-year-old daughter, worked behind the bar. She had the morals of an alley cat. A few drinks and she was anybody's, the original good time had by all. And if he ever passed comment or dared to remind her that she was supposed to be engaged, he'd just get a mouthful of abuse. No respect at all.

Penny was eighteen and a mummy's girl. Miss Goody Two Shoes. Butter wouldn't melt in her pouting mouth. She went out of her way to argue with him, and Carol always took her side. She worked in the kitchen, or was supposed to. Last week she'd taken off to the Glastonbury festival to enlighten herself'. She'd left him short-staffed and had refused to speculate when she'd be back.

No, nobody was going to miss him. They'd be glad to see the back of him. He wouldn't be expecting too many visitors.

A huge roar from the crowd signalled Kitty's naked finale. The handle of the bull whip slowly emerged into view. After a quick bow to all points of the stage, the show was over. Blowing kisses to her cheering fans, like the star she was, Kitty gathered up her discarded clothes and was gone, back behind the heavy drapes and into the number one dressing room, the ladies loo.

Charlie took to the stage. His suit stretched to accommocate his ever spreading waist line, only one button now fastened the waistcoat. When he'd first got the suit, it had fitted like a glove. Carol had said that he reminded her of Tom Jones. Recently she'd commented on how he now looked like a second-hand car salesman.

"Thanks for coming tonight, lads, I'll mop the floor later. Kitty is back with us on Wednesday and don't forget, if you're passing through tomorrow, it's Country and Western night. And remember, we're open at five in the morning to serve you the best breakfast this side of the Atlantic. Thank you and a very good night."

Debbie slammed the shutters down on the bar as the drivers funnelled towards the exit doors. Carol appeared from the kitchen and began collecting up the ashtrays and glasses.

At the till, Charlie cashed up. As he stuffed the bank roll into his pocket, he glanced over at the solitary driver still sat in the bar. He had that smug look on his face that Charlie had seen so often before.

"Debbie, can't you ask him to wait outside?" he asked. "You've got all the glasses to do yet."

"I'll do 'em in the morning," she said, throwing her tea-towel down on the bar. Her mini-skirt was little more than a belt, her blouse struggled to hold in her ample breasts.

"You'll do them now!" snapped Charlie, no longer hiding his irritation.

"In the morning," she said, flicking her long blonde hair back over her shoulder. "I said, I'll do 'em in the morning!"

"But Debs, I need you in the morning," said Carol, returning to the bar with a tray full of ash trays. "I want help with breakfast, you know Penny's away."

"Yeah, I know she's away," Debbie spat. "She's been away all bloody week! How come she gets to go off on the bloody hippy trail for as long as she likes, and I can't even get a fucking night off?"

"Debbie! No need for that sort of language!" said Carol, in her serious voice.

"She just does what she fucking likes, she's always been your bloody favourite," said Debbie.

"Debbie! That's not true!"

"Oh, do shut up!" said Debbie, making for the exit, closely followed by her night's conquest.

"When's Borg due back?" Charlie shouted after her.

A single finger was the only reply he got.

"I've had enough of this," said Carol. "I'm off to bed."

"Well, don't expect me to finish off," said Charlie. "I can't do everything myself."

"I've given up expecting anything from you," said Carol. "Say goodnight to Kitty for me." Then she too was gone.

Charlie sat alone in the empty, littered bar. Alone with his thoughts. Tomorrow he would phone Tommy, his accountant. They needed to talk about damage limitation. Recently, he'd got the distinct impression that Tommy was getting nervous. There could be a slight conflict of interest, and he could well give preference to saving his own skin.

Walking over to the emergency exit he kicked open the door. Looking out into the darkness of the lorry park, he called out, "Kitty! Come on! Let's go!"

A muffled cough came from behind a parked truck as Kitty cleared her throat. "He's just coming!" she shouted.

Charlie laughed to himself as he went to fetch the car round. Best part of the day this, giving Kitty a lift home. He was going to miss Kitty.

***

Tommy was more than nervous; he was crapping himself. Months ago, he'd warned Charlie that the end was nigh. He'd told him then that a runner was the best bet. The only bet. But Charlie wouldn't listen, he thought he was untouchable. Tommy had got him out of the shit so many times in the past, he'd just got blasé about it. But this was it, and if Charlie went down, then he could well be going with him. He couldn't lie for him without incriminating himself. False accounting, fraudulent invoicing, he could even get a longer stretch than Charlie.

Tommy Thomas was Charlie's accountant, financial advisor and confidant. An expert on the thin divide between legal and criminal. He lived in a small flat over his office in Henyard, a small village just north of the truckstop.

They were old friends, him and Charlie; they'd been to school together. Their long friendship, interrupted briefly when Charlie stole his fiancé, paid rich dividends for them both. His advice on tax avoidance had saved Charlie thousands, he'd also put a lot of good business opportunities his way. But now he was trying to dig Charlie, and himself, out of a very big hole. If only Charlie would listen.

"Piss off to Spain!" he'd told him. "When the heat dies down, I'll flog the business and send you the money."

But Charlie didn't trust anyone, not even Tommy. Charlie had spent his whole life conning and deceiving practically everyone he'd dealt with. So, he assumed that, given the chance, people would con and deceive him.

And Charlie had certainly deceived Tommy. It had been more than twenty years ago, but he still carried the mental scars. It wasn't so much the fact he'd stolen Carol away from him, the bit that really hurt was that she'd screwed him. She'd never let Tommy touch her, not even an outside rub. She was saving it, she said, for their wedding night. The wedding night that was only weeks away when he caught them having a knee trembler in the pub car park. And it had been going on for months!

Tommy had been devastated. In all the years since, he'd never had a proper relationship with a woman. His sex life now was lived out in the massage parlour in Shorley. He got a discount for keeping their books.

His relationship with Charlie was shaky for a while, to say the least. But Charlie had told him how Carol had thrown herself at him, and a few of the other lads as well. He convinced Tommy that she just wasn't good enough for him. By blaming Carol instead of Charlie, Tommy had managed to get on with his life and continued to be Charlie's right-hand man.

***

Charlie's Place began life more than twenty years ago, in the early 1970's. Just a tea and butty caravan on the side of a busy road close to the Sussex coast. It was a business investment for Charlie, and a very wise one it turned out to be. He had come into big money by way of a lucrative scam that was to see him well for many years. A cousin of his was the manager of an electrical distribution centre in London. Another cousin ran a chain of electrical shops along the south coast.

Charlie always referred to his villainous mates and fences as cousins. He felt it added a bit of glamour to the business, and differentiated between his straight contacts and the bent ones.

Acting as middle man to his two electrical cousins, Charlie arranged the illicit movement of goods from one to the other and collected a handsome commission from both of them. Charlie never got his hands dirty; he never even saw the stuff; it was all done over the telephone. When the curtain finally came down, he was Mister Clean. His cousins got four years a piece at Her Majesty's Pleasure.

Charlie never liked having big sums of money in bank accounts. He was terrified that someone might want to know where it had all come from. So initially he bought the tea caravan to launder the proceeds of all his dodgy deals, spread it out a bit.

With Carol, his newly wed and pregnant wife, he set up the caravan in a lay-by a mile south of Henyard, in West Sussex. It was an instant success with all the lorry drivers working out of the nearby port of Shorley. Soon Charlie's legitimate business was earning as much as his dodgy ones.

Then, some five years later, when five acres of waste land behind the tea caravan came up for sale, he didn't hesitate. By now he had two young daughters and was looking to the future. He was onto a winner and he knew it.

Three years of legal battles ensued as the residents of little Henyard, just thirty houses, a post office, pub and a church, objected strongly to his plans for a transport café on the site. The local resident big wig, Ted Morrison, led a hard-fought campaign against planning permission.

It was only after Charlie persuaded a dozen or so lorry drivers to park their wagons on the village green every night for a couple of weeks, that the residents saw the need for a proper lorry park and dropped their objections. Charlie got his planning permission.

He designed the whole place himself. Originally, he had wanted the family to live over the café in a modern luxury apartment. Again and again, the plans were rejected. He could build a transport café, not a house. Again, it was local magistrate and Tory councillor Ted Morrison who led the objectors. Charlie had to concede and the truckstop was finally built. In place of the proposed apartment, twelve single bedrooms were constructed as accommodation for Charlie's customers.

It took over a year to build Charlie's Place. During this time the family lived on site in a large static caravan, as Charlie personally supervised the whole project.

His connections with lorry drivers paid off. Most materials, cement, bricks, timber and the like, arrived in the dead of night. Charlie often boasted that the whole place only cost him a few grand to build.

The finished truckstop looked like a giant log cabin. With neon lights on the roof and floodlit parking for more than a hundred trucks. Along with a large restaurant, there was a bar with entertainment six nights a week. Charlie knew just what truckers wanted, and he supplied it. The place was a resounding success and featured in several truck magazines as a blue print for truckstops of the future

Alongsde the lorry park was a large warehouse with a repair shop and fuel pumps, all earning more revenue for the truckstop. In the back yard, behind the kitchen, was a porta-cabin that Charlie used as his office; a place to hide when things got too hectic.

Only Ted Morrison, seething with resentment, noticed that the two large roadside hoardings, strategically placed some one hundred yards or so either side of the truckstop, advertised every virtue of the place except accommocation. Within a week of the opening, Charlie had converted the twelve bedrooms into four doubles, one on-suite, and a huge lounge. The family moved in shortly afterwards

Charlie Wheeler always got his way.

TUESDAY

Charlie's Place opened for breakfast at 5 am. By 5.30, Carol had cooked, and Charlie had served, over twenty Big Breakfast Specials.

By the time Debbie rolled in at 6.30, that number had nearly doubled. She stumbled through the restaurant, eyes down, as a few lewd truckers whistled at her.

"Where the hell have you been?" said Charlie, as he passed a bacon sarnie over the counter to a driver. "No, don't tell me, let me guess."

Ignoring him, she pushed through the swing doors into the kitchen.

"Good afternoon," said Carol, up to her elbows at the sink.

"Don't you start!" snapped a bleary-eyed Debbie. Her hair was knotted, and last night's make up was smeared all over her face, highlighting her sunken eyes.

"Don't start? Don't start? You've got a nerve!" Carol stopped and took a deep breath. "OK! OK! We'll talk about this later, now how about you making a start? Butter that toast and put some more bread in the toaster."

The mother and daughter relationship they had once enjoyed had disappeared long ago. At about the same time that Debbie had discovered sex. She no longer had to beg and plead and throw tantrums to get the attention she craved. She just smiled and rolled those green eyes.

Charlie swept in through the swing doors. "Two Specials, one double egg, no tomatoes, one no black pudding. Debbie, tables need clearing, now!"

"I can only do one thing at a time," she said.

"Then he must have been very disappointed last night. Have you washed your hands?"

"Piss off!" said Debbie.

"Debs! That's no way to speak to your father!" said Carol.

"Why not? You do!"

And breakfast time at Charlie's Place disintegrated into another normal day.

***

Charlie's customers were well used to the streams of abuse that flowed out of the kitchen; it was all part of the entertainment. They were a mixed bunch, mostly truck drivers, but sales reps and other road users made up a good part of his clientele.

There was a hardcore of regular truckers who had been using his services for years. These were the guys who stayed over, sleeping in their trucks, bellies full of Charlie's fine fare. These were the guys who could drink the bar dry, if the entertainment was good enough. Some were locals, working out of the port at Shorley and calling in most days. Others travelled days to get there. Trucks from all over Europe and Scandinavia were regular visitors.

Charlie always made the effort to listen to their moans and groans. They were his friends, they were his customers, they were his meal ticket.

He'd always had a brilliant business acumen. Analysing the business constantly, maximising his assets to the full. The evening entertainment was his bread and butter. Drivers diverted miles off their route to catch Kitty titillating the Monday and Wednesday night slots.

Tuesday's Country and Western Night was a bit slow. A few weeks back Charlie had tried to encourage a local group of line dancers to pop in and boost the till. But when they arrived, in their ten-gallon hats and spur-jingling boots, they got such a piss-taking reception from the truckers that they left early, vowing never to return. The Thursday night comedian never got as many laughs.

But few of Charlie's ideas failed so miserably. When his lunch-time takings started to fall, he fly-posted the local industrial estate in Shorley, offering cheap set meals at Charlie's Place; cheap enough to make the ten-minute journey worthwhile. His lunchtime take doubled.

Friday nights were never busy, most truckers were home with their families then. So, Charlie started 'Karaoke Night at Charlie's Place'. It quickly took off, making a good family night out for the locals from Shorley and Henyard.

The truckstop used to close early on Saturday afternoons, no punters about at all. Then a couple of years ago Charlie had another brainwave. And Saturday night became Band Night. He hired a local band, threw out the fly posters again, and soon Saturday's take was equalling Kitty's Wednesday nights. The clientele left a lot to be desired, and the music definitely wasn't Charlie's scene, but it was a success just the same.

Sunday was another quiet day. They opened at 10am but there was very little passing traffic until early evening. Carol and the girls had wanted to close for the day. Have a day off, like normal people do.

But Charlie wasn't having any of it. A few continental drivers usually week ended at the truckstop. They needed feeding, and boy, could they drink on their day off.

But he agreed that all this downtime wasn't productive. So, he called in on a couple of local old folks' homes and convinced the owners that he could feed their charges a lot more cheaply than they could. But only on Sundays between 12am and 2pm. It would be a nice day out for the old dears.

Now Charlie was guaranteed twenty-five set meals every Sunday. And the rest of the family were guaranteed the sight of twenty-five old incurables being force fed by their keepers. Penny was disgusted by the dribbling old ladies, shouting abuse at one another. Debbie was disgusted by the wandering hands of the old men, as she cleaned up around them. And Carol was disgusted by the disgust of her children.

"They all have God's love," she told them. "You'll have to face up to old age one day. We all will."

***

Charlie sat at the back of the restaurant having a brew, contemplating his future. Calm had descended on the truckstop. Only half a dozen drivers still lingered over their meals, watching the morning news on a large TV set on a table in the corner. The next rush would be for lunch.

The local TV reporter was in Shorley. A new container base was due to open in the port, and the locals were concerned about the large increase expected in traffic. Shorley was only a small one street town, and that one street was already clogged up most of the day with trucks coming and going to the docks.

Charlie watched impassively. He should have been pleased; every truck had to pass the truckstop on the way in and out of Shorley. But he had other things on his mind.

"Alright, Charlie?"

His thoughts were interrupted as a driver shouted a greeting across the tables.

Charlie raised a hand. "Great, Dave, just great."

"Kitty was popular last night," said Dave. He was an old boy, a regular Monday nighter, had been for years.

"Kitty's always popular," said Charlie.

"Yeah, I know, but last night I had to queue!"

A few other drivers laughed knowingly.

Debbie appeared from the washroom, mop and bucket in hand. She was fuming. "Those showers are bloody disgusting!" she yelled, to no one in particular. "And the graffiti! Yuk! Bloody perverts!"

A couple of drivers jeered and gave her a round of applause.

She stormed through into the kitchen and the yelling continued for all to hear. "When's that lazy bitch sister of mine back? I'm fed up doing all her shit jobs!"

"Calm down, Debs," said Carol. "She'll be back soon."

"Not soon enough. Have you seen the drawings in the men's bog? Those wankers can't even spell my fucking name right!"

The yelling entertained everybody in the place, except Charlie. He held his head in his hands in despair. Looking out of the window across the lorry park, he watched trucks from all over Europe and beyond, pulling out. He'd often wished he'd been a truck driver. All that freedom and travel. Just going home every few weeks or so. No nagging family on your back all the time.

Across the yard he saw Donkey, his yard foreman, making his way over for his breakfast. How Charlie envied him. Young, single and free, and with no ties. If he were Donkey, he wouldn't be wasting his time around here. He'd be off around the world enjoying himself. And with Donkey's assets, there was no doubt he could have a lot of fun.

"Got any fags, Charlie?" A young skinny driver stood hovering over the table.

"No, sorry, Steve, should be here tonight."

"Put four hundred Bensons by for me, will you? I'll be by again on Friday."

"Sure, I'll hold them for you."

"Thanks, Charlie," said Steve, ambling off.

Charlie was expecting Borg back tonight. Most of the booze and fags he'd be bringing were already sold.

***

Donkey strolled in and stood at the counter. He was starving, he'd been busy all morning serving diesel at the pumps.

A good-looking stocky lad in his mid-twenties, his long fair hair hung neatly in a pony tail. Wiping his hands down his overalls, he called out through the serving hatch behind the counter. "Morning!"

"Morning, Donkey, alright?" said Debbie, coming out through the swing doors. "How's it going?" She poured him his coffee.

"Yeah, not bad at all, and you? You're looking a bit tender; good night last night?"

"Oh, yeah," she said, sarcastically. "He was a real athlete! Quick off the mark and determined to come first!" She giggled and looked away like an embarrassed school girl.

Donkey laughed. He liked Debbie, bit of a slut, but then he liked that in a woman. He could probably have her any time he liked, but so could most people. She might be a good looker, but she was also the boss's daughter, almost family.

True, that hadn't stopped him with Carol. But that was different. A one off a long time ago. Shouldn't have happened, but it had. Damned alcohol!

Taking his scrambled egg breakfast from Debbie, he went and sat down with Charlie at the back of the restaurant. "Morning, boss."

"Is it?" said Charlie. "How's them tyres going?"

"Yeah, great. Another one this morning, I think."

"Good, can't be that many left now."

"About a dozen or so. Not bad out of thirty."

"Yeah, you've done well."

"I think this is him now," said Donkey, nodding in the direction of the door.

A scruffy driver, fag in mouth, came in and made for the counter. He babbled loudly to Debbie in French.

"No parly voo!" said Debbie, loudly. "Speak slowly! In English!"

"Problem!" said the agitated driver. "Problem!" He made hissing noises and waved his hands about a lot.

"Oh, you've got a puncture! Why didn't you say? Donkey! Customer!"

"Ten minutes," said Donkey, pointing to his breakfast. "Tell him I'll be out in ten minutes."

***

Carol sat with Debbie at the kitchen table. They were having a cup of tea and a well- earned break. Though both had blonde hair, Carol's was natural. The tiredness showed in her face. She was stressed, these were difficult times for her.

Debbie was whingeing again. "So, when's Little Miss Perfect likely to grace us with her company?" she asked.

"If you mean Penny, I've got no idea." Carol sipped at her tea. "I don't know why you two can't get on. She used to idolise you when she was younger."

"We don't get on 'cos she's an idle bitch and..."

"Oh, don't, please! I've got a headache. Isn't Borg back today? You should be so happy, engaged to a handsome Swede, and such a nice lad. You should be thinking ahead to the future and thanking God for his blessing."

"Oh, do shut up!"

"Debbie! I'm your mother, remember that!"

"Well, don't give me all that Jesus stuff. What's got into you lately? You never used to be like this."

"I have discovered true love, and it was Him who gave me this love..."

"Isn't that what you're supposed to get from Dad?" said Debbie. "You see, that's what puts me off the thought of settling down with just one bloke, I could so easily end up like you!"

"There's nothing wrong with our relationship, thank you."

"That's not what you told dad last week. You said you wished you'd never married him."

"You weren't supposed to be listening."

"The whole bloody restaurant was listening."

"Well, I'm sorry," said Carol.

"But you had to marry him, didn't you? Because of me. How do you think that makes me feel?"

"Look, Debs, I'm... "

"Unwanted, that's how I feel. Always have done and always will."

"That's not true, Debs. Of course we both love you." She reached over and took Debbie's hand. "And, yes, we have our ups and downs, but we're OK, we'll get by."

"Yeah? So, when was the last time you made mad passionate love?"

"Debbie!" Carol was shocked. "That isn't something you ask your mother."

"Why not?"

Because, thought Carol, you wouldn't like the answer.

"What about Kitty?" said Debbie. "You not worried when he gives her a lift home?"

"What are you suggesting? You don't for one moment think that he and Kitty..."

"Why not?"

"She's half his age..."

"Yeah, and the rest," said Debbie. "Mutton dressed as lamb, you said last week."

"Kitty is a good friend, to both of us; we've known her for years."

"Don't mean he ain't giving her one."

Carol had no such worries about Charlie. The problem never came up. In fact, that was the problem. Since the day Penny had been born, Charlie had struggled to perform. She blamed the fact that he'd witnessed the occasion. She'd tried everything, dressing up, dressing down, she'd even suggested bondage, but nothing seemed to kindle his fire. No way would he see a doctor, that would mean admitting to a problem. All these years she'd had to find other ways to purge her urge. But now, she no longer needed Charlie, or her vibrator. The good Lord had provided.

"If anybody's morals are due for examination," said Carol, "it's yours. What would Borg say if..."

The back door of the kitchen suddenly opened, and in breezed Barry.

"Morning all, Carol, Debbie. Cup of tea? Love one! Cheers!"

"Morning, Barry," said Carol. "In the pot, help yourself."

Debbie pulled a face and held her nose, Carol kicked her under the table.

Barry poured himself a cuppa, then sat down with them at the table. Debbie moved her chair away. His white boiler suit, soiled with various decaying reds and browns, oozed the smell of death. His Wellington boots were caked in a congealed crust of blood and gore.

Barry worked at the local knacker's yard. He drove the truck that took the old and diseased animals to the plant. Then he drove their remains to the dog food factory. And in between, he helped cut them up.

Reaching deep inside his overalls, he pulled out a bloody, newspaper wrapped parcel and slapped it down on the table. "Pig's liver," he said. "Tell Charlie a fiver, OK?"

Carol picked up the package and, getting up, transferred it to the sink. "Thanks, Barry. He's about somewhere if you want to see him."

"No, it's OK, I'm in tonight, so I'll see him then. Is Penny back?"

"No," said Debbie, "She bloody well ain't."

"I haven't seen her for ages," he muttered.

"I know, Barry, she was only saying last week how she missed you."

"Really? She said that?" He ran his hand through his scraggy, uncombed hair, his big smile showing off his badly-stained teeth.

"Yeah, really," said Debbie. "You must know she fancies you. She's always going on about you, ain't she, Mum?"

Carol smiled but refused to take part in Debbie's little game.

Barry couldn't hide his excitement. "Can you ask her to give me a call when she gets back?"

"Sure," said Debbie. "I bet she'll be on the phone in a flash!"

***

Swinging the sledge hammer high above his head, Donkey brought it crashing down onto the rim of the tyre. His body shook with the impact as the tyre broke free from the wheel. The chain-smoking Frenchman stood close by, repeatedly checking his watch.

Serves him right, thought Donkey, he should have had a spare. The tyre was illegal anyway and shouldn't have been on the road. That's why Donkey had chosen it, in the dead of night as the Frenchman slept, probably dreaming of Kitty. Now he'd have to pay for a new tyre. Good job Charlie had one in stock. Good news for Charlie, another one gone, and good news for Donkey, he got a bonus for every tyre sale. This was the second one this week.

Charlie had intercepted the load of Polish remoulds on its way from Warsaw to Bristol. The Bulgarian truck driver had stopped off for the night at the truckstop and, after a few beers with Charlie, was only too keen to offload 30 of the huge tyres into Charlie's warehouse. In exchange for some hard currency, of course.

Charlie was more like a mate than a boss; he looked after Donkey, especially in the early days. Six years ago, Donkey had arrived at the truckstop as a twenty-one-year-old hitch-hiker, broke and broken. And just plain Richard Wells. He'd left his native Leeds six months earlier after a failed romance. The love he'd given had not been returned. Not to him anyway. It had been the latest in a long line of betrayals. He'd run away from it all and hit the road. A new beginning, he told himself. He planned to see the world and discover his real self. But after a few months on the road he discovered that the world was a shit place, and his real self couldn't handle it.

He was broke and hungry when, one night, a truck dropped him off at Charlie's Place. Unable to pay for his supper, he'd asked Charlie if there was any chance of a little work. That same night he was helping him handball twenty pallets of Chilean wine off the back of one truck and into another. Charlie said he could stay a while, and he moved into the old static caravan, now parked at the top of the lorry park, that used to be the Wheeler family residence.

He started off as the odd job man, unblocking sinks, changing light bulbs and serving behind the bar when things got busy. He learnt early on not to ask too many questions, in fact, best not to ask any at all.

Soon Charlie was calling him his yard foreman and he was putting in a fourteen-hour day, mostly serving diesel. A small kiosk alongside the fuel pumps, with a washroom out back, served as his office. Charlie's diesel was cheap and sold well.

A year after Donkey first began working for him, Charlie put him through his driver training, and he passed his HGV Class 1 first time. It was all part of a grander scheme of course. Within weeks he was working for a multi-national haulage company, delivering electrical goods all over the country. The third day on the job, Donkey diverted his Glasgow-bound load of TV's to a cousin's warehouse in Dorset, and then left the empty truck in a lay-by in Hampshire. Charlie met him in the car, with a big smile and an even bigger bonus.

Donkey got a new job every few months or so. He'd work a few days to suss out the best runs, then when the opportunity came, he'd disappear with a high value load, usually wine or electrical goods, but occasionally fashion garments. Sometimes he'd deliver it to Charlie's warehouse, but mostly the gear would go straight to a cousin.

It was Charlie who had given him his nickname. He'd been in the loo one night, stood at the urinals. Charlie came in, glanced down, as you do, and suddenly exclaimed, "Fucking hell, mate! You're hung like a flaming donkey!"

Charlie then rushed back out into the bar, telling all and sundry what he'd just seen. "Hung like a bloody donkey!" he kept saying, over and over again. The name stuck, and from that day on, everybody called him Donkey.

At first, it was highly embarrassing for young Richard, the laughs, the sniggers and the innuendoes. He'd been there before of course, at school. The showers after rugby were a nightmare. The staring, the jibes, the boisterous grabs at it that made his class mates laugh so loud. Now he knew it was just envy, penis envy. He was more than twice as long as the nearest contender, and a lot thicker than any he'd seen. He left school gratefully and with very few friends.

It wasn't until he worked at Charlie's Place that he realised his abnormal growth was actually an asset rather than a handicap. Especially with his hobby.

Women would be right up front with him. Why the nickname? they'd ask. He could tell when they already knew, it was in their eyes. But they wanted to hear it straight from the Donkey's mouth. It was a turn on for them, just talking about it.

They were all the same, especially the Saturday nighters, the teenage vamps that descended on the truckstop from Shorley to hear the local bands play. Rarely did he go home alone on Saturday nights. It served his collection well. Donkey's hobby was unique, but nobody could ever know about it.

***

"Great! Fucking great!" cried Charlie. "Yes, of course! Go for it, Tommy! Go for it! Well done, Tommy! Well done!"

Charlie slammed the phone down and leapt from his office chair. "Yes! What a result! What a bloody result!" Dancing a little jig, he punched the air. "Yes!"

Carol was right, there was a God! And right now, he was smiling down on Charlie Wheeler.

Good old Tommy! He was in line for a big bonus for this one. He'd found a buyer for the truckstop! A buyer who was prepared to pay cash, in exchange for a discount, of course, and accepted the need for speed and secrecy. He'd be coming to see the place on Monday, while Carol was away doing her good deeds. First she'd know about it would be a postcard from Spain. Glad you're not here!

A deal to end all deals. Couple of week's tops, Tommy had told him. What a bloody result!

***

Manny Baxter, local property developer and entrepreneur of great renown, had been watching with keen interest the developments at the port of Shorley. He knew weeks before the general public that permission would be granted for the container base. It was his business to know these things. He also knew that rumours of a major ferry company, wanting to operate a passenger service to France from the port, were strongly founded.

Manny's original plan was to buy up land close to the port and build a hotel. Couldn't fail, only competition was a few B&B's. Then, while discussing the project with his accountant, a certain Tommy Thomas, it all came together.

He'd often driven past the truckstop, and although he'd never met Charlie Wheeler, he'd certainly heard of him.

Manny's acute business brain sussed the possibilities immediately. It could be a gold mine. With five acres to play with, and an established business already operating, planning permission for a motel and classy restaurant would be no problem. Its roadside location would guarantee its success. Long term, the plan would be to build up the business for a few years, then flog it off to Granada or Trusthouse Forte.

From what Tommy had said, Wheeler was in a bit of a hurry to make a deal and move on. So, the price would reflect that. It could all be done and dusted in a fortnight, if the price was right.

***

Debbie was knackered. Without Penny around she was pretty much doing an eighteen-hour-day. Her dad refused point blank to even consider hiring more staff. Not that anybody in their right mind would want to work for such a slave driver. Now, sat on a stool behind the bar, she couldn't stop yawning.

On stage, Betty Barbell and the Blue Ridge Drifters were tuning up. Drivers had begun to drift into the bar from the restaurant as Betty tapped the mic and did the old "One two! One two!"

Debbie pulled a pint for an Italian trucker. She just loved his accent. Well, any accent really. French, Dutch, Swedish, she liked them all. She couldn't always tell them apart, but some made her knees go weak.

The driver held on to her hand as she passed him his change. They always did that, the Italians. The French would stare into her eyes, unblinking, and speak in a whisper. The Germans, they'd just demand their lager and undress you with their eyes. And the English? They're just as likely to grin and say something stupid like 'Pint and a blow job, please!'

Debbie knew all about truck drivers, and most of them knew all about her. It wasn't that she was easy, she just liked it. A lot. A trucker had once told her she had the morals of a man. Spot on! If a bloke shagged two or three girls a week, his mates would envy him, or call him a bloody liar! But for a girl, well it was different, wasn't it?

It wasn't just the sex that she so rampantly sought. It was the need to be wanted, cuddled and loved. Making love in a truck was a bit like screwing on a parcel shelf. But that was part of it, the closeness of it all. They couldn't just roll over and go to sleep afterwards, no matter how drunk they were. There wasn't enough room. They had to stay close, all night long.

Debbie moved on to the next customer. She had to be good, Borg would be arriving soon.

She knew her life could change tomorrow, if she wanted it to. Borg wanted to marry her. No problems there, she thought that was great. But he wanted to live here, at the bloody truckstop! Kept talking about living in the old caravan and helping to run the business. What about Donkey? Where would he go? And what about her?

Debbie wanted out. She hated the truckstop and all it represented. She'd only said yes to Borg's proposal in the first place because she'd thought he'd take her away. Why couldn't they live in his native Sweden? Too cold, he said. He knew no one in Sweden, all his friends were here, at the truckstop.

If Debbie had to spend the rest of her life behind the bar at the truckstop, no way could she see herself doing it with just one man.

The band struck up with 'King of the Road'. They had done the same set last week, and every week before that. The truckers moved away from the bar and settled at their tables.

***

The steel guitar and the electric drums filtered through into the restaurant where, at the counter, Charlie was serving the last of the evening's specials, liver and bacon casserole.

"Cheers, Charlie, am I OK for a couple of cases of Stella?"

"No problem, Bob, see me before you turn in tonight."

Bob trotted off with his dinner and Charlie went through into the kitchen.

Carol was mopping the floor. "Keep off!" she said. "Floor's still wet!"

"Alright! I can see that, keep your hair on!"

There was a knock on the back door, and into the kitchen strode Borg. The tall, gangly Swede held open his arms and made for Carol.

"And how is my future mother-in-law?" he asked, his English clear and precise.

"Fine, just fine," said Carol, as Borg gave her a hug.

"Borg!" said Charlie, holding out his hand. "Good to see you mate. Everything OK?"

"Sure, no problems," he said, shaking Charlie's hand with both of his. "The truck is over by the warehouse. I see Debbie, then we offload, yes?"

"Yep. Great. I'll get Donkey to give us a hand. Carol, watch the counter, will you?"

"I'm busy," she said.

"I know," said Charlie, as he went off to find Donkey.

When Charlie came back ten minutes later, he found the happy couple stood tongue locked behind the bar, their bodies grinding shamelessly. Drivers leered and jeered as Debbie's hands roamed freely over Borg's body.

"Thank God you're here, Charlie," said Bernie. "For fuck's sake pour us a pint, will you?"

Other drivers told Bernie to join the queue.

"Debbie!" shouted Charlie. "For Christ's sake, put him down! We're running a bar not a bloody exhibition. There's customers waiting." He pulled gently on Borg's arm. "Come on, mate, there's work to do."

Charlie and Borg had a good thing going. Borg drove for a Dutch company, collecting and delivering flowers all over Europe. Once a fortnight he would come by Charlie's Place. On the way he'd stop off in Belgium and do a bit of shopping for Charlie. Just a few cases of tobacco and cigarettes, and lots of cases of beer and wine. It was a very profitable venture for both of them.

It took the three of them nearly an hour to offload all the contraband into the warehouse. Guitar riffs floated across the lorry park, as Borg passed down the last case of Stella Artois from the back of his truck.

"Right!" said Charlie, as Donkey closed up the warehouse doors. "First pint's on me!"

"Bloody generous of you," said Donkey. "You feeling alright? You've been grinning like a Cheshire cat all day."

"Never felt better," said Charlie. "I'll just get cleaned up, then see you at the bar."

"Next time? Same again?" asked Borg, as he pocketed the wad of notes that was his commission.

"Er, not sure. Yes, but not sure how much, let me think about it." Charlie wasn't planning to be around in a fortnight; he didn't want to lay out cash for something he'd never see.

Back in the bar, Charlie got them in as the band howled on. Betty, suitably big-busted and blonde, though a little on the short, dumpy side, encouraged her audience to join in with a sing song. Halfway through Tammy Wynette's D.I.V.O.R.C.E. some drunken Scousers, along with a Jock or two, started singing Billy Connolly's version of events.

Much more entertaining, thought Charlie. Most of his punters seemed to be of the same opinion, joining in loudly when the dog got to bite his B.U.M.

Betty struggled on with the song. Whoever reckoned that truck drivers liked cowboys had never been near one. A cowboy or a trucker. They were bloody hard work. Unless you got your tits out, you had no bloody chance.

Donkey, sat at the bar, tried to explain to Borg why everybody was laughing. He failed miserably.

Barry, already on his third pint, had a go. Although he'd shed his overalls, the smell still lingered. "Same song. Different words. We sing funny version. Yes? Understand?" He spoke haltingly and loudly like he was speaking to a child.

"Yes, Barry," said Borg. "I understand your English, you speak it quite well. I don't understand the humour, that is all. The group, they are good? Yes?"

"No, they're bloody crap!" said Donkey, laughing.

***

As soon as the shutters came down on the bar, Debbie was away. Sod the glasses! Grabbing Borg by the hand, she dragged him out of the bar and into the lorry park.

Jeering truckers wished him luck. Their childish jibes of "We know where you're going," rang with envy. Tonight, she was Borg's.

Borg's wagon was a new Daf Super Space Cab, the pride of anyone's fleet. The metallic blue artwork was covered with a constellation of silver stars. Massive spot lights hung from the chrome bull bars that protected the Daf from straying moose.

As Borg slipped the key into the door, Debbie came from behind and threw herself at him. They face locked as their hands dug deep into the folds of each other's bodies.

Borg pulled her tight to him. "It's been so very long," he said. "I miss you badly."

"Oh Borg, I missed you too," she said breathlessly, unbuckling his belt. There was an urgency about her.

"No, not here! Slow down, we get into the cab, slow down..." Breaking free, Borg held her hands still.

Debbie agreed, reluctantly. She was hot! She wanted it now! As Borg climbed up into the cab, she tugged on his jeans and they slipped down, revealing his tanned buttocks. She slapped his arse and he accelerated his climb. She followed him in and immediately began ripping her clothes off. Borg quickly closed the curtains.

The big Daf was one of the largest cabs she'd been in, and she'd been in quite a few. She didn't like Volvo's. The beds were too small, and you had to lay down to get your gear off. Very unladylike. She didn't like Scanias much, either. The roof was too low, you kept banging your head. Renaults, now she liked them. The Renault Magnum was bloody huge, you could walk about inside them.

She'd once got off with a driver who, to her horror, drove a transit van. He only had a sleeping bag in the back, and when he'd finished with her, he kicked her out!

Bastard! So now, before she got to know anyone properly, she always asked them what truck they drove. They liked her taking an interest.

Standing up certainly wasn't a problem in the Daf. Borg stood behind her, bending her over the steering wheel. She squealed with delight as he took her, fast and furious.

"Yes! " she cried. "Yes! Yes!"

They went through their whole catalogue of positions before, with the cab rocking wildly, Debbie finally rode Borg to a grand orgasmic finale of screams and grunts. Gasping for breath and exhausted, they lay in a tight twist of hot sweaty flesh. Borg was snoring soon after.

***

'Since you came into my life, my lord, my master, the veil of gloom surrounding me has lifted. Like a bright light within me, I glow with thoughts of you. The knowledge of your love for me, and mine for thee, helps me through these long meaningless days. When I offered you my love, you took it as gratefully as I gave. My body still aches from that day. The day I discovered your love. The day I was reborn. That day in church will remain in my mind and heart forever. Your gift of love will always be returned. Amen.

P.S. See you in church on Sunday.'

Carol sealed the letter into an envelope, wrote J.C. on it, and slipped it into her handbag. In the dressing table mirror, the worn-out Carol looking back out at her wasn't the one she felt living inside. The crow's feet, the lines, the dry skin. It was all there. The wear, the tear, the scars and the memories. It had been a long marriage. Twenty years is long enough for anybody. Even Charlie said he'd have got less time for murder.

They only got married because she became pregnant. Charlie said he would have married her anyway, but she'd never believed that. At the time she was just happy to get away from Tommy. She was young and so innocent then.

But now, she'd seen the light. She was tired of living a sham with him. What had they got apart from a crappy business and two arsey kids? Charlie said they were making good money, but he'd never spend any. One day, we'll sell up and move to Spain, he used to say. That had appealed to her when she was in her twenties. Just a few more years, he'd say. Then in her thirties, when the truckstop really took off, with the new building and all, he'd said let it ride, plenty of time left to retire.

Now, in her forties, she saw Charlie for what he was, a wide boy who would never give up the truckstop. His constant wheeling and dealing was as much a part of his life as washing pans at the sink were hers. Only he enjoyed what he did.

The love and romance a wife should expect from her husband had disappeared years ago. She'd tried, the Lord knew how she'd tried. She even used to wear those awful stupid shoes he kept buying her. Every birthday, every Christmas, year in, year out. All he ever bought her was bloody shoes! Her wardrobe resembled that of Imelda Marcos, most of them worn just the once to please Charlie.

Things started to change after Penny was born. She should never have let him see the birth. She was sure that's why he and Penny never got along.

Charlie had been her first lover. She'd left Tommy for him. Or rather Tommy had left her, after catching them together, semi-naked in the pub car park. They'd hardly spoken since. But Tommy and Charlie were still the best of buddies. Strange how things had turned out.

She saw Charlie when he flirted with Kitty, but she didn't care anymore. If Kitty could get him to perform, then good luck to her. Carol had tried everything except splints. She doubted even that would work.

She'd not been an angel herself in the past. But only the once. One night, after a row with Charlie, she'd had a few gins and ended up crying on Donkey's shoulder. He was so kind and understanding. And when she'd kissed him, he'd responded and took her to bed. The bed in their old caravan, her old matrimonial bed! What a night! He was so bloody big. And did he know how to use it! That bed had never seen such action when Charlie shared it with her. She ached the next day. She wanted more, but Donkey had said no. It was a one off, caused by alcohol and distress. No way did he want to destroy his friendship with Charlie.

For a few hours of her life, she'd thought she'd escaped. But she knew Donkey was right. The kids were still young then, and maybe, just maybe, they really would get to Spain one day. And so, her weary existence had continued.

But not for much longer. She had found something that had changed her life. She was blessed, and she knew it. Charlie was right in a way; twenty years was far too long to serve only one master. Her life, from now on, belonged to her saviour.

Wednesday

Penny took a deep breath before going in through the front door.

Her dad was handing a couple of Big Breakfast Specials over the counter when he saw her. "Jesus fucking Christ!" he yelled out. "What the bloody hell have you done?"

The breakfasting truckers all turned away from the TV and stared.

"Oh no!" her mum cried, coming out from the kitchen. "Penny! How could you?"

"Hi!" said Penny. "Nice to see you too!" Standing in the doorway, denim clad, and with her rucksack on her back, she gave a little wave.

Her dad just stood there, mouth wide open in horror. Her mum looked like she was about to burst into tears.

Penny really couldn't see what the all fuss was about. She'd never liked her hair anyway. Nobody did, it was just too stringy and thin. She thought her newly-shaved head looked just great. Although, it was a little on the pink side, where the sun had caught it. Maybe it was the jewellery that upset them. It was only like an ear ring, except it was through her nose, and the stud in her eyebrow, well, it was so tiny you could hardly see it. She'd bottled out of the tongue stud, maybe next time. They should see Killer; he'd really freak them out.

"You look like bleeding Frankenstein!" said her dad, shaking his head.

"Wait 'til you see the tattoo!" said Penny, slipping off the rucksack.

"Oh no! Please God, no!" said her mum, sitting down quickly, looking quite faint.

"Only joking! Ha! Ha! Had you going then, didn't I?"

It was the first time she'd gone away on her own, and it wasn't going to be the last. The whole experience of Glastonbury had blown her tidy little world to pieces. The Wheelers little girl was no more! Now she was a warrior, with battles to fight. And she'd become a woman! She'd lost something very precious at Glastonbury and discovered just what else the world had to offer. Walking over to her mum, she kissed her on the cheek.

"Why?" spluttered her mum. " Why?"

"Because she's bloody stupid, that's why!" said her dad. "Aren't you supposed to have parental permission for that sort of thing?"

"Dad, I'm eighteen, remember? I can do what I like."

"Not while you're living under my roof..."

"Nice to see you, Penny," mocked Penny, flopping her head from side to side like a clown. "We've really missed you."

"We have, Pen, we have!" said her mum, getting up and giving her a hug. "We're just a bit shocked that's all. Did you have a nice time?"

"Too right I did! It was just great! I had..."

"Excuse me," interrupted her dad. "Do you think we could listen to your holiday yarns later? We are running a business, remember? Carol, a Big Breakfast for Cyril, and Pete's still waiting for his sausage sarnie. That reminds me, where's Debbie? She's got to stock the bar, busy night tonight."

***

Charlie couldn't believe what she'd gone and done. She looked like a bloody zombie! He'd told Carol repeatedly that Penny wasn't mature enough to go off on her own. But she wouldn't have it. And now look what had happened. He was sure Carol had only let her go in the first place to piss him off. Still, it wouldn't be a problem for much longer. Not for him anyway. In a few weeks' time he would be retiring. Cashing in on his life's endeavours. Recuperating on a beach in Spain, or maybe even South America.

***

Penny unpacked her backpack in her bedroom, then went for a shower. Looking at her nakedness in the bathroom mirror, she thought of Killer. He'd told her she was beautiful. No one had ever told her that before. And that's just how she felt. Beautiful.

How her life had changed since she was last here. It didn't feel like home any more, it felt like she was just visiting. Now there was a sense of purpose to her life, and a need to stretch out into the outside world. A need to be free.

Back in her bedroom, she listened to the sounds coming up from the restaurant. Drivers laughing and joking, the TV, her dad calling out orders. Reality. She dressed and went back downstairs to the workhouse.

Her mum gave her a hug, then they sat together, at the kitchen table.

"I'm sorry, Pen," said her mum, taking her hand. "It was such a shock, that's all. And you of all people!"

"Why not me? What's wrong with me?"

"Nothing, but it's just not like you to go off and..." She gently touched the razor nicks on Penny's head, then, taking a tissue, dabbed at the red sore spreading out from her nose ring. "Did it hurt?"

"Pain is all relative to what you hope to achieve."

"Is that a yes? Why the haircut? You had such beautiful hair."

"No, I didn't, Dad said it looked like straw!"

"He didn't mean it; besides you were only six at the time."

"It's things like that that shape your life. By cutting off my hair, I'm making a statement. By cutting off my hair, I'm letting the vibes flow into my head more freely. By cutting off my hair..." Penny paused. What was it Killer had said? Statement, vibes... Oh yes. "By cutting off my hair, I am allowing my new persona to grow, along with my new hair."

"All sounds a bit artsy fartsy to me, Pen, sorry!"

"Mum, I'm not the little girl who waved you goodbye last week, I've changed."

"Oh, I see, it's a boy then?"

"How did you guess?" Penny's eyes sparkled.

"What's he like? Tell me all about him."

"Oh, you'd absolutely hate him," she giggled. "I just know you would!"

Mother and daughter laughed together, and the warmth returned.

"So, what's his name?"

"Killer," said Penny.

"Killer?"

"Yeah, it's his nickname."

"Why?"

"Don't ask."

"What's he look like?" asked her mum. "Tall, dark, handsome...?"

"It shouldn't matter what he looks like, I'm in love with his soul. It's what's inside that counts."

"Ugly bugger then!"

They both burst into a fit of laughter.

"Glad you both find it so funny." Charlie came in through the swing doors carrying a tray of dirty plates. "But what I want to know is, when is her Ladyship going to be available for work?" He put the tray down on the table. "I hate to say this but, yes, we actually did miss you. Now you're back, maybe we can all take it a bit easier. Carol, watch the counter, I've some important phone calls to make. Penny, beef burgers, in the freezer, get them out to thaw." He turned to go.

"Sorry, Dad, I can't."

He stopped in his tracks. "What do you mean, can't?"

"I'm a vegetarian now. I don't eat dead animals anymore. And no way am I going to be touching any slabs of butchered flesh!"

"What?" he gasped. "A bloody vegetarian! What's wrong with eating dead animals? It's what they're for, ain't it? This is a café, remember? Our customers eat it, so you can help bloody cook it!"

"No! No way! I'm not touching the stuff!" This was the new confident Penny. Directing her life in the way she wanted it to go. Killer had given her this confidence. He'd picked her up and turned her life around. "Dad, we're shitting in our own nest, we're trashing the Earth! I want to try and change all that!"

"What's that got to do with being a bloody veggie?"

"You can judge a species by the way it treats other species on our planet. Have you ever been to a slaughter-house?"

"Have you?" he jeered back.

Penny ploughed on. "What right have we to devour them? Imprison them, beat them, feed them poisons just so their flesh becomes more tender. It's disgusting!"

"So, what are you going to do?" he asked. "Just serve tea and cereals?"

"I'll work in the bar; Debbie can work in here."

"Oh! So, you've discussed this with her then, have you?"

"No, but I will."

"Well, just make sure I'm not around when you do." He thought for a bit. "What about Bloody Marys?"

"That's right," said Penny. "If you can't win an argument with logic, just take the piss. It's an old parental custom, especially in this family!"

"I don't have to put up with this crap," said Charlie, storming out of the kitchen.

***

Helen Cunningham's day had just gone from bad to worse. First a blazing row with John over breakfast, when she'd had the nerve to disagree with him, and now she'd hit a pot hole in the road and got a puncture! She had so much to do before evensong, and she was already running late.

John was so controlling. Her mother had warned her that the age difference between them was too great. He acted more like a father than a husband. Why couldn't he just accept that she needed more out of life than weddings and garden parties?

She had managed to pull her Mini off the road and into the café, just outside the village. Now she just sat there, on the garage forecourt, feeling quite tearful and wandering what to do next.

A knock on the car door made her jump. A tall young man in overalls, with a long pony tail, stood there, peering in.

"Are you OK?" he asked.

She wound down the window. "Yes. Yes, thank you, but I do seem to have a puncture. Could you repair it for me?"

"Looks way beyond repair to me," he said, poking the tyre with his foot. "Have you got a spare?"

"In the boot, I think," she replied. "Will you, can you change it for me?"

"Well, we don't normally deal with cars," he said, a broad smile lighting up his face, "but how can I resist such a pretty damsel in distress?"

Helen blushed as she handed him the keys for the boot. Getting out of the car, she watched as he effortlessly lifted out the spare and set about changing the wheel. He was a few years younger than her, but seemed the strong and capable type. Quite handsome too.

"Is there a pay phone I could use?" she asked him. She needed to tell John of the delay in her busy schedule.

"No, sorry, but there's a phone on my desk, in the kiosk," he replied. "Help yourself."

John wasn't very sympathetic. Why hadn't she looked where she was going? If the pothole was that big, why didn't she see it? He seemed only too willing to carry on where he'd left off at breakfast. She couldn't hold back her sobs; she felt wretched.

"Don't start your blubbing again," he said. "Did you..."

She hung up. He'd reduced her to tears again. She didn't want to give him the satisfaction of hearing them.

A muffled cough made her turn. The young man was standing in the doorway.

"Your keys," he said, hand outstretched. "All done." He paused, then said gently, "Are you OK?"

"Yes, of course," she replied, dabbing at her eyes with a tissue. "Men! What would we do without them?" She forced a laugh.

"Local, are you?" he asked.

"Yes," she said softly. "I'm Helen Cunningham." She coughed to clear her throat. "My husband is the vicar, in Henyard."

"Oh right, not someone I've met."

"No, probably not."

"He's a lucky man," he said, making her blush again. He was flirting with her, his eyes seemed to bore right into hers.

"And you? Are you local?" she asked him.

"Yes, I live in the caravan, top of the yard." He offered out his hand, "I'm Donkey," he said, with a big grin on his face.

"Did you say... Donkey?" She laughed. "What a strange name."

"It's my nickname."

"Oh really? Why?" she asked, as she gently shook his hand.

"You really don't want to know!"

"Why not? What do you...?" She paused as she suddenly realised the implication. "Oh! You mean...? Oh!" Her hand went to her mouth. She turned her face away as it reddened.

"I'm sorry," he said. "You did ask!"

"No, it's me. I'm sorry!" She hesitated, looking around. "Er, have you somewhere I can wash my hands, please?" Her eyes avoided his.

"Of course, I'll show you."

She followed him round to a grubby washroom at the rear of the kiosk. He apologised for the state of the place. "Bloody truck drivers!"

As she sat on the toilet, her mind was racing. Her body tingled in a way she had long forgotten about. John had stopped flirting with her the day after they'd got married. He never paid her compliments anymore. Donkey. How brazen was a nickname like that? And he was so handsome and rugged. The themes of her teenage fantasies, a life time ago.

She reminded herself that she was a married woman, for better or for worse. How she wished she'd listened to her mother.

After washing her hands and composing herself, she opened the door to find him waiting outside.

"Thank you for helping me out," she said. "Today has been a really bad day for me."

"Well, we all have our shit days," he said, with a grin. "Mine has been a really good day, I met you!"

She could feel the blood rushing to her cheeks. He had a twinkle in his eye that should have frightened her.

"How much do I owe you?" she asked, opening her handbag.

"Oh, just forget it," he said. "See it as a community service. My good deed for the week."

She took a five-pound note from her purse and held it out to him. "Please, I insist," she said, trying to force it into his hand.

He put his hand over hers. "No, I insist... " His hand held onto hers quite firmly.

She could smell the sweat on him, her heart was racing out of control. Looking into his eyes, she whispered softly, "Thank you... Donkey."

He leant forward, so did she. Their lips almost brushed, but she pulled away. Donkey put his hand on the back of her head, and gently pulled her back. A soft moan, more like a purring, emanated from the back of her throat as their lips met.

Her mind was scrambled. What on earth was she doing? How had this happened? May God forgive me, she thought, as she gave in to her desires.

The kiss was hard, forceful even, sending shock waves racing around her body. He gently backed her back into the washroom, kicking the door shut behind them and sliding the bolt. Pulling her back into his arms, his tongue forced her mouth open and his hands began wandering freely over her body.

Undoing the buttons on her blouse, he pulled her breasts free from her bra. She gasped as his cold hands caressed and squeezed. The sensations, surging through her trembling body, made her legs week and her mind dizzy. Then, when Donkey lowered his head and began teasing her nipples with the tip of his tongue, she thought she would explode!

Pushing her back against the wall, he lifted her skirt up around her waist, and his hands began exploring her erogenous zones. Pulling her silk panties to one side, he drove her on, caressing her quite vigorously.

"Ouch!" she cried, as a sudden tug on her pubic hair made her jump.

"Sorry!" said Donkey.

Taking her hand, he guided it into his overalls. She shuddered as his hot erection throbbed in her hand. Oh my God! She released him, and began tugging at his overalls, ripping them open until he was fully exposed.

Leaning back, she looked down and gasped! She couldn't take her eyes off it, it was frightening! John's penis was the only one she'd ever seen or touched. But there was no comparison. None at all! She feared it may hurt her, but there was no stopping now. She was so wet! Taking hold of his erection with both hands, she steered him towards her. As he slowly entered, she cried out and bit into his shoulder.

Donkey began gently, teasing her, testing her, seeing how much more she could take. Seeing how much more she wanted to take. The adrenaline racing through her body peaked as Donkey took her somewhere she'd never been before.

When she started to lose all control, he stepped up a gear. With one hand gripped firmly on her bum, and the other clinging to an exposed breast, he slammed her into the wall with every thrust. With her face pushed into his chest, her muffled screaming reached a crescendo, as he thrust wildly to his own climax. The pain! The pleasure! This was like nothing on earth she'd ever experienced before. Wave after wave of vibrating sensations, exploding within her like a volcano.

As she fought to control her erratic breathing, her legs finally gave way, and together they slid slowly down to the floor. She held tightly onto him as they recovered in silence, sat in a crumpled heap, amongst the debris on the washroom floor.

As the euphoria slowly faded, Helen came back down to earth with a bump.

"Sorry," said Donkey, looking at his watch, "but I have to get back to work."

They climbed slowly back to their feet. Donkey zipped up as she put away her breasts, all in a very awkward silence.

He walked her back to the car.

"Thank you," she whispered, giving him an embarrassed kiss on the cheek. Then she got into her car and drove home to John.

***

Fucking unbelievable! thought Donkey. The vicar's wife! Charlie ain't ever going to believe this!

As soon as she'd left, Donkey returned to his caravan. From his pocket he gently removed three wiry pubic hairs. Placing them carefully on a small white card, he fastened them securely with a thin strip of Sellotape.

Long straight auburn. Nice. He wrote 'Helen' on the card, along with the date, then filed it away in a blue velvet jewellery box.

Donkey's collection had begun with his first love, when he had been just sixteen. Stephanie, so beautiful, so sexy. So easy. It had been a one-night stand on the beach at Margate. A one-hour stand, really. He lost his virginity, and for that whole hour had thought their love was forever. When she said she had to get back to her boyfriend, he burst into tears and begged her to stay, find a flat together, have babies.

She gently explained to him that she was just passing through his life, an experience never to be forgotten. Enjoy the memories, she told him. When he seemed reluctant to let her go, she gave him a gift. She pulled some pubic hairs from her little ginger bush and put them in a cigarette packet. For you, she said, to remember me by. She broke his heart. Never again would he be able to tell a girl of his feelings, for fear of rejection.

His next romance lasted a bit longer, several months in fact. She went off with a mate of his. But not before he'd retrieved several golden pubic hairs from their bed.

And that seemed to set the pattern for young Richard's love life. His refusal to commit, and his girlfriends' refusal to stay faithful. His love life was a disaster. And when it got too much for him, he ran away from it all.

Since his arrival at the truckstop, his attitude to love and sex had changed. No longer did he seek true romance. They didn't even have to be beautiful; they just had to have nice hair.

When Charlie began Band Nights, a few years back, Donkey's collection really took off. Once word got round about his 'affliction', girls threw themselves at him. On Saturday nights he rarely went home alone. Not all of them were one-night stands, some relationships lasted a few weeks or more. But as soon as they wanted commitment, Donkey was out of there! And back on the great pube hunt.

He didn't always have to pull them out by teeth or hand. Normally, after a vigorous session, he'd collect them up from the bed sheets, or in some cases, from their knickers when they weren't looking. The secrecy of stealing such personal items added to the thrill. He used them like they used him.

He was proud of his collection. All different in their own way. Some short and straight, others long and curly. Blonde ones, black ones and ginger ones, and all shades in between. The youngest, his first, Stephanie, just sweet sixteen. The oldest belonged to Carol. Each trophy reminded him of the conquest.

Over recent years his collection had grown rapidly. Helen had the honour of being his ninety-sixth specimen.

Soon he would be celebrating his century, and he wanted it to be something special.

***

As Penny lay on her bed, the photo collage on her bedroom wall took her back to her childhood. Pony tailed at seven, with Thumper, the long-eared Angora rabbit. She confided in Thumper, told him everything. How she hated her dad and loved her mum. And how she wished Debbie would stop bullying her.

When Thumper died, squashed by a truck after escaping from his cage, everybody blamed her. She had been the last to see him alive. That was a catalyst in her life. The guilt she felt, the hate everybody felt towards her. Oh, happy days.

Then, a wedding snap, some distant relative of her mum. The family all stood posing. She was thirteen, buck teeth and flat-chested, in a demur pink trouser suit. Debbie, all tits and make-up, in a mini-skirt. Dad, aka John Travolta, in his white suit and back combed hair, with his arm around her mum. She looked stressed, but then she always did.

She remembered catching Debbie with her hand down some spotty youth's trousers. When she'd told her dad, he'd shouted at HER! Told her to stop causing trouble! Debbie could do what she liked, still did. But she'd always had to toe the line. Her dad's line.

But it was all so different now. That was then, this is now. There was an urgency to her life, with new goals and objectives. Battles to be fought and won. With Killer at her side, she could change the world.

Killer! How she loved him, how she needed him. He'd taken her through to the other side, shown her the true meaning of life.

She remembered so vividly, that first time they'd met. She'd had a really great time at the festival, listening to all the bands, meeting lots of new people, then at night sleeping in her small tent. She felt so grown up at last, away from her controlling dad.

Then, nearing the end of the festival, just as she was passing by a beer tent in the pouring rain, Killer had stumbled out. He tripped over a guide rope and, despite Penny's effort to avoid him, had crashed right into her. They both fell flat into the mud and, in their efforts to get up, they'd rolled about in each other's arms, laughing and giggling to the point that she'd almost wet herself. It was meant to be. His old leather jacket was covered in mud, but he just grinned that stupid grin and said that it didn't matter.

Killer built a fire outside the port-a-loos, using some bog rolls to get it going. They sat around it drying off. They spent the whole day just talking.

He was an eco-warrior, fighting to save the planet. He'd come to Glastonbury straight from the Newbury by-pass protest. Hundreds of protesters had been arrested, he said, trying to stop ancient woodland being destroyed just to save motorists five minutes on their daily commute. The police were acting as a private army for the bastard Tory government! But the people had had enough and were fighting back.

The protest had been front page news recently and Penny had seen pitched battles on TV; they looked pretty vicious and frightening.

Killer commanded a battalion of some fifty troops and had dispatched them all off to various parts of the country, taking the revolution to the people. Some were at Manchester airport, burrowing under the proposed new runway, others were off sabotaging mink farms and disrupting fox hunts. He himself was leading a group of warriors searching the country for secret GM farms. With their Frankenstein plants, they were the new threat to civilisation, he said.

His freedom fighters were spread so thin on the ground, he'd come along to Glastonbury to recruit more troops.

Penny was enthralled. She'd known for years something was missing from her life, and now she just knew she'd found it.

She listened intently as he described all the suffering he'd witnessed in slaughter houses and battery farms, and how he wanted to rid the world of all these animal abusers. Meat is murder, he said, so it was acceptable to kill those involved in the suffering. The farmers who drugged and tortured the animals, the politicians who allowed it to happen, all legitimate targets.

Penny wasn't too sure about the killing bit, but she could see his point. She resolved there and then, never to eat meat again. She struggled with her conscience, and sought solace in a can of lager, for all the animals she had consumed in her short eighteen years.

It stopped raining, the first time in days. The moonlight bounced off his nose stud, the rings in his eyebrows reflected the stars in her eyes.

When he finally fell silent, they lay back and gazed at the heavens together. It was then, as they lay under the stars, side by side on their sleeping bags, that Killer had made a woman of her.

A couple to their left began to make love, noisily. Penny couldn't help but see hands kneading naked breasts. The young girl cried out, unashamedly.

Somewhere behind her, a rhythmical grunt and a slapping of flesh seemed to confirm that everybody was at it. This had a profound effect on Penny. On the one hand it seemed daring, it excited her, she felt a little damp. But on the other, it distracted her from Killer. She found his exploits riveting; he was so inspirational.

Suddenly he leaned over and whispered sweetly in her ear, "Shall we do it?"

She knew straight away what he meant. "OK!" she said.

Killer rolled on top of her and kissed her. His tongue stud rattled her teeth and set off a filling. She just lay there knowing that the moment was right.

He sat up and wrestled her jeans and panties down to her knees, before pushing her T-shirt and bra up off her breasts. The cool wind on her naked flesh, brought out a desire in her she'd never felt before. She could see people watching, staring at her nakedness, but she didn't care, this was love. What she'd been waiting for all her life, it seemed.

When Killer knelt up and pushed his trousers down, Penny was looking at the first erect penis she'd ever seen. It stuck out from under his grubby vest, a stiff, purple-veined pole.

Then he was on her, his weight pressing her into the soft ground. She couldn't open her legs very wide because her jeans held her knees together. Killer seemed to be having the same problem. His hands fumbled in between their bodies; they were so cold!

Then he was in her! Entering her like a stallion, bucking furiously! The pain! Oh, the pain!

Then, with a grunt and a sigh, it was over. He kissed her and rolled off. Penny pulled up her panties and jeans. It was done, she was a woman, and it felt so good.

They lay side by side all night. He told her how good she was, the best he'd had for ages. When she told him he was the first, she thought he was going to cry.

The following morning, before she headed home, Penny became a full life member to the cause. With Killer's encouragement, she got a nose ring and an eyebrow stud. Together, they had their heads shaved. Their relationship would grow, along with their new hair. Killer wanted to have her name tattooed on his forehead, but he was a bit low on cash. In fact, he had to borrow some from Penny, so he could get back to his troops in Manchester. There was to be a raid on a GM farm, warriors from all over the country were gathering ready for the assault. It could all kick off in the next few days; he needed to be there, to lead his troops into battle.

They did it again before they parted. This time in the platform toilet, as they waited for their trains home. They stood, shirts up, jeans down. Killer pushed into her and squeezed her small breasts. Penny held onto him as he thrashed away. If anything, it took even less time than before. Killer sat down on the loo to get his breath back. She pulled up her jeans and sat on his lap. He told her what a wonderful lover she was, and that he loved her. Penny cried; she had found true love.

Killer went off to Manchester to continue the fight, and she returned home to a family that she felt had never known her.

A brief knock at the door tore Penny from her daydreams as Debbie barged straight into her bedroom. She sat up.

"So, you're back then," she said. "About time too. Jesus Christ! What have you done with your hair? Bet Mum had a fit."

"She'll get over it," said Penny, bravely. "Did you miss me?"

"Only in the kitchen at five every bloody morning, any more of it and believe me, I would have walked out!"

"I need to talk to you about that, Debbie, you see, I'm a vegetarian now and..."

"A veggie? Never! You'll break out in zits, and your bad breath will get even worse, just you watch."

"Cheers. But that's not a problem. You are what you feel, even a leper has a soul."

"What?" cried Debbie, throwing her hands in the air. "You on drugs or what? Dad was right, you've flipped!"

"I have not flipped!" Penny yelled back. "I'm in the process of discovering myself!"

"Wow! Like groovy man!" taunted Debbie, waving a V sign above her head.

"Fuck off, Debbie!" said Penny, turning her back to her. "Just fuck off!"

"Oh, and such language too. What would Mummy say if she could hear her innocent little angel now?"

"Not any more I'm not!" Penny spat back. She just couldn't stop herself. Debbie was such a bitch, it was unbelievable.

"Not what?" said Debbie, her face suddenly lighting up. "What aren't you? Innocent or an angel? No, I don't believe it. Yes! You're blushing. You've done it!" She began jumping up and down like a ten-year-old, pointing at her. "Yes! You've had a shag! Great! About bloody time too!"

Penny squirmed under her interrogation. "No! I... But it wasn't like that..." Be true unto thyself, Killer had said. Be true. Bracing herself, she said firmly, "Yes, it's true, I have. Only I'd prefer to say we made love. It's a lot different to... to what you do."

"What was he like?" asked Debbie. "Was he big? What colour? I've never had a black one, I'm told they're very nice."

"Would you mind leaving my room?" said Penny. "You're making me feel sick!"

"Hope you used a condom, there's a lot of dirty men about."

"And you've had most of them. Now piss off!" cried Penny, jumping up and pointing to the door. "Just bloody go!"

A knock at the door and their mum came in.

"Back to normal already, I see," she said. "Good to see her back, isn't it, Debs?"

"Yes, just wonderful. Has she told you the good news?"

"Debbie!" Penny cried out in horror.

"What's wrong?" asked Debbie, in that innocent drawl that she did so well. "You must want to tell Mummy. You tell Mummy everything."

"Penny, what is it?" asked her mum.

"Go on little Princess, tell Mummy."

"Fuck off, Debbie!" said Penny, close to tears.

"Penny! There's no need for that." her mum shouted. "Debbie, will you stop it. Now! You're like a big kid. I'm sick of your constant bickering. You haven't seen each other for a week and you're at it already." She paused for breath. "Have you sorted out the bar?"

"What about the bar?" asked Debbie, suspiciously.

"Oh, so you haven't."

"What's going on?" demanded Debbie, staring straight at Penny.

"Penny wants to work in the bar, on account of her being vegetarian."

"Well, she can just piss off!" said Debbie. "The bar is mine! You won't get me back in that bloody kitchen. No fucking way! Besides, how can she possibly work in the bar looking like that? She'd drive them all away. They'd think it was a fucking freak show. She can go to hell first!" Debbie stormed from the room slamming the door behind her.

As Penny burst into tears, her mother sat down on the bed beside her and gave her a big hug.

***

Down the hall in the master bedroom, Charlie squeezed into his suit, getting ready for tonight's show. He'd listened to the girls doing battle with a smile on his face. If ever he needed confirmation that he was doing the right thing, then this was it. Soon he'd be gone, away from all this trouble and strife. He began humming 'Viva Espana!' as he fastened his bow tie.

***

Kitty sat on the stool in the ladies' loo. Reflecting back out from the mirror, a young and talented actress prepared herself for an audience with her fanatical fans. Kitty only saw what she wanted to see. At thirty-eight, it was her golden rule for survival.

For the first set tonight, she was Cher. And when she hit the stage, that's just who she'd be. At fifteen she'd come third in a talent show, dressed as Cher. She remembered it as if it were yesterday, the applause and the picture in the local rag.

For the second slot she was Tina Turner, knocking out the rock. She had always wanted to be an actress, and every night on stage she was.

This was a good earner for Kitty. Charlie didn't pay so well, but his customers did. In between shows she met her real fans. They paid court to her in the dressing room. They'd arrive like gentlemen, with a bulge in their pants and a £10 note in their hand. They left with neither. These were her regulars. In the lorry park after the show, it was just quickies at half price while she waited for Charlie to give her a lift home.

They were all the same really, just lonely truckers away from their home and families. Some liked to kiss her, some even French kissed. Ugh! They wouldn't if they thought about it. But then, most of them were pissed, and quite a few never came at all. But there were no refunds, they all knew the score. They just got a short-term lease of any available orifice. And if they couldn't use it to the best of their ability, then that was their fault, wasn't it?

She could always tell the married ones. They never kissed and always went for the blow job. Perhaps their little wifeys didn't like sucking cocks. Maybe, as they fired off their frustrations, they closed their eyes and imagined it was the wife.

Kitty never got too friendly with her punters. Some were good lookers, but most of them were fat, smelly, or just plain ugly. Paying her was the only way most of them were ever going to get it. She saw herself as a social service to the community. After a session with her, a guy was much less likely to go off and rape somebody, wasn't he? If she had, just once in her career, prevented such an attack, then it would all have been worthwhile.

Kitty liked Charlie a lot. She knew he was a crook and she liked the thought that she could be his moll. They understood each other, they knew each other's needs. And Charlie had very special needs.

There was a knock at the door and the man himself came in, Southern Comfort in hand.

"Ten minutes, Miss Le Sadé," he said, passing her the drink. He stooped and kissed her on the back of her neck, then checked his bow tie in the mirror.

"Thanks, my darling," she said, sipping her favourite nectar. "Busy tonight?"

"It's always busy when you top the bill," he replied, kissing her neck again.

She turned to respond with a peck on his cheek.

"Mind the suit," he said, brushing his collar and moving away. "Took ages to shift that lipstick last time. Which ones tonight?"

"Red, white or blue?" she teased.

"White!" he replied, without hesitation.

"I thought so."

"Let me see!"

"No! You'll have to wait!" She spoke in an authoritative voice. She knew he liked that.

"Bitch!" he said.

But she knew he didn't really mind waiting, that was all part of it.

***

Penny slowly pushed the trolley into the restaurant. She'd compromised. She'd had to because Debbie never would. She was now the veggie cook and chief washer upper. Her mum would be cooking the meat and serving it, but she would have to clear it away. She steered between the tables. Bits of it lay on the plates, burnt and decaying. All that suffering and abuse and they just leave it on their plates. Her elbow-length rubber gloves weren't enough, she felt ill.

The truckers, tucking into their evening meals, were pleased to see her.

"Nice to see you back," said Ernie. "Been a madhouse here without you."

"Thanks," said Penny.

"Love the hair do," Terry joked. "Nits was it?"

They all laughed. She'd known most of them for years, they'd watched her grow up.

"No, it wasn't!" she said. "You should try it, let's your brain breathe."

"Debbie said you've got a tattoo, that right?" asked Ernie.

"No, it isn't. But have you seen hers?"

"No, I haven't had that pleasure," he replied. "Where is it?"

"It's just below her belly button. It says 'Queue Here!'"

"Miaow!" said Terry, as they all laughed.

"Hallo, Penny," said a familiar voice behind her.

She turned and saw a blood-caked Barry, just a few feet away.

"My God, Penny!" he gasped. "What have you done?"

"Oh, hallo Barry." She could say no more. His overalls were covered in blood and gore. And the smell! She suddenly felt sick.

"Good to see you back," he stuttered, looking quite shocked at what he was seeing.

"I'm sorry, Barry, but... but I feel quite ill." She tried to manoeuvre around him, gulping, trying to keep the contents of her stomach down.

"But, Pen, I wanted to talk to you."

"Later, Barry, later..."

"Well, can you just give this to Charlie for me then?" Reaching into his overalls he pulled out a blood-sodden, paper parcel and pushed it at her.

Barging past him, Penny fled the restaurant, gloved hand to her mouth.

After a few deep breaths in the lorry park, she felt a bit better. The cool evening air flushed out her mind. Trucks were shunting into parking bays, the drivers hurrying to get a pint in before the show started. She made her way over to the fuel pumps.

Donkey saw her coming and came out of his kiosk to greet her. "Hi, Penny, great to see you back. Have a good time? " He flung his arms around her.

"Yeah, just brilliant. So nice to see someone who's actually pleased to see me."

"Wow, you look great," said Donkey, stepping back. "Really suits you."

"Thanks, Donkey. Do you really think so?"

"Of course I do. Bet your dad was pleased."

"Him and everyone else. God, I hate the lot of them."

"Oh, they're just stressed, that's all. They'll get used to it."

"They don't have much choice, do they?"

"It's what's inside that counts, Penny," he said. "As you well know."

She threw her arms around his neck and kissed him on his cheek. That was the nicest thing anyone had said to her all day.

***

Kitty stood in the wings. Well, that's what Charlie called them. He'd slung a heavy black curtain over a scaffold pole and hung it across the back wall of the stage. Gave it depth, he said. A parting, right of centre, allowed her to come and go gracefully. It also gave Charlie somewhere to watch his punters, unnoticed. The show only began when they were all sat with full glasses.

She stayed poised, listening to his warm up.

"So, open your flies and give a big welcome to the one, the only, ladies and gentlemen, I give you, Miss Kitty Le Sadé!"

The applause rose with the loud music as Cher hit the stage, mic in hand, every bit the superstar. Going straight into 'It's In His Kiss', the long red dress hit the deck moments later to the cheers of the crowd. Clad only in skimpy red bra and panties, Kitty twisted and gyrated to every beat of the song. Then off flew the bra, and her nipples swung freely every which way.

Kitty looked out over her audience. No one was looking at her face, not a one. All eyes were transfixed on her wobbling parts. This was the first show of the night; a quick flash of pubes was all they were going to get. Keeps them keen, and in the bar for the next show. Word soon got around that the late show was the one to watch. Kitty had built her reputation on the late show.

The final bars of the number saw her panties slipped off her rounded bottom and waved above her head. As her baying fans called out for more, she took her bows to all points of the stage.

***

Behind the bar, Debbie was dressed to kill. A tight blue mini skirt and a skimpy red top showed off her assets to all the thirsty truckers. But now Borg was back, she knew she had to be good. It wasn't easy; there was a lot of good-looking guys about.

Barry wasn't one of them. Pulling him his fourth pint of the evening, she ignored his lecherous staring.

"Have you seen Penny yet?" she asked him.

"Yeah, but she said she wasn't feeling well," he replied. "I can't believe she's chopped off all her hair. It looks bloody awful."

"It's so her tiny brain can breathe, apparently. What did you reckon on the metal work? I'm thinking of getting Borg to have a stud in his tongue. Can you imagine what that would be like for me?"

Barry's eyes glazed over, and she knew he was doing just that.

Donkey and Borg arrived at the bar.

"Borg! Glad to see you back, mate," said Barry. "Good trip? "

"It's always a good trip when I end up here," he replied, smiling at Debbie.

"Donkey," said Barry. "Do you think I'm in with a chance with Penny?"

"Hard to say. Would you like to be?" Donkey replied tactfully.

"Too right I would. Wouldn't you?"

"No," cut in Debbie, "he bloody wouldn't. He's not into immature, spotty bald types, are you, Donkey?"

"But she's a vegetarian now," said Donkey. "Wouldn't that get in the way a bit?"

"I can live with that if she can," said Barry. "I wouldn't force her to eat meat."

Debbie took Borg's hand. "You'd hate it, wouldn't you," she said. "if I stopped eating meat?"

Barry left the bar and fought his way to the front of the stage as Charlie began whipping up his punters for the late show.

"Stand back from the stage boys, my insurance doesn't cover acts of God! Put your hands together for the one, the only, Miss Kitty le Sadé!"

The cheers were drowned out by the opening chords of 'River Deep, Mountain High' as Tina Turner hit the stage.

Barry was drooling as Kitty went straight into the number. The skirt came off first, so cool and casual. The lacy top soon followed. To cheers from the crowd, Kitty left the stage and sat on Bernie's lap. As she sang to him, he unfastened and removed her sequinned bra. She allowed him a quick grope before moving on to the next lucky driver. Thrusting her tits into his face, she pulled him off his chair and forced him down onto his knees. With his mates loudly urging him on, he struggled to remove her tiny red panties using only his teeth. When he'd got them down to her knees, Kitty pulled his face into her belly, before pushing it downwards. The boys went mad, envious truckers yelling and whistling.

Retreating back to the stage, Kitty lay down on her back. Drivers in the front row leant forward, they knew what was coming. Barry pushed even closer to get a better view.

She carried on miming the words, but all eyes were now on the other end of Kitty, as she slowly devoured the microphone. She left it there for a while as she pulled on her breasts in time with the heavy beat. Then, with the final crashing crescendo of the song, she raised her bum off the floor and spat the mic back out again, sending it skidding across the stage.

"I can't believe she does that!" said Debbie, as the audience went wild.

Kitty stood to take her bow. They loved her.

Debbie brought down the shutters on the bar as Charlie wound up the show.

Barry finished his pint then went off to join the queue in the lorry park.

***

Charlie drove the Merc into the lay-by, the same one he used every Monday and Wednesday night.

"Great show tonight, Kitty."

"You say the sweetest things, Charlie."

"And it's all true."

He leant over and kissed her on the cheek as his hand lunged between her legs.

"Careful, Charlie, slow down," she said, unbuttoning his waist coat.

"Mind the lipstick," he muttered, running his hand down her leg. He caressed her ankle for a moment, then slipped off her white stiletto shoe. As Kitty undid his flies and lowered her head, Charlie held the shoe to his face like a gas mask and took a deep breath.

Thursday

Charlie nearly choked on his breakfast. "The vicar's wife? No bloody way! You've got to be kidding me. I don't believe a bloody word."

"Yep, it's true," said Donkey. "She practically threw herself at me."

"And in the bog? You dirty git!" he laughed. "Hope it was in your tea break and not in company time."

"Perks of the job," said Donkey. "Bed, board and birds. Wasn't that the deal?"

"I dunno how you do it," said Charlie. "Well, yes I suppose I do. I just wish I was twenty years younger, Donkey, I really do."

They finished off their breakfast. Donkey went back out to his pumps and Charlie went off to make a call to Tommy, finalise a few details, sort out a few loose ends before he took off.

***

Carol put the potatoes on, ready for lunch. She found the constant arguing between the girls exhausting. She should be used to it by now, they'd argued all their lives. Is this how motherhood was meant to be? It was like living in a war zone. Charlie was no help at all; in fact, he just wound them up, playing them against one another.

Penny's shaven head looked awful, and that ring in her nose! She could have cried when she first saw her. She knew she shouldn't have let her go off on her own. It was only because Charlie had said no, that she'd said yes. The thought of her youngest having a boyfriend called Killer frightened her.

Debbie was so lucky to have Borg. A fine, handsome lad with a lot to offer. But why on earth did she get engaged if she was just going to carry on as before? Borg would be heartbroken if he knew what she got up to.

Perhaps she shouldn't be so judgemental. If they knew what was going on in her life, they might have something to say as well.

***

Mid-afternoon found Debbie having a late lunch with Borg in the restaurant. Eyes glued to the television, she picked at her food.

Borg looked knackered; she'd kept him up all night. He was back out on the road tomorrow, collecting a load of daffodil bulbs from Norfolk and taking them to Copenhagen. He wouldn't be back for at least two weeks.

"Debbie," he said, "it will be a long time."

"Only a couple of weeks," she said, taking his hand. Her eyes never left the telly.

Penny appeared from the kitchen. Pushing her trolley with gloved hands, she began clearing away the debris from the tables.

Borg sounded desperate. "Debbie, I must have something, some hope. We will wed? Yes?"

"Yes," she replied, watching the fighting on the TV screen.

"But when? You must tell me when so I..."

"Shush a minute, will you?" she said, waving a hand to silence him and pointing at the TV. "Look at that. Hey, Penny! Look at this!" Grabbing the remote she zapped up the sound.

On the TV a mass battle was taking place in a field of turnips. Shield bearing police and tattooed new age protesters fought it out with truncheons and placards.

Penny rushed over to watch as the commentator droned on.

"They later discovered that they had attacked the wrong field! In fact, they were even in the wrong county! The only GM around here is General Motors! They have in fact destroyed a crop of organic turnips!"

"Oh, yes!" said Debbie. "What a bunch of wankers. Hey, Penny, any of your friends there?"

Charlie came out from the kitchen to see what all the fuss was about. He watched in amazement as jewellery-spangled faces spat abuse at the police.

"The police were later called to the protesters' campsite after the farmer returned with a muck spreader and sprayed the entire camp, and its occupants, with liquid pig waste!"

The reporter quickly ended the report and fled the scene, holding his nose.

Charlie roared with laughter. Debbie nearly wet herself. Borg didn't see what was so funny. Nor did Penny; they were all laughing and pointing at her.

"Tossers, the bloody lot of them," said Charlie. "Save the world? They couldn't save coupons!"

Penny burst into tears and fled up to her room.

***

Mole called for silence; he was fuming. This was a nightmare, the worst possible scenario. The wrong fucking field! His motley crew of eco-warriors, over a dozen in all, sat around him in the mud. Stinking! They all stank! The farmer's revenge had caught them by surprise. They were all soaked in the foul-smelling stuff. They'd bathed in a stream, much to the amusement of all the media and the locals, but their clothes still hung on to the atrocious smell.

"Snake! You took us there, you wanker!" raged Mole. "This is all down to you!"

"Dog drew the fucking map! I just drove the van!" Snake snapped back.

"The map was right!" Dog yelled. "Angel said it was the right field. Ask her!"

"It was the right field!" cried Angel, her anger rising. "Killer identified it as GM!"

All eyes turned to Killer.

The spotty, newly-cropped volunteer, leapt to his feet. "It was GM! All this denial is bullshit! We hit the right field sure enough. They control the media, but we are not fooled!"

"Killer," said Mole, patiently, "how did you know it was GM? Where did you get your information from?"

"You can tell by looking, if you know what to look for."

A heavy groan escaped from the despondent warriors.

"Bollocks, Killer!" spat Mole. "You're so full of shit. You're such an arsehole!"

The inquest adjourned, and a heavy bout of comfort drinking began.

***

Killer had only been with them for a month or so. He'd stumbled blindly into their camp one night on his way down from a bad mushroom trip.

Clutching a warn copy of 'The Anarchist's Cookbook', a seventies war manual full of recipes for upheaval and destruction, he quoted from it chapter and verse. He convinced them all he was a raving loony. Too many mushrooms, they said. And too often.

Of course, Rupert, for that was his birth name, didn't quite see it that way. He'd woken up after a week-long high, clutching his new bible and surrounded by new friends. They were a great bunch and they all seemed to like him.

They had all these weird ideas about animals. Meat was murder. They were our brothers, not our dinners. Calling themselves eco-warriors, they were the sworn enemy of all the meat-eating capitalists who were plundering Mother Earth's precious resources. They were a cell of the Animal Liberation League, 2nd Battalion, West Midlands Division.

Killer thought their hearts were in the right place, but they were going about it the wrong way. When he first arrived, he'd tried to educate them.

"Peaceful protest doesn't work," he told them. "Take your fucking politicians for example. You petition them with millions of signatures, you demonstrate outside their fancy mansions and offices, you beg them, you plead with them. Do they give a shit? No, they just laugh in your face. They'll do it maybe, after the next election, or the next, or the fucking next! Now you shove a fucking Kalashnikov up their arse and bingo! It's yes, sir, no, sir, three bags full, sir! Whose fucking laughing now, sir?"

He paused for breath. His audience were captivated.

"And why stop at the politicians? Why release the mink? You just kill the fucking farmers! Do it often enough and people will soon come to realise, that this is not a good occupation to follow. Same with hunting. You wire up the fox dens with Semtex, then when the hunters are all gathered round watching the kill, BOOM! You kill the fucking lot! Adds a certain thrill to the hunt don't you think?

Once the odds change in favour of the fox, they'll prefer to stay at home playing dominoes!"

That gave them all something to think about. Most of them agreed with him but were afraid to stand up to Mole. He'd volunteered to be their battle commander, but they already had one, called Dove.

They had all these weird names reflecting their nature and their abilities. Mole got his because he was good at tunnelling, and Squirrel, he was good up trees, building houses and things. And then there was Dog. Angel said it was because he could lick his own bollocks. Well, she would know.

A unanimous vote backed Angel's suggestion of the name Killer for him. He was really chuffed. He liked the feel of it. A tough no-nonsense name. People knew where they stood as soon as they heard it.

Killer fancied Angel, though they should have called her Rabbit. In the short time he'd been there he'd seen her sleep with every member of the group, male and female! Everyone except him, that was. He'd tried often enough, but she always said no.

In the stream, trying to wash off the pig shit, she'd stripped right off! Naked! He'd kept his underpants on and got as close to her as he could. She was a little plump, and her short dark hair gave her quite a masculine look, but she had huge tits! And she didn't seem to care that he and the lads, along with some startled locals and the world's media, were all watching and staring.

Mole had her last night. He was the leader, a pacifist who always rubbished Killer's ideas. It was only jealousy, that and a fear that one day he would rise up through the ranks and oust him in a bloody coup.

Mole knew Killer didn't like him, that's why he was getting the blame. It wasn't his fault it had all gone wrong. They should have gone in mob-handed like he wanted to, and the farmhouse should have been the target, not a bloody field!

They'd have to listen to him in the future, but right now a blame culture was developing, covering up all their failures. The vibes were pretty bad. They needed to get through it on their own. Best if he let them stew in their own disappointments for a while.

Tomorrow he was going to hitch down to Sussex. That's where Penny lived, the one he'd told the boys about. The virgin he'd picked up and deflowered at Glastonbury. They'd screwed non-stop for days. He told them all how he'd taught her the art of love making, and how she'd begged for more. She'd wept when they'd parted.

Her old man ran a truckstop down on the south coast. A leg over at the seaside would be a welcome break from the battlefront.

***

Putting on his glasses and slowly standing up, Ted Morrison called the meeting to order. Henyard's tiny village hall was packed. Practically the whole village was there, at least forty people. The committee sat together at a table in front of the troubled parishioners. Alongside the grey-haired Ted Morrison, magistrate, councillor and head of the local Tory party, sat the vicar, John Cunningham, and Miss Haplin, spinster and post mistress. Together they were the elected protectors of Henyard.

"Ladies and gentleman welcome to the meeting," Ted began. "Thank you all for coming. I'm sorry it was at such short notice. But I won't waste any time with pleasantries, we all know why we're here." He paused and gazed out among the worried villagers before continuing, "The government has given the go ahead for the container base. Despite our protestations and without a thought to what it means to the local population. Already we have huge juggernauts thundering past our doors all day long. The very foundations of our ancient village are being destroyed. Our homes and our lives. Only yesterday, Miss Haplin had to jump for her very life when a lorry mounted the pavement to go around a parked car."

A soft gasp swept through the hall as Miss Haplin slowly shook her head.

"And the traffic will increase ten-fold! I guarantee it!" Ted continued, banging his fist on the table to emphasise the point. "Twenty-four hours a day! Seven days a week! This is a disaster for Henyard, and for every one of us who lives here! We have to do something, and we need to do it now!"

A ripple of applause was cut short by an angry voice. "But what the hell can we do? It's all done and dusted!" Local cab driver, Willy Evans, had lived in the village all his life. He'd lost a wing mirror to a truck only last week. The wagon hadn't even stopped. "We've made our views known since the beginning," he said, "but no one listens to us, so what can we do?"

Ted waited for any suggestions, but none was forth coming. He knew just what they had to do. He'd given it a lot of thought and even taken some legal advice. He liked to be thorough, think his plans through. The people of Henyard respected him, he was their leader in all but name. Over the years he had served them well, preserved their way of life, stopped new housing projects, and prevented undesirables from taking up residence. The only blot on his reputation, indeed the only blot on his whole career, was Wheeler! Him and his damned truckstop! He'd fought hard to prevent that crook from building that bloody monstrosity. Well, he may have lost the battle, but the war was still being fought. And now there was an opportunity to strike a lethal blow. And save the village, all in one foul swoop.

Ted cleared his throat. "Ladies and gentlemen, I believe I may well have the answer. After consulting with all members of the committee, and having taken the appropriate legal advice, I shall be meeting with members of the county council next week to ask for, no demand, a by-pass for Henyard!"

A grunt of approval was followed by loud applause.

"And I think our plan is such that approval is almost a certainty!"

More applause as Ted sat down and handed the chair over to the vicar.

As John Cunningham rose from his chair he glanced over at his wife, Helen. Sat in the front row alongside Carol Wheeler, who was taking the minutes of the meeting. Carol smiled at him as he tugged nervously at his dog collar.

"Thank you, Ted," he began. "Plans have been drawn up to upgrade the B88, a mile to our west, into a dual carriageway. This would provide a good connection from the coast road to the A27. At the moment, the road, also known as Peacock Lane, is far too narrow for heavy lorries, but open waste-land on either side would mean less costs and disruption. Upgrading a road is a lot simpler than building a new one, in terms of costs and planning permission." He paused for a sip of water, glanced at Carol, then pushed on. "Neither will Henyard be the only beneficiary. The new road will allow traffic to enter Shorley from the west, thus taking it away from the High Street. The people of Shorley have suffered much the same as we have over the years and their obvious support can only add weight to our cause. Shorley Council have agreed whole heartedly to back the plan, so I don't see any objections forthcoming. The possibility of government funding and grants will be explored by the county council."

As the vicar spoke, Ted was watching Carol Wheeler, to see how she reacted. But she didn't seem to be paying any attention at all to what was being said. Or the implications.

As soon as the vicar had sat down, Ted was back on his feet. No time to waste. They must press on.

"When I speak to the county council next week," he began, "I hope to get their initial approval. I will demand that the container base does not go ahead until the by-pass is completed. I also intend to ask for a weight limit through the village,to come into force as soon as possible."

Again, he looked at Carol. No response at all. She seemed to have other things on her mind.

***

"So, what do you give a woman who has everything? Eh? A man to show her how it all works. It's true! You know it is. And you know why women fake orgasms? No? Neither do I. They must think we actually give a shit!"

The truckers howled with laughter as, on stage, Bobby Bent paused to draw on his glowing cigar. His pin-striped suit, creased and covered in cigar ash, stretched to accommodate his roly-poly frame.

"When my wife has PMT, the only difference between her and our Rottweiler is the fucking lipstick! And how can anything that bleeds so much, live so fucking long?"

Charlie sat at the bar listening to his punters having a good laugh. Supping at his pint, he was in a reflective mood. He looked around him at the dream he'd built. Twenty years of sweat and hard work, but a lot of good times too. He was proud of what he'd achieved, and a little sad to be letting it all go. But needs must. He had taken it as far as he could, the time was right to move on; cash in his life's work and retire to a life of luxury.

But he wasn't really kidding himself, he knew he had little choice. Paradise or prison? Only a fool would ignore this opportunity. He'd spoken to Manny on the phone, and he seemed as keen as he was to get on and complete the deal. He was coming round on Monday to have a look at the place. Next week, it could all happen.

He wondered how they would all react to his runner. Carol would probably sob for weeks, but the kids wouldn't care less. Manny had said he would continue to employ them and let them stay on in the apartment. He wanted the truckstop as a going concern, for now.

But did he care? Did he hell! Parasites, the bloody lot of them! Now they would have to manage without him. He'd thought about leaving a letter of resignation as head of the family, but no, fuck 'em. He'd leave out the back door, unnoticed. Then he'd drive down to Spain in his Merc. Take his time, enjoy the freedom. Book into a good hotel while he checked out the real estate.

"Penny for 'em?" Donkey pulled a bar stool up alongside him.

"Never, not for that price. Pint?"

"Cheers. You look happy, won the lottery?"

"No, Carol's night off!" he said. "Debbie! Pint for Donkey!" He was going to miss Donkey. Good mate, good laugh too.

Charlie prepared for the end of the show, slowly walking over to the stage as Bobby wound up his act.

"And I always think a blow job is a bit like a Lobster Thermidor, both very nice but you don't get either at home." He paused as the cheers and jeers rose up. "And lads, as you all stagger off to your bunks tonight, here's something for you to ponder. If you could suck your own dick, would you spit, or would you swallow?"

The truckers roared with laughter, whistling and yelling out.

"Thank you and good night, you've been a great audience. Thank you, Charlie!"

"And thank you too, Bobby," said Charlie, climbing onto the stage and taking the mic. "I've just pissed myself laughing. What a great guy! Bobby will be back with us next week, same time, same place. Thank you, boys for coming out tonight, and for those of you who are around tomorrow, it's Karaoke Night at Charlie's Place! And don't forget we open just for you, at five in the morning. Thank you and a very good night!"

Penny came into the bar and began gathering up the ashtrays and glasses as the truckers filed out of the exits on the way to their bunks. Debbie wiped down the bar while Borg took out all the empties.

"That ring has gone septic," said Debbie, peering closely at Penny's nose. "Look at it. Is that pus or snot?"

"Piss off!" said Penny.

"That's not very nice is it? Only trying to be helpful. Your nose could drop off. Borg, look, it's weeping."

"Leave her alone!" said Carol, arriving home to another family spat. Taking off her coat, she began helping the girls clear up.

"Hallo, Carol," said Donkey, carrying in a new barrel for the bar. "Good night off?"

"Just a parish meeting, that's all."

"God knows what you talk about at these meetings," said Charlie, cashing up at the till. "Just a load of self-important nobodies making noises that nobody listens to."

"No, I don't think so," said Carol, obviously irritated by his dismissive attitude. "The whole community revolves around its' church and its' village hall."

"Is that right?" said Charlie. "Well, I've never been to either."

"Well, that just about says it all, doesn't it?"

"So, what vitally important decisions did you make this evening then?" he asked.

"I don't think you're really interested, are you? You think the world revolves around Charlie Wheeler, don't you? Well, it doesn't, there's a world out there that cares about people other than themselves..."

"Sorry I asked," muttered Charlie.

"It may only be things like weight limits and by-passes, but these meetings address people's fears. Anyway, sod you! I'm off to bed. Goodnight, boys." She turned and walked away.

"Goodnight," called out Donkey and Borg.

Charlie laughed as he counted the night's take. "Silly cow!" he mumbled. Then he stopped. What was that she just said? Weight limits? By-passes?

"Carol? Carol!" he yelled, rushing off after her.

***

The ringing bedside phone dragged Tommy from his dreams.

"Yes? Who is it?" he asked, bleary-eyed and cursing.

"Me! Charlie! Charlie Wheeler!"

"For Christ's sake, Charlie, it's nearly midnight! What's wrong? Can't it wait?"

"No, it bloody can't! A by-pass! A bloody by-pass! They're going to get a by-pass!"

"What? Who?" said Tommy. "Where? What the hell are you on about? You pissed?"

"No, I fucking ain't; I soon will be though! Morrison! Fucking Ted Morrison! He's convinced the village that they need a bloody by-pass! He's submitting plans to the county council."

"Oh my God!" gasped Tommy, immediately seeing the implications. "How? Where?"

"Peacock Lane. They want to widen it to a bloody dual carriageway. And put a weight limit through the village!" said Charlie, breathlessly. "They can't do it, can they?"

"Shit!" said Tommy. "Doesn't matter, does it? The chances of a quick deal are dead. Manny can afford to wait and see. You can't!" And neither can I, he thought.

"What can we do?" Charlie sounded desperate.

"You're back to square one. You've got to do some serious thinking, Charlie. Come and see me tomorrow."

"Damn that tosser! What do they need a bloody by-pass for?"

"Get some sleep, Charlie, come see me in the morning."

"Yeah, OK. Don't think I'll be doing much sleeping though."

Friday

Penny scraped the bits of bacon and black pudding off the plate and into the bin bag. Gritting her teeth and taking deep breaths, she moved her trolley on to the next table.

How her life had changed in the last few weeks. In her mind she was now free, but in reality, she was still chained to the truckstop. To break free completely, to cut the umbilical cord, she'd need strength, and help.

She'd dreamt of Killer last night, her hero laying down his life for her. He was so romantic. She longed to see her lover again, he made her feel whole. But right now, she felt trapped, like a bird in a cage.

Debbie constantly wound her up. She'd told the whole world that her little sister had finally been 'shagged'! What a bitch! It was so embarrassing. And her dad was in a right mood today. He'd bitten her head off for no reason at all. And Barry. Why wouldn't he just take the hint? He disgusted her, and the smell! Perhaps, when he heard Debbie's gossip, he might just leave her alone. And her zits were the worst they'd ever been. Today couldn't really get much worse, could it?

"Hey, Penny, take a look at this." A laughing Debbie skipped into the restaurant with a newspaper in her hand. Borg followed her like a puppy.

"Remember those wankers on the telly yesterday? Well, look at this great picture!" she said, thrusting the paper into Penny's hand.

Penny froze with horror. There, on the front page of the Sun, was Killer! Clad only in his underpants! He was up to his knees in a stream, standing next to a completely naked girl. And his eyes were on stalks. Riveted to her huge bosoms. He was positively drooling!

The newspaper, in the name of decency, had covered her nipples and nether parts with motifs of a smiling sun. The headline screamed out 'WHAT A PAIR OF T*TS!'

Penny was mortified.

Debbie couldn't stop laughing. A couple of drivers came over to join the fun as Debbie began reading out snippets from the report.

"'Are they organic?' Fucking great! And what about this? 'Pig poo pair come clean'. What a joke. Are they mates of yours?" she asked Penny. "Do you know them?"

The paper told of the battle in the turnip field with relish. They quoted the farmer as saying how the pig shit sweetened up the smell in the warriors' camp.

Carol came in to see what all the noise was about. "Debbie! Will you just stop. What is it this time?"

"Penny's mates have made the front page. Look at these tossers!"

Penny could take no more; throwing off her gloves she fled the restaurant close to tears. Running into the lorry park she ran straight into Donkey, on his way over for his breakfast. She just folded into his arms and let go, sobbing uncontrollably

Donkey said nothing. He just held her tight.

Her sobs slowed to a weep and she finally got her breath back, regaining some of her composure.

"Want to talk about it?" he asked.

She shook her head. "Debbie... Such a fucking bitch!"

"What's new? But you're stronger than her, you can cope."

"No, I can't!" she cried. "Why doesn't she just leave me alone?"

"Maybe she's jealous of you."

"What's she got to be jealous about?"

"Your freedom. Her life is all mapped out, Borg and babies. All she ever thought she wanted. But now she can have it, she's not so sure. You're like a butterfly, she envies you."

"Why should she envy me? She can have any bloke she wants."

"Maybe that's her problem."

Penny snuggled tighter into his arms. She loved him like a big brother. "Donkey?"

"Yes?"

"Can I ask you something?"

"Sure, anything you like. Except physics, I was never any good at physics."

She laughed, then hesitated a while. "Do you think my boobs are too small?"

Donkey coughed and stepped back from her. "What? How would I know?"

"Well, you've seen as much as most people. Are they small? Too Small?"

"You're only eighteen, Penny, you're still growing."

"That means yes!" She turned away from him. "I knew it! All men like big boobs!"

"Not all men think that's the most important thing about a woman."

"Do you?"

Donkey trod carefully. "You're a beautiful young girl..."

"With tiny tits."

Donkey laughed and hugged her again. "So, how's that new boyfriend?" he asked. "Is he really called Killer?"

Penny pulled herself together. "Yeah, he's fine. I think you'd like him." She took a deep breath; she had to be strong. The new Penny could handle this; there were more things in her life than the Wheeler family. She had come of age. She was a free spirit, a butterfly, just like Donkey had said.

"You OK now?" he asked.

"Yeah, thanks, Donkey," she said, wiping her nose on her sleeve. "I just needed someone to be nice to me for a change. Thanks." She moved away; she had to get back to her post.

As she went back in through the doors, Donkey called out to her. "Penny!"

She stopped and turned. "Yeah?"

"I just love your tits!"

Penny blushed and felt a warm glow, then retreated back to the kitchen.

***

Tommy felt rough, he'd sat up all night. That light at the end of the tunnel had been totally extinguished. Unless he could get Charlie to do a runner, he was doomed. False accounting equalled a long prison sentence, big fines and being barred from his profession. Damn you, Charlie Wheeler!

"So, what we going to do?" asked Charlie, as soon as Tommy had let him in.

"What you should have done months ago!" said Tommy.

"But I can't go empty-handed, can I? Where would I go? How would I live?"

"Once it's all calmed down, I'll get Carol to sell up and send you the proceeds."

"Bollocks! For a start it'll take years to calm down, and no way will Carol co-operate, she'll not give two shits about me!"

"So, what else would you suggest?" asked Tommy. "I'm expecting a call from Manny any time now saying the deals off. Now he'll be wanting to buy up land alongside the new by-pass."

"And I suppose, as he's also your client, you'll probably help him!" said Charlie.

"Don't get arsy, Charlie, it was me that set you up with him, remember?"

"The deal could still go ahead! We'll get petitions against a by-pass. It hasn't been agreed yet. Can't we demand an enquiry or something?"

"You're clutching at straws, Charlie, all that would do is delay the inevitable. What with the new container dock and all, anyone can see the need for a by-pass."

"Thanks a fucking bunch! I thought you were on my side?"

"I am. But you haven't got the time. Manny can wait for the outcome of any enquiry, you can't! A month from now you could be under arrest. They'd seize your passport straight away, then what would you do? I'll tell you what you'd do, five fucking years, that's what! And I'll be in the next bloody cell. Charlie, you've got no choice, you've got to go. And the sooner the better!"

***

It was late in the afternoon when Barry's truck pulled up by the kitchen door. The swarm of flies that had followed his wagon from the knacker's yard, finally caught up just as Killer got out the passenger door.

"Thanks for the lift, mate," he called across to Barry.

"No probs, any time. Enjoyed the company."

Killer had jumped the trains all the way to Shorley. By pretending to be asleep or drunk, he found ticket inspectors left him alone. His appearance and the smell may well have helped, some passengers even got up and moved away from him. He'd been stood hitching at the crossroads in Shorley for nearly an hour before Barry had picked him up. Nobody had wanted to stop for him. Sign of the times.

Barry went into the kitchen with a wrap of sheep's kidneys, and Killer, carrying his sleeping bag and backpack, went around to the front and into the café.

"Tea please, and an egg sandwich," he asked, politely.

Carol called out the order through to Debbie as she poured him his tea. "If you sit down, I'll bring your sandwich over."

Killer took his tea and sat in a window seat. He was looking forward to seeing Penny again. He was hoping she could put him up for a few days, until things cooled down a bit. The revolution had been put on hold.

"One egg sandwich?" called out Debbie, as she came through the swing doors.

Killer raised his hand like a school boy.

Debbie gasped at the sight of him. Passing him his sandwich her nose twitched as she picked up the scent. Pig shit! "You're not a friend of Penny's, are you?" she asked him, hand wafting in front of her face.

"Yeah, I am. How did you guess? Is she around?"

"Penny! Penny!" Debbie called out, turning back towards the kitchen.

Other diners looked over to see what all the fuss was about.

"Penny! Your friend is here! Come on, he's waiting for you!"

Penny came out from the kitchen. "Killer!" she cried. Rushing over to his table she kissed him on the cheek, then taking his hand, she sat down alongside him. "How are you? I didn't think I'd see you so soon."

"Wow!" said Debbie. "True love, eh? Is this the same Killer that shagged you? Took your cherry? " She began to laugh. "Well, ain't he a handsome one!"

"Fuck off, Debbie!" said Penny. "Why don't you just fucking grow up?" Grabbing Killer's hand, she pulled him from his chair. Dragging him behind her, she made for the door.

"My sarnie!" he cried, "I'm starving!"

Once in the lorry park, Penny turned and grabbed him. Wrapping her arms tightly around him, she lay her head on his shoulders. "I am so glad to see you; I just can't believe you're here. Oh, Killer, I've missed you so much."

"Yeah, well, I've missed you too, baby."

They kissed gently; Penny's nose was too sore for anything more. They stood awkwardly, just holding each other.

"Can I go back and finish my egg sarnie?" he asked. "I'm starving; haven't eaten since Manchester, and that was days ago."

"Oh, Killer, I'm so sorry. Of course, but Debbie, my sister, she's a real bitch and..."

"Yeah, I noticed; well, let me handle her, OK?"

They went back into the restaurant. They could hear Debbie and Carol laughing in the kitchen.

"So why all the bad vibes? What's her problem?" he asked, munching on his cold egg sandwich.

"Debbie's a slag, she'll sleep with anything with balls. That's why we could never have a dog!"

They both laughed.

"Sounds to me like you've got one for a sister." Killer laughed at his own joke, spraying his sarnie across the table from his open mouth.

As soon as Killer had finished, and wiped his mouth down his sleeve, Penny leant across the table and gently kissed him on the lips.

"Look at those love birds, all together now... ahh! They look like fucking aliens." Debbie appeared alongside them. She had the Sun newspaper in her hand. Holding it up, she compared the front-page picture to Killer.

"Yep! Looks like him, smells like him. Yes, it's definitely him. The Pig Shit Kid. Sounds better than Killer."

Diners on other tables joined in the laughter as Debbie stuck the paper under Killer's nose. It was the first time he'd seen it. This was serious, people were laughing at him, the picture made him look stupid.

"Would you like me to autograph it for you?" he asked her, real cool.

"Wow! You can write?"

***

Charlie sat in his office, alone with his thoughts. Was he really going to have to go on the run? He was so close to doing the deal with Manny. Now he would be penniless. He could raise a few grand in cash maybe, but how long would that last him? And what then? He couldn't see Tommy staying loyal. And if Carol did sell up in his absence, he wouldn't be able to claim a penny! Not that she'd offer. He looked out of the window into the lorry park; his empire was crumbling.

"Dad? You got a minute?"

Penny stood in the doorway, a spotty, bald youth in tow. A farmyard smell wafted around his office.

"Good God! Is this him?" he said, looking him up and down.

"Dad, this is Killer. My... my friend, Killer. I need to ask you a favour. Mum says it's OK by her if it's OK by you. Can Killer stay for a few days?"

"Jesus Christ, what? Penny, you can't be serious."

"Dad! Don't embarrass me. You shouldn't judge people by their appearance."

"Shouldn't I? What is he then? A brain surgeon? Or maybe a lawyer? That would please your mum. So, what do you do for a living, Killer?"

"I am an eco-warrior," he replied. "Fighting to save your planet from the destruction of capitalists. While you sit and watch, I lead my warriors against the forces of greed."

"So, you're on the dole, then."

"The state may subsidise me, but they don't control me."

"Didn't do so well in the turnip field, did you?" said Charlie. "So what battles are you fighting now, Killer?"

"I've got troops at Manchester Airport, tunnelling under the new runway. More at the Newbury by-pass. Others are off sabotaging fox hunts and mink farms."

Charlie stopped and took a deep breath. Did he just say...? "So how do you stop a by-pass then, Killer?"

"Easy, stopped loads."

"Is that right? Why don't you sit down, Killer?" said Charlie, pointing to a chair. "Penny, get the lad a cup of tea."

"But, Dad..."

"So, what happens if people want a by-pass, what happens then?"

Killer seemed a bit taken back with Charlie's sudden attitude change. He sat down opposite him at the table. "Well, you convince them that they don't. Flowers or concrete, bird song or diesel fumes."

"Dad..." Penny began.

"Just get the lad a tea..."

"Can he stay a few days?" she said.

"So, what if they won't listen?" Charlie asked Killer.

"Oh, they'll listen. I'm an expert at making people listen."

"They want to bulldoze a by-pass around Henyard; nobody really wants it, they're being bullied into it, by big business concerns."

"Sounds about normal, want help? I can have hundreds of protesters here in days."

"Yeah? Fucking great!" Charlie was ecstatic.

"I'll need somewhere to stay of course, and somewhere for the troops, parking for their buses and vans."

"Yeah, no problem, they can park here, in the lorry park."

"And me?" asked Killer.

"Yeah, well if her mum's OK about it, the spare room..."

"Dad!" cut in Penny. "He stays with me. We're a... a couple."

"OK, OK, if that's what you want. Now could you leave us, we've things to talk about, and make that two teas."

"No, Dad, I'm an eco-warrior too." she said, sitting down. "So, what are we going to do about it?"

Charlie told Killer everything. Well, almost.

"And it's all down to one man. Fucking Ted Morrison. He's a power freak. No one in the village wants a bloody by-pass; they're just too scared to stand up to him. He hates me, God knows why..."

"Where's the by-pass going to go?" asked Penny.

"They want to upgrade Peacock Lane into a dual carriageway," he replied, answering Penny but talking to Killer. "It cuts down from the A27 to Shorley. It's a really narrow country lane."

"Are you sure the villagers are against it?" asked Penny.

The look on Killer's face cut her dead. "If they're not," he said, "then we'll have to educate them."

"I'm told the post office would close, and with no passing trade the pub could be in trouble too!" said Charlie.

"Not to mention the truckstop!" said Penny.

"You don't have to tell me that!" snapped Charlie. "If the by-pass goes ahead, we'll have to close, full stop!"

"Death of the community," said Killer. "And all for some fat cat's bank balance. Building the road is only the beginning. Next will come the developers, stealing the surrounding fields from the birds and the bees, building lavish houses that only they can afford to buy! We've got to stop them!"

"Here! Here!" said Charlie, looking at Penny as though she was out of her depth. "So, what we going to do about it, Killer?"

"Fight the bastards! In the fields and in the trenches... and in the... " Killer struggled to finish so he tried a high five with Charlie. "Yes!" he yelled, as he swiped his hand over Charlie's head. Charlie ducked, thinking Killer was throwing a punch. They both laughed nervously as Charlie slapped him on the back.

"So?" Charlie asked again. "Where do we start?"

"I'll need to round up my troops. They're in Manchester, so I'll need a train ticket."

"Two tickets. I'm going too." said Penny.

"How long before you get back?" asked Charlie.

"Two or three days maybe," said Killer. "I'll have to pull some off the airport. I could maybe bring down a few dozen or more."

"Great! Make it as quick as you can," said Charlie. "Time is important, once a decision is made it will make it that much harder."

"Sometimes these things can go on for years," said Killer.

"I haven't got years!" said Charlie.

"Why not, Dad?" asked Penny. "If they haven't got planning permission yet..."

"I just can't take all this stress." Putting his head into his hands, he rubbed his eyes. "The thought of losing everything. Twenty years we've been here, built it up from nothing. I want to end my days here." Looking directly at Penny, he slowly shook his head, "Your mother couldn't cope if we lost this place. I really worry for her..." His eyes dropped down, fighting back the tears.

Penny reached across and placed her hand on his. "It's OK, Dad, we can fight this together. Right is might. We'll leave tomorrow and be back as soon as we can."

Charlie rose from his chair, eyes still down. "Right, better get on, got a business to run, though I don't know for how much longer. Thanks, Killer, I'll see you before you go, give you some expenses."

They followed him as he shuffled out of the office, heading back to the kitchen. Penny took Killer up to her room.

***

She had been seven when the family moved out of the caravan and into the truckstop. Around the walls of her bedroom, her life was detailed in photos' and memories. Junior school drawings of Mummy and Daddy still hung alongside posters of Michael Jackson and Postman Pat. She felt embarrassed as Killer gazed around her room. It didn't reflect how much she had grown, mentally and physically, in the last few years; or indeed the last few weeks.

Taking Killer's rucksack from him, she threw it on the floor. Then flinging her arms around him, she pulled his face onto hers. As their rings and studs clashed, she felt her body heaving with expectation. Killer's hands went to her bum and began to squeeze. She felt a bit nauseous as the smell from his leather jacket finally overcame her need to be close to him.

"Why don't we shower?" she heard herself saying. She felt brave, confidant, this was the new Penny speaking, full of passion for her lover.

His spotty face lit up. "Yeah? That would be nice."

Penny led him by the hand out of her bedroom and down the hall to the shower. Locking the door behind them, she began ripping off her clothes. She seemed in a daze, unable to believe what she was doing. Penny Wheeler, taking off all her clothes in front of a boy!

Killer just stood there, staring, his eyes locked onto her body. He looked stunned.

She was soon naked. What now she thought? Moving closer to him, she began tugging at his jacket. A lust she'd never known before took over. His jacket fell to the floor, and as she ripped off his T-shirt his hands came alive, roughly groping her young breasts.

Penny backed away; she had been expecting much more. Some tender words maybe, a gentle caress. But she was new to this; she'd never been naked with a boy before. At Glastonbury, and then the railway station, her jeans and panties never went below her knees.

Penny slowed down. Undoing his jeans, she pushed them down to his ankles, exposing his erect manhood. It seemed smaller than she remembered; it was almost lost in his mass of wiry pubic hair.

As she knelt to remove his trainers, he grabbed her head and roughly pushed her face forward into his groin. She resisted and stood up. She wasn't ready for that; he was being a little too pushy for her.

She watched as he sat on the loo, wrestling his jeans off, that big stupid grin lighting up his face. Then a naked Killer stood and wrapped her in his arms. Taking her hand, he held it against his stiff penis. Penny felt it throbbing, heard him gasp, and then with a jerk, her hand filled with a warm, sticky mess.

"Oh wow!" sighed a breathless Killer, sitting back down on the loo. "That was so fucking good! Oh yes! Yes!"

Penny stood looking down at a crumpled Killer, disappointment on her face and confusion in her mind. Surely there was more to love than this.

When Killer had recovered, they climbed into the shower together. She washed every inch of his body, several times over, as he just stood there with a big grin on his face and a renewed erection. She held his face and kissed him, like she'd seen them do on the telly. It felt good. Her body was tingling all over with expectation and desire. Of what she didn't know, she'd never felt like this before, ever. Her knees felt wobbly, they needed to move on.

Out of the shower, she dried him off. Again, he tried to push her head down, again she resisted. She wanted love, and she wanted it to last.

They wrapped themselves in towels and quickly made their way back to her bedroom. Penny locked the door before dropping her towel and pushing Killer onto the bed.

She leapt on top of him, sitting astride and shamelessly grinding her nakedness into him. His hands were all over her, pulling and pinching her breasts. She felt his stiffness, rubbing and teasing her aching vagina. She reached down to help him enter, but it was too late. Killer bucked, then let out a grunt, as she felt the wet, sticky cum splash over her legs. Killer sighed and closed his eyes.

Penny was still flying high, but Killer had already crash landed. Within moments he was emitting a soft snore. Game over.

Penny climbed off and reached for some tissues. Maybe I'm not doing it right, she thought. This can't be all there is, can it?

***

In the lorry park, Debbie held onto Borg as they leant up against the side of his wagon. Lips, arms and bodies entwined, in a farewell embrace, oblivious to the staring truckers passing by.

Borg pulled his face free and pushed her hand away from his crutch. "So, when I get back? We will set a date. Yes?"

"Yup!" she replied, pulling his face back into place.

He emerged again. "I'm so happy, Debbie. I love you so much. Soon we will be together every single day!"

They untangled, and Borg threw his kit up into the truck.

Debbie tried to smile as she watched her fiancé climb up into the cab. She would usually grab his arse at this point, but his words were swirling around her head like a fruit machine, and when they finally came to a halt the winning line read 'Every Single Day!'

Borg fired up the engine. She could see tears of happiness rolling down his cheeks as he blew a kiss and pulled away into the late evening sun.

"Every single day? What did I ever do to fucking deserve that?"

***

Carol put on some make up. It had been a long time since she'd wanted to look nice for someone.

Friday night was Karaoke Night. Charlie had bought the machine and all the tapes and lights from a car boot sale years ago. He compared the show and supplied the prizes of cheap plonk and booze. The audience voted by cheering the loudest.

Most truck drivers were heading for home on Fridays, but Karaoke Night attracted quite a few punters in from Henyard and Shorley, so it wasn't a bad night for the till. The restaurant closed early; any truckers still staying over knew the score and ate early.

This allowed Carol some time off. A whole evening. Tonight, she was helping the vicar with his sermons for the weekend. It was something a vicar's wife would normally do, Carol noted, but Helen was so much younger than her husband, and didn't seem to have his drive or his energy. She seemed to think it was all about garden parties and weddings. Helen always visited her mother on Friday. Carol loved Fridays.

***

"Charlie? It's me," said Tommy, his voice almost a whisper on the kitchen phone.

"Yeah, I know it's you. What do you want?"

"What do I want?" Tommy sounded incredulous. "What do I fucking want? Have you forgotten the shit you're in?"

"We, Tommy, the shit we're in."

"Well, it just got worse, a lot worse. Manny's pulled out of the deal."

"So, we expected that, didn't we?" said Charlie.

"Of course we expected it," Tommy replied, "but what's changed with you? Only this morning you were crying on my shoulder, crapping yourself, and now it's like you don't have a care in the world. What's happening? Have you decided to go?"

"No, I haven't made any decisions yet. Except not to expect any help from you!"

"Charlie, we're in this together..."

"Yeah? So, I fuck off to a pauper's life in Spain, and you stay here, Mr Clean!"

"It's not like that, Charlie..."

"No? So, what are you and Manny up to now? Let me guess. Doing a few land deals maybe? Come on, tell me! You should know because you're his fucking lapdog!" Charlie slammed down the phone. When the shit hits the fan, you knew who your friends were. He could do this on his own. He'd have to.

Carol passed by on her way out. "I've done the sandwiches for tonight," she said, "and the sausage rolls are in the cooler." Then she was out the door and gone.

Charlie stared after her. Twenty years ago, they'd started out, with a bloody tea caravan! It had been hard, but what fun they'd had. Opening the truckstop had been the highlight of his life. The culmination of all his dreams. Their dreams, his and Carol's. Where had it all gone wrong?

Debbie passed through the kitchen, fag in her mouth. "The shower stinks of pig shit," she said. "There's a pile of clothes on the floor, think they might be the problem. No way am I touching them!" Then she too was gone. That's where it all went wrong. Bloody kids!

Right now, he had to make some calls to a couple of cousins. He was going to be around a bit longer than he'd thought. He needed to up his cash flow and move a few accounts away from Tommy's grasp. He still might need to run.

***

The screeching of the sound system, and the odd 'one two, one two' from her dad, reverberated through to Penny's bedroom and made Killer stir. Penny had dressed and was sat patiently at the dressing table while he slept. Looking at herself in the mirror, she saw a young woman, reborn and strong, ready for the fight. Ready to give all to protect her family and loved ones from the wicked capitalists. And on the bed resting was her lover, her leader, her saviour. She'd covered his naked body with a blanket, it seemed a little more dignified.

Her disappointment was confusing her. What was she doing wrong? She'd had no experience at all. Killer had had hundreds of girls; he'd told her so. In the novels she'd read, they made love for hours, and orgasmed every few minutes.

She knew about orgasms. Occasionally in bed as she slept, she'd have these dreams. In the last one, and the one before that, she'd dreamt of Donkey, picking her up into his arms. He'd just hold her and stare into her eyes.

Then she'd wake up, frantically thrashing with her fingers, turning her face into the pillow to stifle her squeals of delight.

Killer rubbed his eyes and farted, then slowly sitting up, he focused on Penny.

"Wow, Penny," he sighed, "you're such a brilliant shag. You're the best I've ever had, honest!"

Penny rushed to him and threw her arms around him. "I love you, Killer!" she said, bursting into tears.

***

"Ladies and gentlemen, boys and girls, welcome to Charlie's Place, the only place to be on a wet Friday night!"

Charlie looked dazzling in his white suit. Just putting it on changed his persona from a wheeler dealer truckstop owner, to the Master of Ceremonies at the greatest venue on the planet.

"Tonight is Sixties Night, and you lovely lot of budding pop stars can choose from any one of a hundred chart hits from the sixties. All of them are listed at the side of the stage and at the bar. For those of you here for the first time, you just write your name and choice of song on the tickets provided and pop them in the bin on the stage. When I pull your name out, you're on! Your three minutes of fame begins! So, get busy with your choice and fill those glasses up. The show starts in fifteen minutes!"

Charlie threw the switch and started off the show with a melody of Beatles' hits. The light show, a mirrored ball with a couple of bouncing colour strobes, began streaking out from the stage.

Karaoke nights were family nights, with a few regular truckers thrown in. Kids and grannies competed for the glory and the prizes. As long as the kids kept off the booze, and the truckers kept off the kids, everyone was happy.

Charlie went back behind the bar to give Debbie a hand. It was a busy night.

Debbie, tight top and even tighter jeans, pulled a pint for Barry. He was already on his third.

"If I'd have known who he was," he moaned, "I'd never have picked him up. Bastard!"

"Who?" said Debbie.

"Penny's boyfriend. Killer. What sort of name is that? Eh? So what's he got that I ain't? He's not exactly tall, dark and handsome, is he?"

"No," said Debbie. "He's short, bald and spotty. And stinks of pig shit. Or he did until they showered." She paused for effect. "Together!"

"What?" Barry looked sickened. "Together? Like at the same time?"

"Yep! Saving water, I suppose."

Barry thought on this awhile. "I ain't got a shower. I got a bath though."

"Big enough for two?" Debbie teased.

"Chance would be a fine thing. Did you see he's got a stud in his tongue?"

"Yup! And one in his eyebrow and one in his nose. They look a right pair. Don't know how they'd get through the airport." Debbie paused. "I wonder if he's got one through his dick? That might be quite nice, I'll have to have a word with Borg."

Barry spluttered on his beer. He just loved listening to Debbie talking dirty.

Donkey joined them at the bar. Denim clad, his long pony tail was held by a gold band.

"Hallo, mate," said Barry. "What you having?"

"It's OK, Barry," said Charlie, "I'll get it. Pint, Donkey?"

"Cheers, boss, how's things going? Looks busy tonight."

"Yeah, not too bad." Charlie moved away from Barry and lowered his voice. "Got a job lined up for you, Monday, up for it?"

"You bet!"

Glancing over at Barry and Debbie to check they weren't ear wigging, he continued, "Good, but I've got to do some checks yet." He passed Donkey his pint. "See me in the morning, should be sorted by then."

***

Pulling Killer by the hand, Penny took him down the stairs and they slipped into the kitchen. It was all closed down. They could hear her dad introducing the first act.

Killer sat at the kitchen table as Penny fried a couple of eggs for her hungry lover. She gazed at him as she buttered his toast. He was dabbing at his nose with a tissue, the reddish sore seemed to be spreading to his lip. He was now dressed in one of her baggy T-shirts and a pair of her old black jeans. Penny thought he looked quite cute, although the jeans were a bit tight around his crotch, and maybe a bit on the short side. But they were a lot better than the ones she'd dropped in the yard bin, along with his jacket. She put his food in front of him.

"Wow! You can cook too. I'm starving."

"It's only eggs on toast," she said modestly, watching as he gorged himself. Egg yolk ran off his chin and on to his T-shirt. Leaning over, she dabbed at the mess with a tissue, like he was a small child. He said nothing, just leaning back a bit, briefly pausing his onslaught.

"So, we'll leave first thing in the morning?" said Penny.

"Yep. Could take us all day," he said, stuffing the final mouthful in.

"Well, I've checked the timetable and a bus from the village at eight-thirty will get us to Shorley Station in plenty of time for the nine-fifteen to Victoria. That arrives at eleven, then we'll need to get to Euston by twelve-oh-seven, and we should be in Manchester Piccadilly by around three."

She paused for breath. Killer was looking at her with a shocked grimace on his face. Oh dear, had she over stepped the mark? After they had spoken to her dad, while Killer had his snooze, she'd phoned around for the times. She thought he'd be pleased, her using her initiative and all.

"Yeah? Great," he said, wiping his mouth on his T-shirt. "Can we go and get a pint now?"

***

"Last week she came second!" yelled Charlie. "This week she wants the title! Give a big hand for Emma Perkinson!"

Little Emma, the shapely teenager from Shorley, bounded up onto the stage. The pretty blonde was hoping that her rendition of Milly's 'My Boy Lollipop', along with red hot pants and a few cute smiles, would win tonight's competition.

Donkey sat with Barry close to the stage. She had their vote before she'd sung a word.

Penny led Killer out of the kitchen and into the bar.

"Two lemonades?" asked Debbie.

"Fuck off!" said Penny. "Why don't you just..."

"Oh my God!" said Debbie, rolling her eyes, "I've never heard you swear so much since you met Cilla."

"It's Killer!" cried Killer.

"She knows that," said Penny. "She's just trying to be funny."

"Oh," said Killer. "Ha. Ha. Ha. Very funny. Now any chance of a pint before I die of thirst?"

"And I'll have the same," said Penny, staring down Debbie.

"A whole pint? Wow! Little sister's on the piss."

Debbie plonked two pints down on the bar. "Any crisps? Got some great new turnip flavoured ones."

Little Emma finished off her act with a flourish of pelvic thrusts that had Barry and Donkey drooling in their pints.

***

If your parishioners could see you now, thought Carol.

John Cunningham, vicar of Henyard, lay naked and spread eagled on his bed. Leaning over him, Carol gently tied his wrists to the bed posts with her stockings.

Slowly raising his head, he inhaled her perfume, then lay back again.

She carefully pulled a pair of black silk panties up his hairy legs and over his rearing manhood, making sure his balls hung neatly either side of the crutch. Then, when his ankles were secured, his helplessness was complete.

Carol removed her clothes, slowly and purposely. As her panties came down, his erection peaked, and he began to groan breathlessly. She mopped his sweating brow with them before stuffing them into his mouth.

Straddling his body, she began playing with her nipples, building up her own sexual tension. Then, when she was ready, she steered his stiff member into her wet aching body and slowly began to ride her lover. She quickened the pace as he began to buck uncontrollably. Faster and faster she went until she felt him explode deep within her. Then she too let go, screaming as her orgasm tore through her shuddering body.

***

Penny dragged Killer away from the bar and they joined Donkey and Barry, sat at a table close to the stage. Penny squeezed in alongside Donkey, and Killer pulled up a chair next to Barry. Shouting to be heard over the music, she introduced him. "This is Killer, my boyfriend."

On stage, much to the amusement of the audience, a twelve-year-year old boy played air guitar to the Shadow's 'Apache'.

"Hallo pal!" said Barry, well on his way to being legless. "We've met before, remember?"

Killer nodded. "Yeah, thanks again for the lift."

"Pleased to meet you at last," said Donkey, leaning across to shake his hand. "Heard a lot about you."

"Glad to be here," replied Killer.

"Why Killer?" Donkey asked.

"Long story," said Killer. "Why Donkey?"

"A very long story," said Donkey. "I don't..."

"Do you kill people?" interrupted Barry.

"Only if they upset me," Killer replied, coolly.

"Nobody ever upsets me," Barry went on. "Good 'ole Barry, everybody likes Barry, don't they, Pen?"

"Sure they do," said Penny, looking to Donkey for help.

Donkey obliged. "So, where you from, Killer?"

"I'm a citizen of the world. No ties, no loyalties. A free man."

"Free to come and go as you please?" Barry spluttered.

"Yeah, that's right," said Killer.

"Then why don't you just fuck off!" shouted Barry, as he half-stood and took a swing at Killer with a clenched fist.

As Killer ducked away, Donkey managed to grab Barry's arm, pushing him back down into his seat. But the table tipped up, spilling the drinks and sending Killer crashing to the floor.

"I'll kill the bastard!" yelled Barry, as Donkey wrestled him away from the table. Charlie jumped off the stage and helped Donkey drag a screaming Barry out into the lorry park.

Killer was all indignant. Brushing himself down, he shouted, "What's his fucking problem? Never met the fucking guy before. If he wants a fight, he can have one!"

"It's OK!" said Penny, holding his onto arm, trying to calm him down. "Killer, it's alright. He's the village idiot, a pisshead! He's gone now. It's over!"

Killer sat back down. "I knew he was mentally deficient as soon as I saw him. And he stinks. Now my pint's gone, bastard!"

As Penny collected up the broken glass, Debbie came over with a dust pan.

"Never had boys fighting over you before, have you, Penny?" she said.

"It wasn't like that."

"Now they know you're not a virgin anymore," she said, "they'll all be after you."

"Fuck off, bitch!" said Penny. Grabbing Killer's hand, she pulled him from his seat, and together they retreated back to her bedroom.

***

Donkey sat with his fresh pint. Now that Barry was in a taxi and on his way home, he could sit back and enjoy the show. Pity it was nearly over. The punters were voting with their hands for the night's winners.

"Ladies and gentlemen," Charlie declared. "There is obviously only one winner tonight, little Miss Emma Perkinson! Let's have a big hand for this very talented and beautiful young lady!"

Little Emma leapt from her seat, screeching with joy and punching the air. Tears rolled down her face as she went up on stage to receive her prize. She held the bottle of Champagne above her head as Charlie congratulated her, planting a kiss on her cheek.

"I want to thank you all for voting for me," she said, breathlessly. "Thank you so very much. I love you all!"

Passing Donkey on her way back to her table, she brushed passed him.

"Well done!" he said. "Need a hand to drink it?"

Their eyes met briefly, and Emma blushed. Donkey smiled, and the connection was made. Five minutes later, as Charlie awarded the consolation prizes, he was sat at her table chatting with her and her friends. When those friends set off back to Shorley, a short time later, Emma elected to stay a while longer. Her friends all teased her causing her to blush profusely. They were all locals; they knew the score. The lads were jealous, the girls envious. Little Emma had won first prize again.

"See me tomorrow," said Charlie, cashing up behind the bar as Donkey and Emma headed for the exit.

"OK," said Donkey, "but not too early."

"They get younger every day," said Debbie. But what she was really thinking was, wish it was me!

Walking across the lorry park to the caravan, Emma held onto Donkey's arm. Neither of them saw Carol sneaking in through the fire exit.

SATURDAY

Penny waited with Killer at the bus stop. He'd reclaimed his old leather jacket from the bin, and the smell was still very evident. She was so excited. In her rucksack were sandwiches she'd made up for the trip, and in her purse the £50 her dad had given them for expenses. What an adventure lay before them. Travelling around the country, rallying the troops, collecting up new recruits. Isn't that what Ché Guevara had done?

She tried not to let last night's disappointment cloud her vision. Killer had grabbed her as soon as they got to her room. They'd thrown off their clothes and dived onto the bed, kissing and rolling around. Her heart was pounding, her desires taking over. But as he climbed on top of her, she heard that familiar grunt, and felt that familiar sticky wet patch creeping across her belly. A frustrated Penny spent most of the night awake, listening to her lover's snoring.

The bus arrived, and they boarded.

"The longest journey begins with the shortest step," declared Killer. "Buddha said that."

"Actually," said Penny, "it was Confucius. And it was the first step."

"What's in the sarnies?" he asked, looking out of the window.

***

Donkey woke with a start as Emma suddenly sat up.

"Oh my God!" she cried, leaping naked from his bed. "Look at the time! She'll bloody kill me!" Grabbing her clothes, she frantically began to dress.

Donkey peered sleepily from the covers, as she squeezed back into her red hotpants.

"I need to phone. My mum will go bloody mad!"

"Your mum? Emma, surely you're old enough to stay out..." he began. Then he saw the look in her eyes and quickly sat up. "Emma? You are eighteen, aren't you?" When she didn't answer, he knew she wasn't. "Oh, fuck!"

Donkey got out of bed and, still naked, pulled her into his arms. "It'll be all right, Emma, calm down. Now the truth, how old are you?"

She sank into his arms with a sigh. Taking a deep breath, she pushed her face into his hairy chest. "Sixteen!" she whispered.

"Oh shit! Shit! Shit!" he said, pushing her away.

"It's OK! I'm legal, honest!"

"You should have told me."

"You never asked. Would it have made any difference?"

"Of course it would!"

Little Emma burst into tears.

Donkey wrapped his arms back around her. "What you going to tell your mum?" he asked, nervously.

The consequences of his night of pleasure were running through his mind. Sixteen-year-olds were great when you were a teenager, but at twenty-seven could well be deemed child abuse. She didn't look or behave her age. Great in bed, and very eager to please. Such a beautiful body, and those tight curls of blonde pubic hair. Number ninety-seven. As soon as she was gone, he'd card and file them in his velvet box. Three to go for his century. But now, he had to get Emma home without too much fuss.

"If I phone my granddad," said Emma, "he'll bail me out. I'll tell Mum I stayed with him."

"Will he do that for you?"

"Well, it won't be the first time he's done it. I'm his only grandchild, he adores me. I'll get him to come and pick me up."

Donkey was as relieved as Emma, until she placed her lips tightly onto his. He broke free. "Sorry, Emma, we shouldn't..."

"It was OK last night."

"But I thought..."

"What does it matter? I'm old enough, I'm an adult now!"

"You're only sixteen, Emma, I can't..."

"Oh, fuck you, Donkey!" she said, pushing him away. "Where's your bloody phone?"

***

"Good morning, Dunstable Electronic Importers. Can I help you?"

"Yes, good morning. My name is Murfett, David Murfett, can I possibly speak to a Mr. Foggerty, please?" Charlie was using his best Irish accent.

"I'm afraid he's not in today, sir, it's Saturday. You've come straight through to security. Best you phone back on Monday."

"Oh dear. So sorry to be bothering you. I'm the M.D. for Murfett Securities, and I wanted to talk to Mr. Foggerty about some satellite lorry trackers we're promoting at the moment."

"Well, sir," said the security guard, patiently. "Like I said, he won't be in until Monday."

"Yes, OK, thank you, I'll try again then. But tell me, to save me wasting my time, and Mr. Foggerty's, does your firm fit any kind of trackers to their vehicles?"

"Oh no, sir, we're only a small family firm. We haven't quite caught up with such modern technology. We've only got three trucks. But you never know, give him a ring on Monday."

"Thank you," said Charlie. "I will. Thank you for your help."

"That's OK. Good luck!"

***

Manny Baxter pulled his red Jaguar into the truckstop. M4NNY read the number plate. A symbol of his success.

He cast his eye over the huge log cabin. So, this was the place he'd nearly bought. Pity it fell through, would have made a nice hotel. Still, the by-pass was a dream come true for him. This time next week he'd have bought up a corridor of land the length of Peacock Lane. Once the road had been upgraded, maybe twelve months down the line, planning permission for a hotel and restaurant at the southern end was almost guaranteed. And for a quick kill, the rest of the land had prime housing potential. This could be his gold-plated pension plan.

He saw his granddaughter crossing the yard towards him. Wearing hot pants and carrying a bottle of Champagne. He winced. A tall fellow with a ponytail strode by her side. He seemed a little old for her, but then nothing surprised him about Emma anymore.

"Hallo, Grandddad," said Emma, leaning through his window to give him a kiss. "Look what I won." She held up the bottle of bubbly.

"What for?" said Manny, eyeing her companion up and down.

"Singing, of course!" she giggled. "This is my friend, Donkey."

Donkey nodded a greeting, but Manny ignored him.

"What we going to tell your mum this time?"

"Oh, we'll think of something," she replied. Rising on her toes, she slipped a kiss onto Donkey's cheek. "Thank you for last night," she whispered.

Then she was in the car and Manny was spinning the wheels out of the lorry park.

***

Charlie sat in his office, a letter from the VAT man in his hand. They wanted, no they demanded, an appointment. They wanted to visit him, see his books. They suggested his accountant and lawyer should also be present. Lawyer? The net was closing. His world was collapsing around him.

A knock on the door and in walked Donkey. "Morning boss. All OK?"

"Yeah, fine," said Charlie, sticking the letter in the out tray, the bin.

"Is it on?"

"Yep, all systems go," said Charlie. "This is a big one, Donkey, a lot of people involved. We've got to get it right."

"Where do we start off?"

"Dunstable. We'll have to travel up early Monday for a six o'clock start. You'll be doing holiday relief. I'll give you all the details on the way up."

"How long do I pack for?"

"Just the one day. This job is load specific. We know what's on it and where it's going "

"Or where it's supposed to be going," said Donkey.

***

The truckstop was never busy Saturday lunch times, just a few local truckers passing by and a few continental drivers, stranded for the weekend, waiting for a new week to start.

Carol was in the kitchen clearing away at the sink. She was feeling happier than ever. Soon all this toil and grief would be over. Last night God had answered her prayers. Her heart, her mind and her soul had all reached an orgasmic peak of happiness. She now knew where her future lay. And it wasn't here at the bloody truckstop! Her body ached from last night; he hadn't been able to keep his hands off her. What a lover! And he'd told her he loved her! Loved her!

Having sex with his younger wife was, he said, so different, so quick. Almost boring, he'd said. Not that they'd done it for ages; Helen just never seemed interested.

And now they had talked of running away together. Soon. Couldn't be soon enough for her. But he had to do things right, that was his way.

"Mum?" said Debbie, as she came into the kitchen. "Mum you alright? You look in a daze."

"I'm fine, Debbie, in fact, I've never felt better."

"Good, I'm pleased for you. Now why didn't anybody tell me Penny's got more fucking time off. She just swans in and out like she's a fucking lodger. I never get time off! It's not fair!"

Carol tuned back into mother mode. Now she knew it wasn't for ever, she knew she could cope. "Shouldn't you be behind the bar, Debs? Your dad won't be pleased if you haven't opened up yet."

"Thanks for your support!" said Debbie, storming back out.

"Egg and chips twice, and a sausage sarnie, brown sauce," Charlie called out, sweeping past Debbie and into the kitchen.

Carol said nothing; she fired up the frying pan and got out the bread.

"Any more news on that by-pass crap?" he asked her.

"Not that I've heard. Most people seemed quite pleased about it."

"Especially that arsehole, Ted Morrison, I bet!"

"They're only doing what they think is best for the village."

"What about us?" said Charlie, "What about our business? You know that if it goes ahead, we're finished, don't you?"

Carol hadn't really thought that much about it. She'd had other things on her mind. The future of Charlie and his bloody truckstop wasn't at the top of her list. Not really her problem, not now.

***

It was a long hot day for Penny and Killer. The trains were crowded, and people kept staring at them, as though they were another species. Killer's behaviour didn't help. He kept pawing her and laying his head on her shoulder, trying to stick his tongue in her ear. Not something that most people could ignore. Then he'd fall asleep, snoring loudly. That was about the only time he stopped eating. Peanuts, sweets and bacon-flavoured crisps.

He said it was OK to eat them because it was all artificial flavours. Man made. If they can do it with crisps, he argued, why can't they do it with the real thing? Artificial cows and sheep. If he couldn't tell the difference, how could anybody?

On the train to Manchester he repeatedly tried to get her to go into the toilets with him. When she refused, he sulked for a while, then tried again. And again. In many ways he was like a child, only more so. He kept staring at girls. Unashamedly so. One girl even got up and changed seats, it seemed he couldn't help himself. It made her feel awkward and concerned for their relationship. She had thought that they'd spend the trip planning for the battles ahead, discussing tactics and strategies, that sort of thing.

"Where do we go when we get off the train?" she asked.

"There's a pub in Moss Side that we use as a meeting place. All the boys will be there."

"What about the ones tunnelling under the new airport runway?"

"Oh, they stay there. They're surrounded by security. We can't get in, they can't get out."

"So where do we get the troops from?"

"Once I put out the call, we'll have volunteers coming from all over the country."

Penny pushed the doubts from her mind by thinking of her dad, practically begging them for help.

Once off the train they caught a taxi to the Hanging Man, a tatty modern pub in the middle of a sprawling, run down housing estate. Loud punk rock poured onto the street from within. Sat on the pavement outside, several tattooed youths swigged from beer bottles, smoking smelly cigarettes. They all seemed to have various metal work hanging from their faces. They just stared silently as Penny followed Killer into the pub.

A pungent smell, along with the loud music, unnerved Penny. A DJ, in the corner of the bar, was scratching some punk classics. The place was packed out. Penny held on to Killer as they squeezed through to the bar. Killer stood there with his hand up, trying to get the barman's attention.

Suddenly, an angry voice cried out behind them, "What the fuck you doing here?"

A tall skinny guy, with short, cropped red hair, pushed his way through to them.

Killer looked nervous. "Er, hallo Dog."

"Mole! Mole!" Dog yelled above the loud music. "Look who's just turned up! Fucking Killer!"

Mole, an angry looking guy with long blonde hair, forced his way through. "Fucking hell! What do you want?" he spat. "You arsehole!"

Penny was frightened. Why had his troops turned against him? This was all going so horribly wrong. She grabbed hold of Killer's arm and held him tight.

"We need your help," shouted Killer. "A by-pass in Sussex; it's capitalism gone crazy. The villagers are fighting it, but they need help, our help!"

"Well, you can just fuck right off!" shouted another angry voice from behind them.

Penny turned to see a long-haired youth, gesticulating wildly with his finger. "Remember what happened last time? I fucking do!"

"Killer!" yelled Mole. "Do yourself a favour, fuck off before Snake rips your fucking head off!"

"Yeah! Fuck off you loser!" said Dog.

Killer looked scared. People were jeering and hurling insults at him. He backed away slowly, dragging Penny with him out through the door.

As soon as they were outside, Penny burst into tears. This wasn't how it was supposed to happen. They sat on the pavement, down the side of the pub.

"What's happening, Killer?" she cried. "What the hell's going on? They were supposed to be your friends!"

"Yeah, I thought so too." He paused in thought for a while. "There's been a coup d'état! While I've been away, there's been a power shift. After that pig shit fiasco, they're feeling low, need someone to blame. 'Cos I wasn't here, I was an easy target. Well, fuck them! The fucking lot of them!"

"But what about the by-pass? What about the villagers? And Dad?"

"We'll do it on our own. We don't need those wankers!"

"But how?"

"I don't know," said Killer. He thought hard for a moment. "Can you go back in and get me a pint?"

"No, I bloody can't!"

***

Donkey leant up against the bar, chatting to Debbie. It was early evening and the local band from Shorley was setting up on stage. Saturday nights could be a lively affair, so Donkey would act as Charlie's bouncer. The young bloods from the town came in many forms, punks, goths and reprobates, all determined to have a good time. They all knew Donkey and showed him respect. But sometimes it wasn't enough.

"She was a bit young for you last night, wasn't she?" said Debbie.

"You can say that again," said Donkey.

"Pretty little thing though; if I was a lezzy, she'd be right up my street "

Donkey laughed. "Could I come and watch?"

"You can cum with me any time you like Donkey. You know that."

Donkey did indeed know that. And maybe one day...

Barry came in, booted and suited, but looking quite ill. "Sorry 'bout last night," he said. "I was pissed."

"Yeah, we noticed," said Donkey. "Still, no harm done, you missed him."

"Three broken glasses," said Debbie. "But it was well worth it just to see the look on Cilla's face. He almost crapped himself."

They all laughed.

"Is Penny about?" Barry asked. "I want to apologise. To her, not to that spotty-faced tosser."

"They left this morning " said Donkey. "Off to Manchester, I think."

"She's off skiving again," said Debbie. "It really pisses me off."

"Do you know when she'll be back?" asked Barry.

"God knows," replied Debbie. "When she feels like it, I suppose."

"She's only gone for a few days, I think," said Donkey. "What you having?"

"Cheers, mate," said Barry. "I'll have a scotch; a big one."

***

Charlie called Cousin Billy from his office, away from all the noise.

"Charlie! How's it going? Everything OK? Ready for Monday?"

"Yeah, of course it is," said Charlie. "Have I ever let you down?"

"The fact that you're still breathing, Charlie, means you've never let me down." Billy's shrill laughter echoed down the line.

"Ha, ha," said Charlie, knowing that it was probably true. Nobody upset Cousin Billy.

"So," Billy went on, "let me know as soon as it's on the way. I've got lots riding on this job, Charlie."

"Yeah, of course, Billy. Going to be a piece of piss. No problem."

"It had better be, Charlie, for your sake."

***

Charlie's Place was rocking. The R's End Band were screaming through their set as over forty youngsters bopped, pogoed and screeched along with them. The pulsating light show bounced off the walls in time to the bass beat.

Donkey sat in a dark corner with Molly, face locked and horny. She was ginger and proud, her locks almost down to her waist. His hand massaged her ample bosoms, her hand never left his crotch. She was so hot for him. She'd tried several times to drag him outside, but he'd resisted. He told her he had to stay around, in case there was any trouble. But when he got up to go to the loo, she followed. And as they passed by Barry, slumped over a table in a drunken stupor, she grabbed Donkey's hand and dragged out into the lorry park. He feigned resistance.

Around the back of the kitchen, Molly pinned him to the wall. With their lips firmly joined and her hands ripping at his jeans, Donkey came alive. As his jeans fell, her skirt rose, and he pulled her scant panties to one side. She was so wet!

Reaching down, Molly grabbed hold of him. "Oh my God!" she whispered. Holding on tightly to his massive beast, she pulled him closer, then slowly guided him in, inch by inch. And when she was full, there was still so much left!

Yanking her legs up around his waist, Donkey span her around and up against the wall.

"Ouch!" she cried, as a sudden pull on her pubic hair distracted her for a brief moment.

"Sorry," said Donkey.

As he began thrusting into her, he felt her body erupt. She let out a long, guttural scream, rising higher and higher, as the fireworks in her head exploded!

Donkey fired into her, adding his cries of pleasure to hers. As the thrusts slowed, they both collapsed into a heap onto the ground.

From inside the bar they could hear Charlie winding up the show, thanking everyone for coming.

Sunday

Penny was cold, wet and hungry. It had been a very long night. They'd slept in a fibreglass castle, in the children's play area of the local park, curled up on the bark chipped floor as the wind drove the rain through the open windows. They'd had little choice. The money was gone. She'd only bought one-way tickets, not thinking of how they would return. It should have been in a triumphant convoy of freedom fighters. But those freedom fighters had told them to fuck off!

It wasn't like Killer had told her it would be. To them, her lover, the one who had made her a woman and had given her so much hope, was a wanker, a tosser and a loser. And now, Penny couldn't help but think, that that was the way it really was. She looked at him curled up and snoring on the floor. She'd hardly slept at all.

Yesterday, after the row at the pub, Killer had had no idea what to do. He'd become aggressive and wanted to go back and 'do' Mole. But by then Penny had lost faith in him completely. Her dreams were shattered.

They'd bought some chips with the last of their money and headed for the park. As it got dark, the rain began, wind driven and relentless. By the time they came across the castle they were soaked to the skin. As she sat on the floor sobbing, Killer had put his arms around her. When she leant into his body, seeking comfort, his hand went straight to her breasts, roughly groping her.

"Fuck off!" yelled Penny, pushing him away. She was really upset, and all he wanted was sex. Moving to the other side of the castle, she screamed at him, "Mole was right. You are an arsehole! You're so full of shit! Why did I ever...?"

Curling up into a ball on the floor, she sobbed her heart out.

***

Charlie sat in his office, mug of tea on his desk. Today was old dears' day. He'd phoned to confirm the figures; twelve from St. Bernadette's and nine from the Shorley Veterans' Rest Home, plus four helpers. twenty-five set places. They'd been coming for years now, for some it was the only time they ever got out. Most of them were like family. Carol had even attended several funerals, but that wasn't for Charlie. His would come soon enough. He went through to the restaurant to give Carol the figures.

Carol and Debbie were busy rearranging the tables. The oldies liked to dine canteen style, one long table, so they could face each other and hurl insults. It also made it easier for their keepers to keep control. It could get pretty rowdy at times.

"Twenty-five," said Charlie. "What we doing for them today?"

"We," said Carol, emphasizing the we, "are doing roast pork."

"Dad?" said Debbie. "Why is Penny off again? I'm pig sick of covering for her. Why can't I have a day off sometimes?"

"She'll be back soon," said Charlie. "When she is here, you only bloody argue. Did Barry bring over those kidneys yesterday?"

"Yes," said Carol. "Bit smelly though; I think they might be off!"

"Bung 'em in tomorrow's casserole; they'll be all right."

***

Penny knew what she had to do. She had little choice really. They'd spent the morning sat in a bus shelter, keeping out of the rain. She'd said nothing, just sat there listening to Killer's diatribe against Mole. Yesterday they were the heroes of the revolution, who were going to help us to victory. Today they were traitors, fascists and sodomites.

The highlight of the morning came when Killer hassled an old guy for some loose change. The guy reacted by punching him hard in the face, knocking him to the ground, then just walked off.

Although shocked and frightened by the assault, Penny resisted the urge to run to Killer's side. She felt no sympathy at all as he lay on the wet pavement, crying and spitting blood. She'd made a huge mistake; she had to accept that and move on. She got up, and without looking back, walked away.

When she arrived back at The Hanging Man, it was nearly mid-day and it had finally stopped raining. Outside, the litter and debris from the previous night cluttered the pavement. Without the crowd and loud music, it didn't seem quite so intimidating. She took a deep breath and walked straight in.

The lights were dim. The smell of stale beer and cigarettes stung her nose. As her eyes refocused, she looked around. A few drinkers stood at the bar, staring back at her. One or two sat at tables, but the place was practically empty.

The tattooed barman, in a string vest, caught her eye. "Yeah?" he asked.

"I'm looking for Mole," she said, slowly and deliberately.

"Yeah?" he said again.

"Do you know where I can find him? Please?"

A long pause, as he looked her up and down, made her feel vulnerable.

"He's in the private bar," he said, nodding towards a closed door behind the bar.

"Can I...?" Penny began.

The clue's in the name. Private."

Penny hesitated. "Could you tell him I'd like to talk to him? Please?"

"And you are?"

"Penny. We met last night."

"Did you now? Hang about here while I go and see if he remembers." He slipped into the private bar, closing the door behind him.

The people in the bar stared at her. Was she really so different to them? Maybe it was her accent. Maybe they were all just like Killer, staring at girls like they were whores.

The barman reappeared. "He'll see you now, ma'am," he said, making a mock bow as he pointed to the private bar. A couple of drinkers laughed.

Taking a deep breath, she knocked on the door and went straight in. The pungent smell in the smoke-filled room hit her nose, and she instinctively covered her mouth with her hand. Sitar music, accompanied by a throbbing drum beat, vibrated around the tiny bar. It was more like a sitting room. A dozen or so people filled a couple of sofas and several armchairs, others sat on the floor. All were arranged around a few low coffee tables, covered with beer bottles and overflowing ashtrays.

Mole was sat on a sofa, wearing a red flamed T-shirt, an arm slung around a girl who seemed strangely familiar.

Penny made her way over, very aware that everybody was looking at her. Mole raised an arm and the music stopped. His eyes bored into hers.

"Hallo. Can I...? I want to ask you something," she said, slowly.

"Can I ask you something first?" said Mole, leaning forward.

"Er, yes, of course."

"What the fuck are you doing with a wanker like Killer?"

The room erupted into laughter and jeers.

Penny breathed deeply, trying to hold back tears. She had to be strong. "I'm no longer with him. It was a mistake." What more could she possibly say?

"Mistake? Yeah, that just about sums that tosser up!" said Dog, sat next to Mole. His friends jeered their approval.

Dog passed a joint to Mole, who hit on it then passed it on to the girl.

"So?" said Mole, exhaling a cloud of smoke.

"So, I need your help. My village, in Sussex, is under threat from the developers."

A hiss went round the room.

Penny pushed on. "Nobody wants it. The pub, the post office, they'll all have to close, and so will my dad's truckstop."

"Your dad's truckstop?" said Mole slowly. "So, this is personal."

"No! Well, yes. But nobody wants it, we don't need it. It's only greed that's driving it on. You see..."

"Woo! Slow down," cut in Mole, pushing Dog further along the sofa. "Here, just sit down and take it easy. What did you say your name was?"

She sat down; it was a tight squeeze. "Penny, Penny Wheeler, I..."

Mole pushed the joint in front of her face, "Here, have some of this and chill out."

"No, no thank you. I don't..."

"Look, I want to help you, OK?" he said. "But you just need to slow down. Ease up, relax a bit. Just take a little hit off this, it's good for you."

He put the reefer to her lips and Penny slowly inhaled.

***

Carol dished up the last of the pork. She was dead on her feet. Only the thought of tonight's service kept her going.

The noise in the restaurant reached a crescendo. Many of the old codgers were deaf, so the ones that weren't, felt the need to shout all the time. They could be quite belligerent at times. Battles were being fought over the bread rolls and the napkins.

Charlie and Debbie put the food in front of them, and the helpers made sure they ate most of it, picking the rest up from the floor.

Their helpers ignored the noise, they were used to it. They dashed from one incurable to the next, dabbing the odd dribble with a napkin and force feeding the slower ones. This was a good day out for the elders of the parish. They never left their rest homes for most of the week.

An irate Debbie stormed back into the kitchen. "If he does that again, so help me I'll punch him!"

"What now?" asked Carol, in the middle of preparing the deserts.

"That fucking filthy old git, Harold!"

"Not again," said Carol.

"Yes again. He put his hand right up my skirt and grabbed a hand full. I had to prize his bloody fingers off!"

"Well, perhaps you should wear your jeans, Debs."

"Oh, so it's my fault is it? If this was McDonald's, he'd be fucking arrested!"

"Debs, they're old men, they don't know what they're doing; most of them are senile. You should be feeling sorry for them."

"Sorry for them? What do you want me to do? How about I sit on their laps and let them play with my tits?"

"Debbie! Stop it! Don't talk like that. Especially not on the Lord's day.

"Oh, God, don't start that again," said Debbie. "Sometimes I think it's you that's going senile." She returned to the battleground of the restaurant with some deserts.

"Hiya, Carol. Alright?" Donkey breezed in from the lorry park for his dinner.

"No, Donkey, I'm not! Bloody kids, bloody husband and bloody truckstop! I've had enough of the whole bloody lot of them!"

Donkey seemed a bit taken aback; she rarely voiced her frustrations to anyone.

"Can't be that bad," he said, throwing an arm around her. "I think you could do with a break. Why don't you take a few days' off?"

"That would be nice," she said, snuggling into his shoulder.

"Oi! Take your hands off my wife!" Charlie cried, as he came in through the swing doors. "You don't know where she's been."

And neither do you, thought Carol, cheering up at the thought.

"Ready for tomorrow?" Charlie asked Donkey.

"Yep, packed and ready to go."

"Good, we'll leave about four o'clock, I'll give you a knock."

"Right, I'll be ready," said Donkey.

***

Donkey sat down at a table with his dinner, as far away from the oldies as possible, not only because of their behaviour, but because they made him feel vulnerable. He just knew that one day it could be him having his chin wiped.

"Hallo, Donkey! Haven't seen you for ages!"

Looking up from his meal, he saw Linda, one of the nurses. She was passing by with Harold, on their way to the loo. Linda was tall, blonde and very fit.

"Linda! Nice to see you again."

"Can't stop," she said, "or else there's going to be an almighty mess. See you on the way back."

Donkey smiled, memories stirring his loins. Luscious Linda. Number fifty-two if he remembered correctly, and not a true blonde. She was loud, raucous, and up for anything.

Linda came back alone. "Left him on the shitter," she said, with a giggle that Donkey remembered so well. "He'll be all right though, he's been groping Debbie, so he'll probably want a wank!" She laughed again. "So, what you been up to?"

"Oh, you know, still pumping diesel. And you?"

"Oh, you know, still wiping bums and emptying bed pans. Night off tonight, though." She giggled provocatively, looking straight into his eyes.

"Yeah? What time do you finish?" asked Donkey, his face lighting up.

"Seven. So...?"
"See you seven-thirty?"
"Yes, please!" she drooled.
"My place or yours?"
"Have to be yours, I'm married now!"
"Wow! Congratulations!"
"Why thank you, Donkey."

***

Penny couldn't remember ever being happier. Angel, the girl, was just great, a real friend. Once she'd got to know her, she loved her. And Mole, and Dog, and all of them. They were such great people. They were interested in her. Wanted to know how she felt about the world. They listened when she spoke, they all loved her.

Mole heard her tale, and straight away was determined to help. He'd taken a head count of all those who wanted to get involved, practically everybody said yes! She was thrilled at such a positive outcome.

Mole was such a great guy; he made her feel like an equal. She never felt that way with Killer. Ugh! Killer! She wished she'd never met him. Or let him... But she had to move on. Be positive. If she hadn't met Killer, then she wouldn't be here now, with all her new friends.

When Mole went off to make some phone calls, Penny spent ages just talking with Angel. As they chatted, Angel stroked her head and held her hand. She felt really close. She had another hit on a joint. It made her feel happy and excited about what was going on.

Mole returned to the sofa, squeezing in alongside Penny.

"We can be ready to leave by noon tomorrow," he told her. "There'll be twelve of us to start with, in two buses and three camper vans. As soon as we've established base camp, others will follow. Our numbers will swell by the day."

Penny was so happy she threw her arms around Mole and planted a kiss on his lips. The room erupted into cheers. Mole held the back of her head and the kiss went on a lot longer than she'd anticipated. His tongue slipped briefly between her lips, sending a familiar surge through her body. Penny suddenly felt quite damp. When he finally released her, she looked towards Angel, feeling quite embarrassed. But Angel just smiled and gave her a kiss on her cheek.

***

As Carol left for evensong, she saw Linda walking up to Donkey's. Lucky bitch! she thought. She knew exactly what fun she was going to have. Unfortunately for her, Helen was always around on Sundays. The most she could hope for was a quick cuddle. But she certainly had a surprise for him tonight.

At the church, she made her why down to the front pew. She always had the same seat, end of the pew, next to Helen. She made small talk with the vicar's young and pretty wife. The weather, the Parish news, the noise from the passing trucks. Everything except, 'Do you know I'm having an affair with your husband?' She wished she could tell her. Then she'd probably leave him, and Carol could have him all to herself.

Selfish she knew, but she'd spent her whole life worrying about what other people thought. She was getting older every day; Helen, damn her, seemed to be getting younger.

The Reverend John Cunningham began the service. As he read the lesson for the day, he gazed out over his flock. His wife sat next to his mistress. What a blessed man he was. A pretty wife on his arm for all to admire, and a wild mistress who understood his carnal needs perfectly.

He gazed into Carol eyes. She smiled, lifted her skirt a little and discreetly parted her legs. Only she knew why the vicar spluttered and lost his place in the text. Because only he saw the object of his desires, staring right back up at him.

***

The warriors spent the rest of the day plotting and planning the campaign ahead. Mole laid out some maps, and Penny pointed out the village and Peacock Lane.

"If we let them get away with this, =" said Mole, "all the surrounding countryside will be swallowed up with houses and factories within a few years, making fortunes for the speculators and turning your village into a ghost town."

"Do you think we can stop them?" asked Penny, taking a joint from Dog.

"Of course we can," said Mole. "Right is might!"

They ordered in a take away and stuffed themselves with beans and rice. It was a real party atmosphere, and the joints never stopped coming round. Penny felt fantastic; she had found true meaning in her life.

Time just flew by. When the pub closed, and everybody left, she tagged along with Mole and Angel; it seemed the right thing to do. They walked to a squat a few streets away. Apart from the fact that they had to enter through a downstairs window, it was a pretty nice place. Others lived in the house, but Mole and Angel had their own room on the top floor.

The heady smell of joss sticks hung heavy in the room. A large mattress lay on the floor surrounded by duvets and cushions. Mole flicked on the sound system, and a gentle chorus of whale music flooded the room. Sitting crossed legged on the floor, he started rolling yet another joint.

Angel sat down on the mattress and beckoned Penny to join her. She was a bit taken aback when Angel put an arm around her and kissed her full on the lips! Her head swam from too many joints, but she wasn't too stoned to realise that actually, it felt really good. Those unfulfilled urges welled up through her body, her heart was beating so fast, she thought it might explode.

Angel gently laid her back on the mattress, and their lips met again. Her hand began caressing Penny's breasts, her fingers teasing her nipples. When Angel's hand slipped inside her jeans, the gentle probing fingers had Penny shivering in ecstasy, sending shock waves through her body.

Angel slowly stood up. With her short, cropped hair and stocky body, she looked quite manly. But when she slipped off her top, Penny was left in no doubt. Her boobs were huge! They swung wildly as she stooped to remove her trousers.

Now she remembered her! She was the girl on the front page of the Sun. The one Killer was drooling over!

Penny had no time to think, she was in a daze, a sensuous tingling daze. She just lay there as a naked Angel began tugging at her T-shirt, slipping it up and over her head. She looked over to Mole, who just smiled and hit on the joint.

Penny raised her hips from the mattress as Angel slipped off her jeans and panties. She lay naked and unashamed, every inch of her body crying out with desire. She never knew she could feel like this.

Angel lay down with her and their lips met again. Penny's hands began caressing those enormous breasts. She'd never touched a girl's breasts before; it felt so good!

Suddenly, a warm hand slipped gently between her legs. Opening her eyes, she saw Mole, kneeling naked alongside them. His hand so soft and gentle, caressing and teasing her, taking her higher and higher. She felt electrified, on fire! Wave after wave surged through her body. It just seemed so right, she closed her eyes and let go.

Monday

As Charlie pulled the Merc out of the yard and onto the road, he passed an envelope over to Donkey. Inside was a driving licence, with an agency ID card in the name of Paul Terry, but bearing Donkey's photo.

Donkey put on the interior light and studied it for a while.

"Ready?" asked Charlie.

"Yep," he replied, closing his eyes.

"Name?"

"Paul Terry."

"Date of Birth?"

"Twelve, twelve, sixty-nine."

"Where?"

"Manchester."

"Agency?"

"Smithson's."

"Load?"

"The one with the most fucking gear on it!" laughed Donkey, leaning back into the passenger seat.

Charlie laughed too, but this was serious stuff. He had to make sure Donkey did his homework. He needed the cash from this job to see him through the next few weeks or so. "Edinburgh!" he said. "You're doing holiday relief to Edinburgh. We can't afford to cock this up, Donkey. Too many people involved."

Charlie's cousins had many talents. One of them was a master forger of documents, another ran phantom firms, such as Smithson's Driving Agency. Another cousin would be receiving the next delivery from Dunstable Electronic Importers.

"When you pull out, head up the A1 and run to Ferrybridge Services. Then give me a bell and I'll fill you in with the delivery details."

Charlie never took chances; if anything went wrong, the less Donkey knew the better.

***

"What?" cried Debbie, from beneath her bed clothes. "No! No! No! First fucking Penny, now Dad. No! I'm not doing it. Fuck off!"

Debbie didn't take kindly to being woken early. And five o'clock was fucking early! She did the bar, late nights. Breakfast was theirs. Now her mum was banging on her bedroom door telling her that Dad was out with Donkey.

"Please, Debs," her mum pleaded. "I can't do it on my own. He'll be back soon."

Debbie stumbled to the door and stuck her bleary-eyed head out. "OK! OK! I'll do it. But when Penny gets back, I'm having some time off! OK?"

"OK, Debs, I'll talk to your father..."

"No! Whatever he says I'm going away for a few days. Right?"

"OK, Debs, OK! Now can you get a move on? There's already drivers in."

***

Donkey was truly knackered. Luscious Linda hadn't left him until gone midnight. Told her new husband she was doing an extra shift. Well, she was! God, she'd worn him out. At it right up to the taxi beeping its horn outside.

No pubic hair stealing from Linda. Hers were already part of his collection. Number fifty-two. He didn't collect doubles. He could hardly swap them with other perverts, could he? Two short and curly brunettes for a rare ash blonde! He laughed to himself at the absurdity of it.

Charlie dropped him off just around the corner from the warehouse. "Phone me," he said, "as soon as you get to Ferrybridge."

Donkey slung his kit bag over his shoulder and went off to work, as Charlie set off back to the truckstop.

***

Driving his Mercedes home through the darkness, Charlie pondered his options.

Plan A was to stop the by-pass, sell the truckstop to Manny for mega bucks and fuck off to a life in the sun. Spain, or maybe even Brazil.

If that failed, and what with the time scale involved, it probably would, there was Plan B. Which was to grab as much cash as he could muster, and run. Anywhere.

Plan C made his stomach sink. The by-pass goes ahead, the truckstop closes down, and a very long holiday at Her Majesties Pleasure. For fraudulent trading, avoidance of tax, and the murder of Ted Morrison!

Arriving back at the truckstop, he parked up the Merc and went through into the kitchen. Debbie collared him straight away.

"Dad, I'm taking some time off. I'm going away for a few days."

"For Christ's sake, Debbie, I've only just got back, give me a break, will you? Later, OK?"

"No, Dad, it's not OK!" said Debbie. "I'm not asking you, I'm telling you!"

"Aren't you supposed to be helping your mother? Look, I can see people queuing."

"But Dad..."

Charlie quickly retreated to the sanctuary of his office. He didn't need all this shit. Too much going on. He'd be hearing from Donkey soon, then he could let Cousin Billy know it was on the way. Billy would be giving Donkey a fat brown envelope. Cash on delivery, as always.

This was a bloody good earner for Charlie. He'd give Donkey a couple of hundred and the rest was his. It was shaping up to be a good day, and Kitty was on tonight. He could do with some light relief.

***

Penny woke, slowly opening her eyes. It hadn't been a dream. Thank God! She lay on her side, her arm around a sleeping Angel. Mole lay behind her, their legs entwined, his hand cupping her breast. She could feel his breath on her back and the softness of his manhood, nestling against her thighs. She felt so fucking good!

The night had been one long explosive orgasm, it never stopped. As Mole had made love to her, so tender and gentle, Angel had sucked on her breasts. Then, when Mole switched to Angel, taking her from behind, Angel had lowered her head between Penny's legs, taking her to even greater heights. After Mole had finished with a flourish and a scream, she and Angel drove each other on to a frenzied orgasmic finale. What would her mother say if she could see her now?

***

"Hallo, boss," said Donkey. "I'm at Ferrybridge Services."

"Well done!" said Charlie. "Well done, son. Any problems? Know what it is?"

"Piece of piss. The paperwork says TV's and audio systems. Full load!"

"Great! Now, go to the Birch Services on the M62, westbound. How long do you think it'll take?"

"Not much more than an hour or so, I reckon."

"OK. Great! Now listen, one of Cousin Billy's boys will meet you there and take you on to a warehouse. Once they've offloaded, they'll want you to run the empty wagon away. Ring me from the warehouse and we'll suss where you can dump it. OK? Well done, Donkey. Well done!"

Leaving the phone box, Donkey felt good. This had been the easiest one yet. A quick look at his licence, then they just gave him the keys and told him to hurry up. Sometimes he'd have to work a few days or even weeks before getting the right load, but not today. Easy. Charlie sounded really pleased. Billy would be too.

Cousin Billy was a thug and a bully who suffered from little man complex. He was only five-foot tall but made up for his lack of height with his psychotic behaviour. His gang terrorised their north London manor. Charlie only dealt with him because he paid hard cash.

Donkey had a piss, bought a burger and ambled back out into the sunshine. What a beautiful day, he thought, as he walked over to the truck.

Only it wasn't there anymore! He dropped his burger in shock. It was gone! The bloody truck had gone! On the ground, broken glass told him that someone had smashed their way in. Shit! Shit! Shit! He looked frantically around the lorry park, no sign of it. God! What the fuck was Charlie going to say?

***

Penny and Angel showered together. They washed each other's bodies, standing tightly together in the bath, under the shower rose. Angel used a razor on Penny's head, shaving away the stubby new growth. There was no lock on the door and several people came in to use the loo and stare. Angel didn't seem to mind, so Penny didn't either. After drying each other off with towels, they walked naked back along the corridor to their room. Penny had such confidence in herself, she was a different person. Someone she had never known before.

The first bus arrived just before 10 o'clock and pulled up on the pavement outside the house. Air horns screamed out from the elderly, multi-coloured bus as Mole yelled down from the window, telling the travellers to come on up.

The eco-warriors, five of them, all hugged and kissed their greetings as they were introduced to Penny. She tried to remember all their names. There was Hog, big, bearded and bold; he squeezed Penny's bum as he hugged her. Then there was Jet, slim with long raven black hair; Penny thought she was quite beautiful. And Deer, her older sister. Then there was Rook with six rings in each ear and two through his nose, or was it Crow? She'd never remember all these names. Her brain was still floating from last night, and they'd had several joints already today. Mole was rolling another one now.

A hoot from outside signalled the arrival of two camper vans. More people poured up the stairs. Fly, Silver, Carrot, Mellow, Penny struggled to keep up, but they all seemed so nice and friendly.

Carrot was a very large girl, but short with it. Her long red hair was pleated into pig tails. She and Angel kept kissing and touching.

More warriors arrived, and a little after midday the convoy was complete. With their roof racks piled high with tents and supplies, the two buses, three campers and a van, carrying thirteen eco-warriors, set off. With horns blaring and lights flashing the convoy pulled away, to the cheers and shouts of those left behind.

Mole drove the lead bus, an orange and green thirty-footer, fitted out with a kitchen, a sound system and a huge double bed. Penny sat up front with Mole, while Angel and Carrot lay on the bed, fondling each other.

Penny was a little confused. The line between sex and love had got a bit blurred. Did she love Mole? Yes, she had to admit, she did. Did she love Angel? Yes, of course she did! Or could it just be the amazing sex? She wasn't so sure. Did she feel jealous watching Carrot with Angel? Yes, she did. Did she want to join them? You bet she did!

***

Charlie took the call in his office.

"Boss! It's gone! Someone's fucking nicked it!"

"What? What's gone? Calm down, Donkey, you're talking gibberish!"

"The fucking truck! While I was phoning you, somebody's fucking nicked it!"

"What? Where? Where from?" Charlie couldn't believe what he was hearing.

"The fucking lorry park! Went out and it's gone, broken glass everywhere!"

"Jesus fucking Christ! I don't believe it! Please, Donkey, tell me you're joking!"

"Wish I could, I really do. What do we do now? What do you want me to do?"

"Shit! God knows, better come back here I suppose. I'd better phone Billy."

Charlie could have cried. Billy was not going to like this.

"Believe me, Billy, it's true! On my kid's life, it's true! He stopped for a piss at Ferrybridge Services, came back out and it was gone!"

Charlie pleaded with his cousin to believe him. But Billy didn't. Not a word of it.

"You've fucking turned me over, Charlie!" he screamed down the phone. "What's the world coming to when one of your own rips you off?"

"But Billy... It wasn't me! Honest! Would I do that to you?"

"You just fucking have, you bastard!"

"No Billy... No!"

When he'd finally finished screaming abuse, Billy told him he'd be down to see him, soon. Get some answers, sort it out.

Charlie knew how Cousin Billy sorted things out.

***

By the time Mole hit the M6, Angel and Carrot were half-naked and noisily pleasuring each other. Penny tried not to look; she was getting those feelings again. Mole was singing along with Carol King, on the CD player. Behind them, the convoy followed on.

She watched Mole as he drove. He was so handsome, suntanned and with long shaggy sun-bleached hair. He was a good leader, the others showed him great respect.

"Oh shit!" said Mole suddenly, as a police car came past and slowed in front of them.

"What's he doing?" asked Penny, nervously.

"Checking us out," said Mole. "He'll probably pull us into the next services. Angel! Stash the gear, empty the ashtrays!"

Angel quickly stuffed a carrier bag into a ceiling light, then went about throwing all the roaches out of the window. Penny felt quite frightened. She'd never been in trouble before. She took some deep breaths to try and clear her dope-fudged mind.

Sure enough, as they approached the next services the police car flashed a 'FOLLOW ME' sign, and Mole, along with the rest of the convoy, followed them into the service station. They all parked behind the squad car, down one side of the lorry park.

"Good afternoon," said the police officer, coming round to Mole's open window. "Your vehicle, is it?"

"Yes, that's right," said Mole, handing down all the relevant paper work. He'd been through all this before, many times. He knew it paid to co-operate. Everything was in order, but if he gave them any shit, they'd soon find something wrong.

A policewoman tapped on the door alongside Penny. Mole pressed a button on the dash and the door hissed open. The WPC stepped up and looked around inside. Angel and Carrot had pulled a blanket up over their nakedness.

"How old are you?" she asked Penny.

"Eighteen," she replied, nervously.

"Where are you going?"

"To Cornwall," cut in Mole. "Going surfing."

"Yeah!" said Angel. "Going to ride them waves!"

"Where's your boards?"

"Picking them up on the way," said Mole.

He took his papers back from the cop at his window, then watched in the mirror as he went around checking the tyres. Inside the girl cop took a few paces up the bus.

"I do like a girl in uniform," said Angel, letting the blanket drop to reveal most of a breast. "Do you do stag do's?"

"Only for my husband."

It was all very good natured.

Her partner came up into the bus and looked around. Angel covered up.

"Your mate behind says he's going to Cardiff," he said. "And your other mate, the one at the back, says he's going to London."

"Yeah, that's right," said Mole, "then we're all meeting up in Cornwall."

"Oh, that's all right then," said the cop. "As long as you all know where you're going." He looked to Mole. "Rear tyre, nearside, get it changed, soon!"

"Yeah, will do. Thanks, mate."

"OK," said the cop. "Now get going, and you don't stop till you're out of Staffordshire. Right?"

"Right!" said Mole, firing up the engine. "Have a nice day!"

As the two officers left the bus, a wave of relief swept over Penny.

"They were cool," said Mole. "They don't want any hassle, nor do we."

"What's with Cornwall?" she asked.

"Never tell them where you're going," said Mole. "If you did, there'd be a reception waiting for us when we got there. They'll know soon enough. They probably think we're heading for Newbury."

"Wasn't she a cutie?" said Angel. "She could handcuff me any time!"

They all laughed, then as they got back on the road, Carrot got the gear back out and began rolling a joint.

***

"Ladies and gentlemen, vagabonds, pimps and truck drivers, welcome to Charlie's Place! Yes, it's Monday!"

Charlie paused, waiting for the cheers to die down. "Miss Kitty Le Sadé is waiting in the wings to titillate your senses and send you all back to your trucks with a smile on your face and a lump in your pants. Empty your bladders, fill up your glasses and take your seats. The horniest show in the country starts in just fifteen minutes!" Returning to the bar, he sank onto a stool.

Debbie put a pint in front of him. "You alright, Dad?" she asked, sympathetically. "You look awful."

"Yeah, I'm fine, just a bit tired, that's all."

"Good," said Debbie. "Now about my time off. As soon as Penny gets back, I'm off, couple of days at least."

"Oh, not now Debbie…"

"Yes, now! I just want to get away from this hell hole."

"Where do you want to go?"

"Anywhere! Just away from here!"

"Better see your mum."

"I have, and I've told her the same."

"What did she say?"

"I don't care what she said. I don't care about anything now! OK? Get it?"

Carol appeared from the restaurant. "Charlie, Penny's on the phone."

"Talk of the devil," he said. "Put her through to the office, will you?"

"Great," said Debbie, "Tell the bitch to get back here, quick!"

"Penny! How's it going?" Charlie asked from his office.

"Great, Dad, just great. We're on our way down. Should be with you tomorrow, around about noon."

"Excellent! Best thing I've heard all day. How many?"

"There's thirteen of us, counting me. Two buses, and some vans."

"Wonderful! I'll cone off the far corner of the lorry park. How's Killer?"

"Not very good; I'll tell you about it when I see you."

"OK then, see you tomorrow. Well done, Penny!"

"Well?" said Debbie, looking over as he returned to the bar.

"Tomorrow; she's back tomorrow."

"Great! Then I'm off tomorrow," said Debbie. "Hear me?"

Charlie didn't reply. Finishing off his pint, he adjusted his bow-tie and returned to the stage.

"Loyal patrons, men of the world, put your hands in your pockets and get ready to rock and roll. I give you, the one, the only, Miss Kitty Le Sadé!"

Kitty stormed the stage with the speakers blasting out 'It's Raining Men'. Dressed in nothing but a mac and a G-string, Kitty rode an umbrella between her legs. When the mac came off, the boys went wild. Opening the umbrella, she twirled it above her head as she thrust her arse into one trucker's face, before allowing another lucky one to kiss it. Laying down on the stage floor, she hooked a high heel into her G-string and slowly peeled it down her legs before twanging it into the audience. Chairs toppled as her fans fought for the prize. When she mounted the umbrella handle and began wildly thrusting, they went crazy. Then the music abruptly stopped. Quickly gathering up her mac, Kitty exited the stage, bowing and taking in the howls of delight from her fans.

***

When the convoy fuelled up at the garage, Penny had called her dad from a phone box. He sounded so proud of her. She felt closer to him now than she'd ever been.

"Dad's ready and waiting, parking all set up," she told Mole.

The convoy pulled out of the garage and shortly afterwards parked up for the night in a lay-by on the A34. The warriors all congregated on Mole's bus. It was crowded and very smoky.

"What's your real name?" asked Jet, passing Penny a joint.

"That is my real name," she replied.

"Oh, you've got to have an earth name!" said Jet. "Birth names are so boring. Hey you guys," she called out. "What about a name for Penny?"

"Princess!" said Silver, dazzling in his silver jacket and boots.

"Piglet!" offered Hog, touching himself.

Names came thick and fast. Nymph, Moonbeam, Rainbow, but none rung true.

Mole silenced the offerings with a wave of his hand. Looking Penny straight in the eye, he said, "Starlite! You have brought a light into our lives. Your earth name shall be Starlite!"

The others cheered their agreement. She just knew it was right. Mole leant into her and gave her a kiss, then she got a hug from everybody, as they all congratulated her.

By the time the warriors had all departed back to their camper vans, Starlite had lost count of the number of joints she'd shared. Mole put on some whale music and they all climbed into the bed. When Mole started making love to Angel, it seemed so natural for Starlite to turn to Carrot.

***

Charlie turned his Merc into the lay-by. A great way to end a very stressful day. Kitty undid his shirt and raked his chest with her plastic nails. Charlie was just caressing her ankle when a car drove by. He recognised it as Ted Morrison's Jaguar.

"Bastard!" he murmured.

"Who?" said Kitty.

"Ted fucking Morrison!"

"Oh! I've always found him to be the perfect gentleman."

"What?" said Charlie sitting up. "You know him?"

"Yes, he's a friend of mine, actually."

Charlie knew that with Kitty, friend meant client. "No! Never! I don't bloody believe it!"

"It's true," she said. "But don't you go telling anyone."

"Of course not. I wouldn't tell a soul."

Charlie would have jumped for joy if his trousers hadn't been around his knees. The day had just got a hell of a lot better. Now he could have Ted Morrison any time he liked. He reached down for Kitty's shoe. Red ones tonight, great!

Tuesday

The breakfast rush was over by the time Charlie got to sit down in a quiet corner of the restaurant with Donkey.

"Tell me again what happened," said Charlie. Not that he needed to hear the story again. Yesterday's phone call from Donkey had played like a tape loop through his head all night.

"Told you, came out and it was gone. Couldn't believe it! Fucking gone!"

Donkey hadn't got back till the early hours; he'd had to hitch-hike home. Took him hours just to get away from the services, and he'd had to walk the last few miles.

"What about the truck?" Charlie asked. "Did it have the firm's name on the side? Any advertising?"

"No, plain white truck and trailer."

"So, we can assume who ever took it, already knew what was in it. Could be an inside job I suppose. Someone could have followed you from the warehouse, just waiting for you to stop. Thieving bastards!"

"What did Billy say?"

"He wasn't too pleased; we'll probably be seeing him soon."

"Look forward to it," said Donkey. "But what about him? Could it have been one of his boys? Perhaps he got greedy, wanted to cut you out of the deal."

"Possible, I suppose," said Charlie. "Come to think of it, his reaction was a bit muted. He only threatened to cut my balls off!"

"The guy's a fucking psycho; don't fancy being around when he comes calling."

"Well, I hope you are," said Charlie. "I might need you!"

A couple of drivers came in and shouted greetings to Charlie. He got up to serve them. "See you later, Donkey."

***

Carol finished off the pans at the sink while Debbie leant against the open kitchen door, puffing on a ciggy.

"So where are you going to go," Carol asked her, "when Penny gets back?"

"Dunno, just away from here. Up to London maybe, do some shopping."

"Borg's birthday soon, isn't it? You could go looking for a present."

"Maybe, but to tell you the truth, I'd forgotten," said Debbie, flicking the dog end out into the lorry park.

"Have you two fixed a date yet?" asked Carol. "You'll have to book the church months ahead, you know."

"Now you're sounding just like him!" said Debbie, sitting down at the kitchen table. "We're still young; we've got all the time in the world."

"So, are you having second thoughts?"

"And third and fourth."

"Oh, Debs, he's a really nice lad, you could do a lot worse. Besides, I quite like the idea of being a grandmother before I get too old to enjoy it."

"No fucking chance!" said Debbie. "Marriage, mortgage and babies are not the future I had planned."

"Then what is, Debs?"

"I don't know, Mum, I really don't know. Anything but this!"

Charlie came through the swing door with a tray stacked up with dirty plates. "Two bacon and egg sarnies and some buttered toast," he called out. "And Dave's knocked over his tea, Debbie; take him another and mop up, please!"

"Shall I do the sandwiches or mop the floor?" Debbie asked. "Can't do both!"

"Of course you can. Penny could."

"No, she couldn't 'cos she ain't fucking here!"

"I'll ask her to give you some lessons later, when she gets back."

"Yeah? There ain't nothing she can teach me!" said Debbie. "But I never thought I'd be pleased to see her. Right, Dad, listen, I'll do the bar tonight, then I'm off tomorrow for a few days. Right? Do you hear me? I'll be back on Saturday, maybe."

"As long as your mother can cover," he replied, "it's OK by me. Now, tea and mop!"

"Charlie!" said Carol. "How can I cover the bar and the kitchen?"

"I'll get Donkey to do the bar, then when you've finished the meals, you can take over. OK? Now, when you're ready with the sarnies."

Carol sighed as Charlie swung back out of the kitchen. Thank God, she thought, all this could soon be over.

***

After a breakfast of muesli and toast, and a quick pee in the hedge, Starlite sat up front with Mole as the convoy pulled out from the lay-by and headed south. She was feeling a bit apprehensive. She knew her dad would be pleased to see them, but she had to learn not to let Debbie wind her up. Her new persona, along with her earth name, made her feel strong and confident, and a real woman for the first time in her life. Carrot had been so gentle with her last night, taking her to such heights, over and over again.

What had happened between her and Killer now seemed like a bad dream. She was young and innocent, and he'd taken advantage of that innocence. And her stupidity. She felt abused. To have lost her virginity to such an... an arsehole, shamed her. She would have to live with that for the rest of her life. She pushed it to the back of her mind.

Shortly after noon the convoy came off the A27 and passed through Henyard on its way to the truckstop. Mole slowed down as Starlite pointed out the post office, the church and the local pub.

"The whole village depends on through traffic to survive," she told them.

A truck coming the other way forced the whole convoy to mount the pavement to allow it to squeeze by.

***

From the window of his large detached house, fronting the main street, Ted Morrison observed the buses and vans causing mayhem in his village. He looked forward to the time when all this traffic would disappear down the by-pass.

He mused over the benefits. The peace and quiet, and the value of his property would probably double. But best of all would be Charlie Wheeler and his damn truckstop going bust. He couldn't wait.

***

The convoy slowly pulled into the truckstop, horns blazing and lights flashing. Her dad came running out and directed them to the coned-off section, at the top of the lorry park. There wasn't enough room to circle the wagons, so they parked side by side.

Starlite jumped off the bus and ran to see her dad. She flung her arms around him and held him tightly. He seemed embarrassed; he didn't quite know how to respond; she'd never done that before. She began introducing the warriors as they piled off the buses.

"Dad, this is Mole, Carrot, and Angel," and as they stepped forward to shake his hand she continued, "Hog, Silver, Jet and Deer..."

"Call me Charlie," he said, looking a little stunned. Apart from Killer, he'd never come across anyone like this before. They were all covered in tattoos and had various studs and rings all over their faces. Some had very long hair of various bright colours, and others had none at all.

"Where's Killer?" he asked.

"Still in Manchester," said Starlite, "and this is Crow and Paradise and Dog, oh, and that's Snake."

"Look, I'm sorry," said Charlie, "I'm never going to remember all these names, sorry. Why don't you all come in; you must be starving."

Starlite linked arms with her dad as they led the motley crew through the lorry park and over to the restaurant.

***

Debbie stared out from the window in disbelief. She'd thought her dad had rushed out to throw them off the lorry park.

"Mum! Mum! Come and look at this! Penny's back and she's brought some of her freaky friends with her!"

Carol joined her at the window. "I don't believe it!" she said. "What's he up to now?"

They watched as the warriors piled into the restaurant. Charlie sat them down away from the other diners.

"It's great you're back," said Debbie, throwing her T-cloth down on the counter. "That's me finished for the day."

"A dozen teas, Debbie," said Charlie. "And Carol, can you knock up a few sarnies for the boys?"

"And girls," said Starlite.

Carol came over and gave her a big hug. "Lovely to have you back, Penny. I've missed you."

"I only left on Saturday, Mum."

"I've missed you too!" said Debbie. "Get your gloves on; you're doing dinner tonight!"

"No, I'm not," said Starlite, firmly, trying to stay calm. "I don't work here anymore. I'm a full-time activist. I've found my calling..."

"You can find what you fucking like," cut in Debbie, "but I'm not covering for you any longer. Do you hear that?"

"Then take it up with Dad," said Starlite. "It's nothing to do with me, I've left home. I'm only visiting."

"Yeah? Is that so? Well, I quit too! Fuck the bar tonight, and fuck the lot of you!" Debbie picked up her T-cloth and threw it back down again, before storming out of the restaurant and up to her bedroom.

"Now come on, Pen," said Carol. "We need you here, I can't manage without you."

"Starlite, Mum. My name is Starlite now."

"What? But you can't just change your name, Pen, can you?"

"Yes, you can, and I have. Please call me Starlite from now on."

"Oh, Penny..."

"Starlite Mum, or I won't answer. It's my earth name."

"OK, OK, if that's what you want," said Carol. "Where's Killer?"

"Still in Manchester, tell you about it later. Mum, this is Mole, Angel, and Carrot..."

"Could we please do the introductions later?" interrupted Charlie. "Carol? Tea? Sandwiches? Please!"

"Charlie," said a puzzled Carol, "what's going on? Who are all these people?"

"These are the people who are going to stop the by-pass!"

"What? How? I don't understand."

"You don't have to understand," said Charlie. "I'll explain it all later. But now they're hungry, they've driven all the way down from Manchester. Can you make them feel welcome? Please?"

A confused Carol went back off to her kitchen.

The warriors held a council of war. Starlite sat alongside Mole, and as they munched on the cheese sarnies, carefully avoiding the ham ones, her dad filled them in.

"So, this local big wig, Ted fucking Morrison, Tory, magistrate, councillor, you name it, he's got a finger in the pie, wants the by-pass so he can bankrupt me. It's all I can think of. No one else wants it. The pub would close, it relies on passing trade. So does the post office, and so do I!"

"Tell us about the proposed route," said Mole.

"Peacock Lane. A narrow little country lane, just west of here, lovely countryside, we used to play there as kids. They want to turn it into a dual carriageway."

"Yes, Starlite has shown us on the map. Is that the only alternative?" asked Mole.

"It's their cheapest option, and the easiest to build. I've heard planning permission is virtually agreed, due to Ted Morrison being on the fucking council!"

"Proving corruption," said Mole, "or even a bias, could overturn any council decisions. We need to check this guy out. We also need to take a trip over to Peacock Lane and have a look. See what's there."

"OK," said Charlie. "When you've finished your grub, we'll go take a look."

***

Debbie seethed in her bedroom.

"This is it, I'm off! Just see how they fucking get on without me. Maybe I'll go to Brighton, or even London. Yeah, why not? It's about time I had some fun. Boy, are they going to miss me!"

She stuffed some clothes into a bag and grabbed her make up. Then, as she reached for the bedroom door, she suddenly stopped. Putting down the bag, she sat back down on her bed and began to cry.

***

Tommy called. Charlie took it in the kitchen.

"Charlie, just got a letter from the Inland Revenue. If we don't make an appointment to see them soon, they'll get a court order to seize all your accounts! And they're talking about a winding up order if you don't co-operate!"

"Tell them I'm ill or something, in rehab, having a nervous breakdown!"

"They'd believe that, wouldn't they? What you going to do, Charlie? This is serious stuff!"

"For you and me both, Tommy, for you and me both. You just hold them back. I need some more time." He hung up.

Returning to the warriors in the restaurant, he said, "Right then, let's go for a ride!"

Mole, Angel and Starlite travelled in Charlie's Merc, the rest followed on behind in the two camper vans. Charlie drove slowly, leading them down along the narrow winding lane. They'd only gone a hundred yards or so when Mole called out for them to stop. The warriors poured out of the motors and swarmed over a fence and into a field. There, just yards from the roadside, was a very large tree.

"Wow!" said Mole.

"Wow!" said Dog.

"Wow!" said Starlite.

Then a communal WOW! from everybody as they surrounded the tree and began gently touching it. Mole took out a camera and began to take pictures from every conceivable angle.

"What's with the tree?" asked a puzzled-looking Charlie.

"This," said Mole, "could be the answer to the problem. This oak tree must be at least three hundred years old! Look at it, it's beautiful! You can feel its power!"

"Yeah? Is that good?" asked Charlie.

The warriors formed a human circle around the tree and started to hum.

"This alone," said Mole, "could prevent the by-pass. No one can destroy a tree of this age. We need to get a preservation order on it, as soon as possible."

"There's more!" said Charlie, with a huge grin on his face.

And there was. In all, eight old oaks lined the route. But the best was yet to come.

At the northern end of Peacock Lane, right alongside the road, lay a barn. An empty, derelict, timber framed construction. Dog, an architect named Robert in his former life, identified it as eighteenth century, possibly earlier. The dovetail joints and the hand-made nails driven into the beams, made this an historic relic.

Charlie stood watching as Mole sat them all down in a circle on the floor of the barn and called for quiet.

"I declare this a council of war. We will peacefully fight for the right of the trees to live. We will fight for the preservation of this barn, so that future generations can see our history. And we will fight for the people of Henyard." He paused and looked around at his warriors. "There is no way we can allow this by-pass to go ahead," he declared. "Plan of action for tomorrow. Dog and Starlite will go to the local library and research the barn. Angel and myself will apply at the county council office for preservation orders on the oaks. Silver and Hog, you will go to the local council and check out how far any application for the by-pass has progressed. And we want to know when the next planning meeting is due. Jet, Carrot and Snake, I want you to organise the printing of anti-by-pass posters and get them stuck up all over Shorley and Henyard. The rest of you come back here and do a field study. I want a comprehensive list of all the flowers and fauna, birds and insects. Everything that lives here must be noted. All of you will report back to me personally. We shall not fail!"

I like this lad, thought Charlie, as they climbed into their motors and headed back to the truckstop.

***

Carol grabbed Charlie as soon as he returned.
"Debbie's gone!" she said.

"What? Where?"

"I don't know. She just packed a bag and went."

"Damn! I'll have to get Donkey to do the bar tonight. When's she back?"

"Didn't say. She does deserve a break..."

"So do I! So do you! But we don't just walk out, do we?"

"She told you yesterday she was going."

"Did she? When?"

"When you weren't listening, obviously."

"Yeah, well, I got a lot on my mind, OK?"

Charlie went off to see Donkey.

***

The bar was filling up as Donkey poured Barry a pint.

"Seen those gypos in the lorry park?" he asked Donkey. "It's a wonder Charlie hasn't thrown them off."

"They're eco-warriors," said Donkey. "They're here to campaign against the by-pass. Charlie invited them."

Barry supped on his second pint of the evening. "Eh? What for? What's wrong with a by-pass? People round here seem to think it's a good idea. So do I."

"Better not let Charlie hear you say that," said Donkey.

"Where's Debbie?" asked Barry.

"Carol says she's taking a break. Gone to London for a few days."

"Oh," sighed Barry. "Missing her already."

And he was. For Barry, Debbie was part of the evening's entertainment. Without her cleavage and miniskirts he could just as well have stayed at home and watched porn.

Betty Barbell and the Blue Ridge Drifters were warming up on stage. The cowboy-clad quartet tuned their guitars and did the old 'one two, one two'. Truckers drifted into the bar from the lorry park and the restaurant. The warriors already occupied several tables near the front.

"Hallo, Donkey!" said Starlite, coming up to the bar with Mole and Carrot. She steered them away from Barry.

"Hallo, Penny, nice to see you. Good trip?"

"It's Starlite now, Donkey; my name is Starlite."

"Wow, what a nice name. It's really you!"

"Yeah? Thanks, Donkey," she said. "This is Mole, and Carrot."

"Nice to meet you all," said Donkey, shaking their hands.

"Hallo, Pen!" called Barry. "Hair's coming on. You look like a bleedin' hedgehog now!" He giggled into his pint, almost spilling it.

Starlite tried to ignore him, but he blubbered on.

"Bought your friends with you, eh? Where's Killer? Eh? Mr Bloody Wonderful!"

"Sorry about him," Starlite said to Mole. "He's the local lush. Works in an abattoir!"

"I can smell it on him," said Mole.

"Shall I punch him?" asked Carrot.

They all laughed.

"Where's Debbie?" Starlite asked Donkey.

"Gone away for a few days, said she needed a break."

"Well, I'm finished here," said Starlite. "I'm never going to work here again."

Donkey poured them all a pint and they went back to their table ready for the show.

***

"Ladies and gentlemen, spivs and truckers. It's Country and Western night! And tonight, for your entertainment, please give a big hand to Betty Barbell and her fabulous Blue Ridge Drifters!"

The warriors cheered loudly as Betty went into 'King of the Road'.

Charlie went back to the bar, unbuttoning his waistcoat as he sat down on a bar stool. "Alright then, Donkey?"

"Yeah, no problem. So how long they staying?"

"As long as it takes to stop fucking Morrison. It's looking good though, Mole and his mates reckon we've got a good case."

"That's great. And what about Billy?"

"Fuck Billy! Ain't heard nothing more. Have to wait and see."

"Awright, Charlie?" Barry called out across the bar. "Seen the tits on that one with the short hair? Cor, could give that one, couldn't you?"

Betty Barbell couldn't believe it. For the first time ever in this hell hole, people were up dancing. They looked a right bunch of freaks and weirdos, but they bopped about like kids, and were having a whale of a time. Never before had the band received such applause. And at the end of the night they did their first ever encore.

***

Walking across the lorry park on his way back to the caravan, Donkey could smell the pungent odour of weed, drifting across from the warrior's camp. They'd got a fire going in an old oil drum and were all sat around it. A couple of them were strumming guitars along with a relentless beat from some bongo drums.

He was knackered. The last couple of days had been pretty long and hectic, and now he was looking forward to his bed. Stepping inside, he suddenly sensed a presence, an intruder. His heart raced as he reached for his hammer. Slowly entering the bedroom, he switched on the light. And there, sat on the bed, was Debbie.

"What the fuck?" he yelled at her. "You frightened the shit out of me! What the hell are you doing here?"

"Don't be cross with me," she said. "I've run away from home."

"Twenty-year-olds don't run away from home. Mostly they get kicked out."

"I'm really sorry, Donkey, but I told them I was going away for a few days. But the truth is, I ain't got nowhere to go. How bloody sad is that? No friends or interests outside this fucking truckstop! I just need a break. Can I hide here for a few days?"

"Hide? Why do you need to hide?"

"They think I've gone to London, having a good time. If they know I'm here, they'll have me back in that bloody kitchen in no time. And I ain't doing fucking Penny's job again! Ever!"

"It's Starlite now, not Penny."

"What sort of shit name is that?"

"It's her earth name."

"Sounds like artsy fartsy bullshit to me. But then, I suppose you're called Donkey." She thought for a moment. "Maybe I could be Rabbit? Yeah?"

Donkey laughed. "Look, you can stay tonight, OK? But after that, well, I don't want to get caught up in any games between you and Charlie, OK?"

"It's not a game! I'm out of there!"

"Well fine, that's OK. But you're not in here," he said, sternly. "Now I've got to take a shower. Give me five minutes."

"I'd rather give you a rub down," said Debbie, slowly getting up. "I know there's room for two in that shower."

"Oh, do you now? Might be a tight squeeze."

"So they tell me," she said. "Can't wait to try."

He just knew this would happen one day, so why not today? Taking Debbie's hand, he pulled her into his arms.

WEDNESDAY

The sun rose over the lorry park as the hungry truckers made their way in for breakfast. They were not a happy bunch.

"For fuck's sake, Charlie!" moaned Dave. "Bloody hippies kept me awake all bloody night with their fucking music."

"Sorry, Dave," said Charlie, pouring his tea. "I'll have a word."

"A word?" said Sandy, a Scottish regular. "You want to kick the buggers out! Didn't sleep a fucking wink!"

"That bloody bongo drummer will need a fucking head transplant if I..." said Dave.

"OK! OK!" cut in Charlie. "I'm sorry guys, OK? I'm sorry. It won't happen again, promise. They're here to stop the damn by-pass. If it goes ahead then we're finished!"

"From what I see," said Tony, "it's inevitable. Henyard is just one big traffic jam all bloody day long. So is Shorley. When the container port opens, it'll be grid locked. People in the village think it's a great idea!"

"Who cares what they think?" said Dave. "What about us? There's no other café for miles around!"

"They say there'll be one in the container dock when it opens," said Tony.

"Who said that?" said Charlie, curtly. "It's rubbish, you know no one gives a shit about you guys. We've been serving you for over twenty years, how about some bloody loyalty?"

***

Debbie lay beside a sleeping Donkey. What a night! She'd waited years for this. She'd tried loads of times to get him into bed. Thrown herself shamelessly at him, drunk and sober. He always declined like a gentleman, citing his friendship with her bloody dad!

Last night was the best ever. Borg was pretty good, but Donkey was in another league. And what a weapon! When she'd first seen it in the shower, she thought it was another leg. She'd heard all the stories about him, but nothing had prepared her for that. He wasn't circumcised, he was circumnavigated!

And now she wanted more. She slowly pulled back the sheets until he was fully exposed. God, it was so beautiful. Reaching down, she gently took hold of him. It began to grow as she caressed it. Donkey stirred as Debbie lowered her head.

***

Carol struggled on in the kitchen. Without Penny or Debbie to help she had to cook, help clear the tables and then there was all the washing up. By then it would be dinner time and the whole thing would start again. Charlie would never dream of getting in more staff. Even on a temporary basis. Why pay proper wages when his slaves could do it so much cheaper. If she dropped down dead from exhaustion, he probably wouldn't call an ambulance until after the breakfast rush.

She couldn't go on like this. If John wanted her to, she would leave all this tomorrow. But she had to be patient. They had spoken of a future together. Away from Henyard. Away from the truckstop. If things worked out, Charlie could soon be running this place all on his bloody own!

Charlie came in through the swing doors. "Two Big Breakfasts, one double egg on toast and a bacon sandwich, when you're ready!" And then he was gone again.

***

The warriors sat around a couple of tables in the restaurant, finishing their breakfast. Starlite listened as Mole ran through the day's orders. They all had their jobs to do. She and Dog were off to the library to research the barn.

Her mind was all a bit fuzzy; she struggled to remember last night's party. After the truckstop had closed, she'd eaten some magic mushrooms that Snake had given her. They'd sat in the lorry park under the stars. Silver had played his guitar, Raven bashed his bongo drums and they'd all danced and sang till the early hours. She'd woken up in one of the camper vans, lying naked with Silver. He too was naked, and their bodies were entwined. She couldn't remember if they'd done it or not.

"We'll all meet back here this afternoon," said Mole, "and report our findings. Good luck!" While Charlie ran some of the warriors up to Peacock Lane, Starlite caught the bus to Shorley with Dog. Mole stayed behind for a while, making phone calls, calling in more troops.

***

Donkey showered alone. He was late for work and needed to get a move on. Debbie was just amazing; he regretted ever fighting her off. She'd exhausted him. She was something else, no comparison to any one he'd ever had before. And he'd had quite a few.

He came out of the shower, naked and proud. Debbie, still in bed, couldn't take her eyes off him as he stood there, swinging free, drying his hair with a towel.

Suddenly a knock on the door made them both jump.

"Donkey!" called out Charlie. "You up yet?"

Donkey quickly darted out of the bedroom, pulling the door closed behind him, just as the door opened and Charlie stepped straight in!

"Fucking hell, Donkey! Cover it up! I've come over all inadequate!"

Donkey quickly wrapped the towel around his waist.

"Overslept, have we? Tony's waiting at the pumps, and there's a guy in the lorry park with a puncture."

"Sorry, Charlie, didn't hear the alarm."

"That fucking Debbie has let me down again," he went on. "Bitch just took off. Me and Carol are working our nuts off to cover for her. Now Penny's not here, it makes it even harder. Can you do the bar again tonight, Donkey? Maybe till the weekend? Just until that lazy cow gets back!"

"Sure, Charlie, no problem."

A noise from the bedroom made them both start.

"Oh yeah?" said Charlie, smiling at Donkey. "Who's the lucky girl?" He lowered his voice. "One of Penny's friends, eh? Not the butch one, with the big tits?"

"Shh!" said Donkey. "She'll hear you!"

"You're one lucky bastard, Donkey. Wish I was free and single again." He sighed. "OK for tonight then?"

"Yes sure, not a problem."

"Don't forget Tony, he's been waiting ages."

"Yep, OK, I'll sort it," said Donkey, ushering Charlie to the door.

"OK! OK! I'm going!" He lowered his voice again. "Give her one for me, will you?"

"Sure thing," said Donkey, laughing.

Charlie chuckled and went on his way.

"Lazy cow, am I?" said Debbie, storming naked out of the bedroom. "Bastard! Maybe I won't ever go back."

"Well, you can't stay here!"

"Oh, why not?" she said, in that baby doll voice, her green eyes pleading.

It was hard to talk to her straight with those nipples starring up at him. "You know why. Now don't you think you should get dressed?"

"No, I don't," she said, yanking his towel off. Grabbing hold of his manhood with both hands, she pulled him back into the bedroom. "Tony will to have to wait," she said.

***

The silence in the library was deafening. The smell of books reminded her of her school days. She'd come a long way since then.

Dog was handsome and funny, cropped hair, dyed bright red, and a weather worn face. Always with a smile on it. He had pierced nipples and a yellow sun tattooed on his chest. Starlite liked his take on life. Laid back and calm. Nothing seemed to faze him.

When she told him that she'd slept with Silver, but couldn't remember it, he replied that, from what he'd heard, she hadn't missed much at all. They laughed together. The librarian hissed a loud "Shh!"

Trawling through the history of Shorley, they discovered that the barn was indeed eighteenth century. It had originally been a wool store, then during the First World War, a munitions store. Various people had owned it since then, but the last proper usage they could find was in the fifties. They were pleased about the discoveries they'd made. Mole would also be pleased.

They had some time before the bus back to Henyard, so they walked along the sea front and down onto the beach. Dog put his arm around her and it felt good. Sitting among the sand dunes, out of the stiff breeze, they shared a joint before laying down together and making love. Dog had a Prince Albert, a ring through the end of his penis. It rattled on Starlite's teeth. Then, when he took her, the added sensations drove her to the edge. Her body jerked in ecstasy as her orgasm flowed from her head to her toes and back up again.

On the bus home, she snuggled up tight to him.

***

They all gathered on the bus. Mole cleared his throat and the meeting began.

"A lot of good things happened today. Myself and Angel applied for preservation orders on the oak trees. We should hear back from the council in a few days. Silver and Hog tell me that the proposal for the by-pass has not yet been considered. There's a council meeting next week when it will be put forward by Councillor Morrison. Our application for the preservation order effectively stops it in its tracks. They cannot proceed until a decision is made on the trees. But that is only a delay, not a victory." He paused as he looked at some notes. "From our survey of the proposed route, eighteen types of bird were identified, but nothing rare. There was also over a hundred species of flowers and herbs.

Unfortunately, none are on the protected list. However, Starlite and Dog have discovered that the barn is one of only three surviving in the UK. The other two are owned and protected by the National Trust. That's a good result; I'll be talking to them today to get their support."

He picked up a pile of leaflets and held them up. "Jet, Carrot and Snake have printed off a hundred 'Fight the By-Pass' posters, so tomorrow I want you all out putting them up, along Peacock Lane, in Shorley and in Henyard. Talk to the people on the street. Tell them what we're doing, get their support. We can win this battle and we shall!"

They all trooped off to the bar; they could hear music, must be a show on tonight.

***

From behind the curtain of Donkey's bedroom, Debbie watched them go. Penny, arm-in-arm with the dyke, laughing, having a good time. Bitch! She could murder a pint, and she was starving.

She'd lived in this caravan when she was nine, before they'd moved into the truckstop. She'd slept in a small box room with Penny. They'd lie awake at night listening to their mum and dad arguing. It was pretty clear that if her mum hadn't fallen pregnant with her, they would not have got married. Both of them used it as a stick to beat each other. Debbie used it as a stick to beat herself.

They never had holidays like other kids; it was always going to be next year, or the one after that. She could never see herself as somebody's wife. And kids? No fucking chance! She'd have to tell Borg soon. She'd strung him along for far too long. He'd get over it. And with guys like Donkey around, so would she.

***

Donkey poured Charlie and Barry a pint, and as they supped, they watched Kitty getting her kit off to the tinny strains of the Stones' 'Let's Spend the Night Together'.

"They never tire of seeing her," said Charlie. "Isn't she great?"

Donkey didn't answer. He'd just had one of the best nights of his entire life and was looking forward to more of the same tonight. And number ninety-nine! Not only that, a first! His collection now included a mother and daughter!

Debbie's were mousey brown, long and straight, Carol's blonde, short and curly. Debbie was by far the better lover, but then she'd had a lot more practice. He couldn't wait to get back to her.

His lust was tempered a bit by the fact she wanted to stay. What about Borg? And Charlie might have something to say if he knew. No, she had to go. He'd tell her in the morning.

Just as Kitty was building up to her big finale, a disturbance broke out. Charlie quickly made his way back to the stage as boos and cat calls rang out.

Kitty had stopped, mid-strip, her G-string down to her knees.

"Shame on you!" shouted Carrot, standing at the front of the stage.

"You're letting the sisterhood down!" yelled Angel, stood alongside her.

Kitty didn't know what to do. She just stood there as the music played on, taking all the insults.

"If you don't like it," cried out Tony, "why don't you just fuck off!"

"Yeah!" yelled other punters.

"You're prostituting yourself and all of womanhood!" shouted Jet from the back.

"Fuck off, you bunch of lezzies!" yelled out Barry, from the bar.

When the music stopped Kitty finally broke and ran crying back to the dressing room.

Mole, realising that the girls may have upset a few people, called for a strategic withdrawal back to the buses. They left quickly, to a torrent of foul-mouthed abuse from the furious truckers, with a shower of fag packets and beer mats raining down on them.

Back in the dressing room, Charlie tried to calm a sobbing Kitty with a big hug.

"But why do they hate me?" she cried, dabbing at her eyes with a tissue.

"Don't take any notice, they're just a load of lesbians!"

"Then why don't they fancy me?" she said, bursting into tears again.

"Come on, Kitty, get your coat on, let's get you home."

THURSDAY

From the kitchen, Carol could hear the truckers at the counter, complaining bitterly to Charlie.

"For fuck's sake, Charlie, did you hear that lot last night?" asked Bob. "Some twat was banging on those fucking drums all night!"

"Sorry, Bob," said Charlie, "I'll get 'em to quieten down."

"Quieten down?" said Will, a regular Wednesday nighter. "Charlie, if you don't throw those fuckers off, you won't have anyone left to serve. Didn't sleep at all last night. This is a truckstop not a fucking hippy commune! Bet they're all on the bloody dole!"

"And what about last night?" said Terry. "Those fucking wasters ruined the show! Kitty was so upset she didn't do the second show, or the lorry park afterwards."

"Look, I said I'll sort it! OK?" snapped Charlie, retreating to the kitchen with some dirty cups.

Carol was at the sink; they'd only been open for a couple of hours and already she felt exhausted. "Why aren't they paying for their meals?" she asked him.

"They're here to help us, OK?" he replied. "Do you want us to go bust? If this place closes, where we going to go? Without the trucks, we're finished!"

As Charlie left, taking Bernie his sausage sandwich, the kitchen phone rang. It was Tommy. Carol was surprised; she'd not spoken to him for a very long time, years even.

"Hallo, Carol, how's things with you?" he said. "Long time no see. Is Charlie there?"

"Hallo, Tommy, yes, it's been a while, hasn't it? He's about somewhere, but he's really busy. Can I get him to call you after breakfast?"

"Damn, I get the feeling he doesn't want to talk to me."

"Why's that, Tommy?"

"'Cos he's in the shit and he's burying his head in the sand."

"So, what's the problem then?"

"If you could just ask him to call me."

"OK then, Tommy, bye."

She wondered what that was all about.

***

The warriors began to drift into the restaurant for their breakfast. As they sat down several drivers got up and moved away from them, scowling.

The TV had the local news reporter interviewing the Shorley public, getting their views on the proposed by-pass.

"Great!" said mother-of-three, Melanie Howard. "Bloody trucks are polluting us all, and their drivers are all maniacs!"

The truckers jeered.

"Only yesterday," said her friend, Tracy Smith, "a huge Juggernaut cut right across me as I tried to pass him on the roundabout. When I beeped at him, he gave me the finger!"

More jeering and abuse filled the restaurant.

"Fuck off, you bitches!" shouted Dave. "Women shouldn't be allowed on the fucking road!"

"Get back behind your sink, you silly cow!" yelled a Scouser.

The warriors stayed silent. They bit their tongues. They knew they were being tested. It wouldn't take much for it all to kick off again.

Last night, after they'd fled, abuse ringing in their ears, Mole had preached tolerance.

"We're here to help them," he'd said. "If we continue to criticise their lifestyle, we could lose their support."

Jet had argued that, entertaining men by taking off your clothes, was prostitution and pornography. It demeaned all women, your sisters and your mother.

Carrot reckoned that they were all perverts, betraying their wives and their daughters. "They probably all have a wank when they get back to their trucks," she said.

Although angry, Angel had agreed with Mole. They had to back off and stay focused on why they were there.

Starlite felt embarrassed and confused. She'd known Kitty for years. She wasn't like they portrayed her. Yes, she could see the seedy side of it, but it was only a bit of fun and nobody was forced to watch.

She was sat next to Jet. She thought she was so beautiful, with her long black hair and her pert little boobs. Dog obviously thought so too. While they all sat around the fire last night, the two of them had made love noisily in one of the camper vans. Starlite had hoped that after their lovemaking on the beach that afternoon, that maybe she and Dog could become a couple. But that wasn't the way it was.

We're all in love with each other, Angel had told her. She'd also told her she'd fucked them all, every warrior, male and female.

"Sex or love?" Starlite asked.

"Love," Angel had replied. "But the sex is fucking great too!"

***

"Scrambled egg for seven, three egg sandwiches and loads of toast," Charlie called out rushing into the kitchen. "And three pots of tea."

"Tommy was trying to get hold of you earlier," said Carol, wearily.

"Cheers. I'll get back to him later."

"He said you had some sort of problem."

"Oh, did he now? He's the one with the problem."

"Charlie, you need to bring in some more help. I'm exhausted, I need a break."

"Oh, God, not you as well! Do you ever hear me crying for time off? The reason we've got this place is because I've worked my balls off for the last bloody twenty years!"

"Can you remember when it was we, Charlie? Seems such a long time ago."

"Oh, Christ! Don't start, please don't start! Just how many people can I take on my back at one bloody time!" he said, storming out of the kitchen.

***

Debbie stared out of the caravan window, careful that no one saw her. She was a princess in a dungeon, waiting for her knight in shining armour to rescue her and take her away to a land of plenty. Somewhere she didn't have to scrub floors or serve pisshead truck drivers. Donkey had told her last night she had to go. After he'd shagged her, of course. She wondered who was using who. She was going to sneak back into her room tonight, then appear miraculously in the morning, after the breakfast rush was over. She'd tell them she'd been in London, having a good time, shopping and partying with all her friends.

Then it would be back to the grindstone, and all the shit that went with it.

***

Starlite found her mum alone in the kitchen. It seemed ages since they'd last found time together. Her mum gave her a long hug.

"Penny, I'm so glad you're happy, I really am."

"It's Starlite, Mum, Starlite!"

"Oh, Penn, I'm your mum."

"It's still Starlite."

"OK then, Starlite it is. Cup of tea? Sod it, I'm taking five minutes, sit down." She poured them both a cuppa then sat down close. "So, what happened to Killer?"

"Don't ask!"

"But you told me you loved him, and didn't he...?"

Starlite blushed. "Yes, he did. The biggest mistake of my life. He was a total fucking wanker!" She didn't normally use such words in front of her mother, it was a sign of how much she'd grown up in recent times.

"So, who's the lucky boy now? Mole? I could see the way you were looking at him."

"No! Well, yes, in a way."

"What way?"

"We all love each other, Mum, it's hard to explain." Especially to your mother, she thought.

"So, what's with all these funny names?" asked her mum, moving on.

"They're not funny. They're appropriate to where we are in life, with no ties to our past. Native Americans have different names all the time. One for childhood, then one when they reach puberty and so on through life according to their position in society."

"Mmm, I can see that, I suppose. So, what would you call your father?"

Starlite thought about it for a bit. "How about Grizzly?"

"More like Gerbil!" said her mum, and they both laughed loudly.

"And Debbie could be Skunk!"

"Not nice, Penn... sorry, Starlite."

"How about Slug for Barry?" laughed Starlite.

"Urggh! And what about me? What would you name me?"

"Difficult. What about Sun? From you comes all life."

"No, I don't feel like a Sun."

"Moon? 'Cos you're loony?"

"Thanks for that." Her mum paused in thought. "What about Slave? Or better still Fool?" The bitterness in her voice betrayed her.

"Mum!" said Starlite, reaching for her hand. "What's wrong? Nobody sees you like that."

"Don't they? I do. Sometimes I wonder why I'm here at all. I don't care anymore. All of this, the truckstop, your father, it all means nothing to me anymore."

"Oh, Mum," said Starlite, leaning over and putting an arm around her. "It can't be that bad, can it? We all love you. Dad's just a bit stressed, what with the by-pass and all. Debbie will be back soon, then you'll be able to take a break. Tell Dad to get some more help in. Stand up to him. Tell him!"

***

"Look, mate," Charlie told Mole. "Last night was right out of order, Kitty was really upset. And I'm getting complaints from my overnighting drivers, they need their sleep, they have long days. They come here to relax and have fun."

They were sat in Charlie's office.

"Sorry, Charlie, but we have strong beliefs, that's why we're here. It won't happen again, and I'll get them to keep down the noise tonight."

"Good!" said Charlie. "Now that's out the way, let's get on. What's happening?"

"There's a council meeting on Monday, in Shorley, where they're going to agree to formally apply to the county council for planning permission. We need to be there, to let them know of our objections. No decisions will be made, the plans will be considered over the next few weeks."

"Can't we jolly it along a bit? The sooner it's turned down the better," said Charlie.

"It'll be a while before they decide. If permission is agreed, we'll appeal. If it's refused, they will appeal. It could take months, years even."

Charlie didn't have that long, a couple of weeks at most, if he was lucky.

Mole carried on. "It's a pity we couldn't find any rare plants or birds along Peacock Lane."

"What sort of plants?" asked Charlie.

"Well, a rare orchid stopped a power station being built last year in Norfolk, and a Montagu's Harrier nest in Cumberland prevented a housing estate going ahead."

"Yeah? How come?"

"They're all protected by law. No one can disturb them. It's their planet as well as ours."

"Of course it is!" said Charlie. "They need people like you and me to stick up for them."

"Right," said Mole, patiently. "The barn and the oak trees are the aces in our hand. I spoke to the National Trust this morning about the barn and they're very excited.

They'll be contacting the farmer who owns it to see if they can buy it for the nation. Preserve it and open it to the public."

"Great!" said Charlie, "I can't see how they could possibly grant permission now!"

"Neither can I," said Mole. "Neither can I."

***

Starlite stretched to pin the poster onto the telegraph poll as Snake passed her the drawing pins.

STOP THE BY-PASS!

SAVE THE OAK'S!

The art work was in brilliant orange and green. Every pillar and post in Henyard was now adorned with the campaign poster.

"Hallo, Penny. I haven't seen you for ages. How are you?"

Starlite turned and was surprised to see the vicar standing right behind them.

"Oh, hallo. I'm fine, thank you. And you?"

"Yes, very fine, and how's your father? Haven't seen him in church lately. And Debra OK?"

"Er, yes, they're all well, thank you."

"Your mother told me you'd cut all your hair off, but she didn't warn me about that," he said, pointing to her nose ring. "Looks awfully sore. Does it hurt?"

"Er, no, not at all."

"So, why don't you want the by-pass?" he asked, studying the poster.

"They're going to cut down lots of ancient trees," said Starlite. "And what about the pub and post office?"

"What about them?" he said. "The post office is going to close anyway, government policy I believe, and the pub landlord was only telling me yesterday he's thinking of turning it into a restaurant. What with the new container base, and all the extra traffic that will bring, I think your father is the only one in the village hoping it doesn't go ahead." He paused. "Who's your friend?"

Snake offered his hand. "I'm Snake, nice to meet you."

The vicar limply shook it. "I must be off," he said. "I'm meeting Councillor Morrison for lunch." He began to go then turned and said, "By the way, you do know there's no apostrophe in oaks, don't you?"

Starlite looked at Snake, then at the poster. Obviously, they didn't.

***

"Carol! Carol!" shouted Charlie. "Someone to see you."

Coming out from the kitchen, Carol was surprised to see Helen Cunningham standing at the counter.

"Hallo, Carol," she said. "Sorry to bother you, I just wondered if I could leave this charity box on your counter? It's for the local hospice."

"Of course you can, Helen. No problem at all. How are you? John alright?"

"Yes, we're both well, thank you," she said, then hesitated, before adding, "In fact more than just well. I'm sorry, Carol, but I've just got to tell someone or else I'm going to burst!" Her face just beamed with happiness. "Even though John said not to!"

"Well, what is it?" asked Carol, wondering what could possibly have made her look so happy.

"We've decided to start a family. Try for a baby! Isn't that just wonderful?" She paused, then went on, "I have to admit that we have been going through rather a sticky patch recently, but that's all behind us now. John is so happy! And he just loves trying!" She let out a childish giggle as her cheeks began to redden.

Carol's heart sank as her entire world shattered into a thousand tiny pieces.

"Con... congratulations!" she heard herself saying. Her throat went dry and she felt nauseous and quite faint. "I'm sorry," she said. "I... I've got something on the stove."

Pushing back through the swing doors into the kitchen, she slumped down at the table. Putting her head in her hands she began to cry.

***

"Borg? It's Charlie. How you doing?"

Borg was feeling great, if a little puzzled as to why Charlie was phoning him, here at his Dutch depot.

"Borg, I need a favour."

"Yeah sure, Charlie. I have good news for you too!"

"Yeah? Great! Now listen, I want some orchids. Rare ones. Can you help?"

"Rare ones? I carry orchids all the time, to garden centres. I don't know if they are rare, but some are much more expensive than others, so maybe they are rare ones, yes?"

"Yeah, they'll do, the expensive ones."

"How many do you want?"

"Just a couple."

"Yes, that will be no problem."

"Great!" said Charlie. "When will you be back?"

"That is my good news! I've quit! I can't live my life like this anymore. I love Debbie and want to be with her, always. So, I've finished! This is my last trip!"

"Oh, er... great! Can you still get me the orchids?"

"Of course. I will be back by the weekend. Can you ask Debbie to call me, please? I can't wait to tell her the good news!"

***

"So, I said to this little boy, 'If I give you some sweets, will you come in my car?' and he said 'Mister, if you give me a fiver, I'll cum in your mouth!"

They screamed with laughter. Bobby Bent had the audience in tears. He was in good form tonight.

The warriors sat quietly at the back of the bar with their beers, on their best behaviour.

At the bar, Donkey poured Charlie and Barry a pint.

"Borg's on his way back," Charlie told them.

"But he's not due till next week, is he?" asked Barry.

"He's quit. Had enough. Wants to come and spend the rest of his life here, with Debbie."

"Arhh!" said Barry.

"Does Debbie know about this?" Donkey asked, knowing full well she didn't.

"Nope," said Charlie.

"She's going to be happy about that, ain't she?" said Donkey, sarcastically.

"Who cares?" said Charlie. "At least it'll be another pair of hands around the place."

"When's she back?" asked Barry.

"God knows," said Charlie. "Lazy cow just does what she wants..." Roaring laughter drowned Charlie out.

"How can you tell if your wife's dead?" Bobby paused before replying, "The sex is still the same but the dishes keep piling up at the sink!"

They howled with laughter. They loved him. Thursday nights at the truckstop was always packed out.

"You know a woman is about to say something intelligent, when she starts off by saying... 'A man once told me...'"

"How about some man jokes?" a female voice called out over all the laughter.

The drivers groaned.

"Got some women in tonight, have we?" sneered Bobby, puffing on his cigar. "Hope you did the washing up before you came out!"

The drivers cheered and applauded.

"Fuck off, you chauvinistic arsehole!" yelled out Carrot, standing up.

"Oh, you're a big girl, aren't you?" he said. "Been eating all the pies?" He took a quick puff on his cigar, then followed up with, "You know why God created lesbians? Eh? You know why? So, feminists like you can't fucking breed!"

The drivers hooted and jeered, clapping and stamping their feet.

Carrot could take no more. Mole tried to hold her back, but she broke free. Moving quickly down to the front, she leapt up onto the stage and floored Bobby with one clean punch.

By the time Charlie and Donkey rushed from the bar, mayhem had broken out. Tony threw his pint over Angel, so Dog decked him. Dave flattened Silver and had to be dragged off of Snake by Donkey. Jet took her chance and, as Donkey held Dave, she connected her boot-clad foot with his nuts. He howled out in pain and dropped to the floor.

Starlite dived under a table, holding her hands over her ears, as tables over-turned and chairs were thrown. Barry rushed in, swinging his arms wildly and shouting abuse. Tripping over Dave, he knocked himself out cold as his head hit the floor.

It took Charlie and Donkey a good while to restore order. Bobby left with a black eye, vowing never to return. Mole, with a split lip, eventually managed to get his troops out into the lorry park. Although he wasn't happy that they'd resorted to violence, he felt that victory was theirs.

Charlie called time on the bar, and as the disgruntled drivers filed out, he slapped Barry a few times until he came round. Then they began clearing up the mess. A couple of chairs were beyond repair and there was food and beer all over the floor. None of them saw Debbie slipping in through the back door.

FRIDAY

"They started it!" protested Tony, nursing a black eye. "That fat lezzie bitch! She whacked Bobby! Anyway, they had it coming!"

"That may be," said Charlie, passing Tony his tea over the counter, "but you boys trashed the place!"

"Well, I'm sorry," said Tony, "but it'll happen again if you don't bar them. How's Barry? He was sparko the last time I saw him."

"He'll live," said Charlie, going back into the kitchen. "Big Breakfast for Tony, two eggs, no sausage!"

Carol was sat at the table; she seemed in a daze.

"You alright?" asked Charlie. "You look quite ill."

Carol got up. "Big Breakfast was it?"

"Two eggs, no sausage. Carol, is there something wrong?"

"No, Charlie, I'm fine. Everything's just fine."

But even he could tell it wasn't.

"Hallo! I'm back. Don't all rush at once!" said Debbie, making her grand entrance into the kitchen.

"Thank God for that," said Charlie. "I have to admit we've struggled without you. Your mother's exhausted, and so am I."

"Hallo, Debs," said Carol, in a slow monotone voice. "Where did you go? Did you have a good time?"

"Yeah, did I? Went to London, it was great. You OK? You sound a bit down?"

"Of course, just tired that's all."

"Where's Penny?" asked Debbie.

"Doing other things," said Charlie. "Oh, and can you ring Borg? He's been trying to get hold of you."

"What's he want?"

"Dunno. Now can we get on? I do have a business to run. Carol, Tony's Big Breakfast..."

"Two eggs, no sausage," said Carol.

***

The mood on the bus was sombre. Last night's fight had shaken them all. They were supposed to be the good guys, so why all the bad vibes? Mole's lip was quite swollen, and Silver had lost a tooth.

"Carrot," said Mole. "Last night you lost control. We all did! We fight our battles with our powers of persuasion, not our fists."

"The guy was a wanker," said Carrot. "But yes, I lost it. I'm sorry."

"Great punch though," said Jet.

Mole silenced the giggles with a wave of his hand. "We're alienating those we're supposed to be helping," he said. "Our numbers will soon swell. Squirrel is on his way down from Manchester; he's picking up more warriors in Birmingham. Word is getting about, soon there will be hundreds of us, so I think we should all move to the barn, set up camp there. That's where our next battle will be. We need to start getting some publicity."

The others nodded in agreement.

Mole went off to see Charlie.

***

With the breakfast rush now over, Charlie sat in his office, staring at the front page of the Shorley Herald.

'By-pass Joy for Henyard!' read the headline. The piece told of the residents' joy at the prospect of an end to all the traffic jams and pollution. Councillor Tom Morrison was quoted as saying that the day the by-pass opened, the village would have a street party. Charlie seethed. A photo of Morrison and the vicar dominated the article.

"Bastards!" said Charlie.

There was a knock on the door and Mole walked in.

Charlie dropped the newspaper straight in the bin. "What the fuck were you lot up to last night?" he asked him, angrily.

"Sorry 'bout that Charlie, but we had a lot of aggravation and..."

"Aggravation? I'm the one getting aggravation! You're here to save my business, not bloody destroy it!"

"No," said Mole firmly. "We're here to save the planet. But it's not an issue any more. We're pulling out."

"Pulling out!" said Charlie, standing up. "You can't do that. The battles just beginning. You can't run out on me now!"

"We're not running anywhere," said Mole. "We're moving to the barn. We need to be on site before the authorities realise what we're up to, or they may try and prevent us. There are more warriors on the way down. We can spread ourselves all the way along Peacock Lane, and get some people up into the trees."

"Sounds great," said Charlie, calming down. "Good idea, good thinking. When you going?"

"Later today; we'll need to set up camp before dark."

***

Carol sat at the kitchen table, her face a ghostly grey. She'd got through breakfast on auto pilot, like a robot. She'd lain awake all night, trying to pick up the pieces of her shattered dreams, trying to find something positive in her life. She'd failed miserably.

Starlite burst through the doors. "Hi, Mum, just come to say goodbye, we're off soon." She paused. "You OK?"

"Yes, just feeling off, that's all. Where you going now, Pen?"

"Starlite! We're moving down to the barn."

"Is that because of the fight last night? What was that all about?"

"Mum, you look really pale, and you sound all spacey. Are you sure you're alright?"

Suddenly Debbie stormed into the kitchen. "He's on his way back! Borg! He'll be here tomorrow!"

"Hallo, Debbie," said Starlite. "You're back then."

"And you're not. How come you can escape this hell hole and I can't?"

"So, Borg's back tomorrow," said Carol. "That'll be nice for you."

"No, Mum," said Debbie. "It bloody well won't! He's quit his job. He wants to move in permanently. Keep's talking about forever!"

"Why don't you just be honest with him for a change?" said Starlite.

"So, what are you, a bloody relationship counsellor?" said Debbie. "I don't see Killer hanging around. You spread your legs for the first spotty kid that comes along, and you think you know everything!"

"Fuck off, Debbie!" said Starlite.

"What language! Mummy, tell her off for using such naughty words."

"You're such a bitch, Debbie!" yelled Starlite. "I hope Borg sees you for what you really are, a fucking slapper!"

Carol slowly got up and walked out of the kitchen.

***

"Shorley Herald news desk, can I help you?"

"Hallo. Yes, I've just seen a Golden Eagle!"

"A Golden Eagle? Wow! Where?"

"I was just walking my dog, by that old barn on Peacock Lane. And it flew overhead, amazing!"

"And you are Mister..."

"Haynes, Trevor Haynes."

"Well, Mr. Haynes, they're very rare indeed. I'll try and get someone down there straight away, see if it's still there. Have you called the RSPB to report your sighting?"

"Who?"

"The bird people. Royal Society for the Protection of Birds."

"No, I haven't, should I?"

"Yes, of course, they'd love to know. Can I have your address, Mr. Haynes, so we can come and interview you?"

"What? Hallo? You're breaking... up... bad line... call you back... "

Charlie hung up and reached for the phone book. "Now, the RSPB."

***

Dog opened the gate to the field, allowing the convoy to pull in. The huge wooden barn was in a state of near collapse. Only two walls remained upright, and half of the roof was missing. They parked the motors across the front of the barn, so they would act as wind breaks.

Starlite and Jet gathered dead wood, as Snake and Dog dug a fire pit in the barn floor. It was good to smell the flowers and hear the bird song, instead of tarmac and diesel fumes. Carrot and Angel hung a white sheet up on the barn wall, facing the road. On it they painted:

'SAVE THE BARN'
'STOP THE BY-PASS'

Purple peacocks and multi-coloured butterflies flew around the words.

Silver and Snake went off into Shorley to get supplies. The others settled down around the fire, smoking joints and listening to Mole on his guitar.

'Starry, starry night, picture palace painted green...'

Starlite's hair had begun to grow again. It was itching and felt prickly. She liked the feel of the breeze on her naked head, and it was true, it really helped free up her mind. She saw things more clearly, understood things easier.

Jet had offered to shave her head for her, and as they listened to Mole, Jet sat behind her and scrapped away with a razor.

"Hallo? Hallo?" A voice from the roadside called over.

Mole spluttered to a halt as they all turned to see a young suit-clad man, climbing over the gate.

"Do you mind if I come over?" asked the man.

Mole got up and walked towards him. "Yes?" he said. "Can I help you?"

"Yes, hi, my name is Dixon, Les Dixon. I'm a freelance reporter, working with the Shorley Herald." Holding up his ID card, he thrust his hand out towards Mole.

"Hallo," said Mole, shaking his hand. "Pleased to see you. You were quick, we've only been here a couple of hours."

"Oh, were you expecting me? Have you seen the eagle?"

"Eagle? What eagle?" asked Mole.

"We've had reports of a golden eagle in the area."

"Yeah?" said Mole. "Wow! That's fantastic!"

The reporter seemed puzzled as he looked around at the warriors. "Then what are you all doing here?" he asked. Then his eyes landed on the painted sheet. "Oh! You're campaigning against the by-pass!" he said, excitedly.

"Yes, we are!" said Mole. "We're defending this ancient barn and woodland from capitalist property developers!"

"Great!" said Les, suddenly realising he'd stumbled on a scoop. "Hang on, I'll get my camera from the car. Can I take pictures? Is that OK?"

Les rushed back to his car. He'd never had an exclusive before.

***

"Anybody seen Carol?" Charlie asked.

It was early evening and the kitchen was empty. There weren't many truckers about on Friday nights, so the restaurant closed early. Carol had the night off, but she should have been making up some sandwiches and snacks ready for the Karaoke.

"Debbie, go see if your mothers upstairs. Sandwiches need doing."

"I'm stocking the bar," she said. "Can't you go? She's your bloody wife!"

Charlie didn't have time to argue. His quickly went up to their bedroom. "Carol? You there?" The bedroom was empty. He looked around and spotted the note stuck to the mirror. He ripped open the envelope.

'Charlie, I've left you. I just can't take any more. I'd like to say that it was a difficult decision for me, but it wasn't. I should have done it years ago. I've wasted more than twenty years of my life with you. Now I'm going to get on with what's left of it. Tell the girls I'll call them in the next week or so. Carol'

Charlie was stunned. He couldn't believe that she'd left him. If she'd only waited a week or so, it would have been the other way around. She'd be back, he just knew she would. Charlie put his suit on, ready for the night's show. When he returned to the bar, Debbie was setting out the ashtrays.

"Nuts and crisps only tonight," he told her.

"Mum knocked off early?" she asked.

"Yeah, something like that."

People were wandering in. Some came in mini buses, others in taxis. Karaoke nights at Charlie's Place were very popular.

***

Les Dixon sweated over his word processor. What a scoop! Eco-warriors, here in Shorley!

They'd been in the news a lot recently. Protesters at the new runway at Manchester Airport had sabotaged earth movers and burrowed under the site. And at the Newbury by-pass, objectors regularly fought pitched battles with the police. Several hundred had already been arrested, and only last week there had been a protest in a turnip field. He'd watched it on the TV.

This was going to be big! Mole had said that, by next week, there would be hundreds of them. They were coming from all over the country. Nice guy, that Mole. They all were, not what you'd expect from their appearance. Only trouble was, the Shorley Herald came out weekly, on Fridays. By this time next week, the whole world would know they were there, so it wouldn't be much of a scoop. He knew just what he had to do. It was time to step up into the world of the tabloids. He phoned the Sun newspaper! Offering them exclusive photos and copy, he also hinted that he could arrange an exclusive interview with Mole, their charismatic leader.

Then he called the local BBC news station.

***

Donkey was trying his best to avoid little Emma. She was back on stage trying to defend her title. 'Love, Love, Me Do,' she sang, staring over at him, trying to make eye contact. With a tight tank top and a micro yellow mini skirt, she'd won most votes before she'd even sung a note. Ending the song, she blew kisses to her fans, soaking up the applause

"Thank you, Emma! What a great song. And now, please welcome Tim and Tina Carter, giving us the definitive version of 'Bridge Over Troubled Waters'. Thank you, take it away!"

Back at the bar, Charlie pulled Donkey to one side. "She's gone, Donkey, Carol's gone. She's left me!"

"What? Never!"

"Yep, just walked out. Gone!"

"Did she say why?"

"Probably the change, bloody hormones! Been acting real strange lately."

"Someone else maybe?"

Charlie laughed. "No, I don't think so. Who'd have her?"

"Who'd have who?" asked Debbie, coming over.

"Your mum's gone," said Charlie.

"Where?"

"She's left us, run out on us."

"Oh my God!" said Debbie. "What are you going to do?"

"Well," said Charlie, "Borg's back tomorrow; do you know if he can cook?"

***

Walking home across the lorry park, Donkey could hear Charlie announcing the winners. Little Emma had done it again. He'd sneaked out early to avoid her. He needed a break. Debbie had been fantastic; she'd worn him out! He couldn't believe he'd kicked her out. But tonight, his big double bed was all his.

Entering the caravan, a familiar perfume teased his nose. No, he thought, please no! He put the light on, and there she was, sat on his sofa.

"Hallo, Donkey, Sorry to do this to you," said Carol, before bursting into tears.

Donkey sat beside her and wrapped his arms around her. "It's OK! It's OK!" He held her tightly.

"Sorry, Donkey," she sobbed. "I've left him!"

"I know, I know. Just let it go."

And she did. By the time she'd pulled herself together, some twenty minutes later, Donkey's shoulder was wet through.

"Do you think I did the right thing?" she asked him, in a stuttering whisper.

Donkey was between a rock and a hard place. Charlie was his mate, as well as his boss. But he did treat her badly, no doubt about that, more like staff than a wife. And his reaction to her leaving didn't do him any favours at all.

"Only you know if it's the right thing," Donkey said, diplomatically. "What are you going to do? Where are you going to go?"

"I don't know, Donkey, all I know is that I'm never going back!"

"So, what made you do it?"

"Everything! The whole bloody lot of them. Nobody sees me as a person anymore. I'm the cook, the mother, the obedient slave. Yes, Charlie! No, Charlie! Three fucking bags' full, Charlie!"

Donkey had never heard Carol swear like that before. Well, maybe the once, a long time ago.

"I want to have some fun in my life. Is that really too much to ask, Donkey? You work hard, and you're supposed to get some kind of reward. Do I really have to wait until I get to heaven?" She snuggled closer to him. "From now on, I'm only going to think of me. I'm going to enjoy my freedom. No thoughts for any of them, sod 'em!" She paused, pushing her head deeper into his arms. "Do you know the last time I had real fun, Donkey? Remember?"

Donkey knew where this was going. It was the last time he'd heard her swear.

"Remember?" she said. "Me in tears, you consoling me? It's all very déja vu."

"A long time ago," said Donkey, his loins stirring at the memory.

"I remember it like yesterday," she said. "Every last detail."

Carol lifted her head. Their eyes met, then their lips. Donkey knew he'd regret it, but he just couldn't help himself.

SATURDAY

The smell of burning toast wafted out into the restaurant as Debbie rushed around the kitchen, unable to keep up with the orders. Saturdays were never busy, but without her mum, and that lazy bitch, Penny, she was struggling.

"Debbie!" yelled Charlie, rushing back into the kitchen. "Toast's burning!"

"I know! I fucking know! I'm trying my best." she yelled back at him. "I can't do all this on my own."

"Your mum did."

"That's why she fucked off!" said Debbie.

"And Dave said his sausages were cold."

"Tell Dave to..."

"Morning all." The back door opened and an overall-clad Barry strolled into the kitchen. He slapped a carrier bag down on the table. "Kidneys, a couple of kilos, alright, Charlie?"

"Yeah, great, Barry, just put them in the sink. Look, do me a favour will you? Can you give Debbie a hand? Just for an hour or so."

"Yeah, sure, no probs," he said. "Where's Carol?"

"She's fucked off!" said Debbie. "And I'm off soon if he don't get some help in."

"Where's she gone?" asked Barry. "She gone for good?"

"Look," said Charlie. "Can you just give us a hand and leave the inquest for later. I'm sure Debbie will tell fill you in with all the details."

Barry peeled off his blooded overalls. "Right, Debbie," he said, rolling up his sleeves. "Where do you want me to start?"

***

Carol woke up alone. She could hear Donkey in the shower. Dear God! What had she done? She'd left him! She'd finally done it after all these years. She knew she'd done the right thing, but maybe she should have planned her escape better. She'd just stuffed a few clothes into a carrier bag, grabbed her credit card and fled.

Since her conversation with Helen, she'd been living in a vacuum. John, the bastard! How she'd loved him! He'd convinced her it was more than a fling. He told her he was prepared to give up his wife and the church for her. Now she saw him for what he was. A man! They'd say anything to get you into bed.

She'd been like a love-struck teenager when he started flirting with her. Helen was so much younger and prettier, yet he wanted her. And he'd got her! When he first revealed his penchant for wearing silk underwear, it had actually turned her on. And he wanted to be dominated, a role she found so exciting. Then, when he introduced her to his secret lust for bondage, her soul and body exploded! Apart from her vibrator, it was the first sex she'd had for years. She'd got carried away, thought it was for real. She believed him when he said it was forever. What a stupid fool she'd been!

And now what? Here she was in her old matrimonial bed, with Donkey. Aching and sore from a night of wild, abandoned sex. All her anger and frustrations blown away in one fantastic night. But Donkey had made it abundantly clear that she couldn't stay. His loyalties lay with Charlie.

His job and his home relied on it. Why would he want to run off with someone old enough to be his mother?

***

Starlite woke up in the barn, surprised to find a naked Jet in the sleeping bag with her. They'd partied until sunrise, dancing around the fire to Mole's guitar and Silver's bongos.

She'd had too many joints and she struggled to remember how she'd ended up with Jet. Others lay around them, covered in blankets and duvets.

Jet stirred and pulled herself closer, her warm nakedness pressing into Starlite. She liked Jet a lot, just being around her made her feel so good. Pity she couldn't remember anything.

Was she now, she wondered, a fully-fledged lesbian? It was just great having sex with Angel and Carrot. But Mole was pretty good too, and so was Dog.

She was confused. Maybe she was bisexual. A confused bisexual, but a very happy one.

The air horns on the multi-coloured bus, pulling up outside the gate, signalled the arrival of Squirrel. Mole ran from his bus to open the gate.

"They're here!" shouted Angel, running up to the bus as it pulled into the field.

In the barn, people quickly got up and ran out, hooting and whistling. Starlite and Jet threw some clothes on and quickly followed them.

Even before the bus had rolled to a halt, people were jumping off. Squirrel, shaven-headed, but with a full beard, threw himself into Angel's arms. They fell on the ground and rolled around hugging each other. Then there was Cat, a big black guy with dreadlocks, followed by Sparrow and Hawk, two blonde sisters. Warriors just poured off the bus. They all seemed to be old friends, hugging and kissing. Starlite was introduced to them all, one by one. Everybody was so pleased to see one another.

Then off the bus stumbled Killer!

"Oh, shit!" said Mole, as a communal groan went up from the warriors.

Starlite felt her heart sink. She stepped back behind Hog, trying to hide herself behind his massive frame.

"What the fuck do you want?" snarled Mole. Not at all friendly like.

Killer, still in that tatty leather jacket, had that stupid grin on his face, the one that she had found so attractive, a life time ago.

"I'm here to help," he said. "The more the merrier. Right?"

"Wrong!" said Snake. "Fuck off or you die!" He obviously didn't like Killer much either.

"Oh, come on," said Killer. "We have a common enemy; we should be friends." He caught Starlite's eye and smiled at her. "Alright, Penny?"

"It's Starlite!" said Jet, defensively stepping in front of her.

"Carrot and Silver are going into town for supplies soon," said Mole. "They'll give you a lift to the station."

"I don't want to go to..."

"It's that or you die!" spat Snake, moving towards him.

"OK! OK!" said Killer, stepping back. "Can I eat first? I'm starving!"

While the warriors sat in the barn, swapping stories and listening to Mole filling in the newcomers on the situation, Killer sat outside on the grass eating a bowl of muesli.

Starlite looked over at the pathetic youth that had abused her mind and body so badly. His head was now covered with a dark shadow of stubbly hair. She felt sick to her stomach that he'd...

Jet, sensing her unease, put an arm around her and pulled her close. "That was great last night, wasn't it?" she said, gently kissing her on the cheek. "I really enjoyed it."

Starlite leant into her. "Yeah... so did I."

***

Donkey finished fuelling up the German truck. The driver signed for his diesel and pulled away from the pumps.

His mind wasn't on the job today. He was in an impossible situation. How could he possibly face Charlie after screwing his wife all night? And what happened now? She had nowhere to go. She couldn't possibly stay on in the caravan. Someone would suss it sooner or later, then he'd be out of a job and homeless.

A Danish wagon and drag pulled onto the pumps. Out of the passenger side, lugging a suitcase and backpack, climbed Borg. After thanking the driver for the lift, he rushed over to say hallo to Donkey.

"Hallo, my friend," he said, shaking Donkey's hand vigorously.

"Hi, Borg! Good to see you back."

"Yes, back for good. This is my home now. I am so happy."

"Come on then," said Donkey. "Let's go find Debbie."

They found her mopping the restaurant floor. Borg sneaked up behind her and grabbed hold of her.

"Oh! Borg!" She flung her arms around him and tried to show how pleased she was to see him.

"I'm here forever," he said. "I am so very happy." He hesitated. "Are you OK? You seem a bit... a little..."

"Mum's gone," she said. "She's left him. Walked out. I'm just so worried about her. Sorry, I'm really glad to see you, but..."

"Oh, Debbie, I'm so sorry. Do you know where she has gone?"

Charlie came in from his office. "Hallo, mate! Great to see you," he said, shaking Borg's hand. "Got the flowers?"

"Yes," said Borg, handing him a carrier bag.

Charlie peered in. Two plastic-encased orchids sat securely inside. "Great!" he said, slapping Borg on the back.

"Sorry to hear about Carol," said Borg.

"Yeah, so was I," said Charlie. "What's your cooking like?"

***

It was a busy morning at the barn. Squirrel had checked out all the oaks, and was now busy with Mole building a platform high up in one of them. They intended to thwart any attempts to cut them down. Mole knew that that was probably a long way off yet, but they had to be ready to face the threat, and to show they were serious.

Jet flirted with Squirrel constantly. Starlite recognised her feelings as jealousy, an emotion she needed to contain. We're all in love with each other, she reminded herself.

Killer had gone. She had certainly been unnerved at seeing him again. He disgusted her. Everyone made mistakes, and she hadn't known any different. She eased her soul searching by seeing him as a stepping stone. Without Killer, she wouldn't be here now. Without him, she wouldn't be the person she now was.

Les Dixon arrived just before noon, accompanied by a couple of guys from the Sun newspaper. One of them, a photographer, just wandered around the camp taking pictures of everything and everyone. He seemed to concentrate on the girls, especially those not wearing a bra. He only spoke to ask them their names, jotting the information down on his pad.

The other guy, Jeff Harris, top environmental reporter on the paper, interviewed Mole and Starlite on the bus.

"So how long before the bulldozers arrive?" he asked.

"There's no planning permission yet," said Mole. "When there is, we'll fight it through the courts. Our presence here will tell them the size of the battle that they face if they go ahead. We're here for the long haul."

"What about the locals? Are they behind you?"

"I'm a local," said Starlite, "and I can assure you..."

A commotion outside made Mole go to the window. Through the open gate drove a new convoy. A local BBC outside film unit, complete with a catering van and crew bus, pulled into the field and began setting up behind the barn. They soon had the cameras up and running, filming around the campsite and interviewing various warriors. Things had really taken off. The battle had begun.

Starlite returned to the fireside, sitting down with Hog and Silver. Silver was playing his bongos, laying down a constant slow beat. The heartbeat of the planet, he said.

"Hallo? Can we come in?"

Three elderly gents weighed down with cameras and equipment stood by the gate.

"Is this where the Golden Eagle has been sighted?" one called across.

"Yes," said Starlite. "Somewhere around here."

"Have you seen it?" asked another.

"No, but it was here yesterday, I think."

**

"Hallo, Charlie! How ya doing?"

Charlie looked up from his lunch. "Killer! Nice to see you. Sit down, cup of tea?"

"Yes please!" he said, sitting down alongside Charlie. "Love an egg sarnie, if there's one going."

Debbie was wiping down the tables, ciggy in her mouth, one eye on the TV set.

"Well, look who's back in town," she said. "Lover boy!"

"Debbie! You heard the lad, egg sandwich and a tea."

Walking over to the kitchen door, she leant through and called out, "Borg! One egg sandwich!"

"So, where you been, Killer?" asked Charlie.

"Well, I got delayed, had to check on our troops at Newbury. See how many of them have been nicked. Nearly got arrested myself!"

"Yeah?"

"Yeah, close run thing."

Debbie came back to the table with the tea. "How's Starlite?"

"Who?" said Killer.

"Starlite. You know, Penny. Your girlfriend?"

"Oh yeah, her. She's alright I suppose."

"So, what's happening at the barn?" asked Charlie, waving Debbie away.

"Just come from there now," said Killer. "Must be more than thirty of us now. We're all ready for whatever they throw at us, Charlie. Bring it on!"

"That's great!" said Charlie, patting him on the back. "Things are starting to look up."

Borg brought out Killer's sandwich. Yes, thought Killer, they certainly are.

"Dad! The news!" Debbie yelled, turning up the volume on the TV. "It's Penny's freaky friends again."

"… fighting to stop the Henyard by-pass. We go over to our reporter at the scene."

On screen, the local TV reporter stood in front of the barn, surrounded by warriors. He introduced Mole as the leader.

"Tosser!" hissed Killer.

"Mole," the reporter continued, "tell us why you're here."

"This barn is eighteenth century; the trees are nearly three hundred years old. Should we allow them to be destroyed just so some property developers can make a killing?"

"But from what I've heard," said the reporter, "the locals all want a by-pass."

"Because they haven't been told the truth. They're being deceived. If the by-pass goes ahead, in five years' time all you see around you will be destroyed and replaced with factories and housing. Speculators stand to make millions on the back of our environment. We will stop them!"

As Mole spoke the camera swung around the camp. Dog, Snake and Carrot stood around the fire. Starlite and Jet sat on the step of a bus watching. When Jet saw the camera pointing at them, she pulled Starlite towards her and gave her a lingering kiss.

Charlie gasped!

Debbie cried out, "She's a lezzie! My little sister's a bloody lezzie!"

Killer nearly choked on his sarnie.

***

Carol peeped out from behind the bedroom curtain as the truckstop filled up ahead of Band Night. All those young kids out on a Saturday night, having fun, enjoying themselves. When she was their age, she already had two kids. She never went clubbing or whatever they called it these days. She never regretted it then. It was only now she knew what she had missed out on. Charlie always told her the rewards would come later. In her twenties she really believed that one day they'd sell up and retire to Spain. Live off the fruits of their labour. But Charlie had conned her. The last twenty years had been one big lie.

Now she was free. But free to do what? Free to have incredible sex with Donkey! But she knew that was only short term. She had to plan for the future. But first, for the sake of her soul, there was one last thing she had to do.

***

Killer wasn't sure of his next move. He was skint so his options were limited. It was pretty obvious he wasn't welcome at the barn. Fuck knows why, common enemy and all that. They'd forgotten who it was that kicked all this off in the first place. Maybe Penny has been poisoning their tiny minds. What did she know anyway? She was just a bleedin' kid.

He'd spent most of the afternoon sat in the restaurant drinking free tea. Now it was closing, so he made his way to the bar. He was dying for a pint.

***

Borg was so pleased with the way things had worked out. Debbie was a bit subdued, but he could understand that, what with her mum leaving. It must have been a real shock for her. But this was now his home and already he was working for Charlie. He'd been in the kitchen most of the day, and now he was helping out behind the bar. He watched Charlie opening the show.

"Ladies and gentlemen, boys and girls, welcome to Charlie's Place. Tonight, live on stage, back by popular demand, I give you, Centipede Express!"

The kids leapt from their seats as the band opened with a long and loud distorted guitar solo.

Covering his ears, Charlie pushed his way back to the bar where Borg had his pint waiting for him.

"Cheers, Borg," he said, sipping at the pint. "How was today? Think you'll manage till Carol gets back?"

"Debbie doesn't think she will."

"What does she know?" said Charlie. "Once she's had a break, she'll be back. You'll see."

"Hiya, Charlie," said Killer, coming up to the bar.

"Killer!" said Charlie. "Pint?"

"Cheers, Charlie, Nice one."

***

Donkey arrived at the bar, bouncer for the night.

"How's it going, mate?" he asked Borg.

"Yes, it's good. I feel at home already."

Donkey turned to Charlie, lowered his voice and asked, "Heard anything from Billy?"

"No, not yet, but I'm sure we will," he replied.

Donkey looked around at all the teenage vamps, dressed in their skimpy outfits. There was a couple of them he'd like to get to know better. His collection now stood at ninety-nine. He wanted his century, but the girl had to be something special, not an up-against-the-wall'er. But with Carol as a house guest, he couldn't really take anyone home tonight, could he?

Killer was telling everyone about his escapades at Newbury, how he'd fought in a pitched battle with the police, narrowly escaping arrest.

"My God," said Debbie. "Forget about the pig shit, all I'm getting now is bullshit!"

By the time Centipede Express had played out their loud finale, Donkey was ready for his bed. His ears had taken enough. Once the cheering had died down, the goths, punks, and other assorted weirdos made their way to the exits. Charlie reminded them of next week's band and wished them all a very good night.

Donkey helped Debbie clear the tables as the band carried out their gear. Charlie was cashing up as Killer sat, finishing his last free pint of the evening.

"Charlie?" said Killer. "Anywhere I can crash out tonight? Bit late for me to get back to the barn."

"Yeah? Well, I don't suppose Penny would mind you having her room tonight, she seems to have moved out anyway."

"Wow! Cheers, Charlie," said Killer. "I won't tell her if you don't!"

Donkey said his good nights and headed off home. When he got back Carol was waiting for him, in bed. She'd found a bottle of wine in the fridge. Now it sat with two glasses at the bedside. How could he deny her? He yanked the duvet clean off the bed. She lay naked and exposed and, as Donkey stripped off, she reached out for him.

***

Killer could smell Penny on the pillow cases, as he snuggled up under the quilt. In the next bedroom he could hear Debbie and Borg going to bed. Debbie giggling, Borg whispering. Lucky bastard! Then the bed began to creek, knocking on the wall. He heard flesh slapping on flesh, and Debbie crying out for more.

Killer reached over and opened Penny's bedside draw. Reaching in, he pulled out a pair of panties, pink silk ones. He put them briefly to his nose before slipping them down under the covers. As Debbie and Borg strove towards their orgasmic finale, Killer beat them to it.

SUNDAY

"Killer! Killer! Get up!" shouted Charlie, banging on Penny's bedroom door. Stepping in, he saw Killer still sleeping and gave him a shake. "Come on! We've things to do!"

"What? Where am I?" Killer looked at Charlie, then around the room. "What's wrong?" he asked.

"Things to do. Come on, I ain't got all day! See you in the kitchen, five minutes!"

After a quick cup of tea and some cold toast, Killer found himself in Charlie's Merc heading to the barn. They pulled up alongside the gate and peered in.

"Blimey!" said Charlie. "Looks like a bloody squatter camp!"

"That's 'cos it is," said Killer.

There was no sign of life; it was too early in the morning. There were now over a dozen brightly coloured vans and buses, along with several tents and a tepee. All scattered haphazardly around the barn and in the field. Behind the barn they could see a couple of BBC wagons, one with a satellite dish on the roof. On the floor of the barn, several sleeping bags with various heads sticking out could be seen. The fire smouldered, surrounded by empty beer cans and take away cartons.

Charlie pulled away and drove slowly down the winding lane.

"Where we going?" asked Killer.

"Here," said Charlie, pulling over onto the grass verge.

They both got out. Charlie opened the boot and took out the carrier bag and a spade.

"What we doing?" asked a puzzled Killer.

"You do ask a lot of questions, don't you?" said Charlie, handing him the spade. "Just follow me."

They clambered over the fence and through a thorny hedge. There, behind an old beech tree, Charlie chose the spot.

"Dig two holes, just here," he told Killer.

"How big?"

"This big," said Charlie, pulling the orchids from the bag.

"Oh, I see," said Killer, finally getting the plot. "Wow, that's clever!"

"You don't say a word to anyone, hear? Now get on with it, I ain't got all day."

"No! Yeah, of course I won't! Great idea."

Killer had never dug a hole before, now he found himself digging two. Charlie kept looking at his watch, and when the job was done and the orchids planted, he scattered a few dead leaves over the freshly dug earth. Then they returned to the car.

"I'll drop you off at the barn," said Charlie.

"No! Er, it's a bit early, don't want to disturb them, do we? Can I come back with you? Maybe have some breakfast, then I'll come back down here later."

They climbed into the Merc and Charlie drove back to the truckstop.

***

Carol watched out of the bedroom window for the taxi. She'd waited until Donkey had left before calling for one. She hated goodbyes. But she knew she had to go, the longer she stayed here, the more likely it was she'd go back. She shuddered at the thought.

But where could she go? For the past two decades, Charlie had been her life. She had few friends outside the truckstop, and her relatives had all disowned her when she'd married him. How she wished she'd listened to them.

She'd written a quick thank you note to Donkey. He'd always been there for her, ever since that first time. He'd made her laugh when she was sad, gave her hope when there was none. He was an amazing lover, though perhaps lover wasn't the right word. She could love him so easily, if he'd wanted her to. But he didn't.

The taxi pulled into the lorry park and came up alongside the caravan. She had to be focused. There were things she needed to do.

After checking that no one appeared to be watching, she quickly left the caravan and slipped into the back of the taxi. "The church, please," she said.

***

Borg helped Debbie arrange the tables. It was old dears' day. He was so happy, but Debbie so wasn't. She'd hardly spoken to him this morning, but he just needed to be patient with her.

Charlie and Killer came in from the lorry park.

"What we doing for the oldies?" asked Charlie.

"Steak and kidney casserole," replied Borg. "I hope they like it."

"And there's ice cream in the fridge for afters," said Debbie.

"Sounds great, they'll love it," said Charlie.

"Heard from mum yet?" asked Debbie.

"No, just give her a few days, you'll see, she'll be back. Can you rustle up a sarnie for Killer? The poor lad's starving."

"Bacon, please," said Killer.

"Bacon?" said Debbie. "Thought you were a bloody veggie?"

"Whoever told you that?" said Killer. "Lots of ketchup, please."

***

"My, my, Carol Wheeler! How the devil are you?"

Carol stopped at the church door and turned to see Tommy Thomas. He looked a lot older than she remembered.

"Tommy! How are you? It's seems like years."

"Yes, it has been, must be nine or ten at least, probably more."

Tommy had been her first boyfriend. Until Charlie had stolen her away. How different might it all have been if she'd married an accountant instead of a crook?

"You're looking well," she said. Out of politeness really, he looked awful.

"You're looking good yourself," he said, smiling wistfully.

"Oh, don't, look I have to get in, the service is about to start."

"Maybe we should get together sometime, meet up for a coffee, talk about the old days."

"Yes, that might be nice. Where are you now?"

"Still in the flat over the office, pop round sometime."

Yes, thought Carol, maybe the good Lord has provided. But first she had to do something quite wicked.

***

The elderly incurables filed in, assisted by their helpers. Wheelchairs and Zimmer frames were parked up and the diners seated.

Nurse Linda looked around for Donkey. Last Sunday had been so bloody good and she fancied more of the same tonight. She'd already told her hubby she was on the late shift again.

"Fuck off!" yelled Debbie. Harold was groping her again.

Linda apologised and tried to tell Harold off. He just grinned as he played with himself. At ninety, you can pretty much get away with anything.

Charlie brought out the meals and Debbie passed round the bread and napkins, carefully avoiding Harold. She was glad she was wearing her jeans today.

***

Carol took her usual seat in the front row, next to Helen. "Morning," she nodded.

Helen looked so young, so pretty. And so happy. She almost felt sorry for her. Poor bitch!

Carol spent the whole service staring into John's eyes. He seemed quite surprised to see her there. Not her usual time, normally she'd be behind the sink now.

She smiled at him, looking forward to what was to come. Helen always visited the hospice after church on Sunday afternoon.

As soon as the service ended, Carol busied herself collecting up the hymn books while the church emptied.

"Where have you been?" John asked, trying to sound concerned. "I've been trying to call you."

Carol knew he was lying, but it didn't matter anymore. "I've been poorly," she said.

"Oh, I am sorry, and are you feeling better now?"

"Yes, a lot better thank you. I've taken the day off."

"Have you?" His eyes lit up. "Helen will be gone soon..."

"I know."

"Do you want to...?"

"Yes, please, I'm really looking forward to it!"

"Yes, so am I," he said, discreetly stroking her bum.

***

Above all the noise and mayhem of feeding time, Donkey and Linda conversed in loud whispers.

"Sorry," said Donkey, with obvious regret. "Can't make it tonight; I'm working." He didn't think Carol would take too kindly to a threesome. Although Linda would, no doubt about it!

"Damn! I was really up for it too!"

"So was I," he said, casting an eye over those magnificent breasts. And he just loved the uniform.

Linda looked towards the loo's, then whispered, "Fancy a quickie? I'm as wet as hell!"

She gave her charges a quick glance, then backing away, made for the ladies.

Donkey waited for a moment or two, when he was sure no one was looking, he followed her in.

***

"Is Charlie about?"

The two guys standing at the counter looked hard. Debbie thought they might be the police. She called her dad out of the kitchen, before nipping outside for a quick fag.

"Yes? Can I help you?" said Charlie, although his gut already told him who they were.

"Billy sent us," said the big one, staring hard into Charlie's eyes. "Can we have a word?"

Charlie's heart raced as he looked around for Donkey and Borg. "Yeah," he spluttered, "Go ahead. Look, it was nothing to do with me! I'm the one who got fucking ripped off!"

"Best we go somewhere private, don't you think?" said the smaller one, looking around the restaurant. "Don't want to frighten your punters, do we?" He cracked his knuckles.

"Better come out to the office then," mumbled Charlie.

He led the way out into the yard. If his legs hadn't been like jelly, he'd have run. He knew what was coming.

***

John Cunningham slipped on the black French knickers. They were his favourite pair. He loved the feel of silk on his balls. The matching top, sleeveless with a little bow, was a bit tight though. Lying down on the bed, he spread his arms and legs, ready for Carol to tie him. She seemed in quite a hurry today. She must be gagging for it.

"Ouch! That hurt!" he said. "Careful, Carol!"

Normally she was so gentle. There was no need to tie him so tight. It wasn't as if he was resisting. The stockings tying his wrists to the bed posts were cutting off his circulation. And now she was double knotting his ankles! His erection quickly disappeared. Pain was so close to pleasure, but...

"Carol! You're hurting me! What are you doing?"

"How's Helen?" she suddenly asked.

"What? Carol, what are you on about? What's wrong with you today?"

"She told me you're trying for a baby. That right?"

"Oh, dear God, no! Carol, I just said that to placate her! To keep her happy!"

"Well it worked, she's certainly happy now. You never were going to leave her, were you?"

"What? Of course I was! I am! Honestly, Carol! Just untie me, please! Please!"

"You bastard!" she hissed. Searching through the laundry basket, she found a pair of Helen's knickers and pulled them over his head. Then she put on her coat.

"Carol? What are you doing? Don't leave me like this!" There was panic in his voice. "Please! Helen will be back soon!"

"I know," she replied, looking at her watch. "In about an hour, I believe. Give you time to reflect on your sins, wont it?" She opened the bedroom door. "Goodbye, John, give my love to Helen."

"No! No! Oh, dear God, please no!" he wailed out, as he heard her go down the stairs and out of the front door, slamming it shut behind her.

"No!" he screamed. "No!"

***

"Charlie! Charlie!" cried Donkey. "You alright?" He so obviously wasn't.

He'd found him in the office. The place had been trashed, and so had Charlie!

"Billy's boys!" said Charlie, spitting blood and teeth as Donkey helped him to his feet. His eyes were both raw and dried blood caked his face.

"Where the fuck were you?" he yelled at Donkey.

"What did they say? What did they want?"

"They want twenty grand!" Charlie replied, breathlessly. "That's how much Billy says we've cost him."

"What? Fucking hell! Did you tell them it wasn't us?"

"No, of course not! I said it was!" He pushed him away. "Bloody hell, Donkey, what do think I fucking told 'em?"

Charlie staggered out of his office and into the showers. He was hobbling and holding his nuts. He shoved his head under the running water, trying to flush away the blood and pain.

"Twenty grand!" said Donkey, handing him some paper towels.

"Yep!" said Charlie. "And they'll be back to collect!"

***

Tommy was surprised to find Carol Wheeler standing at his door.

"Hallo, Tommy," she said. "Thought I'd take you up on that offer of a coffee. Can I come in?"

He welcomed her into his grubby flat, apologising profusely for the state of the place.

"The truth is, Tommy," she told him over coffee, "I've left him!"

"Oh, Carol, I'm so sorry," he said, even though he clearly wasn't.

Carol reached into her handbag for a tissue and dabbed at her eyes. "These past few years have been just awful, I wish I'd never met him!" she said, bursting into tears.

Quickly moving to her side on the sofa, he put an arm around her. Damn that Charlie Wheeler, he thought. Although it was a long time ago, the memories had never left him. He and Carol had been engaged, the wedding just weeks away, when he'd caught her with Charlie, at it like dogs in the pub car park!

For reasons of business and friendship, it suited both him and Charlie to blame Carol. He'd believed Charlie when he told him she'd thrown herself at him. It had helped him cope. And now, here she was, crying in his arms.

"I need somewhere to stay," she said. "Just for a few days, till I sort myself out."

"No problem," said Tommy, not believing his luck. "You can stay for as long as you like."

"Oh Tommy. Thank you so much." She hugged him.

Better move my porn stash from the bedroom, he thought.

***

Mole had spent most of the day giving interviews. The Daily Mirror, The Sun, The Shorley Herald and the BBC, all queued to hear the words of Mole.

More people, just ordinary people, had come along to support the warriors in the fight. They'd seen it on the TV and read about it in the press. They came from all over the country. Birdwatchers appeared at regular intervals, looking for the golden eagle.

Locals from Shorley brought their kids along to stare at the weirdos over the fence. The camp had taken on the atmosphere of a village. On the road, just outside the gate, a burger van had set up and was doing a brisk trade.

Starlite was helping Squirrel, Cat and Carrot set up a sound system. There was going to be a party tonight, to celebrate the full moon. A festival of love and peace.

She liked being around Cat, the Jamaican, he was so easy to talk to. She told him about Killer and he'd helped her deal with it.

"You are the sum total of your life experiences," he told her. "Learn from it and move on. Don't let your past destroy your future."

Starlite felt he'd touched her very soul. Looking into his eyes her body tingled, and those desires began rising again. She'd never slept with a black guy before. Until a few weeks ago, she'd never slept with anyone at all. Now she found herself fancying almost everybody. She just felt horny all the time. But she had to get over wanting a loving relationship with everybody she had sex with. She knew it wouldn't happen, she had to enjoy it for what it was.

***

Donkey tried to get Charlie to go to hospital, but he wouldn't have it. He'd been pretty badly beaten up; he could hardly walk. Donkey had to help him up the stairs to his bedroom. He left him sprawled out on his bed.

When he returned to the caravan, late in the afternoon, he was surprised to find it empty. Carol had gone. He found a note.

'Thank you for everything. You convinced me I've done the right thing. There's
more to life than Charlie Wheeler. I'll keep in touch. X'

He felt for Carol and worried where she might have gone. But he was also quite relieved. Now he could concentrate on more important things, like Billy's boys. He was lucky he hadn't been around when they'd come calling, otherwise he'd have been short of a few teeth as well.

Suddenly, he heard a car pull up outside and his heart went into overdrive. Going to the window, he peeped out, but couldn't see anything.

There was a faint knock on the door. Picking up an empty wine bottle, he held it behind his back and slowly opened the door.

"Hallo, Donkey," said a tearful Helen.

***

Starlite was buzzing! The party had started early in the evening and was now in full swing. The beer and wine flowed, and the joints keep rolling on by. Around the large fire the warriors were singing and dancing along to their favourite rock anthems. Silver DJ'd as air guitars were plucked and imaginary drums followed all the beats. Angel danced wildly, close to the flames. She tore off her T-shirt to cheers of approval from the warriors. Sparrow and Hawk soon followed suit, all the time bopping to the rhythm.

Angel upped the tempo, ripping off her jeans and pants. Naked and proud, she danced around the fire, encouraging others to do the same. Carrot, and then Jet, stripped off and joined her.

When Starlite saw Cat throwing off his clothes, she quickly followed suit.

Soon the whole camp seemed to be dancing naked, in wild abandonment around the fire.

Everyone that was, except the guy from the Sun newspaper. Armed with a camera and hidden behind one of the buses, nobody seemed to notice as he shot away at the naked revellers.

Starlite danced until she was dizzy. The cool breeze on her naked body excited her. Knowing that people were watching her just added to the buzz. She danced alongside Cat, his beautiful ebony body, covered in sweat, filled her with desire.

A naked Hog stepped between them and began to shake his stuff at her. Starlite laughed as his eyes flashed all over her.

Cat stopped dancing and moved away from the fire. She watched him as he climbed up into Mole's bus. She gave him a while before she followed; she didn't want to seem too keen, too obvious. Walking slowly over to the bus, her naked body still bouncing with the beat, she was ready for some love.

On the bus scented candles gave off a flickering eerie light. Her eyes slowly focused on the bed. A blanket covered a human form. Taking hold, she gently pulled it from the bed.

Cat, in all his naked glory, was exposed. And so was Mole! They lay in an intimate pose, legs entwined. They smiled up at her.

Starlite froze! It was all she could do to stop from crying out. She couldn't hide the look of shock on her face.

Cat reached out for her hand. "Don't be scared," he said, softly.

"Why don't you join us?" said Mole.

They parted so she could lie between them.

***

Helen sat on his sofa sobbing her heart out, her make-up smudged all over her face. Donkey patiently supplied the tissues and coffee. It seemed his caravan had now become a refuge for distressed women. Word must have got around.

He had no idea what she was doing here; he'd only ever met her the once. She'd been there for over an hour, and he still hadn't managed to get more than a few words out of her. Then, as the sobs finally slowed, Donkey made her yet another strong coffee.

"So," he gently asked her, "want to tell me about it? What happened?"

"He, he..." she stuttered, before bursting into tears again.

Donkey sat down beside her, putting an arm around her shoulders.

Burying her head into his chest, Helen managed, bit by bit, to blurt out the shocking sight that had blown her tidy little world into pieces.

Donkey listened in a stunned silence.

"...and he had a pair of my panties on his head!" she cried. "I screamed! I just couldn't help it! And he'd pooed himself. Can you believe that? The place stank! And all the time he was crying, saying sorry, over and over again!"

Donkey couldn't believe what he was hearing. He'd never met the guy, but his picture was always in the local paper.

"So, who tied him up?" he asked.

"I don't know, I didn't ask... I was speechless!" She began crying again. "He, he looked so pathetic, weeping and pleading with me to untie him."

"And did you?"

"Yes, though I don't know why. I cut one hand free with a pair of scissors... it was blue and limp. Just touching him made me feel so... so dirty. I screamed at him 'How could you?' Then I just ran from the house. I drove around for hours not knowing what to do. All my friends are his friends. How could I tell them? How could I tell them that my husband is a pervert?" The sobbing started again.

Donkey pulled away as she dabbed at her eyes.

Taking deep breaths, she slowly steadied herself. "I'm sorry... but you're the only one I could think of. The only place he wouldn't think to look for me. I don't ever want to see him again, ever!" She paused. "Can I stay? Just for a day or so, please? Just till I get my mind sorted. I don't know what to do, I really don't. I just need some time."

"Sure, of course," said Donkey. "No problem, you stay until you're ready. I'm just glad I can help."

***

"Fucking hell!" cried Killer. "What happened?" He'd found Charlie sitting in the darkened kitchen with a beer.

"Fell over," said Charlie, not bothering to look up.

"Looks to me like someone's beaten the shit out of you."

"You heard me!" Charlie snapped back. "I fell over! Right?"

"Yeah, sure, Charlie, anything you say."

"What do you want, anyway? Shouldn't you be at the barn?"

"Just wondering if there's any food about, I'm starving!"

"You're always starving, must have bloody worms." Charlie went to laugh then held his ribs as the pain shot through him.

Killer opened the fridge and began poking around inside. "Can I stay again tonight, Charlie? Please?"

"Do what you like, son, I don't care anymore."

"Thanks, Charlie," said Killer, taking out some cheese and a pot of yoghurt. He took a spoon from the sink. "Night, Charlie, see you in the morning."

He made his way up to Penny's room. He wanted to get settled before Debbie and Borg got started.

***

Tommy threw some blankets and a duvet onto the sofa. He'd been hoping for a more intimate arrangement.

"Thank you, Tommy," said Carol, as he made up a bed for her. "I don't know what else I'd have done if I hadn't bumped into you."

He'd made it quite clear that she could share his bed, if she wanted to. But she hadn't wanted to. He understood. He'd spent most of the evening just listening to her dissect her life. Emotionally, she was in pieces. Twenty years of her life wasted, she'd said. Give her time, he thought, give her time and who knows?

He wouldn't be needing his porn tonight; he had some new fantasies to work on.

Monday

The first drivers of the day were coming in as Charlie hobbled down into the kitchen. Every step seemed to crush his swollen balls. Debbie had already begun serving, as Borg fired up the cooker and toaster.

"Bloody hell, Dad! What happened to you?" said Debbie.

"Charlie!" said Borg. "Are you all right?"

"Yeah, 'course I'm alright!"

"What happened?" asked Debbie, trying to touch his bruised face.

He pushed her away. "Fell down the stairs, OK? Now stop making a fuss; there's drivers out there waiting to be served."

"But Dad, you look awful. Shouldn't you go to casualty or something?"

"For Christ's sake give it a rest, will you? I said I'm OK, OK?"

He slowly limped back upstairs and into Penny's room. "Killer! Killer!" he shouted, shaking him till he woke up.

This was the sort of room service that Killer could do without. "What?" he whined. "What do you want?" Looking at Penny's bedside clock, he cried, "It's only half five! What's going on?"

"Need you in the kitchen," said Charlie. "Come on, you can earn your keep and a few bob as well."

"What if I don't want to?"

"Then you can start walking back to the barn. Now! Make your mind up."

Charlie went to lie down. He felt awful. Every inch of his body ached and throbbed.

***

Carol had hardly slept. The sofa was really uncomfortable, and Tommy's loud snoring had reverberated around the whole grubby apartment all night. Now he was in the small kitchen, noisily making a cup of tea.

She'd done a lot of thinking during the night. She felt in limbo, in between lives. End of the old, start of the new. She had no regrets. Maybe she should have planned it better. Found somewhere to go first, got some cash together. But no way was she ever going back.

She felt low, but cheered up considerably as she recalled her revenge on John. It was so wicked. Far too wicked to tell Tommy about.

For now, she needed Tommy. He'd tried to paw her last night. He repulsed her. The body odour, his greasy hair and his grovelling manner. And the way he'd kissed Charlie's arse all these years. But her options were limited.

"Morning, Carol," he said, coming in with a cup of tea. "How you feeling this morning? Still glad you did it?" His dressing gown and slippers looked like they'd belonged to his granddad.

"Of course, Tommy, should have done it years ago." She sat up and took the tea from him. "Thank you. It's so good of you to put me up." She paused, then added, "Please don't tell Charlie I'm here, I know you're his friend but..."

"He's no friend of mine," cut in Tommy. "Client yes, friend no!"

Carol was pleased to hear that; it would help with her next request.

"Tommy, I need to get some money together," she said, "so I can go away for a while. Charlie limited my credit card to a hundred pounds a day. But that's nowhere enough. I need to buy some clothes, maybe a small car. I'm going to divorce him, Tommy, I've made up my mind, but these things take time." She smiled sweetly. "Tommy, you have access to our accounts, is there any way you could...?"

***

Starlite slowly opened her eyes. Thank God, she hadn't been dreaming. She lay between them. Cat's legs were wrapped around her, his soft manhood lay across her belly. Mole, gently snoring, lay alongside them, a hand on her breast.

And she remembered everything. Her with Cat, so gentle, but strong. Her with Mole, teasing and pleasing. And Mole with Cat! She'd never seen men kissing before, let alone having sex. Girls did it together all the time, so why not boys? It was a real turn on for her.

Her body stirred and a warm glow swept over her as she recalled having sex with both of them. At the same time! Did she really do that? Although a little shocked by what she had done, she had no regrets at all. It had been amazing, just great!

The Wheeler's little girl had come a long way in the past few weeks.

***

Killer stood at the kitchen sink, up to his elbows in the washing up. His hands were all wrinkly and pale. No way was he going to wear those stupid pink gloves. He'd been at the sink for hours. The plates just kept on coming, and his feet were killing him. And now his nose stud was weeping again.

Borg brought him another tray of dirty dishes. "OK, my friend?" he asked. "Another half hour or so and the rush will be over."

"Cheers," said Killer, picking up a rejected sausage from one of the plates. He devoured it in a couple of bites, then went for a bit of leftover toast.

Borg was OK. Killer liked him. Fuck knows how he puts up with Debbie whingeing on all the time.

Debbie came in. "One big breakfast, no black pudding, and an egg sandwich for Tony. And where's Freddy's bacon sarnie? He's been waiting ages."

"I'm going as fast as I can," said Borg, rushing back to the stove.

"So, Killer," said Debbie. "One of the staff now, are we?"

"Just helping out Charlie," he said, trying not to stare at her cleavage.

"What happened to him?" she asked.

"If he said he fell down the stairs..." Killer began.

"Then he's bloody lying," she said. "How he expects me to run this place on my own I don't know."

"That's why I'm here," said Killer, "to help you out."

"Cheers," said Debbie. "I don't know how we ever managed without you."

***

Donkey crept around, trying not to wake her. She'd slept on the sofa, but only after crying herself to sleep. He felt so sorry for her. What a shock. What an arsehole to have as a husband. He wondered who'd tied him up. Maybe a call girl he hadn't paid. But then, knowing the church, it didn't have to be a girl. He'd better not test that theory with Helen, she was distraught enough. She stirred just as he was about to leave.

"Donkey..." she said, quietly.

"Morning, Helen. How are you feeling?"

"Don't know. I feel sick to the stomach every time I think of..."

"Well, try not to think too much about it. Look, I have to go to work, help yourself to anything you want. Loads of food in the kitchen."

"You don't mind if I stay?"

"No, not at all. Stay as long as you need to. I'll pop back later, OK?"

"Donkey?" She knelt up, holding the sheet to cover her nakedness.

Donkey leant towards her and she kissed him on the cheek.

"Thank you, thank you a thousand times."

"That's OK," he said. "See you later."

As he made to leave, she said, "Donkey, please don't tell Carol I'm here. I wouldn't want her to tell John where I am."

"No, of course not. But she's gone. She left him on Friday. Just walked out."

"Oh," said Helen.

"Must be the weather," said Donkey. "Lots of it about."

He went off to work with a smile on his face. He couldn't wait to tell Charlie.

***

Charlie watched from his bedroom window as trucks pulled out of the lorry park. How he wished he could join them, just fuck off and leave all this behind. Life was catching up on Charlie Wheeler. A sudden knock at the door made him jump.

"Dad!" called out Debbie. "Someone to see you downstairs."

His racing heart beat painfully against ribs. "Who is it?" he called back nervously through the closed door.

"Says he's from the Shorley Herald. Wants to talk to you about the by-pass."

"Oh, OK." Charlie breathed again. "Give him a cup of tea and sit him down in the restaurant; be there in two minutes." He wiped his face over with a wet flannel before going down.

"Hallo, Mr Wheeler. Les Dixon, Shorley Herald." Les stood and held out his hand, but he couldn't hide the look of shock on his face.

"Hallo, Les. Nice to meet you." He shook his hand. "Please, call me Charlie."

They sat down.

"Sorry about the horror show," said Charlie. "Had a car accident. Emergency stop, dog just ran out in front of me. Stupid me, no seat-belt, hit the screen with my face!" He laughed a little. "Not as bad as it looks."

"Oh, I am sorry. Perhaps I can do a story, with a picture, highlighting the dangers of uncontrolled dogs."

"And stupid idiots not wearing seat-belts, no, I think not. How long have you been with the Herald, Les?"

"I'm freelance really, working with the Herald. It was me who alerted the Sun newspaper to the eco-warriors on Peacock Lane."

"Yeah? Well done! So, shall we talk by-pass?"

"Yes, right. Now it seems to me that a lot of people want the by-pass. What do you say to them?" He sat, note book in hand, ready for the answer.

"Yes," said Charlie. "Everybody can see the need for one, what with the new container port and all, but at what cost? The barn, hundreds of years old. Do we just knock it down? And the trees, been there since forever. I heard the other day about an eagle nesting there, and what about the orchids?"

"Orchids?" said Les. "I haven't heard about any orchids."

"That's because nobody knows about them." Charlie lowered his voice. "Can you keep a secret, Les?"

"Sure," said Les, leaning forward. "Of course."

"When I was a kid, we used to play in those woods. Me and my sister, and all our mates. I was climbing those oak trees when I was about four years old. Anyway, my sister always used to pick flowers for our mum. One day she picked some pretty orange and white ones. They were so unusual, my dear old mum looked them up in the library." Charlie paused to let Les take it all in.

"And..." said Les.

"They were orchids! Rare bloody orchids. They had a weird long Latin name. My mum phoned some famous gardening guy off the radio, and he came to see us."

"Can you remember who he was?"

"No, I was only bloody four. I didn't understand what all the fuss was about."

"So, what happened?"

"I remember they sat us all down and told us that they were so rare we had to promise not to tell anybody about them, ever. Or else someone would come and dig 'em up. Steal them! So, we kept quiet about them."

"Gosh! That's an amazing story."

"But you can't tell anyone. We promised. I'm only telling you now, because my dear old mum passed on recently, and I have to tell someone or they might concrete over them."

"Can you remember where they were?" Les could hardly contain his excitement.

"I can draw you a map if you like," said Charlie, reaching for his pen.

***

The two guys in Barbour coats, with their cord trousers tucked neatly into their socks, shook hands with Mole and introduced themselves.

"Peter Carter, National Trust, Ancient Buildings Department. This is my colleague, Paul Bowyers. We've come to check out the barn. It certainly looks good from here."

"Great to see you! Glad you could come so quickly," said Mole, leading them around the vans to the barn.

As they passed the smouldering fire, Paul suddenly dived into the ashes. "What's this?" he said, holding up a charred piece of wood with a bolt in it.

"Firewood," said Mole. "We've got to cook and keep warm."

"This," said Paul, angrily, "is part of the very barn you're trying to save!"

"Oops!" said Mole.

A quick tour of the barn enraged them even more. It was evident that people had been urinating up against the outside wall. And someone called Jet, had carved their name on an overhead beam.

"Really, Mole, this is quite unacceptable," said Peter.

Carrot and Silver were still asleep under a large patchwork quilt. As Peter took photos and Paul took measurements, Carrot stirred. Sitting up, she yawned and had a good stretch. Paul dropped his tape as her huge bosoms swung free.

"Morning!" she said, sticking a finger in her ear and having a good scratch.

"There really should be as little disturbance as possible in the barn," said Peter. "We need to cordon it off, to keep people out."

Paul tore his eyes away from Carrot. "There could be ancient artefacts buried a few inches under the surface of the floor," he said, bending down and picking up a couple of roaches. "And someone," he said, "has been smoking drugs!"

"Artefacts like what?" asked Mole.

"Like nails and bolts from the eighteenth century," he replied. "You must keep people out; it's so easy to damage history."

Silver slept on as Carrot slowly stood up. The duvet dropped away, revealing her complete nakedness. Turning her back on the duo, she bent to pick up her clothes.

Peter spluttered, Paul just stared, taking in as much as he could.

"So, we'll cordon off the barn then," said Mole.

"Yes," said Paul, still staring. "I've got some tape in my car."

"Well," said Mole, "do you want to go and fetch it?"

Paul tore his eyes away from Carrot as she squeezed into her jeans. "Yes, I'll fetch it now." And off he went, unable to quite believe what he'd just seen.

***

"French knickers? I don't fucking believe it!" said Charlie, trying not to laugh. It hurt too much.

"Yeah, it's true. She's at my place now, crying her heart out," said Donkey.

They sat in Charlie's office. Donkey had spent most of the morning clearing it up and wiping the blood off the walls.

"He's quite a bit older than her," said Charlie. "Dirty old git. If Carol knew about this, it would really blow her away. Can't wait to tell her!"

"Have you spoken to her? Is she coming back?" asked Donkey.

"Bound to, sooner or later. Tell me more. Who do you think did it?"

"Dunno," said Donkey. "What about Kitty? Is she into that sort of thing?"

"She's into everything," said Charlie. "I'll ask her tonight."

The phone rang. It was Mole.

"Hallo Mole, how's it going?"

"Great. The National Trust have just left. They're going to apply for a preservation order on the barn."

"Great news!" said Charlie.

"Yes, takes a while, but it stops dead any planning permission till it's heard."

"Yahoo!" said Charlie. "That's that then, right?"

"Not quite. The planners could just alter the route slightly, to avoid the barn. And you can't always trust the National Trust. They could just dismantle it and put it up in one of their open-air museums. And we've yet to hear about the preservation order on the oaks. We need to fight on and protect the whole route."

"Hear, hear!" said Charlie.

"We're all off to the council meeting in Shorley later today. Morrison is submitting his plans. Once they're approved, they can apply to the county council for planning permission. They won't know about the National

Trust's interest in the barn yet, but we still need to stop them in their tracks, and make them aware of the opposition. Are you coming along?"

"Love to, but I've been in a car accident. I'm a bit shaken up."

"Oh, nothing serious I hope."

"No, I just need to rest for a few days. Good luck at the meeting. Let me know how it goes."

"Yeah, sure," said Mole. "You take it easy."

***

John Cunningham sat in the vestry. He still felt the need to rub his wrists, and he had little feeling in his feet.

How could she? The bitch! Such language didn't come easily to him, but his whole life had been torn apart. He'd had to cancel the remaining services yesterday, citing ill health, and it had taken him ages to clear up the mess in the bedroom. He'd lost his mistress and his wife in one foul swoop. He didn't care anymore about Carol. He'd actually, God forgive him, wished her dead! Helen was probably at her parents in Cornwall. He couldn't see her ever coming back, and if she did it would only be to collect her things, and maybe serve divorce papers on him. How could he ever look her in the face again? He prayed she hadn't told anyone. He couldn't bear it if his parishioners found out.

***

Starlite ran breathlessly into the kitchen.

"Debbie! Where's Dad? What happened? Is he OK?" Then she saw Killer standing at the sink. She froze. "What the hell is he doing here?" she cried out.

"Killer's helping us out," said Borg.

"He's your replacement," said Debbie. "Bit slow, but very entertaining."

Killer kept his head down.

"What? Are you completely insane?" She paused and took a deep breath, trying to regain her composure. Don't let the past destroy your future. "What happened to Dad? Mole said he'd been in a car crash! I came as quick as I could."

"He is OK," said Borg. "He fell down the stairs. He will be OK."

"And Mum's gone!" said Debbie. "On Friday, she just fucked off. She'd had enough. Didn't even say goodbye or anything."

"What? But why?" Starlite was really shocked. She knew her mum was down; the last time she'd seen her she looked really pale and tired. But leave Dad? She found that hard to take in.

"Dad reckons she'll be back," said Debbie. "But not if she's got any sense. If I knew where she was, I'd join her; I've bloody had enough here."

Borg put his arm around her, but Debbie pushed him away.

"Where's Dad now? " asked Starlite.

"Try the office," said Debbie. "Hardly seen him all day."

She found him, head slumped down over his desk. He looked awful.

"Oh, Dad," she said. "How are you? What happened?" She put an arm around him.

"Nothing, I'm OK. Stop fussing," he said, shrugging her off.

"Mole said you'd had a car accident. Borg said you fell down the stairs. What really happened?"

"Both, but I'm all right now. OK?"

"What did the doctor say?"

"Take a six-month holiday!"

"Oh, Dad!" She wrapped her arms around him and gave him a big hug.

"Go on, get away," he said. "I'm busy."

"I've just heard about Mum. Is she OK? Have you heard from her at all?"

"No, I haven't, but don't you worry, she'll be back, just wait and see."

Poor Dad, thought Starlite. He's being so brave.

She went up to her room; she needed to pick up some clean clothes before going back to the barn. As soon as she entered, she smelled him! Pig shit and body odour! Killer! He'd been here! In her room! There on the floor were a pair of his grubby underpants, and she could see he'd been sleeping in her bed. She could have screamed! She ripped the duvet off the bed in a rage. How could he? How dare he?

Then she saw them. There, at the foot of her bed, lay a pair of her panties. Her favourite pink silk ones. She picked them up, they felt damp. She held them to her nose briefly, then dropped them as she gagged! Falling to her knees she grabbed the waste paper bin just in time as she threw up.

Storming back down into the kitchen, she grabbed the first thing she saw, a small saucepan, and running at Killer, whacked him sideways on his head, knocking him clean to the floor. "You bastard! You filthy little bastard!"

As Killer writhed in agony on the kitchen floor, she stood over him and took another swipe, catching him hard on the back of his head.

"Ow! Stop! No!" he cried, trying to cover his face as he rolled away.

Borg leapt across the kitchen and grabbed the pan out of her hand. "Penny, stop! What is wrong?"

She stood over Killer. "You pervert!" she yelled, lashing out at him with her foot. He screamed out in agony as it connected with his balls.

"You dirty little arsehole! I'm going to fucking kill you!"

"Yes!" yelled Debbie. "Go girl, go!"

But Borg wasn't having it. He grabbed hold of Starlite and pulled her away. "Stop, Penny! You must stop! What is wrong?" He held her tightly around her waist, lifting her from the ground.

She was kicking the air and yelling abuse. "That dirty little bastard's been sleeping in my bed!"

"Charlie said I could!" cried Killer, staggering to his feet, holding his balls. Blood trickled down his face from a gash on the side of his head.

"Did he say you could fucking wank into my knickers as well?" she screamed, trying to wriggle free from Borg. "You fucking little shit!"

"Woo!" said Borg. "Let's cool down! Yeah?"

"And that's my T-shirt you're wearing! Get it off, you moron! Now!"

"Yeah! You tell him, little sister!" Debbie hadn't had so much fun in years.

As Killer pulled the T-shirt off, up over his bleeding head, Debbie spotted something. Going up behind him, she quickly slipped a hand down the back of his jeans, and grabbing hold of his underwear, yanked it up, giving him a painful wedgie.

Killer screamed out in pain, standing on tip toe as the yellow G-string cut into his arse.

"I think these may be yours as well!" said Debbie, before letting go.

Starlite screamed out, then, breaking free from Borg, she attacked Killer again, this time with her fists. "You fucking arsehole! You... you..."

Killer could only cover his face with his arms as she rained down blows with her clenched fists. When Borg finally managed to pull her off again, she ran crying out of the kitchen.

***

Carol sat with Tommy at the desk in his office below the flat. Tommy had opened a bottle of wine and poured two glasses. Spread out before them on the desktop were Charlie's accounts. Unethical yes, but Charlie had screwed them both and now it was his turn. The books were bad. Bad and bent. Tommy told Carol that Charlie was heading to prison, for a very long stretch.

"No! Really?" she said.

"Yes, really. Tax evasion mainly, but they're looking at money laundering as well."

"Oh, my God!"

"That's why," said Tommy, "he was going to do a runner!"

"What? Are you serious?" Carol could hardly believe what she was hearing. She'd had no idea this was all going on.

"Of course, you know I shouldn't be telling you all this, but I can see what he's done to you, and enough is enough."

"He was going to run out on us?"

"Yep," said Tommy. "Not only that, he was going to sell up first, grab the cash and fuck off to Spain. Leaving you and the girls homeless and penniless."

"The bastard! I don't believe it!" She paused. "Well, yes, I suppose I can. What stopped him?"

"The by-pass! Now the truckstop is virtually worthless."

"So that's why he's fighting it!"

"Yep! Not to save the truckstop, but to flog it. All behind your back!"

Carol was shocked. She knew he was capable of bad things, but this was pure evil.

The phone on the desk rang. It was Charlie.

"Tommy, it's me!"

"Yes, I can tell. What's the problem, Charlie?"

Looking at Carol, he put the phone on speaker so she could hear. She winced.

"Fucking VAT men have been snooping around. Debbie told them I was in hospital after a car accident. I think they bought it, but they'll be back."

"Oh, no doubt about that. So, what you going to do?"

"That's why I phoned you! That's what I pay you for isn't it? So, what we going to do now?"

"Thought about declaring bankruptcy? Or you could always sell the business to Carol, for a nominal fee. Then the problem's hers, not yours." He winked at Carol.

"But would she co-operate?"

"Why don't you ask her?"

"She's away at the moment, visiting her relatives. I'll think about it."

"OK then, Charlie, let me know when you've spoken to her. Bye."

"Woo! Hang on! Have you heard from Manny?"

"Don't think he's in the game anymore."

"But if the price was right, I would accept a lot less than I originally wanted."

"I'll ask him next time I see him."

"You could phone him now! I'm desperate!"

"Yes, I can tell. I'll let you know, OK?"

"Yeah, but don't take too long."

"Bastard!" said Carol, as the phone went down. "The dirty rotten bastard!"

***

The warriors were all in stitches; they just couldn't stop laughing. They were sat in Mole's bus, listening to Starlite recalling her clash with Killer.

She hadn't expected them to laugh at all; she was still fuming. She'd never ever been violent before. Even when Debbie used to hit her as a kid, which she did frequently, she'd never retaliated. But they all agreed she'd done the right thing.

"Brilliant!" said Dog. "Bet he wishes he'd gone back to Manchester now."

"Yellow G-string! Far out!" said Angel. "Good old Debbie; hope they sliced his balls off."

"My yellow G-string!" cried Starlite. And when the squeals of laughter rang out again, she joined in. Loosening up a bit, she started to see the funny side. Jet put an arm around her and gave her a loving hug.

After everyone had stopped giggling, the warriors climbed into a couple of camper vans and set off for the town hall.

***

"Can I call the meeting to order, please!" said Ted Morrison loudly, as he stood up.

The town's councillors were all sat along the table, raised slightly above the public seating. About sixty people had crammed into Shorley Town Hall to hear plans for the by-pass. Les Dixon sat at the front, note book in hand.

Ted was really pleased with the turn out, though he was expecting trouble from the hippies at the back. He looked at his watch; he was waiting for the vicar to arrive. He must be running late; he'd have to start without him.

"Thank you all for coming today, I know you're busy people, so we'll get on. I hope you've all taken the trouble to look at the plans in the foyer for the proposed route. I feel I have little need to tell you, the good people of Henyard and Shorley, the benefits the new by-pass will bring. Only last week an accident outside Henyard post office caused gridlock and mayhem for miles around. The emergency vehicles struggled to get through. No one could get in or out of Shorley or Henyard for hours. With the new container base expected to open soon, we can expect events like this on a weekly basis. That, ladies and gentlemen, is not scaremongering, that is a fact!"

A murmur of agreement swept across his audience.

"I'm told a simple upgrade on Peacock Lane would only take a few months to complete," he went on. "and the cost would be well within our government restraints."

"What about the trees?" a voice from the back called out.

"And the barn?" said another.

"Can I ask who's speaking?" Ted enquired, looking to the back of the hall.

A long-haired hippy stood up. "My name's Mole," he said.

"And are you a ratepayer in this parish? Do you and your friends actually reside in this area?" he asked.

"I am a citizen of the world," replied Mole. "My concern is for the damage your plans will do to our environment, and the hundreds of years of our history you wish to destroy."

"So, you're not a ratepayer then, or even a resident. I'm afraid your opinions aren't valid or relevant to this meeting. It was called so the residents of Shorley and Henyard could have their say, put their views. Not for some publicity seeking troublemakers to cause problems."

"We don't want to cause any trouble," said Mole. "But I'd like to know what gives anybody the right to cut down these ancient trees, just so they can cut a few minutes off their journey times."

"I'm sorry," said Ted, though he clearly wasn't. "Only rate payers can speak..."

"Why don't you want to hear what we've got to say, you pompous bastard?" called out Angel.

"Yeah, dickhead!" yelled Carrot. "What about the millions the property developers are going to make on the back of our environment?"

"Why don't you just shut up?" came a voice from the front.

"Yeah," called out another. "What's it got to do with you lot anyway?"

Ted called for order, but people were now standing and yelling insults at the warriors.

Silver stood up. "All your countryside will be swamped with houses and factories if you don't put a stop to this madness now!" he shouted.

"What's wrong with that?" someone yelled back. "Jobs and houses? That's what we all want, isn't it?"

The whole hall seemed in agreement with that. Ted was happy to let the flack fly.

Les stopped his scribbling and stood up to take a few photos. He found this all very exciting.

Eventually the abuse from the crowd forced the warriors into a strategic withdrawal. To the cheers and jeers of the local residents, they exited the hall.

***

Charlie left off the waistcoat. Far too tight on his poor ribs. He looked at himself in the bedroom mirror. Battered and bruised, but not beaten. He'd given a lot of thought to what Tommy had said. Bankruptcy wouldn't help him flee, and in nick, your financial status counts for nothing. Now, if he could empty what accounts he could, move his funds overseas, then it might be worth transferring the business over to Carol. She didn't even have to know. He went on down to the bar. It was filling up ahead of Kitty's first show.

"My God, Charlie!" said Bernie. "What the fuck happened to you?"

"Bloody hell!" said Jock. "You alright? You look bloody awful!"

"Thanks for that, Jock. I'm fine, fell over that's all."

"Shouldn't you be lying down?" said Bernie. "You look in agony."

"Listen, I said I'm alright, OK?"

Debbie poured him a pint as Barry called out from the opposite end of the bar, "Sorry to hear about your fall, mate!"

Debbie was telling Donkey, and anyone else listening, about Penny's attack on Killer. "She got him right in the balls," she laughed. "Should have heard him scream!"

Barry was laughing louder than any of them. "Yellow G-string?" he shouted. "I knew he was a nancy boy the moment I saw him!" He laughed so hard he spilt his beer.

"Poor Penny," said Donkey. "I've never seen her violent before."

"Well, you missed a good one," said Debbie.

"Hey! Look who's here!" cried Barry. "It's the G-string Kid!"

They all turned to look at Killer as he timidly approached the bar.

"How's your balls?" asked Barry, laughing out loud.

"He wouldn't have any left if I'd caught him wearing my knickers!" said Debbie.

Killer didn't like being laughed at, but he had no choice but to front it.

"Give him a pint, Debbie," said Charlie. "Wages for the day."

"Charlie," said Killer. "I've got a problem."

"I've heard," said Charlie, taking a sup of his pint.

"We've all heard!" said Barry, giggling away.

"Penny's locked her bedroom door," said Killer. "Got nowhere to sleep tonight."

"Then you have got a problem," said Charlie.

"But I'm working for you now," he said. "So, I need a place to sleep, right?"

"Do you now? Well, I suppose you could sleep in the restaurant, push a couple of tables together. You'll have to be up by five though."

"Oh, Charlie, c'mon..."

"You can always go back to the barn," said Charlie.

"Oi, Killer!" cried Barry. "Don't get your knickers in a twist, will you?" He almost fell off his stool, howling with laughter.

Show time. All the drivers were sat with full glasses, waiting for Kitty to fuel their bedtime fantasies.

Charlie took centre stage. "Ladies, gentlemen, pimps, spivs and truck drivers..."

***

Helen could hear strains of music coming up from the truckstop. She'd calmed a little and was managing to assess her predicament. She never wanted to see John again, divorce was inevitable. She felt nauseous every time she thought of him. That first image, when she entered the bedroom to investigate the smell, would be lodged in her mind for the rest of her life. Yes, she'd been unfaithful, but only the once. And as fantastic as it had been, it was normal sex. Not cross dressing and bondage! She racked her brain to think of who could have tied him up, and under what circumstances. Donkey had hinted at a prostitute. He'd never asked her to do that for him, and of course she would have refused. So maybe he did pay some... some whore! Was there a brothel in Shorley? She'd not heard of one.

And to think they'd been planning for a family, while all the time...

So, what now? She could always go to her parents, in Cornwall, but what would she say? She couldn't possibly tell her mum. She needed to stay here for a while, sort herself out. Plan her next move.

She went for a shower, and as she tried to wash away the tears and heartache, her thoughts drifted back to the time she and Donkey had first met. It had been a really awful day, starting off with a blazing row with John, then the puncture when she was running so late.

John acted so proud of her in front of his parishioners, but behind closed doors it was very different. He was so controlling. She was just a chattel, a possession, to have and behold. Maybe it was the age difference that made him treat her like a child. Her mother had been against their relationship from the very start.

He was her first lover. A virgin, deflowered by the vicar! She felt so special; he was such an outstanding member of the local community. But it all changed as soon as they were wed. Their lovemaking became so brief. He'd roll on top, take his pleasure, then roll off again. No hugs, kisses or kind words. She was left feeling so alone and unloved. But what could she do? She felt trapped.

So, when Donkey started flirting with her, something inside her just snapped. She'd lost all control; it was like she'd been possessed by demons. Having illicit sex with a complete stranger, up against the wall in a filthy little toilet. She really knew how to sin!

And she had sinned again that very same night. As John took his pleasure from her in his favourite position, the appropriate missionary, she'd thought of Donkey, and actually had an orgasm with John for the first time since their honeymoon.

She didn't want to sleep on the sofa tonight. And now her marriage was over, she wouldn't have to handle the guilt. She slipped the sponge down to her aching thighs and closed her eyes.

***

Kitty finished off the late show completely naked with her back to her fans. Bending over and looking at them through her open legs. All the time miming to Rod Stewart's 'Do You Think I'm Sexy?' The boys just loved it.

Afterwards in the dressing room, she dabbed at Charlie's wounds with a tissue. "You poor thing. Does that hurt?" she asked, pressing a little.

"Ouch! Of course that fucking hurts! Careful!"

"Were you drunk when you fell over? Where was Carol?"

"No, I was not!" he said, indignantly. "Carol's away for a few days."

"Oh, is she now?" Kitty's eyes lit up.

"Yeah," he said. "So how about you staying over tonight?" He slipped his arm around her waist.

"That would be nice," she said. She'd never done that before.

"Better wait until Debbie's gone to bed."

"Well, I do have people waiting, you know. I told Barry I'd see him in the lorry park, and Jock wanted..."

"Yeah, OK, OK!" he cut in. "Well, just don't be too long. As soon as Debbie's out the way I'll give you a shout, OK?"

***

Donkey smelled her as soon as he stepped in. Chanel Number 5, his favourite. Helen was sat on the sofa wearing his dressing gown.

"I hope you don't mind," she said. "I found it in the bathroom."

He saw the twinkle in her eye and knew she was feeling better. "And what if I do mind?" he said, mischievously.

"Well then," she replied, "you can just have it back."

Rising up from the sofa, she slowly removed his dressing gown and, standing there naked, held it out to him.

Taking it from her, Donkey threw it back down onto the sofa. "Glad to see you're feeling better," he said, taking her in his arms and planting his lips on hers.

Tuesday

The sound of a stressed-out Debbie, yelling at Borg in the kitchen, filtered through to the restaurant and dragged Killer from his dreams. Nightmares really. He was at Wembley Stadium, stood alone in the centre of the pitch. The packed terraces were all chanting his name. Killer! Killer! Killer! And waving yellow G-strings!

"Oi! Cilla!" shouted Debbie, poking her head through from the kitchen. "Get your arse out of that sack and into the kitchen. There'll be drivers in soon, they won't want putting off their grub by the sight of you. Move it!"

Killer lay across two tables. Poking his head out from his sleeping bag, he looked at the clock. It was only ten to five!

Reluctantly, he crawled out of the sleeping bag, fully clothed, and shook himself awake. That Debbie needs to learn some respect, he thought. Just 'cos Charlie talks to me like I'm shit, doesn't mean she can.

Putting on his trainers, he rolled up his sleeping bag and trudged off into the kitchen to start work.

***

The shouting from the restaurant below woke Kitty. Charlie lay beside her on the king-size bed, mouth open and snoring. His poor battered face and heavily bruised body told her it had been more than just a fall. But then Charlie never told her the truth. It was Barry, in the lorry park last night, who told her that Carol had left him. She looked around the plush en-suite bedroom. She could so easily be her replacement, if he wanted her to. She'd even consider giving up her regular job. He hadn't been up to much last night, just a little gentle light relief, but even that had seemed painful for him.

When Charlie eventually woke up, they showered together. She washed his aching body with a soapy sponge. But when she knelt down in front of him, he pushed her away. He must be feeling really bad.

"Going to come back tonight?" he asked her, as she helped him dress.

"Oh, I'd love to, but..."

"You're busy, right?"

She could see he was annoyed. "I do have a previous engagement."

"Can't you cancel? You can see I need you; I can't even put my trousers on."

"Well, maybe..."

"Who is it?" he asked, sarcastically. "Who's the lucky man tonight?" He was such a charmer.

"Actually, it's Ted..."

"What that fucking bastard Morrison?"

"Yes, as it happens. But I can cancel, I'll tell him I'm sick."

"No! No, wait! Let's not be too hasty," said Charlie. "I mustn't be so selfish; it's what you do for a living, after all."

"Yeah, thanks. But I'll just cancel anyway, I'd much rather be with you." She went to put an arm around him, but he moved away.

"No don't! What time's your appointment? Is it an all-nighter?"

"No, just an hour, ten o'clock," she replied.

"Well, that's OK then, isn't it? Come over when you're finished. Country and Western tonight, by the time we get cleared up, you'll be back. OK?"

"Well, yeah, Charlie, if that's want you want, if you don't mind."

"Why should I?" he said, with a smile on his face. "Now I must get down to the kitchen. Can you leave through the fire exit? Wouldn't want Debbie to see you, would we?"

***

Down in the kitchen, Charlie found all his staff, Debbie, Borg and Killer, stood round the table looking at a newspaper.

"What the hell's going on?" he said. "You're always moaning you're over-worked, but you can still find time to read the bloody newspaper!"

"Look Dad, it's Penny!" said Debbie. "And she's naked!" She moved aside so he could see.

There, on a double page spread in the Sun, with lots of pictures, was an article about the warriors. The report concentrated mainly on Sunday night's full moon party. All the pictures had smiling sun motifs strategically placed to avoid any problems with the Obscene Publications Act.

Charlie was gobsmacked! Penny appeared in several of the pictures, in one dancing naked with a black guy! And she had a joint in her hand! In another she was hugging a naked girl!

Killer drooled as Charlie snatched the paper away in sheer disbelief.

"Back to work, now!" he said. "Jesus fucking Christ! This is all I need. What's her mother going to say?"

"Looks like she's having a ball," said Debbie.

Since Debbie had witnessed Penny beating up Killer, she'd seen her sister in a different light; felt a little respect maybe.

***

Donkey gently pulled himself from Helen's arms, trying not to wake her. Slipping on a pair of jeans, he crept out to the kitchen and put some coffee on. He was exhausted. Helen was so beautiful, and what a body! Any inhibitions she may have had, soon went right out the window. The vicar was a bloody fool to play around when he had a wife like that.

Arms suddenly slipped around his waist from behind. "Morning," she said, laying her head on his shoulder.

He turned to hold a naked Helen. "How you feeling today?" he asked, gently kissing her neck.

"Much better, thank you," she said, politely.

"I have to rush off to work..."

"Ooh," she said, stroking his bare chest. "Do you have to?"

"Unfortunately, yes," he replied, gently squeezing her smooth bum and giving it a little slap.

"Mmm!" she purred. "Can I try and persuade you to stay?"

"No, duty calls. But you'll still be here tonight, won't you?"

"Yes, please, if that's what you want..."

He answered her with a lingering kiss as his hands cupped her glorious breasts.

***

Carol had spent another uncomfortable night on the sofa. Tommy had tried to get her drunk last night. He'd bought a bottle of Jack Daniels, to celebrate, he said, her new life without Charlie. The real reason was so he could get her into his manky bed. He'd made a big deal about changing the sheets. But it was him who got drunk, and after only two glasses. He kept going on about the good old days, when they'd been together. He certainly saw it all through rose-tinted glasses.

It was a long time ago, but her memories were so very different to his. She'd only agreed to marry him because he was the only one to ask. She didn't want to be left on the shelf. She was a shy virgin, with very little confidence or self-esteem. She knew she'd made a mistake as soon as she'd accepted his proposal, but she didn't have the courage to call it off. They'd never had sex; she wouldn't even let him touch her. All he got was goodnight kisses. They were bad enough; his breath was awful and his body odour... Yuk!

Then when Charlie, Tommy's best mate, made a pass at her, she felt flattered. He was a real jack the lad and all her friends fancied him. She was like putty in his hands. When he'd first kissed her, she felt something she never had with Tommy. And when she let Charlie put his hand up her skirt for the first time, she came alive, and realised what she'd been missing. When Tommy finally caught them, behind the pub, it had been going on for several months. She was glad he found out. Another few weeks and they probably would have wed. She just wished she'd never married Charlie either.

Today Tommy was running her down to the bank in Shorley. He'd forged Charlie's signature on a £1000 cheque and she was going to open her own account with it. For now, she needed Tommy, but she wanted to move on, and the sooner the better.

***

The warriors were gathered on Mole's bus, discussing yesterday's council meeting, plotting and planning their next moves. Cat and Sparrow arrived back from town with some supplies.

"Hey, take a look at this," said Cat, spreading out a copy of the Sun newspaper on the bed.

Spread over two pages, their full moon party was revealed in all its naked glory. They all crowded round, looking in amazement at the story.

"Wow! That's me!" said Carrot, pointing at one of the many pictures.

"And that's me!" cried Squirrel. "Look at them abs!"

Starlite was shocked. Oh, God! There she was naked for all the world to see! And she was smoking a joint! What would her mum think?

Mole stopped the laughter with a wave of his hand. "This is not good!" he said. "Neither is it funny!"

Like children they hushed.

"How can people take us seriously when they see pictures like this?" he said, sternly.

"It shows we have a free spirit," said Cat.

"It shows we have no discipline," said Mole. "It shows we smoke drugs."

"It shows our bums!" said Jet.

Everybody tried to stifle their giggles.

Mole lightened up a bit. "OK! OK! We can all have a good laugh, but now we can expect a visit from the drugs squad. So, let's just be aware, OK? Stash all the gear and no more smoking out in the open, right?"

Carrot leant over and pointed to one of the pictures. "Does my bum look big in that?"

***

Debbie was having a fag by the open kitchen door. She was feeling really down. Borg had all these plans for the future, and they all revolved around the bloody truckstop! He kept telling her he'd never been happier.

Well, she had, loads of times. In fact, now she'd never felt unhappier. She felt trapped. Shackled.

He was behaving like a husband already. Asking her if she really needed to put on so much make up. Saying her skirts must have shrunk, because they seemed a bit short. And if she spent too long chatting to any of the drivers in the bar, he would come over and introduce himself as her fiancé.

And now he was talking about having kids! What? No bloody chance! Stretch marks and nappies had no place in her dreams. If she felt trapped now, how would it be with a couple of screaming brats to care for?

Mum had escaped, so had Penny, but she had nowhere to go. The only friends she had were truckers. And they were only friends for one reason. Most would run a mile if she suggested moving in with them. Their wives would probably object too.

In a way, she envied Penny. They'd never got on as kids, mainly because Penny was a snotty-nosed kid who was always telling tales. But now she was free! The pictures in the paper showed just what a good time she was having, partying all night and dossing around all day. And some of those freaky friends of hers looked quite tasty.

All she had to look forward to was another day in the kitchen with Borg and Killer. Apart from staring at her tits, all Killer did all day was eat and whinge. And the bullshit that spewed from his mouth. Bragging how he'd shagged every one of the girl warriors. Mostly in twos and threes of course! He said Penny only left him because she couldn't handle his popularity with all the other girls.

But Debbie knew just how to shut him up. She'd ask him, "What colour you got on today?"

***

Starlite sat crossed-legged on the grass behind Squirrel.

They all sat around the fire because the barn was now out of bounds, all cordoned off with tape. The National Trust guys had given them a real hard time over it.

Jet sat on the ground behind her, shaving and scrapping at her scalp, while she did the same to Squirrel. She'd slept with him last night. Nothing too exciting, but he'd comforted her after her return from the truckstop. He was a shoulder to cry on. She was going to walk into Shorley soon and check out the charity shops.

"Excuse me! Can I speak to your er... leader? Whoever is in charge?"

They all turned to see two suit-clad heavies standing by the gate.

"Pigs!" said Jet. "Quick, get Mole!"

Starlite ran off to get him as Cat and Squirrel walked over towards the gate.

Mole was quickly on the scene. "Can I help you?"

"Are you in charge here?" said one, aggressively.

"I'm the spokesperson, yes. And who are you?"

"We've come to serve you, and anyone else occupying this land, with an eviction order." He handed Mole a large white envelope. "You have seven days to comply and vacate this property. If you fail to do so you could be forcibly removed. Is that clear?"

"Quite clear," said Mole. "And let me make it quite clear to you, we have no intention of leaving. We are here as a peaceful protest, but we will defend ourselves using the courts and any other measures it takes."

"So, you understand then?" said the bailiff.

"Yes," replied Mole.

Mole was a veteran of these campaigns. He'd seen it all before, many times. But he was a bit surprised at the timing. Usually it would be many months before any court action. And then, not until planning permission had been granted and the bulldozers were ready to come in.

The court order had been filed on behalf of the landowner, a Mr Manfred Baxter.

***

Charlie and Donkey sat with a cup of tea in a quiet corner of the restaurant. Debbie wiped the tables down while Killer mopped the floor.

"She still there?" asked Charlie.

"Yeah, could be for a few days yet. Got to sort out her life."

"I bet she's sorting out yours!" He laughed briefly, then held his ribs.

"Still painful, eh? Heard anything more from Billy?"

"I'll let you know, believe me. Thinking of getting a shotgun for under the bed."

"Better hope you're in bed then," said Donkey, "when he comes calling. What about Carol? Heard from her yet?"

"No, but she'll be back soon, just you wait and..."

"Mr Wheeler, how are you feeling today?"

Charlie looked up to see Les Dixon approaching, hand outstretched.

"Hallo, Les! Yeah, getting better all the time." He shook his hand then turned to Donkey. "So, catch you later then."

Donkey took the hint and went off back to his diesel pumps.

"Debbie! Two teas to my office, please!" Charlie called out, as he led Les away.

Les could not contain his excitement. Before they'd even sat down, he spurted out. "I found them, Mr Wheeler! I found them!"

"Please, call me Charlie." He put his finger to his lips as Debbie brought in the teas. When she'd gone, he said, "Didn't touch them, did you? It's against the law to disturb them. And you can't say where they are, or some bugger will nick them!"

"Yes, I know. No, I just took pictures so they can be identified. Hopefully before the print deadline, so it can be in Friday's issue. I've already written the piece, sort of. It certainly changes things as far as the by-pass is concerned."

"Yeah? You think so?"

"Of course, no way can they disturb them. Can they?"

"I hope not," said Charlie, trying to hide his glee. Today was going to be a good day. Now it was going to get even better. They sipped at their tea.

"Do you know Ted Morrison?" Charlie suddenly asked.

"Yes," said Les. "Met him yesterday, as it happens. A Conservative councillor and magistrate. He's leading the campaign for the by-pass. Lives here in Henyard, I believe."

"That's right, just up the road."

Charlie took another sip of his tea. He needed to be cautious; he had to choose his words very carefully. "Did you know he uses prostitutes?"

Les spluttered, spilling his tea. Charlie thought he was going to choke.

"No! I find that hard to believe. Are you sure?"

"Couldn't believe it myself!" said Charlie, passing him a box of tissues. "Pillar of the community, and all that."

"Good God!" said Les.

"Something like that could destroy him," said Charlie.

"Yes," said Les. "It certainly could."

Charlie looked him straight in the eye. "Could be quite a scoop for somebody, don't you think?"

Les smiled as he took out his note book.

***

Tommy dropped her off at the bank in Shorley, telling her he'd pick her up in an hour. Carol had all the forms she needed to open her own account, plus the cheque for £1000. Charlie's signature certainly would have fooled her. She felt perhaps it wasn't the first time that Tommy had forged it. Still, not her problem, not anymore. She was looking forward to doing some shopping. Her clothes were taking on the smells from Tommy's flat.

"Mum! Mum!"

Carol turned to see Penny running across the road towards her.

"Mum!" she screeched, as she flung her arms around her. "Oh, Mum! Where have you been? Are you all right?"

"Oh, Pen!" Carol hugged her; she was really pleased to see her.

"Mum, are you OK? What happened? I've been so worried about you."

"Pen, it's so lovely to see you. Are they coping all right without me?"

"I think so, I haven't been there much. Where have you been? Why did you go? Was it that bad?" She paused, then asked suspiciously, "Or was it something Dad did?"

"All these questions, Pen. Look, I've got time for a coffee, but it'll have to be quick. It's so good to see you, Pen."

"It's Starlite, Mum, Starlite!"

They sat with their coffees in the bus station café.

"...and I just couldn't take any more, it all got too much. Sorry, love."

"I understand, I really do. I don't blame you, I don't. But since his accident..."

"Accident? What accident?"

"Didn't you know? Well, he told me he fell down the stairs, but he told Mole it was a car accident."

"So probably neither," said Carol. "What's the damage?"

"His face is like a balloon, black eyes, fat lip and a couple of teeth missing. He hobbles a lot, holding his ribs. He refuses to go to the hospital."

Carol tried not to feel sorry for him. It was easy. "Sounds like he was beaten up. Must have upset the wrong person this time," she said. "How's Debbie coping?"

"OK, I suppose. Borg is helping out. He's quit his job and moved in. Apparently, he's the manager now."

"Debbie must be pleased."

"Yeah, right!" said Starlite. "So, where are you staying?"

"With a friend, an old friend."

"Oh, Mum no, you're not..."

"No! Certainly not!" Carol was shocked that her daughter would even think such a thing. "I'm sleeping on the sofa, and as soon as I can get my own place, I will. The last thing I need in my life now is a man!"

They both laughed together, just like they used to in the old days.

***

Killer left his sink and went looking for Charlie. He found him in the busy restaurant, sat chatting to some truckers, all suited up, ready for Country and Western Night.

"Hallo, sweetie," said Tony, getting a cheap laugh.

Killer ignored him. "Charlie, can I have a word?" He had to shout over the TV. They were watching the local weather. Rain for tomorrow.

"Yeah? What's the problem this time?" asked Charlie, not looking away from the telly.

"I need some cash, need to buy some new clothes, and maybe a ticket back to Manchester."

"Oh, not much then. And tell me, why should I fork out on such luxuries for you?"

"I work for you..."

"Oh, right! When did you start?"

"Monday," said Killer.

"And what day is it today?"

"Tuesday!" said Killer, clearly irritated by Charlie's manner.

"Two days?"

"Yes!"

"Minus bed and board, and at least ten pints..."

"And all the knickers you want!" laughed Bernie.

They roared out loud at that. Killer, eyes down and deeply embarrassed, stood his ground.

"But Charlie, you said..."

"Shh! The telly... Look boys, it's that wanker Morrison!"

The drivers hissed as Ted Morrison spouted his mantra on the by-pass to the local TV reporter.

"Believe me," he told the camera, "I represent the people of Henyard, I am one of the people. Nothing will stop the by-pass! Nothing!"

"Wanna bet? You bastard!" shouted Charlie.

Tony threw his fag packet at the TV. "One of the people? Ha!" He was a local and knew Morrison well.

"Apart from him being a judge and a bloody Tory, he lives in the biggest house in the village, with a new bloody Jag on the drive. And he says he's one of us? Well, he can just fuck right off!"

"Hear! Hear!" said Charlie.

"Want me to do him?" Killer suddenly interjected.

"What, you?" said Charlie. "Yeah, maybe you and a few of your dyke friends could beat him up!" He began to laugh. "Stop before I wet myself!" He got up, holding his ribs. Nudging Killer out of the way, he made his way back to the bar. He had to start the show soon, Betty Barbell was already warming up.

Killer felt snubbed. He needed to demonstrate his worth to Charlie.

***

John Cunningham opened the door of the vicarage to find Ted standing there. He'd hoped against hope that it would be Helen.

"Evening, John, feeling any better?" Ted said. "God, you look awful! Trust you to fall ill while Helen's visiting her parents. Still, she'll be back soon, wont she?"

"Yes," said John. "Come in, saw you on the television earlier. Good show!"

"Thank you, John, but I've got some even better news!"

"Good! Sherry?"

"Don't mind if I do," said Ted, sitting down.

"So," said John, passing Ted his glass. "Cheers!"

"Cheers!" replied Ted, sipping at the sherry.

"So, come on, you're obviously bursting to tell me something."

"Meripilus Giganteus!"

"What? What on earth is that? Sounds like some sort of condition."

"Spot on, John, spot on! It's a disease of trees." Ted paused, sipped at his sherry again, then said slowly, "Specifically oak trees!"

"No! You mean..."

"It's a fungus that attacks the roots, and it's fatal. And yes, the by-pass oaks, all bloody eight of them, are riddled with it!"

"Oh yes!" said John. "Perhaps God wants this by-pass as well. How did you find out?"

"Well, you know how thorough I am, John, I had to explore every avenue. A friend of mine is an arboriculturalist. He had a look and took some samples. No doubt about it, all the oaks are doomed! The diagnosis is that over the next few years they will all weaken and be susceptible to strong winds. And, as they're alongside a public highway, they are a danger to the public," he paused, "and must be felled immediately!"

"Well done, Ted, well done! We knew we could rely on you."

"Thank you, John. I've informed the county council and they're having their own independent survey done on them. Then they will chop them all down!"

"Wonderful! Well done, Ted! More sherry?"

***

Carol sat opposite Tommy at the dinner table, eating their takeaway. She'd enjoyed her trip to Shorley. She now had her own bank account, for the first time in more than twenty years. And she'd certainly bashed her new chequebook. The first thing she'd bought was a suitcase, and now it was full of new clothes. Clean underwear, bliss! She'd kept Tommy waiting for over an hour.

"Saw Penny today," she told him. "She said it looks like someone's beaten up Charlie. Pretty bad by the sound of it."

"Upset the wrong person..." he replied, munching on his Kentucky Fried chicken.

"That's what I said," said Carol.

"Couldn't have happened to a nicer person," sniggered Tommy, wiping his fingers on the tablecloth.

Carol didn't laugh. Yes, she hated Charlie, but she didn't much like Tommy either. He kept touching her; several times she'd had to remove his hand from her knee. She was sure he was looking through the bathroom keyhole last night, when she had a shower. She could see his shadow moving under the door.

"Probably a husband," said Tommy, casually.

"What? I'm sorry, did you say...?"

"You must have known he was screwing around," said Tommy. "Everyone else did."

"Well, I didn't!" said Carol.

"It's true; there was Kitty for a start."

"What? No!"

"Yeah, he used to boast to me about giving her a lift home. They used that lay-by, just up the road from your place."

Carol was shocked. She'd had her suspicions of course, but never really wanted to believe them.

"And she wasn't the only one."

"Tommy, please! I really don't care anymore. It's over now. Please don't rub it in how much of a fool I've been."

"I'm sorry, Carol, I didn't mean to..." He got up and put an arm around her. "I'm so sorry Carol, I..."

"Look, Tommy," she said, pushing him away. "I'm going to my sister's in Devon tomorrow. Just for a few days. I need to get away from Henyard, I need to get myself together, sort out where I go from here."

"Oh!" said Tommy, realising he may have just over done it a bit.

***

Silver and Squirrel had found them in one of the lower fields, hundreds of them. Magic mushrooms! Squirrel danced around the fire as he handed them out.

Cat warned Starlite not to eat too many. "You'll know when you've had enough" he said, before eating a large handful.

Angel and Carrot dragged over some dead tree branches and the fire took on a new dimension. The sound system belted out Techno as the party got into full swing.

***

Les Dixon sat in his car opposite Morrison's house. A shiny Jaguar sat in the driveway. The house was in darkness except for an upstairs bedroom window, indicating the scene of the crime. Les checked his watch, eleven o'clock, Charlie had said. A few snaps of her leaving the house, that's all that was needed to destroy him. Charlie's words, not his.

Les felt a moral dilemma coming on, in fact it had been with him all day. There was no doubt Morrison's reputation would be shattered. How could a magistrate possibly keep his post, when he associated with the very people he punished in court? Les had already done his research and found several cases where Morrison had heavily fined local prostitutes. Les was sorry a long career of serving the local public was about to end, but the word hypocrite featured heavily in the first draft of his exposé. He wound down the window and pointed his camera, getting the focus right.

***

Killer entered the garden through the neighbouring property on his belly. He'd show Charlie what he was about. Your enemy is my enemy.

Staying in the shadows, he crawled closer. His hand went into something soft. Dog shit! He gagged as he furiously wiped his hand on the grass.

Rolling sideways, he covered the last few yards commando style. Then he was there, hidden in the shadows alongside his objective, Morrison's capitalist trophy. The Jag!

From inside his jacket he pulled out the box of fire lighter's. He tore open the packaging, exposing the white blocks, before reaching underneath the car and placing the box directly under the fuel tank.

"Bona la Vista, baby," he whispered, as he struck the match. The packaging caught first, then a block, then another.

Time to exit stage left, he thought, as he rolled away from the car. He followed the same route out as he'd come in by. Only this time he put his other hand in the dog shit.

***

Les checked his watch again. Anytime now, he thought, as he aimed his camera at the front door. That's when he noticed a yellow glow at the rear of the car, just moments before the explosion. It lifted the Jaguar's rear end several feet into the air, spinning it around onto the front lawn. Within seconds the whole car was ablaze!

The shock-waves rocked Les' car; he could feel the heat. His journalistic instincts took over. Leaping from the car, he began taking photos, getting as close as he could to the raging flames, which were now as high as the house.

Ted Morrison came running out through the front door. Wearing just a pair of boxer shorts, he was jumping up and down, panicking and screaming.

Les carried on shooting like the professional he was.

Suddenly, the upstairs bedroom window opened and a distraught, flimsily dressed blonde, leant out and screamed, "Ted! Ted! You OK?"

Les suddenly remembered why he was there. He turned his camera onto the prostitute as the sound of the fire engines grew closer.

***

The warrior's camp fire was huge, flames streaking right up into the night sky. Starlite could see rainbows in the flames. In fact, she could see rainbows everywhere. In the sky, in the fields, and in the eyes of everyone she looked at. She felt fucking great!

Everybody was up and dancing to the loud throbbing beat of the sound system. Carrot and Angel were naked, as usual, and Mole was sliding down a rainbow with a joint in his mouth.

The fire got bigger, filling her whole world. They'd removed the tape from around the barn, and people were making love on the dirt floor, in time to the heavy Techno beat. They were surrounded by rainbows and flames.

Suddenly, the rainbows began to fade, and the flames seemed to take over. The heat was becoming unbearable. There was a sudden, urgent change in the vibes.

Starlite sensed the fear! People were screaming and running! This wasn't fun anymore! She wanted it to stop! Please stop!

She ran and found Cat. She was freaking right out. Her heart was racing, her mind was scrambled. "What's happening? What's wrong?" she screamed at him, holding tightly onto his arm.

"Fucking barns on fire!" he yelled, his eyes glowing with fear.

The music stopped abruptly, replaced by wailing sirens. Starlite's whole world suddenly turned a shade of blue, flashing and pulsating. Strangers clad in yellow invaded her space, shouting and shoving.

Starlite could take no more. She ran off screaming into the darkness of the night.

WEDNESDAY

Flaming hell! thought Donkey. Hope Penny's OK.
  Wow! thought Debbie. Bloody heck!
  Ah, Gode Gud! thought Borg. How terrible!
  Fucking great! thought Killer. Hope Mole got burnt!
  Shit! thought Charlie. That's fucked it!
  They sat with the drivers around the TV in the restaurant, silenced by what they were seeing. Last night's inferno was captured by the local BBC news unit, already at the scene. It showed the raging barn collapsing into a heap of flames and sparks. It was mayhem. Most of the warriors ran around in panic. Mole and Squirrel were seen moving buses and vans away from the flames.

  Then they went over live to Hugh Baynes, their intrepid reporter, standing next to the smouldering remains. Behind him the fire brigade dampened down the embers.

  "...and as you can see, the barn is totally destroyed. Thankfully, no injuries have been reported. It's believed that sparks from the protester's fire may have started the fire, which quickly spread through the 260-year-old barn. It has been a busy night for the Shorley Fire Brigade; earlier they'd been called to a car fire in Henyard. For more on that, back to Diana in the studio."

  "Thank you, Hugh, yes, we are getting reports that the car fire in Henyard last night may well have been arson. The car, belonging to Councillor Morrison, was totally destroyed."

  "Yes!" screamed Charlie, leaping from his chair. "Yes!" His joy countering the pain searing through body.

  Killer smiled, but said nothing.

Ted Morrison appeared on screen, looking drawn and very shaken. "I was in bed, about eleven o'clock, when I heard an almighty explosion. I looked out..."

The vicar, standing by his side, comforted him.

Charlie was elated. But if it was arson, then who...?

***

Starlite lay hidden amongst the scrub, waiting for Cat to return. She felt stunned, in total shock. She kept hoping she'd wake up and find it had all been some terrible nightmare.

Last night had really freaked her out. She just ran and ran. Cat had found her, hours later, hiding in bushes a couple of fields away from the fire. He was pretty freaked out himself. As they came down from the mushroom trip, they comforted each other. When dawn finally came, Cat had left her to go and see what was happening. It was some time before he returned.

"Man, it's a fucking mess!" he said. "The barn's just a heap of ashes, totally destroyed! But everyone's OK. One or two of the buses are a bit singed..."

She just listened, not saying a word. She couldn't. How quickly had her heaven turned to hell.

The police and fire brigade were still there. Mole and Squirrel had stayed at the scene, by police request, the others had all regrouped a few fields lower down, around one of the oaks. They went off to join them.

***

"So, it wasn't you?" Donkey asked him.

"No! Wish I could take the credit, but I can't. Bet Morrison shit himself!"

Charlie and Donkey were eating breakfast together at the back of the restaurant.

"And what about the barn?" said Donkey. "Good job no one was hurt, but it changes things a bit, doesn't it?"

"Yeah, now they won't have to knock it down. Stupid bastards were supposed to save it, not burn the bloody thing down," he said, pushing his plate away.

"There's still the trees..."

"Oh, I ain't given up yet," said Charlie. "If that by-pass goes ahead, I'm finished. And if I'm finished, then we're all in the shit!"

"Heard from Carol yet?" asked Donkey, not wishing to think too much about what would happen to him.

"No, but once she sees what real life is about, she'll be back. How's the vicar's missus? Kicked her out yet?"

"Now why would I want to do that?"

***

Killer scrubbed away at the pan. He felt really good. Something had gone right for a change. And the fact that Mole had fucked up big time, only added to his joy.

Debbie came in and started on at Borg again. He just took it from her. Killer had tried to give him some advice. A woman like Debbie needed to know who was the boss, needed to know who was in charge. He could handle her, show her what a real man was like. She was always flirting with him, flashing those amazing tits. If Borg wasn't about, he'd be in there like a shot. That's why Borg never left them alone for too long.

Barry suddenly barged in through the back door. "Hallo Debbie, Borg," he said, slapping a bloody parcel on the kitchen table. He sneered in Killer's direction then turned to Debbie, "Kidneys. Charlie about?"

"Somewhere," said Debbie. "Try his office."

"What about last night then, eh?" he said, "The barn and Morrison's car! Must be some right nutters about!"

"The police say the barn, it was an accident," said Borg.

"They say it was a bomb under Morrison's Jag!" Barry said, excitedly. "Fancy that. And in Henyard! Nothing exciting ever happens here."

Killer smiled to himself. Maybe not in your world, tosser!

***

Helen lay on the sofa, wrapped in Donkey's dressing gown. She could smell him on it. She'd just seen her husband on the TV. Someone had blown up Ted's car. Her feelings of disgust returned and she felt quite ill. The last time she'd seen him he'd had a pair of her knickers on his head. She began to weep; her life was in ruins. Turning off the TV, she let go, sobbing into the dressing gown.

A gentle knock at the door made her sit up. Then in through the door, carrying a suitcase, walked Carol.

"Oh!" said Carol.

"Oh!" said Helen.

It was difficult to tell who was the most surprised.

"What...?" they both said together.

"I'm sorry..." said Helen, quickly standing up, "I'll get dressed. Excuse me." Dashing into the bedroom, she quickly threw on her clothes, all the time breathing deeply, trying to control the feelings of complete panic. What would she say? How could she explain why she was here? Oh God! She was bound to tell John!

When she returned, Carol was sat on the sofa. "Donkey's not here," she said, stupidly.

"I can see," Carol replied.

Helen sat gingerly at the other end of the sofa. "I'm sorry to hear that you've left your husband."

"Don't be," said Carol. "I'm not. Does John know you're here?"

"No! You see... I've also left my husband... and I'm not sorry either!" She felt stronger now that that was out of the way.

"Oh," said Carol. "Must be the weather."

"That's what Donkey said. He should be back soon. Can I get you a coffee?"

"I'll get it. I know where everything is, " said Carol.

Helen followed her into the kitchen. "Where have you been staying?"

"With an old friend, but I'm off to see my sister tomorrow, in Devon. I was hoping Donkey would let me sleep on his sofa tonight," she said, getting out some cups. "But I assume it's already booked."

An embarrassed glance and blushed cheeks told Carol it wasn't.

"Oh, I'm so sorry," she said. "I didn't realise. I don't want to intrude... I'll just have this coffee, then I'll go."

"No I... Please wait till Donkey gets back."

They took their coffees back to the sofa and sat quietly for a while.

"How long have you been here?" Carol asked.

"Since Sunday," said Helen. "Since I..." She promptly burst into tears.

Carol put down her coffee and passed Helen some tissues.

"You won't tell him I'm here, will you?" said Helen, dabbing her eyes.

"No, of course not."

"Did he tell you I'd left? Does everybody know I've gone?"

"To be honest, Helen, I haven't seen him since Sunday myself. And I had no idea you'd left until you just told me."

"There was someone else!" she suddenly blurted out.

"No! I don't believe it. Who?"

"I don't know, and I don't really care. Someone who obviously could give him something I couldn't. Or wouldn't!"

"Oh dear," said Carol. "I'm so sorry."

***

"Les! What the fuck happened?" asked Charlie, on his office phone. "Were you there?"

"Yes of course I fucking was!" snapped an angry Les. "You sent me there, remember? You set me up, didn't you? You knew..."

"Les, on my kid's life, I'm as shocked as you! I had no idea."

"Bollocks! You knew Charlie, you bloody knew."

"Then why would I want you there? I knew about Kitty, but that's all."

"Kitty? Who's Kitty?"

"The girl, the prozzie. I knew she'd be there, but not anything about the car, honest, Les, believe me."

"The police wanted to know why I was there. They've taken my camera and film for evidence."

"What did you tell them?" asked Charlie, unable to disguise the fear in his voice.

"Don't worry," said Les. "I told them I had a tip off about him using prostitutes. I refused to name the source of my information."

"Well done, son!"

"Professional principle," said Les. "Don't mean I won't, though!"

"Oh!"

***

Mole sat alone at last in his bus. He was exhausted, mentally and physically. He'd been quizzed by the police, the fire brigade, the BBC, and the local media. At one time they were actually queuing to hear his story. The excuses, the regrets, and how he felt now that he and his warriors had destroyed the very barn they'd come here to save. His head ached; his brain hurt. He tried to ease the pain with the knowledge that no one had got hurt; it could have been a lot worse!

No, it fucking couldn't! After the turnip field fiasco this was all they bloody needed. Sparrow and Hawk had left with Hog this morning, going back to Manchester. Jet and Squirrel were set to go tomorrow. The whole protest was breaking up, and everyone was arguing. He himself had told Angel to fuck off this morning. Damn those bloody mushrooms!

***

Tommy answered the phone in his office.

"Tommy! It's me, Charlie!"

He had hoped it was Carol. "Yes Charlie, what can I do for you?"

"Tell me what's happening. Have you spoken to Manny yet?"

"Manny's out of the equation; you're clutching at straws."

"Yeah? OK then, listen, this is what I want you to do. Merge all of my accounts, transfer it all into my number one account, OK?"

"You're going then. About time too! I told you months ago..."

"I didn't call for a bloody lecture, OK? How soon can you sort it?"

"Well, I'll have to get the appropriate forms from the bank first, and then I'll need some signatures," said Tommy. "Carol will have to sign for some of the joint accounts."

"Yeah? Well, if you can drop them off here, I'll get it all sorted. How long before it's all goes through?"

"Once you've signed, a few days maybe. When you thinking of going? And where?"

"Even if I knew myself, I wouldn't be telling you, would I?"

"No, I suppose not. How's Carol?"

"Fine, why do you ask?"

"Just haven't seen her for ages. Perhaps I will when I come over, to get her signature."

"Yeah, OK, Tommy, must go, see you tomorrow."

***

Donkey headed back to the caravan for his break. He was hoping Helen was still in bed. Last night had been so good, she'd really loosened up. Game for anything. As he went in through the door, he stopped dead. In shock!

"Sorry, Donkey," said Carol.

"What...?"

"I just came by on the off chance..."

Helen was sat at the other end of the sofa, looking acutely embarrassed.

"How are you?" asked Donkey, unable to think of anything else to say. His mind was racing. This was just so surreal.

"I was hoping to borrow your sofa tonight, but..." Carol began.

"Er, would you like me to make some coffee?" said Helen, getting up and heading for the kitchen.

"Cheers, that would be nice," said Donkey.

"I'm sorry," said Carol, as soon as she'd gone. "I just wanted to see you before I left." She got up and Donkey put his arms around her.

"I thought you'd gone. Your note..."

"I got delayed, but tomorrow I'm going to my sister's for a while, I just... Why is she here? I didn't know you knew her."

"She's left her husband, needed a shoulder to cry on."

"Sounds familiar. Your dressing gown looks better on me!"

"Look, I'm sorry," he said. "You should have called me, if I'd known you were coming back..."

"You'd have turned her away?"

"Er, no, probably not."

Carol stepped away from him. "So, I'm stuck. Sorry. Too late to catch a train, so can I have the sofa tonight? I promise to stick my fingers in my ears!"

Donkey laughed. "Of course! Sit down, I'll have a word with Helen." He went into the kitchen.

"Do you want me to leave?" asked Helen, quietly. "I don't want to cause you any problems."

"No, of course not," he said, putting an arm around her. "She's an old friend. She can have the sofa; it's only for one night."

"And then?" she whispered. "What about me?"

"I was hoping you'd stay around for a while."

"Oh, Donkey," she said, snuggling closer into his arms.

***

"Mr Wheeler?"

Charlie turned and saw the two guys stood at the counter. He nearly had a heart attack. He looked around; only Bernie was still sat in the restaurant, not much good in a fight.

"Shorley Police," said one, holding up his ID card. "I'm DC Roberts and this is my colleague, DC Phillips. Can we have a chat?"

As Charlie's heart rate began to slow, he led them out to his office.

"Been in the wars?" Phillips asked, studying Charlie's bruises.

"Fell down the stairs."

"Must have been big stairs."

"They were. Now can we get on? I'm a busy man."

"I believe you know Councillor Morrison," said Roberts.

"Yes," said Charlie.

"Are you aware of the car fire at his house in Henyard last night?"

"Yes," said Charlie. "Saw it on the telly. Pity he wasn't in it."

"You don't get on with him then?"

"Nobody does; the guy's a wanker. And before you ask, no I didn't. But I'll shake the hand of the man that did."

"Could have been a woman," said Phillips.

"I was here all night; compered the show. Loads of witnesses."

"Any idea who might have a grudge against him?" asked Phillips.

"Stick a pin in the local phone directory, could have been anyone."

"Strange, we got the impression he was pretty well-liked in the area."

"You've obviously been asking the wrong people. Now is that all? I do have a business to run, you know."

"Thank you, Mr Wheeler," said Roberts. "We may well come back."

"Yeah, no problem. Bye"

Charlie waited till they were leaving before calling after them, "You know he uses prostitutes, don't you?"

***

The restaurant was filling up, drivers filling their bellies before the show. Debbie was flirting with a Frenchman. As she passed him his sausage sandwich, his hand lingered over hers, gently stroking as she pulled away. All the time his eyes were on her nipples, jutting out freely through her tight white T-shirt.

If Borg wasn't here, she thought, I'd have you. Oh, for the good old days. Looking around the crowded restaurant, she saw several other guys that she'd like to make out with, and a few that she already had.

And they would all be feeling horny. It was Wednesday. Kitty was already warming up in the loo. Debbie knew what Kitty got up to in the lorry park. Maybe she should ask her for some career advice, turn her favourite pastime into a business. But then no, she couldn't handle the fat ones, or the smelly ones. Ugh! And what about Barry? She knew Kitty 'serviced' him. Yuk! No fucking way! If she was going to be a hooker it could only be with rich, handsome men.

She went back into the kitchen where her fiancé was busy cutting up kidneys.

***

"...and that's why I didn't come over last night," said Kitty. "It was so scary! Bang!" She waved her hands in the air and screwed her face up.

Charlie stood behind her, checking his bow tie in the mirror.

"By the time the police had finished with me, it was gone one o'clock, so I went straight home. Ted got me a taxi."

"I was really worried about you," said Charlie. "What did the police say? Who do they think did it? Have they got any clues?"

"Ted thinks it's probably them eco whatsits, the press was there waiting. All very frightening, I think Ted may have wet himself. He was just about to..."

"Enough detail, thank you!" said Charlie. "So, what did he tell the police about you? Who did he say you were?"

"His daughter-in-law; told me to say I was in the back bedroom."

"What a creep!" he said, kissing her on the back of her neck. "Staying over tonight?"

"If you'd like me to." She leant to kiss him, but he pulled away.

"Mind the suit!"

***

Killer watched from the bar as Charlie introduced Kitty, whipping up the drivers to a mild frenzy. Bit old for him was Kitty, he preferred them young, willing and able. Like Debbie.

As Kitty got them out, Charlie came off the stage and sat beside him at the bar.

"Pint please, Debbie," he called.

"Better make it two," said Killer.

"And why would I want to buy you a pint?" asked Charlie.

"Boom!" said Killer, clapping his hands together then waving them above his head. His stupid grin spread across his spotty face.

Charlie looked at him with a puzzled frown on his face. "What the fuck you on about?" Then he paused, "No... I don't fucking believe it! You?"

"Well, you'd better believe it," grinned Killer. "Didn't need no fucking dykes to help me neither!"

"Fucking 'ell!" said Charlie, slapping him on the back. "Well done, son! Well done! Debbie!" he called out, "Pint for the lad!" Lowering his voice again, he whispered, "Ain't told anyone else, have you?"

"Do I look that stupid?"

Charlie didn't answer.

***

Carol lay under the quilt on the sofa. She could hear the bed gently knocking on the wall. Bitch! That should be me in there. Helen had unwittingly ruined it for her and John, and now she'd taken Donkey off her as well. She'd only wanted one last night with him, before she left Henyard forever.

How strange that John had driven them both into Donkey's arms. She wondered how he would feel, if he knew his pretty young wife was being serviced by a well-endowed young stud. Perhaps someone should tell him.

The knocking began to accelerate. She wasn't even screaming. What a waste! Now if that was me, she thought, slipping her hand down under the duvet...

THURSDAY

Starlite stirred as Squirrel nestled up behind her in the sleeping bag. Dawn was breaking. They lay together under the sky, alongside a great oak. She kept still as his erect penis slid into her. His hand squeezed her breast as he pumped away. Her eyes remained closed as he gasped his way to a jerking orgasm. When he'd finished with her, he rolled away and went back to sleep. He'd done the same last night. He was leaving today with Jet. She was going to miss Jet.

How her world had changed. The vibes around the camp were just awful. Mole and Angel had had a screaming match yesterday and Angel had stormed off back to Manchester, along with Silver and Snake.

The whole thing had really freaked her out. The barn was gone. And they were responsible! But there was still the oaks. And as Mole said, if they all left they would be defenceless and doomed. She was determined to see the fight through. For her dad's sake if nothing else. What else could she do?

Once she'd said her goodbyes to Jet, she was off back to the truckstop. See her dad and pick up some clean clothes.

***

Carol heard Donkey getting up, ready to go to work. When she heard him go into the kitchen, she draped the duvet around her and followed him in.

"Morning, Carol, sleep OK?" he asked, putting an arm around her.

"Yes, I was fine," she said, snuggling into him. "I won't see you again. I'll be gone when you get back."

"You don't have to go," he said, with little conviction. He knew she had to. So did she.

"It's OK, I understand," she said, pulling away. "Is Helen staying long?" She knew she had no right to ask. Nobody owned Donkey; that was part of the appeal.

"Just 'til she sorts herself out."

She'd heard that one before. When it was her who needed to sort things out. She still hadn't. Her sister in Devon didn't exist; it was just an easy exit strategy. She wrapped both her arms around him, half-hoping Helen would come in. Then she might leave and she could stay.

"Got to go," said Donkey. "The diesel pumps are calling."

"I can hear them. Bye, Donkey." She pushed her lips towards his, but he broke free.

"Bye, Carol, keep in touch. Hope things work out for you, I really do."

***

In the kitchen, Borg was furious, Debbie had never seen him so angry.

"Why?" he kept asking. "Why?"

He'd found her contraceptive pills; she'd dropped them in the bathroom.

"Why did you not tell me? We want children? Yes? Why did you not speak the truth, Debbie? Tell me!"

Killer, at the sink, kept his head down. He'd never seen Borg like this either.

Debbie just swept in and out the kitchen with meals and dirty plates, not ignoring Borg, but trying not to crank it up. Maybe today was the day to tell him the truth, if that's what he wanted. She knew that if she were to get pregnant her life would be mapped out for ever. And she hated kids!

Charlie came in to see what was going on. "Some of the boys want to know what time the fight is."

"Tell 'em to fuck off!" said Debbie.

"No, you can tell them when you take Jock his breakfast. He's been waiting half an hour! Can you two not keep your domestics to yourself? Or at least keep your voices down!"

"Like you and Mum did, you mean?" said Debbie.

"Exactly. Now I've got backache, headache and ball ache, so can we just have a peaceful, calm day today?"

"Charlie! Charlie!" Jock called out from the restaurant. "Come look at this!"

Debbie followed Charlie back into the restaurant just in time to see a gloating Ted Morrison on the TV, telling the world that the oaks were doomed, diseased and rotten. "A danger to the public," he said.

"Bollocks!" said Charlie.

"Does that mean the by-pass goes ahead then?" Debbie asked him.

"I don't care anymore," he said. "No one else seems bothered, so why should I be?"

Debbie knew he was right. She didn't really care what happened to the truckstop. If it closed down, then she wouldn't have to work here anymore, would she?

***

Carol sat behind the curtains, watching the truckstop. Trucks coming and going, some of the drivers she'd known for years. Perhaps she should take a lift from one of them. Start a new life wherever they dropped her off.

But she'd decided what she was going to do, for now. She had to be practical. She'd go to Brighton, some twenty miles away, book into a B&B and look around for some work. Loads of hotels there. Maybe get a live-in job as a cook or a cleaner. Then she'd divorce Charlie, maybe get some money out of him. If he was still around, that is. Just enough to start over. When she'd run the idea through her head last night, it had seemed like a good idea. But now she realised it was probably her only option. Apart from going back.

Suddenly, she saw the fire exit at the rear of the truckstop open. And out popped Kitty into a waiting taxi.

The bastard! So, Tommy was telling the truth. She wished she'd taken more than a grand from him, a lot more.

"Morning, Carol. Was it OK on the sofa? Did you sleep all right?"

Helen was standing behind her, two cups of coffee in her hand.

"Yes, thank you. I'm just waiting for the coast to be clear, then I'll be gone."

"Er, pardon?"

"I don't want Charlie to see me. Don't think I could stand him begging me to go back."

"Is that likely to happen?"

"No, of course not, I was joking. He's probably glad to see the back of me."

They sat at the table with their coffees.

"What about John? Will you take him back?" she asked Helen.

"No! Not ever!" she replied firmly. "I never want to see him again."

"Men! Who needs them?" said Carol, sipping her coffee. "So, what are your plans?"

"I don't really have any. Can't face going to my parents, not yet anyway. Donkey's been really kind, letting me stay here."

"I'm sure he enjoys your company."

Helen blushed. "I shouldn't feel guilty, should I? If it wasn't for... If he hadn't..." She took a deep breath to hold back the tears. "Well, I wouldn't be here now, would I?"

Perhaps you should be grateful, thought Carol.

They finished their coffee in silence.

"Can I run you anywhere?" asked Helen. "I need to get out and buy a few toiletries and things. I left in a bit of a hurry."

Sounds familiar, thought Carol. "Well, if you could drop me at the bus station, I'd be most grateful, thanks."

***

"Charlie? Can I speak with you?" Borg stood at his office door.

"Sure Borg, come in, as long you're not after a pay rise."

Borg looked nervous. Closing the door behind him, he sat down.

"So," said Charlie. "What's the problem?"

"First, Charlie, I have to ask you something. People are saying, the truckstop, it is finished. When the by-pass opens, we will close. Is that true?"

"Nonsense, Borg," said Charlie. "That is never going to happen, believe me. It'll take years before any permission is granted, and if it is, then we'll appeal, taking another few years. Then, if it does go ahead, where are all these trucks from the new container port going to park up overnight? Where are they going to eat and take their breaks, eh? So, they might have to divert a few extra miles, so what? Where else are they going to find another Kitty?"

"Good!" said Borg, a huge smile lighting up his face. "That is what I wanted to hear."

"Yeah?" said Charlie.

"Yes," said Borg. "I want to become your partner. Come into the business with you."

"Oh!" said Charlie, a bit taken aback. "Er, why?"

"It would show Debbie how serious I am about providing for her. She doesn't think we can afford children. I want to spend the rest of my life here. Marry Debbie and raise a family. Just like you did."

"Oh, I see," said Charlie. "Well, I'm not sure I..."

"I have money that I can invest. I would not want to be an equal partner straight away, but eventually, yes I would."

"Yeah? So er, how much were you thinking of investing?"

"I can raise £20,000, maybe a little more. My life savings, so far."

"Wow!" said Charlie.

"So, what do you say? I could run the place for you. You could relax, take a holiday maybe."

"Mmm, now you've got me thinking, Borg. I like the sound of that," said Charlie. "Maybe you could just take a small stake at first, then build up, and who knows, by the time I retire, you could own the lot!"

"Yes!" cried Borg. "So, your answer is?"

"Yes, my son, you've got a deal!" Charlie leant forward and shook his hand. "Best not tell anyone till we've got it all sorted, right? Keep it hush hush."

"It will be difficult not telling Debbie," Borg said, shaking with joy. "But yes, you are right. We tell no one."

"Good!" said Charlie. "How soon can you get the money?"

***

Starlite stood with Cat and Mole as they said their farewells to the last of the warriors. Then she watched as the convoy of buses and vans pulled out of the field. They were off to fight other battles, battles they felt they could win. Mole's bus was now the only vehicle left. This morning's news about the oaks had been the last straw. Mole had declared the by-pass unstoppable. The barn was gone, the oaks were dying, and it was so obvious that the locals really wanted it.

Carrot and Dog, along with Squirrel and Jet, were off to Newbury, to join the protest there. They had begged Starlite to go with them. But it wasn't the same anymore. The bubble had burst.

Mole and Cat only stayed because they didn't want to go with the others. There had been a lot of bad vibes and blame flying around last night. They were going to stay for a few days, then take off, maybe up to Scotland. They said she could go with them. She said she'd think about it.

***

"Hallo, Carol, fancy seeing you again. How's your sister?"

Tommy pulled up alongside her in his car.

"Oh! Hallo, Tommy. No, I got delayed, I'm just off to the bus station now." She nodded towards her suitcase to give her explanation some truth.

The truth was she was off to the bank in the hope of arranging an overdraft before she left. Helen had just dropped her off.

"Got time for a coffee?" he asked.

"No, Tommy, I'd love to, but my bus leaves soon and..."

"How's the money going?" he suddenly cut in. "You haven't spent it all already, have you?" He managed to laugh and leer at the same time. "Need some more? In fact, Carol," he said, "I have a little plan where you could have a whole lot more. Fancy that coffee now?"

Sitting in the bus station café, Tommy told her of his plan.

"Charlie's ready to run. Wants all his money in the one account, ready to transfer abroad. I'm on my way to see him now, sign a few forms, make it all happen. Soon as the money's there, he's off! Two to three working days at most!"

"The bastard!" said Carol. "And?"

"So," said Tommy. "What if that one account was your account?"

"Yes?" She liked the sound of that. "You could do that?"

"Of course!"

"How much are we talking about?"

"There's more than £20,000 spread across six accounts," he said. "In two or three days, it could all be yours!"

"Gosh!" said Carol, a little overwhelmed by the thought of so much money.

"Some are joint accounts held with you," he said.

"But I don't know anything about those."

"Of course you don't. He used your name to get loans, then he'd get them paid into a joint account. There's still a couple of loans outstanding. When he's gone they'll become your responsibility."

"Damn him!" said Carol. "How long has he been doing that?"

"Oh, about twenty years!"

It was pretty shocking hearing the extent of Charlie's lies and deceit. Tommy was enjoying this, she could tell. She could also tell there was more to his plan.

"What's in it for you?" she asked.

"Not money." He smiled wryly, leering at her as he spoke.

She knew what was coming. "So, what then?"

"It would be nice if my, er, friendship was reciprocated."

"You mean you want me to sleep with you?"

"In a word, yes!"

***

His editor was holding the front page of tomorrow's edition. This could be the defining moment of his career. Les took a deep breath, turned on the tape recorder and picked up the phone. He'd never done this before. It rang for ages before someone answered.

"Yes?"

"Councillor Morrison?"

"Yes, speaking. Can I help you?"

"This is Les Dixon, from the Shorley Herald."

"Oh yes, I think we've met."

"Yes, we have." Les took another deep breath. "I'm calling to inform you that in tomorrow's Herald we're running a story on you."

"About those bastards blowing up my car?"

"No."

"About those damned oaks?"

"No. About your use of prostitutes."

The silence was dramatic. Les waited awhile. He could hear him breathing. "Councillor Morrison? Are you still there?"

"What? What are you on about? I've never been with a prostitute in my life! Who is making such outrageous suggestions? I'll sue!"

"Do you know a girl called Kitty? I believe you were with her on Tuesday night. Did you know she was a prostitute?"

The line went dead.

***

Borg held Debbie in his arms and kissed her. Killer, peeling spuds at the sink, watched his hands gripping her bum.

"I'm sorry, Debbie, my fault. I should not have rushed you."

"It's just that I'm not ready for babies, Borg, not yet."

"Things will change soon, I promise you."

"The only thing that will change is when this place closes down. How can we have kids when we could soon be homeless?"

"That will not happen, Debbie. Charlie will not let that happen. Soon everything will be OK. I love you, Debbie, so very much," he said, squeezing her tight.

Looking over Borg's shoulder, Debbie saw Killer poking his finger down his throat in a mock gag. She mouthed the words 'Fuck Off!' before openly groping Borg's balls. Killer nearly choked.

"Charlie will retire one day," said Borg, stepping back from her, "then I will take over. We will run this place together, you and me. Just think what we could do."

All Debbie was thinking was that, sooner or later, she'd have to tell him she wanted out.

***

Starlite arrived at the truckstop. She couldn't face seeing Debbie or Killer, so she went to see Donkey at the pumps. He saw her coming across the forecourt and came out to meet her.

"Great to see you again," he said, as she threw her arms around him.

"Oh, Donkey," she said. "Good to see you too." She held onto him tightly. He had to prise her off.

"You look really down," he said. "Things not going so well, eh?"

"It's just awful," she told him. "You heard about the barn?"

"Yes," he said. "It was on the telly. It must have been terrifying."

"Yes, it was, really horrible. And now, the oaks have all been condemned and everybody's leaving."

"I'm sorry," he said. "But what about you? Are you going with them?"

"I don't know yet. One thing's for sure, I'm not coming back here!"

"Good on you," he said. "You've come too far for that."

She loved Donkey. He knew her so well.

A truck pulled in for diesel, so she left Donkey to it and walked over to the workhouse.

"Hallo, Debbie. Hallo, Borg," she said, entering the kitchen. Killer sat at the table, eating a ham sandwich. She blanked him.

"Hallo, Penny," said Debbie, coming over to give her a hug. She'd never done that before.

"Starlite! It's Starlite!"

Borg also gave her a hug. "So sorry to hear about the barn," he said. "It was good no one was hurt."

"And the trees," said Debbie, glaring at Borg. "Looks like we're going to get the by-pass after all."

Killer caught her eye and grinned. He made her feel sick.

"Saw you in the Sun," said Debbie. "Who's the black guy? Nice!"

"Did Dad see it?" Starlite asked, anxiously.

"Yep!" said Debbie. "And Tony's got you stuck up in his cab."

"Oh, God!" She put a hand to her mouth.

"We saw you on the telly as well," said Debbie. "Don't you ever wear clothes?"

Starlite felt embarrassed. Be true to yourself, she thought. Then she remembered who had taught her that mantra. Every time she glanced at him, he was staring back. She needed to be strong.

"I saw Mum on Tuesday," she said.

"What?" said Debbie. "Where? How was she? Is she coming back?"

"In town. She looked a bit low, but otherwise she seemed fine."

"Where's she staying?"

"Didn't say, a friend or something. She's on the sofa."

"Do you think she'll be coming back?" Debbie asked again.

Charlie came through the swing doors. "Debbie, Dave's at the counter, if you could just find the time to... Oh! Hallo, Penny. Back, are we? Haven't come to burn us down, have you?" He laughed, holding his side. "Your head looks bloody awful. Are they scabs?"

"Nice to see you too, Dad. I've just come back for a few things."

"Lovely. Debbie, two teas to my office, once you've served Dave. Pronto!" Then he was gone.

"No," said Starlite, looking at Debbie. "I don't think Mum will ever come back. And neither will I!"

***

Tommy passed Charlie the forms. "Sign there," he said, pointing with his pen, "there and there. Alongside the crosses. And get Carol to sign there, there and just there."

"And then what?" asked Charlie.

"Two to three working days and it will all be in the one account. So, when you off?"

"Two to three working days," said Charlie.

Debbie came in with the tea. "Hallo, Tommy," she said. "Long time no see."

"Too long," replied Tommy, staring at her cleavage as she bent to place the tray on the table. "Still engaged to that Dane? He's a lucky fellow."

"Yes, I am, but he's Swedish..."

"Thank you, Debbie," interrupted Charlie, looking towards the door.

"Right," he said, when she'd gone, "I'll get Carol to sign these tonight and I'll drop them round tomorrow, OK?"

"Yes, but I thought she was away, with relatives."

"She is, but I'll be seeing her tonight. Don't worry, see you tomorrow, OK?" He held out his hand and shook Tommy's. "Well done, Tommy," he said. "Well done."

***

The phone on his desk just kept on ringing. Les ignored it and pressed on. His editor was waiting for the final draft, his exposé of Councillor Ted Morrison! They had already extended the print deadline, everything was on hold, ready and waiting. This was the biggest thing that had ever happened to him. Even bigger than his eco warrior scoop.

He could ignore the ringing phone no more. Snatching it up, he yelled curtly, "Yes?"

At first there was nothing, then a small cough. "Hallo? Mr Dixon?"

"Yes."

"This is Councillor Morrison. I wish to make a statement."

***

"A pint of bitter and a gin and tonic, please Debbie," said Donkey.

Debbie peered out across the smoke-filled bar. "Who's the lucky girl tonight?" she asked him. "Ain't seen her before."

"Just a friend. Bit shy though, so you'll have to excuse me if I don't introduce her."

"Ooh, Donkey, you're talking all posh, does that mean she's posh? We don't serve many G&T's here."

Donkey laughed as he left the bar. He'd had quite a job persuading Helen to come out for a drink. She was terrified that someone would see her. Someone she knew. He'd worked hard to convince her that the church and the truckstop were so far apart in their clientele, that's she'd be more likely to bump into the Devil than a churchgoer.

"They ate the last Christian who came in here," he joked. But Helen had insisted on sitting at the back, in the shadows.

"Cheers!" he said, as they touched glasses. "I must, first of all, apologise for tonight's entertainment. I forgot it was Bobby Bent."

"Bobby...?"

"Bent. Bobby Bent, he's a comedian."

"Oh good," she said. "I like a good laugh, don't you?"

"Oh, he's a good laugh all right!"

The noise levels dropped as Charlie came on stage. Then the whistling and cat calls began.

"What happened to his face?"

"Fell down some stairs," said Donkey.

"Ladies, gentlemen, hookers, whores, thieves, scallywags and truck drivers," Charlie paused until the jeers subsided. "Tonight, returning by public demand, I give you, the one, the only, give it up for Mister Bobby Bent!"

The crowd went mad, they loved Bobby. He came on sucking on his huge cigar. His black eye had almost faded.

"Good evening my cock sucking, arse licking cowboys! How are we all tonight?"

They let him know that they were feeling good.

Helen couldn't hide the look of shock on her face.

Not quite her everyday language, thought Donkey.

"It's good to be here tonight, boys. I'm just happy to be away from the wife. She's like a bloody laxative," said Bobby. "She irritates the shit out of me!"

Helen giggled, holding her hand over her mouth.

"She's just like a condom; she spends more time in my wallet than she does on the end of my dick!" He paused to draw on the cigar, waiting for the laughter to stop. "You know, when I was a kid I was always told, don't play with yourself in bed 'cos Jesus is watching. Only later did I realise that it was really Uncle Fred! And Jesus certainly wasn't watching him!"

Helen laughed out loud, glancing at Donkey like a naughty school girl. She was enjoying this. "This is such fun," she said.

"Even better last week, somebody punched him!"

"What! Why? Why did he punch him?"
"Wasn't a he, it was a she!"

***

Starlite sat in the driver's seat of Mole's bus. Looking out through the screen at the star-lit sky, she hit on a joint. It was the first she'd had for a while. Cat and Mole lay in bed together, behind her. They'd wanted her to join them, but she'd declined. Now she could hear that they'd started without her.

They were leaving for Scotland tomorrow and wanted her to go along with them. Rest and recuperation, said Mole. Just let the mountain air cleanse away all these negative vibes. Starlite wasn't so sure. But the only alternative was to go back home. To the truckstop, the very place she thought she'd escaped. She could soon be as stir crazy as Debbie.

She needed to make up her mind. Was the fun really over now? Was that it? She could spend the rest of her life looking back with regret.

***

Carol sat on the edge of his bed. Tommy was in the shower. He'd wanted them to shower together, but she'd refused. She showered first, knowing full well he was spying on her. Now she was waiting for him. She'd prostituted herself, sold her body and her soul. May God forgive her.

She felt she deserved something out of the truckstop. Why should she have to spend the rest of her life in servitude? That's how she'd spent her last twenty years. Was she doing it just for the money? Or to get even with Charlie? The money would give her a new start in life. Revenge on Charlie would make it that much sweeter.

When she heard the shower stop, she removed her new nightdress; she didn't want to spoil it. She slipped down between the sheets, her heart racing.

Tommy came into the room naked, and stinking of aftershave. She could see his ribs, and his hips seemed to protrude out from his waist. She avoided looking any further. Oh, God, please make it quick, she prayed.

He climbed into the bed and clambered straight on top of her. His hands were freezing as he plugged himself in and set off like a race horse.

Two to three working days, thought Carol, as Tommy squeezed her breasts.

***

Two to three working days, thought Charlie, then he'd be gone! Fuck the tax man! Fuck Billy! And fuck the fucking by-pass!

He lay in bed, resting his broken body. Yes, it broke his heart to lose the truckstop, but he'd rather be weeping in Spain than in prison. It was finished anyway.

With Borg's money, he'd have close to £50,000. Not a lot in real terms, but better than nothing. Maybe he could buy into a bar, start again.

There were still a few things to be done before he took off. He needed to cover his back.

Friday

COUNCILLOR MORRISON RESIGNS!

***

The Shorley Herald headline had the breakfasting drivers howling with delight. Their cheers and jeers brought Charlie and Debbie out of the kitchen. Charlie snatched the paper from Tony and soon he too was dancing a jig.

"Yes! Yes!" he yelled with glee. "Got you! You bastard!"

The front-page picture showed Morrison's burning Jag, lighting up the night sky. And there, in the background, clearly visible through the thick smoke, was a scantily dressed blonde hanging out of the bedroom window.

The paper told, how, after the car fire at his home on Tuesday night, questions had been asked about the councillor's private life. These questions had gone unanswered, declared the paper's top investigator, Les Dixon. Then, in a dramatic late-night phone call, the councillor had resigned and announced he was also stepping down from his position as a magistrate. The paper printed his letter of resignation.

"Listen to this, boys," said Charlie, reading out the best bits. "'Rumours of a liaison with a call girl are completely false. The arson attack on my car and these lurid allegations are an attempt to silence me, an attack on democracy itself!'"

"Oh yeah?" said Dave. "Then why the fuck has he resigned?"

"Thinks someone's out to get him," said Charlie.

"Here, hang on a minute," said Tony. "That bird, she looks like Kitty!"

"Yeah, does a bit, doesn't it?" mumbled Charlie, feigning surprise.

"It is," yelled Dave. "It's Kitty!"

"What a dirty old git!" said Tony. "Fancy using prozzies!"

"What?" cried Debbie. "What a bunch of fucking hypocrites you lot are! I think I'm probably the only one here who hasn't shagged her!" Glaring over at her dad, she gathered up some plates and headed back to the kitchen.

"Not only was someone out to get him," said Charlie, studying the paper, "but they fucking well did! The teas are on me, boys! "

**

Starlite stood by the bus with her rucksack at her feet. Fighting back the tears, she hugged Cat and Mole. They wished her luck and again tried to persuade her to go with them. But she had decided. Not what to do, but what not to do. She couldn't go with them; the dream had ended. They were all moving on, and so must she.

They offered to drop her off at the truckstop, but she wanted to stay awhile. She needed some time alone with her thoughts.

As the bus pulled out of the field she sat down and, leaning back against the oak, she closed her eyes. Was it really only three weeks ago that she'd first met Killer at Glastonbury? And she'd known Mole and the others for even less. It seemed like a life time. It didn't seem possible that she could change so much in so little time. Things would never, could never, be the same again. She listened to the bird song; she could smell the honeysuckle in the hedge.

Slowly standing up, she picked up her rucksack and set off for home.

***

"Hallo, Charlie, its Les." He sounded quite curt.

"Hallo mate, well done, what a scoop!" Charlie took the call in his office.

"Thank you."

"I see you got your film back, good shot."

"Yes," he said abruptly, "but I still think you set me up."

"Les! Why would I do that? I told you, I knew nothing about the car. And if I do hear anything, you'll be the first to know."

"Cheers, but that's not why I called. They've identified the orchids."

"Yeah?" said Charlie. He'd forgotten all about them.

"Yes. They're very rare. They're White Himalayan Beetle Orchids."

"Wow!" said Charlie.

"Only found in two places in the world."

"Where?"

"The Himalayas…"

"Obviously," said Charlie.

"And B&Q Garden Centres!"

"What? What are you saying Les?"

"I'm saying that when the experts magnified the pictures, they saw a little plastic tag amongst the roots!"

"And…?"

"And it said fucking B&Q!"

"Oh!" said Charlie.

"Oh!" said Les. "I think my next exposé could well be on you."

"Look, mate, it's not what you think."

"Don't mate me! You've conned me from the word go. You've taken me for a fool. And that's exactly how you've made me look, a bloody fool!"

"Look, Les, I'm sorry if you feel that way, I really am. But look, I've got something else you might be interested in. How about a transvestite vicar?"

"Fuck off, Charlie!"

The phone went dead.

***

Donkey carried the case of wine back up to the caravan. Charlie had let him have it cheap.

He needed to restock. Recent events had taken its toll on his wine list.

Tonight was party tonight, just him and Helen. He loved having her around. Great body and so keen. He was in danger of burn out.

She threw her arms around him as soon as he stepped in. After a lingering kiss she pulled away. "Bad news, I'm afraid," she said.

"What? What is it?"

"I called Mum this morning, Dad's in hospital. Broke his hip."

"Oh, I'm so sorry..."

"It's OK, it's not life-threatening, but I need to be there for Mum. I can also take the opportunity to break my news to her, gently."

"When you gonna go?" asked Donkey, holding her tight.

"This afternoon," she said, unbuttoning his shirt. "But not for an hour or so."

***

Carol watched nervously out of Tommy's office window. They were waiting for Charlie to show up. He was due anytime now with the forms. The forms he was getting her to sign. She was going to hide in the loo and hear what he had to say.

"Ha ha," laughed Tommy, sat with the Herald spread over his desk. "What about this then? Morrison's got his comeuppance at last."

She looked over his shoulder. "That looks like Kitty."

"So it does," said Tommy. "Filthy old sod. Never did like him."

Then she saw it. There at the bottom of the page, below the main article, was a picture of the barn on fire. "What?" she gasped, snatching the paper off the desk. "That's where Penny is!"

"Didn't you know?" said Tommy. "It happened Tuesday night. Stupid idiots burnt the bloody thing down. It's one of the things that forced Charlie's hand. Along with the trees being diseased, the by-pass is now practically guaranteed."

"But Penny's there!"

"It's OK, calm down," he said. "No one got hurt. They're all still there, dossing around naked and taking drugs. Huh, the youth of today, eh? Maybe we were born too soon." He smiled up at her and placed his hand on her bum. She moved away.

Carol felt a parental guilt. All she'd been concerned about these last few days was herself. She'd run way from her children as well as Charlie. As soon as she was settled, she'd call them, explain her reasons, tell them the truth about Charlie. But for now, she had to stay focused. She had to be strong.

Last night had been just awful. Tommy had groped her all night, slobbering over her, poking and probing her. His breath reeked of onions and his aftershave was intoxicating. And he had the smallest penis she'd ever seen. Not that she'd seen many.

"Here he is now," said Tommy, going over to the window. "Quick, in the loo!"

Carol locked herself in the small toilet and stood close to the door, listening. She heard Charlie come through the door.

"Morning, Charlie," said Tommy. "God, you look terrible!"

"Yeah, cheers, I know. Can we get on?"

"How's Carol? Did she sign up OK? No awkward questions?"

"Of course she did. She does as I tell her. The recipe for a lasting marriage."

"Yeah? Good, can I have the forms?"

Carol could hear the rustling papers as Tommy ran through them.

"What about Morrison then?" said Charlie. "What a pervert, eh?"

"Each to their own, Charlie, each to their own. Pity about the car though. Nothing to do with you was it?"

"Why does everybody think it was me?" said Charlie. "Wish I could take the credit, I really do."

"Right, all in order," said Tommy. "I'll place these with the bank this afternoon and the whole process can get started."

"When do you reckon it'll all be in?" asked Charlie.

"Should all be merged into the one account by, say, Monday earliest, Tuesday latest."

"Good, and what about that fucking VAT bloke?"

"If I make an appointment for the end of next week..."

"I should be long gone by then."

"Exactly!"

"Good thinking," said Charlie.

"Going to tell Carol?"

"Good God, no. Why would I want to do that? She'll know soon enough."

"Not even a post-card?"

"Nope. Not even that," said Charlie. "So, what are you going to do, Tommy?"

"Well, when you've disappeared, so will all your files and records. I'll report a burglary; they'll probably blame you."

"You just make sure you do that, OK? Now I must go, things to arrange. Can I use your bog before I go?" he said. "I'm dying for a piss."

"Er, no!" said Tommy, panic in his voice. "The loo's blocked, and there's rats coming in. Got to keep it locked until it's sorted." He knew Charlie didn't like rats.

"Oh, OK then," said Charlie. "Have to piss in your yard then, wont I? See you, Tommy, talk to you before Monday, right?"

"Right, Charlie. Give my love to Carol."

Carol watched carefully out of the loo window as Charlie pissed up against the back wall. His face looked awful! Someone had given him a real beating. But she felt nothing but hate for him. She waited until Tommy told her the coast was clear.

"So, look at these signatures," he said. "Almost as good as yours."

"But not as good as yours," said Carol. "What now?"

"I'll drop these down the bank now. And maybe by Monday, all Charlie's funds will be in the one account."

"And then?"

"And then I will give you a cheque, signed by Charlie, for the full amount in that account. Around £20,000!"

"Wow! " said Carol. She'd never seen that much money before.

"You'll have three or four days to cash it before he realises that he's been duped." Standing behind her, Tommy started stroking her bum. "Why don't you go back up to the flat?" he said. "I won't be long. I may even fetch a bottle of Champagne. Would you like that?"

Carol tried to smile. Perhaps getting drunk would help. Monday seemed a long way away.

***

Debbie and Borg were cutting sandwiches in the kitchen, ready for the Karaoke tonight. Killer was mopping down the floor.

"Borg, can I have a word?" Charlie poked his head through the kitchen door.

"Sure," said Borg, following him out to the office.

"So," said Charlie, as they sat down, "have you thought any more about that investment? Are you still interested?"

"Yes, of course," said Borg. "I have made calls to my bank, and I can have the money to you by Monday."

"Great!" said Charlie.

"All I need are your account details."

"No problem, got them all written down here," he said, handing Borg all the numbers on a scrap of paper. "My number one account."

"OK, I will phone this through now."

"Great! Well done, partner!" Charlie shook Borg's hand vigorously. "I'll set a meeting up with my accountant for the end of next week and we'll make it all legal. Right?"

"OK, Charlie. But it's not a problem, I trust you."

"Good. Now look, Borg, I might be taking a few days off next week. I want you to know that while I'm away, you'll be in charge, OK? You're the manager now, understand? I want you to do the menu, run the till and introduce the shows. Can you do that?"

"Yes, of course I can! It's what our partnership is about. I cannot wait to get started."

"Well, you can get started tonight. Think you can run the Karaoke? All you do is introduce them, stick on the music, then hand out the prizes. Easy! OK?"

"I've watched you doing it, it seems simple."

"Great. Come and watch me set up, and I'll show you how to run the lights."

Borg followed Charlie into the bar, bouncing along behind him.

"Don't you tell Debbie I'm going off," said Charlie. "Best wait till I'm gone. She'll only get all blubby, what with her mother gone and all. I'm counting on you to look after her while I'm away. OK?"

Borg threw an arm around Charlie's shoulder and hugged him. "OK, partner!"

***

Donkey sat with Barry at the bar. Debbie poured him a pint as Borg, in his smartest suit, opened up the show.

"Ladies and gentlemen, welcome to Charlie's Place. My name is Borg and tonight I am your host."

"Oh my God!" said Debbie. "What's he doing?"

"Very well," said Charlie, coming in behind the bar. "He's giving me a break. Christ knows I deserve one."

Debbie looked surprised; her dad had never done that before. He must be feeling ill.

The disco lights bounced around the stage as two fat ladies kicked off the show, yelling out 'Gimme! Gimme! Gimme!' Abba they were not.

"Imagine them two in your bed," said Barry. "Cor!" Then he joined in with the chorus, loudly singing, "Gimme, Gimme, Gimme a shag after midnight!"

Killer snuck in alongside Donkey, keeping well away from Barry.

"Alright mate?" said Donkey. "How's the job going?"

"I'm bloody knackered," he said. "On my feet all day, and my hands are all dry and cracked!"

"Stop whingeing!" said Debbie, "I'll lend you some of my hand cream."

"Better lend him some of your knickers as well!" said Barry, giggling away.

Killer glared over at him.

"Pint, Killer?" asked Charlie.

"Yeah, sure, thanks," said Killer. "Could I have a sub till pay day, please, boss? I fancy a day off tomorrow, think I might go to Brighton."

"Sure mate, thirty quid enough?" said Charlie, pulling a bankroll from his pocket.

"Yeah, that'll do nicely," said Killer, snatching it off him. "Cheers!"

"What?" said Debbie. "Why are you giving him time off? I wouldn't mind going to Brighton myself, but I just can't up and go, can I?"

"Oh, for Christ's sake, give it a rest will you," said Charlie. "Don't you ever stop?"

"Cheers, Charlie," said Killer, raising his pint. He grinned at Debbie and winked.

"Hallo, Donkey, how ya doing?"

Donkey turned to see little Emma stood right beside him at the bar.

"Oh, hi, I'm great, and you?"

"All the better for seeing you," she said, pouting her cherry-red lips. Her breasts were bunched up and heaving under a thin yellow T-shirt. The pink mini-skirt she was wearing barely covered her pert bottom. Her white bobby socks made Donkey feel like a paedophile.

Killer's eyes were popping out of his head. "Can I get you a drink?" he asked.

"No, thank you," she said, looking him up and down, "I don't do boys."

"Yes?" said Debbie, "What can I get you?"

"Two cokes, please."

"How's your granddad?" asked Donkey, unable to think of anything else to say.

"OK, thank you, he's picking me up later. Who's the guy doing the show? Quite a cutie, don't you think?"

"My fiancé!" said Debbie, slapping down the cokes. "And he doesn't do little girls. Anything else?"

"A packet of crisps," said Emma, firmly holding her ground.

***

Sat in his office, Charlie could hear Emma declaring 'I Will Always Love You' to her adoring audience. He was finalising his paper work, feeding it into the shredder. This time next week he'd be in a beachside bar, enjoying the rest of his life, slowly. But there were still a few things he had to sort out. He couldn't be trusting Tommy to tidy up things after he'd gone.

A light knock on the door made him jump. The door slowly opened.

"Mr Wheeler? Charlie Wheeler?" An elderly guy in a sober grey suit came in, hand out-stretched. "Manny Baxter, we've spoken on the phone."

Charlie rose and shook his hand enthusiastically. "Manny! Of course, sit down. Can I get you a drink?"

"No, no, thanks, I'm driving. I'm here to pick up my granddaughter."

"Sorry about the horror show," said Charlie, seeing the look on Manny's face. "Fell down some stairs."

"Big stairs..."

"Yes, they were. So, is this a social visit or...?"

"Depends," said Manny, sitting down. "Have you given up your fight against the by-pass?"

"No," said Charlie. "How can I? It's my livelihood."

"Full planning permission will be granted at the next county council meeting, in a month's time."

"How do you know that?"

"I make it my business to know. Now the trees and the barn are no longer a problem, the bulldozers will roll in before winter, and this time next year the only traffic passing this place will be the local bus service, once a week." Manny paused to let his words sink in. "So where does that leave you?"

"You tell me," said Charlie. "You seem to know most things."

"Well, I would say you're finished."

"Thanks for the summary. Have you just come here to gloat?"

"No, not at all. I might be able to make you an offer, a way out."

"Yeah? I'm all ears!"

"When I look to the future," said Manny, "maybe five or six years hence, I see the by-pass, with housing along its entire length. I know this because I now own that land, and that is the way it will go!"

Charlie listened intently, wondering where all this was going.

"I also see the truckstop," Manny continued, "closed down and abandoned. You might survive for a while as a tea house or even a nightclub, but you'll never make a living out of it."

"You really know how to piss a guy off, don't you?" said Charlie.

"I didn't come here to do that," said Manny. "A five-acre site, just outside Shorley? All that new housing? I think that in a few years' time, one of the big supermarkets could well be interested in this place.

"Great!" said Charlie. "But I don't think my bankruptcy will wait that long. Once this place closes, I'm finished."

"I know," said Manny. "That's why I'm here."

"So?"

"So, I'm going to make you an offer. I will purchase an option from you. An option to buy the site any time in the next five years." He paused to let it sink in. "For market price at the time of sale, less forty per cent."

"Wow! That's a big cut!"

"Forty per cent of fuck all is fuck all!" said Manny. "You'll still own the place of course, until I exercise my option."

"So, what would you offer for this option?"

"£25,000. Non-refundable of course. If I don't take up the option within five years, you keep it."

"Fucking hell!" said Charlie, a bit stunned by the unexpected offer. "So, what happens if I..."

"If you go bust? Then with my option I'd get preferential terms from the liquidators."

"And you'd get it even cheaper!"

"Correct. Good business for us both, wouldn't you say? Short term for you, long term for me."

Charlie couldn't help but feel some admiration for Manny, he could see bits of his old self in him.

"Well?" said Manny, looking at his watch.

Charlie hesitated for precisely one millisecond. "Deal!" he said, holding out his hand. "How soon can we...?"

"Seal the deal?" said Manny, shaking his hand. "Come see me at my office first thing on Monday. I'll prepare the contract and arrange a bank transfer. If you give me your details now, it can be in your account the same day."

Charlie's head was spinning. What a bloody result! He scribbled his details down on a piece of paper. Charles Wheeler. Number one account.

***

Donkey headed for home early, as Borg was presenting the prizes. He wanted to avoid Emma. She had won again for the third week running. True, she had a good voice, but that wasn't what got her the votes. She'd slobbered all over Borg as she accepted her prize, leaving lipstick all over his face and neck. Debbie looked furious.

Halfway across the lorry park, he suddenly noticed a light on in his bathroom. Maybe Helen hadn't gone after all. Or it could be Carol back again. Please, no!

He crept up and stood outside the bathroom window. The shower was running, and he could see a figure through the steamed-up glass. A female figure. He became aroused, feeling like a peeping Tom.

Sneaking into the caravan, he heard movement in the bedroom. Suddenly the door opened and out stepped Penny, naked, except for the briefest of pink panties!

"Aargh!" she screamed, quickly pulling a towel to her body. "Donkey!"

"Aargh!" yelled Donkey in surprise, quickly averting his eyes. "Penny!"

"Oh shit! Sorry, Donkey!"

"What the hell are you doing here?"

"Sorry, Donkey!" she cried. "I've come back, but I just couldn't face seeing them yet." She wrapped the towel around her. "Hope you don't mind about the shower, I haven't had one for at least a week. And I used your razor, sorry."

Donkey laughed. "That's OK! No problem. You just gave me a fright, that's all."

"I just thought that if I could stay here tonight, then I could just ease back into normality in the morning. Is that OK with you? Please?"

"Of course it is. I understand "

"I'd better put some clothes on," she said, and went to turn away. But then she hesitated.

Donkey just couldn't help it. There was something really erogenous about a beautiful young girl with no hair. Her nakedness was surreal. He could feel his unfurling manhood reaching out for her. Their eyes met, his embarrassed, hers inviting. She dropped the towel and stepped towards him. Donkey opened his arms and she slipped in between them. As he wrapped them around her, their lips came together and his hands went to her bottom.

Then it hit him! Number 100! Not only that, but now he'd have a mother AND two daughters! What a century! The ultimate prize!

There was of course, just a tiny bit of guilt; this was Penny, after all. He'd watch her grow from a child to a woman. But she'd certainly come of age recently.

Gently lifting her up into his arms, his eyes locked onto hers as he carried her into the darkened bedroom. She said nothing as he lay her down on his bed. He could see she wanted this as much as he did.

She watched him undress. A whispered gasp as she saw what was about to come her way.

Donkey lay down naked alongside her. Their lips teased and their tongues danced as his hands began exploring the intimate curves of her body. He gasped when her cold hands gently took hold of him.

Leaning over her, his lips went to her breasts, teasing and nibbling her pert nipples. Moving slowly downwards, his tongue probed her belly button, tracing wet circles and kisses. She giggled, running her fingers through his hair.

Donkey's fingers began stroking her silk panties, gently caressing the folds of her young pussy. Slowly pulling them to one side, he felt for his prize.

What! No! It can't be! Donkey almost cried out in shock. He pulled away and sat bolt upright. He couldn't believe it. Penny's pussy was completely clean-shaven!

SATURDAY

Debbie was seething. Crashing in through the swing doors with a tray of dishes, her face was like thunder. "Big Breakfast, no sausage!" she yelled out, dumping the dishes noisily in the sink. "Bacon sandwich, brown sauce!" She stomped around the kitchen, slamming things down and muttering obscenities.

Killer kept well out of the way.

Borg had never seen her like this before. "Debbie, I am sorry," he cried for the umpteenth time that morning.

"Yeah? So am I!" she snapped back. "That little cow was all over you last night. She's only a fucking kid!"

"What could I do? She was just so happy to win." Borg looked exhausted. He'd spent most of the night trying to calm her down. He'd failed miserably.

"But you didn't have to look so fucking happy about it!" she yelled. "Bet you had a bloody stiffy!"

"Debbie, I did not! How can you be so crazy?"

"Borg, you fucking loved it!"

Even though she wanted out, there was no way she was going to stand by and watch him with that... that child. She practically had her tongue down his throat!

Why couldn't he just stay driving his bloody truck? Once a fortnight was just about right, allowing her to live a little in between his visits. But now he was the 'manager' and wanted to spend the rest of his life here. He was the only one here who didn't see that everything was going tits up. The by-pass would kill the place stone dead. The end was nigh.

Borg tried to put an arm around her. "Debbie, I love you!"

"Don't touch me!" she hissed. Grabbing the Big Breakfast, she pushed him away and barged out through the swing door.

***

Donkey quietly slipped out of the bed, trying not to disturb her. She looked so young, so vulnerable. Her scrapped head, sunburnt and with the odd scab or two, looked pretty awful in the light of day. She'd removed her studs, but the sore on her nose looked painful.

What a shock finding her here last night. Never in a million years did he ever think he would get it on with Penny. It was an even bigger shock to find a naked pussy! He'd thought he'd got his century. The only hairs on her body were under her arms. Couldn't really add those to the collection, could he?

What the hell would Charlie say? Probably, you're fired! And Carol? What would she think?

But Penny wasn't an innocent child anymore. She certainly knew what she was doing. And boy, was she good! No inhibitions at all, in fact she took the lead role most of the night.

Penny stirred, stretching her arms. The covers fell away exposing her firm little breasts as she slowly opened her eyes.

"Donkey," she whispered, reaching out for him.

"Have to go to work," he said, voice full of regret.

"No! Oh, please stay... just a little longer." She sat up, eyes pleading.

How could he resist?

***

Carol had pretended to be asleep when Tommy got up. Now she could hear him in the kitchen, cluttering about. Last night had been so bloody awful! She'd made a pact with the Devil and was now paying the price. Three times during the night he'd rolled on top of her, had sex, then rolled off again. Each time no longer than a minute or two. But to Carol the disgust and shame had lasted all night, and probably would do so for the rest of her life. Now she lay in a soggy wet patch, wondering if she could last the distance. Two or three more nights of this in return for £20,000, and a new start to life. She'd come this far, she just had to see it through. Not a lot of choice really.

She worried what would become of Debbie and Penny. They were about to lose everything. Their dad and their home. And they had absolutely no idea what was going on. And what about Donkey? Where would he go? And Borg? He'd given up his job to be at the truckstop. Charlie had no conscience at all about the lives he was destroying.

She'd thought about going back after he'd left. But Tommy had convinced her that a winding up order from the tax man would probably close the place within weeks. And, as he'd also pointed out, once Charlie sussed he'd been ripped off, he could well come back looking for her.

She didn't trust Tommy at all. She knew he must have his own plans; he wouldn't want to hang around either. It was pretty obvious he'd been ripping off Charlie over the years, and now he'd got what he wanted from her, he could double cross her as well.

"Morning, Carol." Tommy came in with a cup of tea. His dressing gown was open, exposing a new erection. "Sleep OK?" he asked, putting the cup on the bedside. Reaching under the covers, he fondled her breasts.

"Tommy, no! I..."

But he wasn't listening. His dressing gown fell to the floor and he climbed back into bed alongside her.

"Tommy, please..."

Paying no attention to her resistance, he clambered on top of her and plugged in.

***

After Donkey had left, Penny stood under the shower, just letting the hot water wash all over her. He'd said she could stay for a few days, as long as her dad didn't know. She'd have to stay out of sight. This suited her, she needed time. She needed to slow down and learn from the past few weeks. She'd come a long way, too far to ever go back to 'normal'.

And Donkey! He was everything she thought he would be. What a night. And God, everybody knew he had a big one, that's why he was called Donkey. But until you saw it, well, it was just bloody enormous! She'd thought he might hurt her, but he was so gentle and considerate, so attentive and eager to please.

She'd had a lot of lovers in recent times, and she'd enjoyed most of them. But she'd quickly learnt not to expect lasting relationships. Take it for what it was, nothing was forever.

But with Donkey, she allowed herself a dream or two.

***

"Got any Benson's, Charlie?"

Steve joined him as he sat at the back of the restaurant with his breakfast.

"Yeah, mate, just see Borg."

"Feeling any better?" Steve asked. "Looks worse, if you ask me."

"Well, I didn't," snapped Charlie.

"Sorry I asked."

Charlie got up and took his plate into the kitchen.

"Alright, boss?" said Killer, peeling spuds at the table.

Charlie sat down with him. "Thought you were going to Brighton?"

"Yeah, well, I just thought I'd stay for Band Night. Have a few jars, maybe pick up a chick or two." He dabbed at his nose; it was oozing something. "Charlie," he said, "those tables are so bloody hard. I rolled off onto the floor last night. Any chance of a proper bed?"

"Nope," said Charlie.

"Aw..."

"Look, quit the moaning, I might have a little job for you soon, you up for it?"

"Yeah, of course! What is it?"

"Shh! Tell you when you need to know," said Charlie. "But it'll be worth a few bob to you, OK?"

***

Donkey sat in his kiosk. He'd hardly served a litre all day. Not many trucks about on Saturdays, that's why the pumps closed at noon. Then he could get back to Penny.

The phone rang. It was Helen.

"Hi! How's it going? How's your dad?" he asked her.

"He's fine, should be out of hospital soon, in the next day or so."

"Good!"

"And I've told Mum I've left him."

"Oooh! How did that go?"

"Well," she said, "I obviously didn't go into any details, but I did tell her that he'd er... been unfaithful. She's upset of course, but she never really liked him anyway."

"Well done. How you feeling now?"

"Fine, I know I'll get over it, with a little help from my friends."

"Good, " said Donkey.

"I'm thinking of coming back early next week," she said. "Pick up some clothes and things from the house. I certainly don't want to spend the night there. Could I stay over at yours?"

"Of course you can. But you must call and let me know when you're coming."

"Oh," she giggled, "you'll know when I'm coming!"

Donkey knew just how lucky he was. His home had recently become a refuge for lost, horny women. No complaints there. Life was good for Donkey, though he knew it couldn't last. He'd been forced into doing a bit of thinking, recently. The truckstop was his life, his job and his home. The place was bound to close now. He just wasn't sure when, a few months, a year maybe, but not much more. Charlie kept telling him it would all be OK, but he didn't think even Charlie believed that anymore.

Charlie would be OK, no doubt about that. He'd often told him, 'Look after yourself, son, 'cos no one else ever will.' Charlie wasn't just his boss, he was his best mate. Donkey wondered how their relationship would be if he knew that he'd not only slept with his wife, but with both his daughters as well.

He could feel change in the air. There was little he could do except hang around and see how it all panned out.

***

Carol just had to get out of the flat. The thought of spending all day sat in front of the TV with Tommy made her feel suicidal. She told him she needed some 'woman' things. He sneered and suggested some racy underwear.

"Look, Tommy," she said. "You know I hate what you're doing to me."

"Yes," he said. "I do."

"I hate you touching me, and when we..." She faltered.

"And when we fuck?"

She could see he was getting off on it he had his hand in his pocket, touching himself.

***

"It's really awful," she said. "I feel sick just talking about it."

"Well, Carol, you don't have to stay you know." He had that leery smile on his face. "You're a big girl, you can leave whenever you like. I'm not exactly keeping you a prisoner, am I?"

"But if I leave...?"

"Before Monday? You leave with nothing. Simple."

Simple, thought Carol, so damn simple.

Tommy dropped her off in Shorley, said he'd be back in a couple of hours. She went straight to the nearest bar and ordered a large white wine. She found a table in a quiet corner and sat down. She needed to be strong, she had to be mercenary about it. Needs must, means to an end and all that. She struggled to convince herself. She now had no husband, no home, and she'd abandoned her children. And she was sleeping with someone she despised for monetary gain. And revenge! The next time she'd see Charlie was when they were both in hell!

"Hallo, Carol!" said a familiar voice.

Looking up, she was horrified to see John! Stood right in front of her! Glass of wine in one hand, his umbrella in the other.

"May I join you?" he asked, rather politely. He was no longer wearing his dog collar.

Carol said nothing. She couldn't, she was speechless. Her body tingled with goose bumps.

John sat down opposite her at the table and just stared. His eyes appeared to have sunk a little into his head. His hair was unkempt, and his skin was a deathly grey.

Putting down his wine glass and taking a deep breath, he slowly said, "You've destroyed me, Carol. My life is worthless! Why? Why did you do it?"

Carol gulped at her wine, trying to regain her composure. She thought about what he'd said, before giving a calm, but firm, response. "You deceived me. You lied to me; you had no intention of leaving her. It's you who's destroyed me because I believed you!" She paused before adding, "You bastard!"

"I've resigned from the church!"

"Good!"

"And Helen's left me. She wants a divorce!"

"Good!"

The wine gave her the strength to say what she felt. She was feeling quite belligerent. She wondered what it would be like to slap him. She'd never slapped anyone before. He seemed so puny, so weak. How could he have seduced her? She must have been really desperate for love.

"Does she know it was me?" she asked him.

"Good Lord no!" He seemed shocked at the very idea. "She's at her mothers. I phoned her yesterday." He paused and his eyes went down. "But all she would say was, that it's in the hands of her solicitors." His eyes picked up. "And it's all your fault!"

Carol thought he was going to cry. She leant towards him. "John?"

"Yes?" he answered.

Her voice rose up. "Why don't you just fuck off and leave me alone!"

"What? Carol!" He'd never heard her speak like that before!

"If you don't fuck off right now, I'm going to start screaming. I'll shout that you've touched me up!"

People were looking over as he quickly got to his feet, dropping his umbrella.

"You, you bitch!" he spat, as he headed for the door.

Carol remembered the last time he'd said that to her, then ordered another glass of wine.

***

Debbie stood at the back door of the kitchen having a ciggy. Borg was stocking the bar, ready for tonight. She watched a couple of German trucks pulling out. One of the drivers blew his air-horn and waved. She waved back.

"Alright, babe?" Killer had sneaked up on her. "Borg giving you a hard time?" His eyes never got past her tits.

"No. And if he was, what's it got to do with you?" She was a bit surprised by his approach.

"You should try a real man, not a weedy Swedey!"

"I'll tell him you said that."

"Go ahead. Bet he wouldn't say fuck all!"

Debbie couldn't believe that this spotty, runny-nosed, little cross-dresser, was making a play for her. Maybe if she responded, Borg might get jealous. If he caught them at it, he might even leave. No, even that wouldn't be worth it.

"I know exactly what you're after!" she said. "You're just after my knickers, ain't you? Well, you got no fucking chance! Besides, Penny's told everyone you've got a really tiny prick!" She crooked her little finger and waved it in his face, then went back inside laughing.

***

"Ladies and gentlemen, boys and girls, I give you the Dickie Didoes!"

Borg stepped away from the whistling mic as the band blasted off with a scream of electronic feedback. The kids all started to bop.

Debbie was having a sly fag behind the bar. Her dad had been acting quite strange all day, and now he was on the wrong side of the bar buying drinks for all his mates. Most unusual, that bang on his head must have been worse than they'd first thought.

"When are you going to resume normal service?" she asked him, raising her voice to be heard. "Borg thinks he owns the bloody place. He's got all these ideas about saving costs and cutting down on waste; it's doing my bloody head in."

"He's the manager now!" said Charlie. "I'm taking things easy for a change. I'm delegating all my responsibilities. Any complaints, see Borg."

"Thanks a bunch, Dad!"

"Now how about a couple of pints for Killer and me?"

"Only if you pay cash. Borg says no more credit for anyone. All tabs are closed."

Donkey came up to the bar with Barry.

"And whatever the boys want," said Charlie.

"Cheers," said Donkey. "Make mine a pint."

"Same for me, bootiful," slurred Barry.

Barry had been the first one in the bar tonight, and he'd probably be the last one to leave. He clambered up onto a bar stool. He loved Saturday nights, all those skimpy dressed teenage girls, bopping up and down.

"How ya doing, lover boy?" he shouted over to Killer. "What you wearing tonight? Stockings maybe?" He laughed loudly, slapping the bar with his hand.

"Come on, Barry," said Donkey, trying to quieten him down. "Bit of an old joke now, not funny anymore."

"Yes, it is!" he said. "I'm laughing, ain't I?" Sliding off his stool, he staggered off towards the loo, muttering, "Must have a piss."

Borg came back up to the bar. "Well, Charlie, what did you think?"

"Great!" said Charlie. "You're a natural. Pint?"

Nobody saw Killer discreetly slip an empty beer bottle into his jacket pocket. Nor did they notice him as he left the bar and went into the loo.

Barry was lent against the open cubicle door, pissing into the pan. He never saw what hit him. Falling headlong over the pan, his piss mingled on the floor with the blood flowing from his head. Killer pulled the cubicle door shut.

It wasn't until the Dickie Didoes were playing out their finale that someone complained to Debbie that the loo was blocked. Donkey went to investigate and found Barry, out cold and covered in blood.

Debbie phoned for an ambulance as Donkey helped Charlie drag Barry out into the lorry park.

When Barry came around, he couldn't remember a thing.

Donkey had seen the broken bottle and had a good idea what had happened.

"Must have slipped," Barry told the medics, as they took him away to the local A&E.

SUNDAY

Debbie and Killer moved the tables around, ready for the old dears. Killer was shameless, his eyes never left her nipples, poking proudly through her tight white T-shirt. Part of her liked to be stared at and admired; she liked guys looking her up and down. But Killer was just a letch.

She hadn't let Borg screw her last night. She couldn't remember the last time she'd said no to sex. She'd been working herself up for days, trying to find the guts to tell him it was over. One of the things stopping her was the thought of staying on here after she'd told him. It would be hell. One of them would have to go, and she couldn't see Borg leaving his new-found utopia. If she knew where her mum was, it might be easier, she could perhaps join her. She'd thought about getting another job. She'd seen adds in the Herald for live-in help. Might be an option. Maybe she could become a maid for some rich bloke with an ugly wife!

As they carried a table across the restaurant, she caught Killer ogling her tits again. Enough was enough. Stopping suddenly, she dropped her end of the table and whipped up her T-shirt! "There!" she said, giving her tits a jiggle. "Seen enough? Now you've really got something to wank about tonight!"

As Killer stared open-mouthed, he dropped the table and it landed on his foot. "Ow! Ow! Ow!" he yelled, holding his foot and dancing on one leg.

"That'll be two swellings you've got now then!" said Debbie, pulling her T-shirt back down. "Catch you again and I'll poke your fucking eyes out!"

***

Carol's head was throbbing. She'd woken to find herself alone. The flat was empty, Tommy had gone out.

When he'd picked her up in town yesterday, she was already half-cut. She liked the way the wine numbed her brain, stopped her thinking too much. She'd carried on drinking when they got back. She had very little recollection of last night. She thanked God for small mercies. Her thighs were sticky and her nipples sore, so she knew Tommy hadn't been too pissed. She tried not to think of what he'd been up to.

Carol needed a shower, to try and wash away her sins. Looking for one of her slippers, she knelt down and looked under the bed. There, pushed right underneath, was a suitcase. Sliding it out, she put it on the bed and opened it up. Inside, neatly packed, was a set of clothes, shoes and a wash bag. In a side pocket she found brochures for a Caribbean cruise and two passports. One was Tommy's, the other had his photo, but was in the name of Benjamin Black.

So, Tommy was ready to run as well! She guessed he didn't want to be around either when Charlie came back looking for his money. Pushing the case back under the bed, she went for her shower.

Carol soaked under the lukewarm flow for a while, trying to wash Tommy from her soul. She had this awful feeling that once Tommy had finished with her, he'd rip her off as well. No honour among thieves, as Charlie used to say.

She heard Tommy coming back into the flat, then saw the shadow under the bathroom door. Be strong, she told herself, be strong!

***

Amongst the noise and the mayhem, Debbie and Killer served up Sunday lunch. Borg had prepared twenty-four roast beef and Yorkshire pudding dinners, and the oldies loved it.

Doris didn't like Morris, so she swore at him. Morris didn't like peas, so he threw his at Leonard. Leonard just stared at Debbie as he fondled himself. The nurses fought to keep control over their charges.

Killer was a bit shocked by the old folk's behaviour.

"It's all right, it's normal," said Debbie. "Just don't mention the war."

Killer had his eye on Linda, one of the nurses. Blonde, with huge knockers. Yes please, he thought. She saw him staring and came over, side-stepping the peas.

"Hi, is Donkey about?" she asked.

"No," he said, "But I am. My name's Killer." He offered out his hand.

She picked some plates up from the table and gave them to him. "Is he likely to be about?"

"No," said Killer, taking the plates. "It's his day off. Anything I can do?"

"No," she said, turning away. "Glenda! Stop it! Now!" She went off to stop Glenda from undressing.

"Do they like it?" Borg asked Killer, as he dumped the plates into the sink.

"Hard to tell. They all look like psychos to me," he said. "One of the old blokes keeps touching my arse!"

"That's Harold," said Borg.

***

Donkey had cooked Sunday lunch.

"That was wonderful!" said Penny, finishing off the last of the vegetable curry.

"I know," said Donkey. "I'm well-known around here for my curries."

They'd spent most of the morning lying in bed, just talking. She'd told him all about her adventures. About Killer, and what an arsehole he'd turned out to be, and how Mole and the others had really turned her life around. In the space of just a few weeks her life had changed so dramatically. Now she saw the world through very different eyes.

Donkey cleared away the dishes and opened another bottle of wine. Squeezing her hand gently, he raised his glass. "To the future, and whatever it may bring!"

"Whatever!" said Penny, raising hers.

"So," he asked her, "how would you like the future to unfold?"

She thought for a while. "I'd just like everybody to be happy," she sighed.

"Bah humbug!" said Donkey, pulling a face. "That's a cop out. Everybody would like everybody to be happy. So that's a given."

She pondered awhile. "Well, how about... how about I meet a tall dark handsome prince who takes me off to live in his castle."

"Now, that's more realistic," he said, laughing.

"Yeah? Oh, and he'd have to have a big willy!" she said, bursting into a fit of giggles.

Monday

Charlie lay in his bed listening to the sounds of the restaurant, drifting up from below. The TV, the banter, Debbie yelling at Borg. He was glad they were managing without him. Today was D-day! Departure day. Just a few things to sort, then he'd be away.

He ran through it all again, like he had all night long. Check Borg's money was in, then a meeting with Manny to seal the deal. Everything should be done and dusted by close of business at the bank today. Then a quick visit to Tommy, to pick up all the paperwork needed to move his funds anywhere in the world. The world that was now his oyster!

He showered, washing his aching body, before packing his suitcase. He was taking his white suit. Once he'd settled down, he'd drop a few pounds, fit him better then. He'd tone up in the sun, beside the pool.

Twenty years of his life gone. His mind drifted back to the day Charlie's Place opened. The champagne, the fireworks, the culmination of all his dreams. He'd made a good living out of it, but now it was over. Time to move on, while he still could. The by-pass, the tax man, Billy, they'd all come together to destroy him. And Carol had left him! He still couldn't believe she hadn't come back.

But none of that mattered any more, did it? He was going to slip out the back door unnoticed. He hated goodbyes. What could he say? He wondered how long it would be before they realised he'd gone. He laughed; he really didn't give a shit. Fuck them all!

He began humming, 'Regrets, I've had a lot, but then again, too many to mention'.

The stress was making him go gaga. He was getting out just in time.

***

Carol had lain awake for most of the night. Tommy's snoring had refused her the escape of sleep.

Please Lord, let today be the day this all ends, she prayed. She'd spent the last few days trying to be positive. If she gave in now, all this... this suffering would have been in vain. She just knew she would be going to Hell. A lifetime of Godliness ruined. How would the kids feel if they knew what she was doing?

But the feelings of guilt were due to her methods, not her aims. Charlie was running out on them all. Did he care about her? Or the kids? No, he was just saving his own skin. He would be sunning himself in some foreign land while his family would be destitute. Would he even think about them at all? Well, Charlie Wheeler, you've got a big shock coming!

Tommy's snoring spluttered to a halt. She felt his arm wrap around her.

"Morning, babe," he whispered.

His hand tried to cup her breast. She pushed it away.

"Today could be our last day together," he said, shoving his hand back.

"Tell me again what happens," she said, again removing it.

Tommy sat up, rubbing his face. He cleared his throat with a growl. She thought he was going to spit.

"When the bank confirms all the funds are in Charlie's account, probably this afternoon, I'll give him all the paperwork necessary to transfer his account to any bank he so chooses.

"And?"

"Charlie leaves town, pronto!"

"And then?"

"I'll give you a cheque, signed by Charlie, for the exact amount in his account!"

"Then I leave town, pronto!"

"You don't have to leave too quickly," he said, his hand running over her thighs. "Charlie's paperwork is such that it will take four or five days for any new account to be opened. By which time, you'll have emptied his account, right?"

His hand forced its way to its objective. The ringing bedside phone saved Carol.

"Charlie!" said Tommy, his face lighting up. "How are you?"

As he spoke with Charlie, he grabbed Carol's hand and tried to place it on his erection. She pulled away, quickly getting out of bed.

"Yes, Charlie, it couldn't be going any better."

He leered after her as she went into the bathroom. Locking the door behind her, she listened as he arranged an afternoon appointment. When he'd finished the call, she saw the shadow under the bathroom door.

***

Penny's gentle kiss on his cheek woke him. Slowly opening his eyes, he saw her standing by the bed. Wearing one of his T-shirts, she had tea and toast on a tray.

"Morning," she said, putting the tray down.

Donkey sat up as she climbed in beside him.

"Last night was just wonderful," she said, leaning into him.

"Mmm, I know, I was there," he replied, kissing her on the top of her head.

They quietly ate their toast. He knew things needed to be said, but it wasn't easy.

"So," he started, "when are you...?" He faltered.

"Going back to the workhouse?"

Donkey laughed. "But you can cope with that now."

"No, I can't, Donkey. I just..." She stopped herself and stuffed a piece of toast in her mouth.

"You're not the Penny that left, remember that."

He knew it would be hard for her, after all she'd been through. But she just had to go. He felt guilty about the pleasures he'd enjoyed with her. Charlie would go apeshit if he knew she was there. Besides, Helen would be back soon.

"I know I can't stay," she said. "I know I've got to go back. But I also know that it's not forever. I will move on, and sooner rather than later."

The confidence in her voice helped ease Donkey's conscience. "Of course you will, Penny. In times to come you'll see all this as a beginning."

"Thank you, Donkey," she said, wrapping her arms around him and laying her head on his chest.

"So when...?"

"One more day? Please?" she pleaded. "I'll return to my workstation tomorrow. That OK with you? Please?"

"OK," said Donkey. "OK, one more day it is then."

She slipped her hand down under the covers. "And one more night!"

"Sorry, got to get to work or Charlie's gonna come looking for me." Moving her hand away he slipped from the bed. He really was sorry, but he was also quite relieved she'd agreed to go.

***

"It'll be in your account by close of business today," said Manny, shaking his hand.

"Great!" said Charlie. "Good to do business with you, Manny. You're a gentleman."

"Thank you. I hope this deal will help you overcome any er, cash flow problems you may have." Manny smiled as he gathered up all the paperwork.

"Oh, it will certainly help, no doubt about that. I hope we can maybe do some more business together, in the future."

"Yes, who knows?" said Manny, glancing at the clock on the wall.

The scepticism in his voice made Charlie wonder just how much Tommy had told him.

Leaving Manny's office, he felt good, bloody good. Close of business today. Yes! And Borg's money transfer would already be in; things were really coming together.

Popping into the travel agents, he checked out the ferry times. While he was there, he picked up a few brochures on Cyprus. He'd leave them around his office and bedroom, to lay a false trail. Just the one thing left to take care of. He couldn't be relying on Tommy to cover his back.

***

The phone had stopped ringing by the time Donkey got back to the kiosk. Damn! Maybe it was Helen. He'd been busy at the pumps all morning. All the drivers could talk about was the bloody by-pass. Everyone thought that the truckstop would now close; just a matter of time, they reckoned. Charlie was in denial, kept saying everything would be OK. Donkey had no plans, so perhaps he was also in denial. This place was his life. His prospects were dire. He had no savings, had never seen the need. He could see himself with just a backpack and a sleeping bag, hitching a lift out with the last truck to leave.

A truck pulled in. It was Barry.

"Hiya, Donkey," he called, getting down from the cab. A filthy bandage clung to his head. "Fill her up, will you?"

"Hallo, mate, how's your head?" asked Donkey, setting up the pump.

"Still sore and I've got quite a bump," he replied. "They had to put twelve stitches in. Can't remember too much about it though."

"Probably just as well," said Donkey.

"Yeah, s'pose you're right."

"In tonight?"

"Of course. It's Kitty, ain't it? I love Mondays!" he said, thrusting his hips obscenely.

Donkey finished off and got him to sign for his fuel.

"You seen Penny lately?" Barry asked. "Did she go off with the rest of them bloody hippies?"

"Dunno. They all split up I think, went their different ways."

"That tosser Killer's still here, working in the bloody kitchen too! How unhygienic is that?"

"Well, Borg's running the show now, Charlie's taking a rest."

"So he should, he ain't seemed his old self since his accident. I think the stress must be getting to him. He was buying everybody drinks Saturday night!"

"Yeah, that was weird. What do you think 'bout the truckstop? Think we'll close?"

"Talk in the village is that he's going bust. They seem quite pleased about it too!"

***

"Look mate," said Killer, pausing from the washing up, "you've just got to stop begging forgiveness. You ain't done nothing wrong!"

He'd spent the last few days keeping his head down, but enough was enough. Debbie had been slagging off Borg all weekend. So he'd kissed Emma! So fucking what? Debbie was a bitch and she needed to be told.

"But I love her!" Borg said. "I want to spend the rest of my life with her."

"You're crazy," said Killer. "You gotta show her who's the boss and..." He stopped short as Debbie came rushing into the kitchen.

"Killer! Mop! Terry's knocked his tea over! Quick!" she yelled.

"Yes, Debbie," said Killer, being as quick as he could.

"Two casseroles, one spotted dick and one double egg sarnie."

Debbie sat down at the table; she was exhausted. Her dad hadn't shown up at breakfast and then he'd gone out just before lunch. She was run off her feet. And she'd still be expected to run the bar tonight. Borg sat down beside her and put an arm around her. She pushed him away. She couldn't go on like this for much longer.

***

Tommy had returned from the bank an hour ago.

"All systems go!" he said. Charlie's number one account now held £20,000! "This time tomorrow," he said, "it will all be yours!"

"Wow!" said Carol. "That's an awful lot of money."

"And you deserve it, Carol, for all you've had to put up with," said Tommy, sympathetically.

Yes, I do, thought Carol. Especially the last few days.

Now they were waiting for Charlie to show, to collect his paperwork.

Carol watched as Tommy straightened his tie the mirror. He ran his hands through his greasy hair and brushed some dandruff off his shoulders. He disgusted her.

"He'll be here shortly," he said, checking his watch. "Stay away from the windows." He sprayed himself with deodorant. "Here we go." Picking up his briefcase he went downstairs to the office.

Oh, to be a fly on the wall, she thought. Please Lord, make it all happen.

A car pulled in and, peering from behind the curtains, she watched as Charlie parked the Merc and walked into the office below. He looked even worse. His face was swollen in various shades of yellow and blue, and he hobbled as if in pain. Carol felt no sympathy at all.

She heard them greeting each other like old mates. Rushing into the kitchen she knelt down on the floor, ear as close to the floorboards as possible. The voices rose up, muffled and not very clear. Tommy had put the fan heater on; that didn't help.

***

"So, Charlie, coffee? Glass of wine? Or maybe some Champagne?"

"Let's just get on with it, shall we, Tommy? I've got a lot on today."

"Yes? So, is today the big day?"

"Of course not! And if it was..."

"You wouldn't be telling me!"

"Exactly!" said Charlie. "So, all done then?"

"All done. You now have only the one active bank account. But there is something..."

"What? What's wrong? I thought you said..." Charlie tensed up.

"There's over seventy-five grand in there!" Tommy lent back in his seat and looked Charlie straight in the eye. "A few days ago, it was less than twenty-five. Is there something you haven't told me, Charlie? Where did all that lot come from?"

"You mean you don't know?" Charlie laughed. "But I thought you knew everything?"

"Obviously not." He paused. "And?"

"And mind your own business. Now let's get on." Charlie put his hand out.

Opening his briefcase, Tommy passed over all the relevant paperwork. "You just sign where I've marked it," he said. "There, there and there."

Charlie did as he was instructed.

"And now?"

"And now you just write a cheque and present it with the paperwork to any bank worldwide, and after a few days to clear, you'll have access to your funds." He sat back and smiled.

"Great! Well done!" said Charlie. His swollen face forcing a smile.

"Oh, and by the way," said Tommy, "you have an appointment with your friends from the Inland Revenue on Friday morning, ten thirty."

"No problem."

"So, gone by then, eh?"

"Ha, ha. OK! OK! I'll tell you," laughed Charlie. "After all, you are one of my oldest mates. Yes, I'm off in the morning, to Cyprus. Over at Dover, then I'm going to drive down to Italy and catch a ferry. Don't expect a postcard!"

"Great!" said Tommy.

"Yeah, it is, isn't it!" said Charlie. "So, I was going to ask you, fancy a few beers and a meal tonight? I feel we should do something. You know, for old time's sake. We've known each other for a life-time. It's unlikely we're ever going to meet up again, so let's have a last drink together."

Tommy was surprised and flattered. But then, who else could he have a farewell drink with, when nobody else knew he was going?

"Well, thank you, Charlie, that's very good of you, I'd be delighted." He lent across the table and shook hands with his old friend.

"OK then, say eight-thirty at the Station Arms, then we can have a drink or two before nipping over to the Chinky. Or Indian, if you'd prefer. I'm paying, it's on me."

"No, Chinese would be fine. I've had two Indians already this week."

"Lucky boy!" said Charlie, getting up to go. He slipped the paperwork into his jacket pocket. "Right then, Tommy, see you tonight. Looking forward to chatting about the old days."

"Me too," said Tommy, as they shook hands again at the door.

Tommy couldn't help the self-satisfied, smug smile that crept across his face. Not only was he shafting Charlie's wife, he was shafting him too! And the fool was even going to buy him dinner!

***

Carol heard him coming back up the stairs. She hadn't been able to hear much at all, just a lot of laughter. But they'd both seemed pretty happy when they were saying their goodbyes. She was sat back down on the sofa when Tommy came in.

"What an idiot!" spat Tommy, as he came in through the door. "What a complete fucking idiot!"

"What?" she said, puzzled. "What's he done now?"

"His bloody passport was out of date! I can't finish off the paperwork until I have a photo copy of his bloody passport!"

"Oh!" she said, trying to hide her suspicions. "So, what happens now?"

"He's got to drive to the passport office in Newport tomorrow and renew it."

"Can't he get one at the post office?"

He looked at her and shook his head. "Takes weeks. If he applies in person, it just takes a few hours."

"So when..."

"He should be back before the bank closes tomorrow. Then I can complete, and everyone gets their dues."

She knew he was lying. They were laughing and joking, not cursing and swearing. But she didn't want him to know that she doubted him.

"Damn fool!" she said. "What else did he have to say?"

He sat down beside her. "He's off to Cyprus, tomorrow night. Already booked his ferry ticket." He moved closer, that filthy smile spreading across his face. "That means just one more night, my sexy lover!" His arm slipped around her waist.

Is that why he's lying? she thought, pulling away. Just for one more night?

***

"Dad! Where the hell have you been? I've been working my tits off none stop since five this morning! I just can't go on!"

Debbie was stocking up the bar when Charlie finally got back to the truckstop.

"Don't start! I've got a headache. If you must know, I've been to the doctors. He thinks I've broken my ribs. I've got to take it easy. No lifting, no stress."

Lying came easy to Charlie, after all, he'd done it his whole life.

"Oh, Dad, I'm sorry." She went to give him a hug.

"Ouch! Mind! They're very tender."

"Sorry!" She moved away from him. "But look, I need a break, or some help at the very least. Have you heard from that lazy bitch Penny? Is she ever coming back or what?"

"I don't know. She's deserted us, Debs. It's just you and me against the world now. I'll get Donkey to give you a hand in the bar tonight. I've got to sit down. I'll be in the office if anyone needs me. Love a cuppa and bacon sarnie! Ain't eaten all day," he said, slowly shuffling out of the kitchen.

***

Killer mopped the floor around the stage. Debbie was driving him crazy. Do this! Do that! Still, he had the show to look forward to tonight. Kitty wasn't that bad, bit old and saggy maybe, but he'd give her one. He'd seen her in the lorry park after the show, maybe he'd join the queue. He could always close his eyes and imagine it was Debbie.

"Oi! When you've finished your daydreaming," called Debbie from the bar, "Charlie wants to see you. He's in the office."

Killer lay down his mop and ambled out, trying his best not to stare.

"Killer!"

"Charlie!"

"How's it going, son?"

"Not too bad, but she's a slave driver, that Debbie. Thought Borg was in charge?"

"He is. She's just a bit stressed that's all. Losing her mother and all."

"She's heading for a nervous breakdown if you ask me."

"Well, I didn't," snapped Charlie. "Look, I want you to come and see me, 'bout eight o'clock tonight, OK? Got a little job for you."

"Yeah? Of course, Charlie. What is it?"

"Eight o'clock," said Charlie. "I'll tell you then."

***

"The phone rang a couple of times today," said Penny, as Donkey came in through the door. "I didn't answer in case it was one of your lovers." She laughed out loud.

"Yeah, best not to," said Donkey. "Wouldn't want you fighting over me."

She threw her arms around him. "They'll have to join the queue, tonight is mine. Why don't we just have a shower and retire to bed? We can eat later."

"Sorry, Penny," he said. "But Charlie's asked me to work in the bar tonight. Debbie's struggling, she's been on since breakfast."

"Ah, poor little Debs! My heart bleeds for her." She pulled away from him in a huff.

"Now, now, she is your sister."

"She's a bitch who's made my life hell since the day I was born!"

"Don't beat about the bush..."

"It's not funny, Donkey. Here I was feeling happy and confident and..."

"I'm sorry," he said, stepping back from her. "But whatever may happen, now or in the future, for the next period of time in your life, you're going to have to work and live with her. And you have to decide whether that's going to be easy or bloody difficult."

"Oh, well, that's all right then, I'll just forget all the shit I've lived through then, shall I?"

"Yes, if you're going to move on, you're going to have to." He smiled at her, then added, "There endeth the lesson for today."

"I know you're right," she said. "You always are. But tonight, you'll be with her behind the bar and I'll be here on my lonesome."

"You're not jealous, are you? You don't think I'd...?"

"She would!" she cried. "If you gave her half the bloody chance, she would!"

***

"Ladies and gentlemen, truck drivers and everyone else! Please fill up you glasses and take to your seats. My name is Borg and tonight's show starts in ten minutes!"

Borg stepped down from the stage to the jeers and whistles of the rowdy truckers. Full house tonight, he'd never seen the place so busy. Good job Donkey was giving a hand. His new role as partner in the truckstop was a dream come true. And in his new suit he looked every bit the part. He was feeling good.

"Where's Charlie?" Donkey asked Debbie, as they rushed around the bar. It was hectic. The place was throbbing.

"Been in the office most of the day," she said, serving two drivers at a time. She'd only just closed up the restaurant, but there was no time for a break.

"Looked pretty rough when I saw him," said Barry. The filthy bandage on his head looked disgusting.

"Doctor says his broken his ribs," added Debbie. "Must be in agony."

Borg pushed his way back to the bar. "Well, how was I?"

"You only told 'em to fill up and sit down," said Debbie. "Even Killer could have done that!"

"Cheers!" said Killer, sat at the far end of the bar. "I thought you did all right, Borg. You're a natural."

"Thank you, Killer. Can I get you a beer?"

"That worked well, didn't it, Killer?" said Debbie.

"No thanks, Borg," Killer replied, staring down Debbie. "I've got to go and see Charlie. Maybe later."

"Better take Kitty her medicine," said Debbie, passing Borg a Southern Comfort. "She needs this to convince herself she's beautiful."

"Miaow!" said Barry.

***

There was a knock on the dressing room door.

"Come!" called Kitty, pausing from her make-up routine.

"Miss La Sadé," said Borg, coming into the ladies' loo. "Southern Comfort?" Placing the glass down, he picked up the two empties.

"Thank you, Borg. My, you're looking good tonight. New suit?"

"Yes. Do you like it? Not too, er, flash? Is that what you say?"

"Yes, that's what we say, and it isn't. You look gorgeous!" Her hand ran over his tight buttocks.

He moved away. "Please. If Debbie saw you..."

"She's just an amateur, honey. Ever had an older woman? No, I can still see the innocence in your eyes." Standing up in just her bra and panties, she put her hand on his shoulder. "Why don't you come and see me in the interval? If you're taking over from Charlie, you've got to go the whole hog."

As she tried to pin him to the door, he made his excuses and left. Did she normally drink so much before the show, he wondered?

***

"I'm so sorry, my love," said Tommy, brushing his hair in the mirror. "Unexpected business. Old client. There's a pizza in the fridge, do help yourself. I should be back by eleven, then we can carry on with the party." He lent over her, as she sat on the sofa. "Last night tonight, so let's make it special, eh? There's a bottle of bubbly in the fridge, to celebrate the successful conclusion of our little plan."

She moved her face away as his breath hit her nose.

"And I've got a little surprise for you later," he said. "You're going to love it."

She sat listening to his footsteps going down the stairs. She could so easily have cried. One more dreadful night; she had to be strong. She wondered where he was off to. Maybe he was… No! Please God, no! She rushed into the bedroom and reached under the bed for the suitcase. Relief. It was still there, thank God! At least she knew he would be coming back. He hadn't done a runner. Yet.

This time the case was locked, but he'd left his office keys in the bedroom draw, and she soon found one to fit the case. She opened it up on the bed. And there on top was an Ann Summer's carrier bag. She tipped out the contents, and immediately felt sick to her stomach. A pair of handcuffs! A blindfold and a rubber gag! And, oh dear God, a black rubber dildo that would put Donkey to shame! A wave of fear and disgust flashed through her. Taking deep breaths, she managed to suppress her rising stomach. So, this was his little surprise.

It had been different with John; he was the one tied up. Even though she hated herself for it now, at least she'd been in control. If Tommy managed to get those cuffs on her, there was no telling what he might do. She shuddered at the thought.

His two passports were still in the side pocket. But in with them was an airline ticket for a flight to Paris in the name of Benjamin Black. From Gatwick, two o'clock tomorrow afternoon.

The bastard! So, after a night of sordid sexual assault, he was going to run out on her. How could he meet up with Charlie tomorrow afternoon if he was on the plane to Paris? He was going to leave her sitting here. The bloody bastard!

She'd always known deep down it wasn't going to work out. She never was going to get her hands on any of Charlie's money. Why would Tommy want to share it with her? He'd already got what he wanted.

Carol rummaged down through his clothes, and at the bottom of the suitcase found a large sealed brown envelope. Ripping it open she emptied it out on the bed. And there amongst all the legal documents was a cheque for £75,800. It was made out to bearer and signed by Charlie. Her heart raced. Tommy had told her £20,000!

God! That was an awful lot of money. Where on earth had Charlie got all that from? Was that really his signature? It didn't really matter, did it? If she couldn't tell the difference, how could anyone else?

Her mind was spinning. She had to act fast. Quickly packing up her own suitcase, she began running through her options. She just had to deposit the cheque in her own account, then move away. Change her name and start all over. With seventy-five grand in the bank!

Woo! Slow down! She felt dizzy. Sitting down on the bed, she tried to pull herself together. Was she going to run, just like Charlie was doing? Desert the girls, just like Charlie was doing?

Maybe, she thought, if Charlie's off tomorrow, she could meet up with the girls after he'd gone, tell them just what had been going on. Plan a future together, away from Charlie and his bloody truckstop.

But first she had to get away from here. Maybe Donkey could put her up. He also needed to know what Charlie's up to. She knew Helen wasn't there; John had told her she was at her mother's.

She rang Donkey's phone. No answer, maybe he was working. She'd just have to go over. She had to be gone before Tommy got back.

***

Penny stepped naked out of the shower and into the bedroom. Donkey's phone was ringing again. Maybe he was trying to call her. She was tempted to answer, but what if it was her dad? That would be pretty awkward. More than likely a lover, then she could tell them he was busy, call back tomorrow. She'd laughed, but deep down...

She was out of knickers. Several pairs were soaking in the bathroom sink. Donkey wouldn't mind if I slipped on a pair of his boxer shorts, she thought, in fact he'd probably love it. Especially if that was all she was wearing.

Tonight was going to be their last night, tomorrow she'd be back in the asylum. She wanted it to be special.

The first draw she tried was full of T-shirts. She selected a bright red one and slipped it on. It was big enough to be a mini-dress. The next drawer was his underpants drawer. She dug deep, she wanted smaller ones, more hot pant than Y-front.

At the back of the draw she felt a box. Pulling it forward she saw it was a beautiful, blue velvet jewellery box. Taking it out, she placed it on the bed and slowly opened it.

***

Carol shut the front door behind her and took a deep breath of fresh air. It helped slow her racing heart. She walked as far as the post office before putting her suitcase down. Taking an envelope from her handbag she checked the address, 'Shorley Police Station', before pushing it into the post box.

There was no way Tommy could do a runner now, not without his passports and plane ticket. Let's see him lie his way out of that one to the police. Bastard!

Carol would never forgive Tommy for what he'd put her through. Ever. But her revenge would go a long way to healing the wounds. Just as it had with John. And the cheque would also help. Charlie's money, stolen by Tommy, was now hers.

She tried calling Donkey again from the phone box, but there was still no answer; he must be working the bar. She'd just have to turn up and hope for the best. She'd taken the champagne from the fridge; maybe Donkey would help her drink it.

Walking up through the village, she thought she saw Killer on the other side of the road. But he had his hood up and the light was fading, so she couldn't be sure. She carried on walking towards the truckstop.

***

"Ladies and gentlemen, boys and girls. My name is Borg and I am delighted to introduce you to the one and the only Miss Kitty Le Sadé!"

As Borg jumped down from the stage, Kitty bounded out from behind the curtains to the amplified strains of Abba's 'Mama Mia'. Clad only in fishnet stockings, G-string and a tiny waist coat, it wasn't long before she was totally naked. The boys loved it. Barry whistled and grunted from the front row.

Some of the drivers had bought a few cases of Stella Artois from Borg, and had now begun working their way through them. Charlie only sold them as takeaways, he knew only too well what would happen if they got stuck into them in the bar.

***

DC Phillips and DC Roberts hadn't quite given up on Charlie Wheeler. They thought he knew a lot more than he was willing to admit about Councillor Morrison's car. Their boss was a personal friend of the councillor, or ex-councillor as he now was, and he wanted results. They had to put pressure on Wheeler. So tonight, they were paying him a little visit, just to let him know that they hadn't forgotten him. They parked out the front, then stood peering in through the windows.

Inside the place was rocking. Jeering and whistling punters surrounded a small stage on which a naked woman was strutting her stuff.

"Corr!" said Phillips. "Bit rough, eh?"

They watched as the stripper thrust her crutch into a drinker's face.

"Lucky bastard!" said Roberts. "Ere, hang on a minute! Ain't that Morrison's daughter-in-law?"

"Blimey, you're right!" said Phillips. "At least, that's what he told us!"

They watched on as a drunk with a bandaged head clambered up on stage and began dancing with the stripper, removing his shirt and waving it above his head. Other punters stood up, cheering and egging him on. A guy in a suit, the compere, pulled the drunk off the stage. The audience booed and threw empty beer cans and fag packets.

"I think this is getting out of hand," said Roberts. "Wheeler could well lose his licence over this. What do you think?"

The woman was now dancing stark naked amongst the tables. Men were openly grabbing at all her wobbly parts.

"I think you're right," said Phillips. "This is a disorderly house if ever I saw one! We'd better call for back up, this could get nasty!"

***

Tommy looked again at his watch, nine o'clock. What the hell was keeping Charlie? Why didn't he answer his bloody phone? Standing at the bar, he began to feel that something wasn't quite right. As soon as he heard the fire engines, he knew!

"No! Please, no!" he cried as it hit him. "The fucking bastard!"

"You OK, sir?" asked the barman.

"No, I bloody ain't!" yelled Tommy.

Rushing from the bar, he watched as the fire engines tore past. Leaping into his car he set off after them. He already knew where they were going.

"Charlie Wheeler, I hope you rot in fucking hell!"

***

Charlie smiled as he heard the fire engines tearing past the truckstop. The perfect day, everything was falling into place.

He was stood out the back, alongside his Merc, suitcase in his hand. Watching in through a window, he could see Borg struggling with Barry, trying to get him to put his clothes back on. Kitty had left the stage, but Barry, with everyone's encouragement, had climbed back up on stage and carried on. Charlie laughed, then looked over at Donkey and Debbie working the bar. It certainly looked busy tonight.

"Goodbye, losers," he sneered. "And good fucking riddance!" Opening the Mercedes' boot, he threw the suitcase in.

"Going away, Charlie?"

The voice behind him chilled his very soul. The blood drained from his body as he slowly turned to find Billy and three of his goons standing there grinning.

"No! I... I..." he stuttered.

"Liar! Liar!" yelled Billy, coming straight at him. Standing on tiptoe, he thrust his face right into Charlie's. "Tell me my money's in the post, Charlie! Go on! Tell me!" His face reddened, the muscles in his neck were pulsating. He was dribbling.

"No... no, it's not. I..."

"No? No?" Billy screamed, poking his finger into Charlie's chest. "Didn't we have a little agreement?" His spittle sprayed Charlie's face.

"Yes, yes..." Charlie began to weep. His whole body was numb with fear. His knees were weak and he felt quite faint.

"That's right! Yes, we did! You owe me money! You pay me money! Remember?"

Charlie lowered his head with a sigh. He'd been so close. If only he'd left ten minutes ago.

"But Billy... It wasn't me!" he pleaded desperately. "Honest! On my kids' lives!"

"Get in the boot, Charlie!" barked Billy.

"What?"

"You fucking heard! Get in the fucking boot!" His eyes bulged right out.

"But Billy, come on! We can work this out! I can get you the cash tomorrow! Honest!"

"No you can't," he sneered. "And I'll tell you why, shall I? Shall I tell you why? 'Cos you won't fucking be around tomorrow!"

Laughing out loud like the psycho he was, he nodded to his goons. They stepped forward, and after a short struggle, bundled a screaming Charlie into the boot of the Mercedes. When they tried to close it, his fingers got in the way. Crying out in pain, Charlie pulled them back in and the boot slammed shut.

Charlie's muffled screams faded as Billy drove the Mercedes out of the lorry park.

***

Carol arrived at the truckstop. It had been a long walk, but it had given her the time to think. She just wanted to stay over for a few days with Donkey. Then, when she was sure that Charlie had gone, she'd be able to see Debbie and Penny again, tell them the truth about Charlie. It was probably too late to save the truckstop, but then, why on earth would she want to do that? Maybe, with Charlie's money, she and the girls could start up somewhere else, a bed and breakfast maybe.

She couldn't really think straight; her mind was scrambled with all the recent events. She felt dirty; she could smell Tommy on her clothes and in her hair. She just needed time and a few friendly faces.

Coming up through the lorry park, she stayed in the shadows. She heard the music and the noise from the bar; it sounded like there was a party going on. Donkey will be working, she thought, I hope he's not too surprised when he finds me here.

Opening the caravan door, she stepped up inside.

"Oh my God!" said Penny, jumping up from the sofa.

"Penny!" said Carol. "What on earth are you doing in here?"

"No, Mum," said Penny, pointing at a blue velvet box on the table, "I'm asking you, what on earth are you doing in there?"

***

Donkey had never seen the place like this before. It was heaving. Kitty had really wound the boys up and they were gagging for the late show. Barry, sat topless at the bar, had nearly caused a riot earlier, stripping on stage. It wouldn't have happened if Charlie was here. So, where the hell was he? He hadn't been around since the bar opened.

"Pint please, Donkey," said Killer, squeezing up to the bar. "What's happening? Whose party is it?"

"Borg's first night in charge," shouted Donkey, above the noise. "Some of the boys bought cases of booze off him, and they've opened them up. If Charlie sees them, he'll go bloody mad. Nothing I can do now; they're all pissed out of their tiny minds!"

Debbie struggled through to the bar with a tray of empty glasses. "Donkey, this is getting out of hand!" she yelled. "Anybody seen Dad?"

***

Helen drove into the truckstop. She'd been trying to phone Donkey all day, he just wasn't picking up. She was longing to see him again. Every night that she'd been away, she had rocked herself to sleep with her memories. She'd picked up a couple of bottles of wine, tonight was going to be bliss.

***

"Ladies, gentlemen and truckers!" yelled Borg, struggling to be heard over the noise.

The boys whistled and cheered. Someone threw a crushed can at him. He ducked it and carried on.

"Introducing the sexy, the beautiful, the one, the only... Miss Kitty Le Sadé!"

The Troggs classic hit 'Wild Thing' belted out of the speakers as Kitty stormed the stage cracking a bull whip. The crowd went wild as she strutted around the stage in leather hot pants and sequinned bra.

"Too loud!" shouted Debbie, as glasses in the bar rattled on the shelves.

"He can't hear you!" yelled back Donkey.

Next thing they knew, Barry was up on stage again.

"...you make my thing swing!" he yelled, in time with the chorus, thrusting his hips wildly at Kitty.

The truckers jeered and whistled. They stood clapping, urging him on.

Kitty cracked the whip a couple of times over Barry's head before wrapping it tightly around his neck and forcing him down onto his knees. The boys just loved it!

Pulling his face into her crutch, Kitty held it there, stomping to the music, as the crowd went mad. Drivers at the back stood on chairs to get a better view.

Pushing Barry away, Kitty removed her bra and, after waving it around her head a few times, threw it to her fans. Chairs flew over as they fought for the prize. The hot pants soon followed leaving her as naked as the day she was born.

The boys were stamping their feet and calling out for more.

Barry, playing to the crowd, began removing his trousers, falling over as he tried to pull them over his boots. Then, clad only in his shabby grey Y-fronts and odd socks, he danced around the stage playing air guitar. Kitty, cracking the whip, ordered him down on all fours, and began riding him around the stage, waving her whip in the air. The music stopped suddenly, but the show just carried on.

When Kitty climbed off Barry and yanked down his Y-fronts, Borg had seen enough. Leaping up onto the stage he tried to prise them apart. "Stop! This cannot go on!" he shouted, pulling Kitty away from Barry. "The show is over!"

The boos rang out and beer cans began to fly.

Donkey pulled the shutters down on the bar, shouting to Killer, "Where the fuck is Charlie?"

Debbie tried to calm them all down. "Come on, boys," she pleaded. "Fucking cool it! Calm down!" Pushing her way past the drivers, she squeezed through to the front of the stage. "Party's over!" she yelled. "We're closing! Everybody out!"

"Get your tits out!" somebody shouted. Then a chorus rose up, 'Debbie get your tits out! Debbie get your tits out!' Over and over again.

Killer stood up on his bar stool and joined in with them, chanting and clapping.

Barry was now naked, except for his socks, and as Borg struggled to pull him from the stage, Kitty came up behind him and started tugging at his trousers. With a roar from the crowd, she yanked them clean down to his ankles. When Borg fell to the floor, trying to pull them back up again, Kitty quickly sat astride him, waving the bull whip in the air. The boys were screaming out, urging her on.

"Borg! Borg!" yelled Debbie, from the front of the stage. "Stop it! What the fuck are you doing?"

Borg was no longer resisting. She could swear he even had a smile on his face as Kitty leant forward, rubbing her tits in his face.

Debbie was horrified. "Borg!" she yelled. "Stop it! Stop it now!"

"Why don't you join us?" shouted Barry, groping his crutch.

Debbie felt physically sick. She had never been so humiliated in all her life. "Fuck you, Barry!" she screamed. "And Borg? Fuck you too! It's over! Do you hear me? It's fucking all over!"

Bursting into tears, she pushed back through the chanting truckers and ran out into the lorry park. Hiding behind a truck, she fell to her knees sobbing. "That's it! That is fucking it! Borg, you're fucking history! And fuck the fucking truckstop as well!"

Slowly pulling herself together, she made her way up to Donkey's place. He wouldn't mind, she thought, and if he played his cards right... Opening the door, she slipped in.

***

DC Phillips had seen quite enough. Backup had now arrived. DC Roberts and eight uniformed colleagues stood ready by the front door. Phillips had his team, six PC's and two WPC's, ready to go in through the fire exits.

***

Donkey pushed through the crowd to the stage, yelling at everybody to calm down. "Party's over!" he shouted. "Come on boys, we're closing! Let's go! Back to your trucks! You've all got work tomorrow!"

They were not listening; the drunken truckers were having a ball. Someone had put the music back on.

"Where's Charlie?" yelled Killer, helping Donkey to pull Barry off Kitty, and Kitty off Borg.

"Fuck knows!" Donkey shouted back. "He'll go fucking apeshit when he..."

A shrill whistle and a loud crashing sound made them all spin around. The place was suddenly swarming with police!

"What the fuck... " said Donkey.

"Everybody stand still!" screeched Roberts through a megaphone.

"It's a raid!" cried out Bernie.

"It's the fucking pigs!" screamed Killer, throwing an ash tray at the nearest uniform.

"Stand still!" yelled Roberts again, as his officers moved in.

Some drivers made for the doors trying to escape, others attacked the police with chairs and fists. Punches were thrown and truncheons were wildly swung as beer bottles, ash trays and cans flew everywhere.

Donkey grabbed hold of Kitty and was trying to drag her clear, when suddenly a bottle glanced off the back of his head, sending him spinning round into the stage curtain. As he fell, he grabbed the curtain and it came down on top of him. The supporting bar crashed down, cracking him on the head and knocking him out cold. The falling curtain covered his lifeless form.

***

The riot carried on. Amid the noise and mayhem, the two WPC's rushed at Kitty with a blanket, trying to cover her up. Kitty hit one over the head with her bull whip and bit the other on the leg, as she was wrestled to the floor.

Borg, still trying to get his trousers up, was grabbed by two police officers and dragged forcibly off the stage. Killer quickly sprang into action. Leaping up onto a table, and with his best blood curdling scream, he dived at the officers just like he'd seen in the movies. His cry alerted the cops who sidestepped, allowing Killer to crash face first into the side of the stage. A boot from one of the cops caught him in the ribs as he rolled away in agony.

Barry, in a drunken stupor, stood naked in the centre of the stage wondering what the hell was going on. "Charlie ain't going like this," he mumbled.

Killer, on all fours, made his way towards the exit. Scrambling around the upturned tables and broken chairs he paused to pick up an unopened can of larger.

"Stand still!" screamed DC Roberts through his megaphone, just inches away from Killer's head.

Killer looked up just in time to see the truncheon coming his way.

All around, drivers were bloodied and bruised. Several lay unconscious on the ground.

The police finally got the upper hand and gained control. One by one, the boys were handcuffed and led out. Borg and Barry, along with a battered Killer, were among the first to be thrown into a paddy wagon and taken away. As an ambulance carted off the wounded, Kitty, wrapped only in a blanket, was driven away in a police car.

***

By the time Donkey came around, several hours later, it was all over. There was silence. His head hurt like hell and he could hardly breathe. He was trussed up in the curtain like an Egyptian mummy. He lay still for a while, gathering his thoughts, recalling the events.

Slowly pulling the heavy material from his face, he felt the cold air rushing down into his lungs. Peering out into the darkened bar, he saw that the place had been completely trashed! Tables were overturned and broken chairs littered the stage. Windows were smashed and there was blood on the walls. But no police. The place was empty and in darkness.

Wriggling free from his cocoon, he crept carefully over to a window. There was a police car parked out the front, with two officers sat inside. Another two sat in a van across the truckstop entrance. Blue crime scene tape ran around the building.

Creeping on his hands and knees over broken glass, he made his way through the bar and restaurant, and into the kitchen. Checking out through the window, all seemed clear. Opening the kitchen door, he slowly crept out, slipping silently under the police tape and into the pitch-black lorry park.

Where the fuck was Charlie? He wasn't going to fucking believe this!

Using the shadows, he crept up through the lorry park, heading for home. If anyone asked, he'd been at home all night.

The lights were on in the caravan, Penny must still be up. Then he heard laughter and music; it sounded like there was a party going on. Sneaking around to the side window, he carefully peered in.

There, sat around his table were Carol and Helen! And Debbie and Penny! And there, to his absolute horror, in the middle of the table surrounded by empty wine bottles, was his blue velvet box!

THE END

Lightning Source UK Ltd.
Milton Keynes UK
UKHW020442200620
365268UK00004B/676